Circle of Three

Also by Patricia Gaffney

The Saving Graces

Circle of Three

A NOVEL

Patricia Gaffney

SIMON & SCHUSTER
A VIACOM COMPANY

First published in Great Britain by Simon & Schuster UK Ltd, 2001
A Viacom company

3 5 7 9 10 8 6 4 2

Simon & Schuster UK Ltd
Africa House
64-78 Kingsway
London WC2B 6AH

Simon & Schuster Australia
Sydney

A CIP catalogue record for this book is available from the British Library

ISBN 0-684-85873-8

Printed and bound in Great Britain by
Omnia Books Ltd, Glasgow

You and me, Jen.
Separated at birth, no question.

1

Nature's Way

It's natural to feel guilty after the death of a loved one. Guilt and grief go together—that's what they say. Because you're still alive, I suppose. Well, lots of things are "natural," including infanticide in some cultures. My teenage daughter's extremely odd friend Raven recently shared with me that the female coot pecks to death all but two of her baby chicks because feeding them just gets to be too big a hassle. It's nature's way.

The presumption behind the guilt-is-natural bromide is that one hasn't actually done anything to precipitate the loved one's death. And there's the rub. I provoked my husband into an argument five minutes before he smashed the car into a tree and killed himself. (That wasn't the only thing I did, but it's the showiest.) An incredibly stupid argument: why couldn't he drive Ruth to her soccer tournament the next day, why did I always have to do it? When was the last time he'd gone to a parent-teacher conference, a science fair, anything? In six years Ruth would be twenty-one and out of his life; did he really want to spend the rest of his only child's adolescence shut up in his office grading papers and writing—yes, I said this—obscure articles on mathematical minutiae that even more obscure journals only published once in a blue moon?

It was eleven o'clock, a Friday night. We were driving home after dinner with my parents, a dinner Stephen hadn't wanted to go to in the first place—but then he never did, so I don't take that so much to heart; I forgive myself for that. He said he was tired, but I thought nothing of it. Ruth, thank God, thank God, wasn't with us;

she'd gone to a birthday sleepover at a girlfriend's. I'd spent the evening keeping a tense peace, smoothing over this, rephrasing that. My mother always liked Stephen, I'm not sure why, but he never liked her, and to this day she doesn't know it. That's my doing. For eighteen years, the length of our marriage, I constantly respun and reinterpreted his rudeness to her, at times his outright contempt. "He's thinking higher thoughts," I'd joke when he couldn't bother to come out of his study when Mama made one of her (admittedly irritating) unannounced drop-ins. And she's so easily intimidated by what she takes for intellectual superiority—except, interestingly, where my father's concerned—so it was never hard to make her believe that Stephen wasn't cold and disdainful, no, he was a genius. Geniuses are eccentric and brusque, they keep to themselves, they don't have time to be ingratiating to their mothers-in-law.

What triggered the argument in the car was fear. I had seen something that night that scared me: a sickening similarity between my husband and my father. Getting angry at Stephen, trying to get a rise out of him, trying to make him yell at me—that would've been ideal—was a way to convince myself I'd seen no such thing.

My father, George Danziger, taught English literature at Remington College for forty years. He recently retired, to write a book with a colleague on some minor eighteenth-century poet whose name I've forgotten. My father is a short, heavyset man, balding, slope-shouldered; he has a paunch; he slouches; pipe ash usually litters his vest or his coat sleeve. He frequently wears a vacant expression, and I suppose he's as close to the cliché of the absentminded professor as a human, as opposed to a cartoon, can be. But there's still a rumpled dignity in his sagging face and his gentle, phlegmatic movements, at least to me. Stephen was his physical opposite. Medium tall with a hard, compact, runner's body, he had handsome, sharp-pointed features—like Ruth's—and a full head of crisp, curling, sandy-gray hair. Quick, economical gestures. And always a restlessness about him, an impatience with his surroundings that could be insulting if you took it personally.

Mama and I did the dishes while the men went outside so Pop could smoke his pipe, a forbidden pleasure in my mother's house. I watched them idly through the kitchen window, standing beside the wrought iron table in the late-August hush, their shoulders hunched, chins pulled into the collars of their short-sleeved shirts. They didn't have much to say to each other, but then, they never did. The college was all they had in common, and Stephen still, after three years, secretly resented Pop for his help, such as it was, in getting him his teaching appointment. They kept a manly distance apart, and even when they spoke they never looked at each other. They shuffled from foot to foot, hands jammed in their pockets, and squinted up at the night sky over the roof as if they were watching a movie.

Just in that moment, as different as they were, they looked the same to me. Identical. I had my hands in hot water, but I remember the coldness that came into me, like the flat of a blade on bare skin. The chill thought crept in that they *were* the same.

Impossible—Stephen had stubbornness in him, a temper, a mean streak, Stephen was *alive*. I thought of my mother's discontent and disappointment, what they've turned her into and who she blames them on, and I thought, What if, by marrying a man as absent and unreachable as Pop, I've made the same mistake she made? Not a similar mistake, *the exact same mistake*.

So I started a fight. Unlike my father, Stephen could give as good as he got—better. His trusty weapon, cold, withering logic, always trounced my teary, incoherent furies, no contest, a sword fight with a balloon. But that night I didn't care, I wanted noise, racket, action. I waited until we were driving home on Clay Boulevard, a straight, well-lit stretch of four-lane highway, no distractions. It didn't matter to me what we fought about, but I was tired, and driving Ruth to her soccer game in Charlottesville on Saturday would mean getting up at six in the morning. So I chose that.

Stephen never said a word. It's been four months, and I can't recall anything he said that night in the car. That makes me inexpressibly sad. I, on the other hand, had quite a lot to say before he rolled down the window—the first indication that something was wrong. It was chilly, I was still fiddling with the heater knobs trying to get warm, I thought he was opening the window to thwart me. "Aren't you going to say anything?"—I can still hear the shrill nastiness in my voice. He made a face, a grimace, but I couldn't see his coloring in the dark, only that his mouth was contorted. "What's wrong?" I still wasn't worried, only puzzled. He said my name, "Carrie," and nothing else. He never clutched at his chest, that cartoon gesture of a man having a heart attack; he clutched his arm, before he slumped over against the door. It happened very fast. One second we were driving in our lane, the next we were careening across the grass median with headlights in our eyes, horns blaring, cars swerving. I grabbed the wheel and we slowed slightly, but Stephen still had his foot on the gas and I couldn't get my legs untangled fast enough to kick it away. Panic swallowed me. Under it, I remember feeling sad because here was the end, the end of me, broken and smashed in high-velocity metal and glass. Ruth wasn't a conscious thought, but she was the weight, the shadow in my brain closing down over everything. *Oh, my baby.*

Steered isn't the right word, somehow I *got* us across two lanes of eastbound traffic without hitting anything. We lurched onto the verge and down a gravel embankment, bumped up a shallow rise. The car's violent motion shoved Stephen back, finally threw his foot off the accelerator. We might've come to a natural stop, but we clipped a line of trees just over the top of the ridge. The car spun around when the bumper caught, and smacked in back against a tree trunk. My head hit something, I think the window on my side before the door snapped open—my seat belt kept me from flying out.

Lights, noise. I was out cold until two boys, Remington students, unbuckled me and pulled me out of the car. They wouldn't let me sit up, made me lie flat on the ground. "Where is my husband? How is he, my husband?" They wouldn't say. Then the police, the ambulance, the rescue squad truck. "Is my husband dead?" I asked a young man in a paramedic's jacket, holding on to his sleeve, not letting go until he told me. "Ma'am," he said, "we're doing everything we can." They were at that moment doing CPR, I discovered later, trying to restart Stephen's heart. But it never beat again.

That's what I did. One can make a little or a lot of it, I'm aware. I've done both, countless times. Either way, I think it's plain that my guilt, alive and well four months after my husband's death, goes beyond the province of "normal." Ruth and my mother say it's time I pulled myself together, started functioning again, found a real job, got on with life. Is that heartless? It's true I'm a mess, no good to anyone, and my daughter needs me now more than she ever has.

What they don't know is that there's more. The argument in the car was only the most conspicuous of my numerous failings and regrets. One in particular pains me. It's a little thing in itself, quite petty. Commonplace. But shabby, you know, distressing to admit. Although nothing truly shameful. Oh, well, it's only this—Stephen and I made love the night before he died. That ought to be a kind memory, a comfort to me—*at least we were intimate that one last time*—a blessing, an incremental notch in favor of life on the big, overbalanced scale. But I ruined even that. I know it's a little thing, but I can't forgive myself. The very last time my husband's body came inside my body, I shut my eyes and dreamed he was someone else.

2

Not Enough Points to Be Anything

I left my mom this really chirpy note on the counter before school. "Yo, yo, I made killer tuna fish salad, eat it for lunch or else! XXOO, Ruth. P.S. Jamie and Caitlin might come over this afternoon to do homework. OK?" I drew two big puffy lips and wrote "smooch" underneath, with an exclamation point.

That was, like, code. It meant, "Eat something healthful for a change, and when I get home could you please have some clothes on so my friends don't have to see you in Dad's old bathrobe."

Well, Jamie and Caitlin didn't come home with me, that was more of a trick anyway, but it didn't work because Mom was nowhere in sight and she'd left her own fake-cheerful note in the exact same spot as mine. "Hi! Drinks and snacks in ref.—don't overdo." She drew a smiley face. "I'm taking a little nap, so could you guys work downstairs? You don't have to be quiet. (Within reason.) Love & kisses, me. P.S. Want to get a pizza tonight?"

Since Dad died, this is so par for the course. She's asleep when I go to school, she's asleep when I get home. I don't know what she does during the day, except that it's not cooking or cleaning. Eating—I know she's doing that, because she's gained about ten pounds in four months. She eats spaghetti with butter on it, mashed potatoes and gravy, Minute rice in a can of mushroom soup with no water—really gross stuff, nothing but carbohydrates. She'll eat right if I'm watching or if I make it, but otherwise it's hot cereal, couscous, popcorn, and pasta. Comfort foods, I guess.

The other thing she does when I'm at school is make flower

arrangements. She has a "job" with a craft shop in town owned by this woman who pays her like two cents per flower arrangement, so you know it's only a matter of time before we're living in a packing crate under the Leap River bridge. *God.* I guess I can't talk, though, because I haven't found a job yet either. I baby-sit for Harry, the next-door neighbor's one-year-old, but the Harmons don't go out that much at night so it's not like I'm getting rich.

I don't know what's going to happen. About a month after the accident Grampa came over without Gram, which was pretty scary in itself, and had a long talk with Mom that I wasn't allowed to hear. After he left, she sat me down and gave me the bad news. Bottom line, we're poor. I thought it was sort of cool at first. "You mean, like, destitute?" No, just poor, which in a way is worse because there's no, like, drama. Apparently my dad didn't teach at Remington long enough to get a pension, so all we have is savings, Social Security, and his tiny little insurance policy.

I don't let Mom know I'm disappointed, but I was supposed to get a car, either a nice used one or a cheap new one, next summer when I turn sixteen. That's out now. Also, I might have to go to Remington. Which is the worst, nobody who lives in Clayborne goes there unless they have to—not because it's terrible or anything, just because it's local. All my life I wanted to go to my dad's alma mater, Georgetown (if I could get in), or else UNC, but they're both impossible now. UVA maybe, but wherever I go it has to be in-state.

I can't stop thinking about what might've happened if I'd been there the night he died. For one thing, I'd probably have been driving, because I've got my learner's and Mom usually lets me drive, even at night, to practice. So even if he'd still had his heart attack, the car wouldn't have crashed, so I could've driven him to the hospital and he'd probably have been saved. Or, I think it's entirely possible he wouldn't have had the attack to begin with, because everything, the atmosphere, the whole night, would've been different if I'd been there. I just have this really strong feeling that if I hadn't gone to Jamie's, he'd still be alive. His fate would've changed. Who's to say the blood in his heart wouldn't have stayed to the correct path or beat in the exact right amounts if he'd been sitting in the car relaxing, looking up at the moon instead of down at the road? I could make him laugh sometimes. What if he'd been listening to me tell some stupid story instead of to Mom or the radio? I just think things would've been different.

I have this picture, I keep it on my bedside table, of Dad, Mom, and me, about three Christmases ago, right before we moved to Clayborne, which is the town my mom grew up in but left when she was like eighteen. The three of us in this picture are lined up outside the old house in Chicago, showing off our new presents. Mom has her coat sleeve pulled up and her arm out, to show the watch Dad gave her. I gave him a green scarf and matching mittens, so he's posing with his hands straight out, with the muffler wound around half his face so only his eyes show. I look even sillier in my new jeans, boots, and down parka, grinning and pointing to my ears to show they're pierced. What a dork.

Sometime around when this picture was taken, maybe the next day but definitely during those same Christmas holidays, my dad and I went ice skating on the lake. Mom was supposed to go with us, but at the last second she said what she'd really like to do was have the house to herself for one whole afternoon. So it was just the two of us. I felt shy around him at first. We hadn't done anything alone since . . . well, I don't even know when. I felt sort of giddy, having him all to myself, almost like a date. I pretended we were a couple, and I watched other people watching us, wondering if they thought he could be my boyfriend. He was forty but he looked pretty young then, it wasn't impossible.

After the skating, we went for hot chocolate in a fancy silver diner on the shore, and I had the feeling, sitting across from him in the red vinyl booth, fingering my sore ears, putting quarters in the jukebox to play fifties songs like "Hound Dog" and "Lipstick on Your Collar," that this was the beginning of our real, true relationship. My dad had just been waiting for me to grow up. I talked a lot, told him about school and my teachers and even this guy I liked in history and how math was my favorite subject by far, a slight exaggeration, and how I'd probably major in math at Georgetown and then go on to teach at some prestigious university.

It was so great. He talked, too, and laughed at my jokes, and told me things I didn't already know. Like one time he and some of his friends from high school cut class to go sledding down Cashbox Hill, which is out in the country in New Jersey where he was from, and he slid into a barbed wire fence and cut his neck in back, under his hairline. He showed me the scar, which for some reason I had never seen before in my life, and just in that moment, everything felt right. Nothing was left out or dangling or mysterious, everything belonged.

The funny thing is, though, nothing ever came of that day. When it was over, we went back to who we'd been before, and it was like nothing had ever happened. He was nice to me, same as always, but he never again suggested we do something together, just the two of us. He went back into his study, you could say, and closed the door.

What I think happened was that I hadn't grown up enough then—I was only twelve—and what's sad is that now I'm probably finally old enough to be his friend and he's gone. We lost our chance. It can never be the way I dreamed it. I thought—maybe this sounds stupid—I thought we'd be partners after I got my degree, my doctorate and everything. I saw us teaming up, having an office in some funky old building in Georgetown and writing books together, solving complicated formulas that have stumped the entire math community for years, for centuries. I could see us with our feet up on either side of his desk when the day was over, drinking coffee, giving each other compliments on our work, planning the next day. VAN ALLEN & ASSOCIATE, it would say on the door. Stephen and Ruth Van Allen, Mathematicians.

No, I can see this is stupid. I don't even know what mathematicians do, not really, except teach, which my dad complained about all the time. He made fun of the other professors in his department, who got ahead by kissing up or playing politics, whereas he just did his job and took care of business. He was sort of a loner.

That's why it would've been so cool to be partners. I feel like, once I was older and had my math degrees and everything, I could've cheered him up, plus he'd've been proud of me. I hate that this is never going to happen.

I have got to do something about my clothes. I took this quiz in a magazine to find out my own personal style. You could be Fun, Preppy, Grunge, Goth, Corporate, I forget what else. Caitlin and Jamie took it, and they were both Fun, but when I added up my scores I didn't have enough points to be anything. God, how pathetic. I can see the same thing going on in my room, which I now hate. I have a Dixie Chicks calendar—yuck! I can't wait till it runs out!—and a picture of Leo D., and a poster of Natalie Imbruglia and some cutouts of Claire Danes and George Clooney and Siouxsie Sioux and the Banshees. I mean, what is that? Exactly what does that mean? So I'm going to take everything down, clear it all out, just have nothing, blank walls, and let my room fill itself back up organically. Then we'll see.

Because Raven came over after dinner tonight, and for the nanosecond Mom let us be alone in my room, his face went into like total disgust and he mumbled, "Happening. Not."

But that wasn't even the worst. I told Mom afterward, if she can't get dressed in regular clothes, daytime clothes, her *own* clothes, not her dead husband's—I almost said, but that sounded mean, and plus we try to avoid the *D* word these days unless there's a good reason—then she can just stay in her room when I have company over. It's funny, I used to worry about what she thought of Raven, and tonight all I could think was what he must be making of *her.* She had on a pair of Dad's old sweatpants, one of his plaid flannel shirts, and his gray wool bathrobe. Oh, and a pair of his running socks. I mean, *God.* No makeup, of course, and I don't know when she last washed her hair. She has goldish brown hair, very long and stick straight, and until now I was always jealous of it. Mine's curly, which I hate, and not as nice a color I don't think, more of an ashy blond like Dad's. Anyway—and her complexion's changed, she used to have very delicate coloring, but now she's like totally gray, probably because of all the junk she eats. She's just washed out. "Um, my mom's still kind of wrecked," I told Raven when he was leaving, and he said, "Obviously." Which I thought was unnecessary.

But he was nice, he came by to lend me a book, some selected stories by Edgar Allan Poe. He likes anything that's creepy. After Poe his favorite authors are Anne Rice and Edward Gorey. I was not feeling that great to begin with, and he wouldn't get off the subject of how everything ends, everything is loss, the only appropriate humor in life is melancholy, which did not exactly cheer me up. But I think it's too cool that his real last name is Black. His first name is Martin, but his last name is Black. Raven Black. It's like a sign.

After he went home, Mom came in my room and sat on my bed, where I was trying to do homework. She's definitely not herself, because she hasn't even been getting on me lately about what a sty my room is.

She didn't say anything, so I kept reading, figuring she'd get to the point eventually. She started picking at the quilt she made me for my thirteenth birthday. It has blue and green stars, and it's about the only thing I still like in my room. "*What?*" I said finally, and she smiled this really shaky smile and said, "Sorry about tonight. Guess I'm not doing so great."

"You're okay," I said.

"I'll be better soon."

"I know."

"How are you, baby?"

"Fine," I said.

"Really?" She touched my cheek with the back of her hand. "Tell me about school."

"It's the same. I got a B on my French test." I didn't tell her about my algebra test, she'd've freaked. That's supposed to be my best subject. "What does it mean when you have a sore in your mouth that won't go away?" I said.

"Let's see."

I showed her the inside of my cheek, which has this tender white spot I keep accidentally biting.

"Oh, that's just a canker sore. It'll go away."

"Canker. That's like cancer."

"It's not like cancer."

I have spots in front of my eyes, too, which could be a warning sign of glaucoma. One of my ankles is bigger than the other.

"So," she said, stretching out on her stomach. "What's with you and Raven."

"God. Nothing, Mom, there's nothing *with* us."

"Does he go to school in that makeup?"

"They won't let him."

"Huh. Do you like him?"

"Jeez, he's not my boyfriend or anything. He's just Raven."

"Oh. Okay. Where does he live?"

"*God*. I don't even *know*."

She punched up one of my pillows and shoved it under her chest and folded her arms around it. "Well, anyway."

"Anyway." I sat up and started giving her a back rub, which she loves. "You're incredibly tense. Your shoulders are like marble. Did you do flowers today?"

"For a while." She groaned into the pillow, and I thought she was enjoying the back rub, but then she said in a pretend-panicky voice, "I have got to get a real job soon."

"You will. I will, too. People are looking for Christmas help, I can get a job in the mall after school."

"Mm. Except you'd need a ride to it."

"You could drive me," I said.

"Not if I'm working, too."

"We could get a job in the same place."

"Hey, that would be neat."

It would be. Well, depending on the place. I could feel her finally starting to relax; the back of her neck wasn't like a block of concrete anymore. When I was little I used to think I was helping to save her life when I'd rub her feet or do some chore for her. Like, if she'd ask me to run upstairs and bring down the aspirin bottle or go down in the basement and get something out of the freezer, I'd grumble and procrastinate, but inside I'd be glad because I had this idea that anything I could do instead of her would save minutes on her life. So if I set the table or got the paper off the front porch or ran and answered the phone before she could get to it—that gave her a couple of extra minutes at the end of her life. It all added up.

"Hey, Mom, did you know that when you pet your dog, it lowers your blood pressure?"

"Mmm."

"But the cool thing is, they found out it also lowers the *dog's* blood pressure. Don't you think that's cool? Can we get a dog?"

"No."

"Why?"

"Oh, honey. We just can't."

We couldn't before, either, because my dad was allergic to anything with hair—dogs, cats, gerbils, whatever. I was just thinking maybe now. . . "Jess has four dogs," I said, "and about fifteen cats.

And a crow that comes up to his back door and lets him feed it. Jess would give us a kitten, I bet. Cats are easy."

"Ruth."

"I know, but he's got all these animals and we don't have any."

"Jess lives on a farm."

"So?"

Jess is great. He's a friend of Mom's from the olden days when she was growing up in Clayborne, and he has a farm right on the Leap River that's over six hundred acres with about two hundred Holstein cows. Last year I had to do a civics paper on a local industry, and I picked Jess's dairy farm and learned all about cows. Then for my science fair project I decided to do a working model of the four stomachs of the cow (the rumen, the reticulum, the omasum, and the abomasum), and he helped me with that, too. I love to go out to his farm and just hang, although I haven't seen him since Dad died—Mom's been too wasted. I miss going there. I miss seeing Jess.

She rolled over, and we stretched out next to each other. "That was great," she said. "Thanks. And by the way, this room is a sty." We smiled up at the ceiling. She made me a mobile that hangs from the light, seven horses galloping or cantering or loping, cut out of thin wood and painted in different colors. It's from my horse phase. I should take it down, but I still like it.

"Mom? Christmas is going to be sad, isn't it?" Thanksgiving was bad enough.

She said, "Yeah," and I was glad she didn't lie. "Because it's the first. But we'll be okay. Some things—we can't go around them. I'm afraid we just have to go through them."

"Do you miss Dad a lot?"

"I do."

"Me, too. Will we still go to Gram's for dinner?"

"Yes, of course."

"And we'll still have presents?"

"Absolutely. Although. . ."

"I know." Not as many.

"The main thing is that we're together. We've still got us."

"Yeah."

Except I don't have her. She's still got me, but she's about half the mother I used to have. When Dad died I lost him and part of her. I'm almost an orphan.

She says she's getting better, but I say not to the naked eye. Well, maybe Christmas will miraculously cheer us up. But I don't think so. I think she's right. Some things we can't go around, we just have to go through them.

3

The Power of Nostalgia

The phone jolted me out of a comatose sleep on the living-room couch. I answered instantly, heart pounding, forgetting to clear my throat first and say hello cheerfully. "Carrie honey, is that you?" my mother's worried voice asked. "What's wrong?"

This happened all the time. Something about my phone voice; if I didn't make an effort to sound bright and clearheaded, people thought something was the matter with me. Are you sick? Were you sleeping? Have you been crying? Today I could've answered yes to all three.

"Oh, hi, Mama. No, I'm fine, how're you? How's Pop?"

"What are you doing?"

"Right now?" The mantel clock said ten after twelve. "I was just getting ready to go out. On my way, in fact. Chores, got things to do, the bank, post office, this and that . . ." I carried the phone into the kitchen and sank down in a chair at the table. Out of steam.

"I was going to run over before the women's club luncheon with one of these casseroles I made. It's Ruth's favorite—scalloped potatoes."

"Mmm. Well, that—"

"I've got enough for an army. You'll be there another half hour, won't you?"

I put my head down on the oak table. God, look at all the crumbs and jelly stains and water marks. How long since I cleaned this table? My nightgown sleeve was stuck to it. "Um, you couldn't just drop it off, could you? Since I'm going out . . ." My mother made wonderful scalloped potatoes. They'd get me through the day. The logistics would be embarrassing, though; I'd have to hide upstairs and wait for her to come in, stick her casserole in the refrigerator, and go away. No, no, it wouldn't work anyway, I realized—she'd see the car.

"Well," she said, "if you're not even going to be there, never mind." Affronted. "Maybe after my luncheon's over, although I can't promise they won't eat everything."

"That might be better. And if you come late enough, you can see Ruth."

That perked her up. "How's my baby? I want you two to come to dinner next Friday night, Carrie. You need to get out of that house."

"Friday. . ."

"Just you and Ruth, a family dinner. It's been ages."

"It's been four months." To the day. Since Stephen died.

She realized it, too. She said too quickly, "Friday night for sure, we'll have a good time, I promise. And now I'll let you get on with your important chores."

"So—you're coming by later?"

"Only if it's not too much *trouble*. If it won't put you out."

I tried to balance the phone on my ear without touching it, so I could drop both arms and go limp. Stay like that all day, lax and drooling, head a complete blank.

"Carrie? I was kidding, I could come over right now if you want. Honey, do you feel like talking?"

I couldn't even make my tongue work. Did I feel like talking? Involuntarily, I snorted into the phone. I turned it into a cough and said, "I'm fine, I'm better today, actually. I should go now, but I'll definitely see you later, okay? 'Bye, Mama."

I would love a vacation from my mother's mind. If she would bump her head—not seriously, nothing fatal or painful or long-lasting, just something to give her amnesia for about six weeks. Lovely, lovely, no calls, no visits, no casseroles, no life advice. No bullying. When I'm in my mother's head, I'm only half myself; she sucks out the other half and swallows it. And I'm so weak these days, I'm lucky if it's only half.

I hung there over the table until my neck hurt. Then I got up slowly, a little dizzy—low blood sugar? pressure? Low something. I put a cup of water and a tea bag in the microwave. Couldn't drink coffee anymore, too harsh; I wanted to *be* awake, not slapped awake. I carried the cup and a handful of Fig Newtons into Stephen's office. Slumped in the doorway, I stared around at the mess I'd made of it.

Six weeks ago I had an idea it might be a comfort to turn his sanctum, his favorite room in the house, into my new flower-arrangement-and-wreath-assembly workroom. A way to stay close to him, I thought, keep his memory vivid, not be so lonely when I was alone. Wrong on all counts, and now I'd ruined his room. He'd kept it neat as a laboratory. I littered his pristine techno-gray carpet with Scotch broom branches and wild grapevine, tansy and goldenrod stalks, crown of thorns, witch hazel. Except for his desk, every surface was covered with pods, nuts, branches, stems, twigs, flowers, containers, driftwood, twist ties, pipe cleaners, wire, silica, sand, salt, borax, clay, vermiculite. And over everything an invisible mist, an allergy sufferer's nightmare fog of dusty dried flower and seed pod detritus. Stephen would've died in here.

But I never touched his desk. Why not? Directly in front of his steel-and-vinyl chair were the notes he'd been taking for a paper on the computation of definite integrals. I hadn't given his clothes away, either, or cleaned out his side of the medicine chest or his bedside table. Ruth said nothing, but she had to think this was bizarre behavior. I thought so, too. I wasn't sure what was behind it, but I didn't believe it was my sad, wistful way of holding on to my husband a little longer. Something more complicated. Less commendable.

I sat down on the floor in my usual place. Even with the blinds open, the light was poor, but I hadn't gotten up the energy yet to drag a floor lamp in from another room. I kept forgetting. Until recently, Margaret Sachs had been paying me eight dollars apiece for dried wreaths and Christmas arrangements, which she sold at a comfortable profit at Clayborne Crafts 'N Candles, her shop on Myrtle Avenue. Last week I began to run low on supplies, so I had to switch to miniatures. I had no choice, it was either downsize or go out into the world and look for more materials, the cattails, teasel, laurel branches, etc., etc., that were the tools of my not-very-lucrative-to-begin-with trade. I couldn't face it. Some kind of agoraphobia; I hoped it was temporary. At any rate, now Margaret was only paying me four dollars per arrangement.

I rationalized the cutback by telling myself I could make twice as many in the same amount of time, so I wasn't really losing money. But that wasn't true—if it were, I'd run out of supplies in half the time, wouldn't I? No, I was just in a miniature frame of mind.

The afternoon dragged by. I could drift into a trance when I made these little arrangements. When I floated up from it because I was out of pinecones or it was too dark to see or my rear end had gone numb, I'd find I had made six or seven tiny floral compositions and they were all identical. Round, fan-shaped, S-curved, pyramid—whatever design I'd chosen for the first, all the rest were exact replicas of it. I found that vaguely appalling. Margaret thought I did it on purpose—"Oh, *these* are cunning, they'll go like hotcakes," she'd say, and ask me to do more of whatever shape I'd unconsciously mass-produced. But I didn't. Not on purpose, anyway.

Hunger nudged me out of my trance today. Stiff-necked, stiff-legged, I hobbled into the kitchen. Almost three; Ruth would be home soon. The cottage cheese had a funny smell, but I scraped off the top and ate in the middle, staring out the window over the sink at my neighbors' house. In our shared driveway, Modean Harmon was unloading her one-year-old from his car seat and carrying him and a bag of groceries inside. I wished I'd thought to ask her to pick up a few things for me while she was out. She was wonderful about that. Wonderful about everything. Modean was shy and quiet, younger than me, very reserved; it was only since Stephen died that we'd become friends. And I wasn't much of one; she did all the initiating. Stephen never cared for Dave, her dentist husband, so we never socialized as couples. But after the accident, Modean was a lifesaver. She didn't say much, and she never tried to draw me out. What she did was leave groceries in the refrigerator, rake the leaves in my yard, drive Ruth to school when she missed the bus. I tried to repay her later by taking care of Harry when Ruth wasn't available, but that was no hardship even for me. He was a big grinning egg of a baby, all he wanted to do was laugh. The hard part was giving Harry back when his mother came home.

The doorbell rang.

Who? I thought, tiptoeing into the foyer. *Who's torturing me now?* It couldn't be my mother, she never knocked, and if the door happened to be locked she had a key. Long stained glass panels bordered the door on both sides—I'd taken a class and made them myself, last year, when screening visitors wasn't a priority. All I could see through the soldered yellow and blue panes was a tall shadow. I opened the door an inch or two. Jess Deeping peered in at me, then took a step back, gray eyes startled. "Hi. Is this a bad time?"

I put him in the living room and excused myself to go make coffee. Wouldn't Ruth revel in this? *I told you,* she'd say, *I told you to get dressed.* I looked ghastly anyway, but more so in Stephen's red Bulls jersey over my oldest, rattiest flannel nightgown. I wasn't vain, but I still had some pride, a shred, a vestige. Measuring coffee into the maker, I watched two fat, humiliated tears spatter on the counter. They weren't remarkable; I cried almost every day about something. *Maybe this is as low as I'll go,* I thought hopefully. *Maybe this is the bottom.*

When I came back in the living room, Jess was bent over with his hands behind his back, studying some small watercolors I did of Ruth when she was a little girl. They weren't very good, but I couldn't part with them; I framed them and put them in a grouping behind the gateleg table, half hidden by the tole lamp. He'd taken off his heavy coat—I'd forgotten to ask him for it. He'd dressed up; he wore pressed slacks and a blue crewneck sweater that looked brand-new. A Christmas present? He had no family, no wife anymore. Who gave Jess presents? His hair was a little thinner now, and darker, a caramel shade, but when we first met, age eleven, he was a towhead blond. In high school it was streaky gold and down to his shoulders. In my illicit dream, the one I can't forgive myself for, it came down around the sides of his face, and my face. It covered us like a tawny curtain.

"These are good," he said, straightening. "Why did you stop painting?"

"How do you know I did?"

"Ruth told me."

"Ah." Should've known. I sat down on the piano bench, crossed my legs, folded my arms. "I have a cold," I said. True, but it didn't explain half of what I wanted it to.

"I've been thinking about you," he said carefully. "How've you been getting along?"

"All right." I nodded a lot, trying to make it sound truer. Something old pulled at me to make him my confidant. How easy to say, *I'm dead inside, Jess. Ruth's all that keeps me going, and I'm failing her.* "I've been all right. Getting by, you know. It's hard," I finally admitted. "But we're okay, Ruth and I. Basically. Tell me about you, what have you been doing?"

He smiled a bit grimly, to let me know he hadn't bought any of that. "Oh, the usual. It's the slow time of the year, so I've been taking it easy. Getting lazy."

"I doubt that. Don't you still have to milk two hundred cows twice a day?"

"Not quite that many."

"Ruth told me that. It's not true?"

"I've got over two hundred head, but not all of them get milked. Maybe a hundred and fifty."

"What happens to the other fifty?"

"Calves, stud cattle, heifers. A few old ladies." He put his hands in his pockets and looked around the room. "I like your house."

"It seems funny that you've never been here before." Because I'd never invited him. Seeing him on his big, busy, wide-open farm, that was all right, and Ruth was always with us. But here in my house, just Jess and me? Not allowed. You didn't have to say the rules out loud to know what they were.

"You did all the remodeling yourself?" He stood stiffly, rocking on his toes a little. Uncomfortable, I realized. Most unusual for Jess. I hadn't seen him since Stephen's funeral. He'd phoned one time. Ruth answered, and they talked for quite a while. I shook my head and waved my hands when she said, "So do you want to talk to my mom?" Then it was awkward, because he said yes and she had to come up with a reason, quick, why he couldn't. "Gosh, she was here a minute ago. Well, I guess she went out. I guess she left while we were talking." He hadn't called again.

"Most of it," I told him. "Ruth helps me paint sometimes. It's not finished. I guess now . . ." I let that hang, weighing how frank I should be. Was it too personal to tell him I might have to sell the house? Ruth loved it, though. Even if we sold it, after only three years of ownership, there wasn't much escrow in our overpriced circa-1880 money sink on the state of Virginia's Historic Register. I smiled at Jess. "Some of my plans have been pushed back, put it that way."

"You need a job."

"God knows I do. Excuse me a sec . . ." I stood up and went to get the coffee.

He followed me into the kitchen. "This is amazing," he said as I filled two mugs with coffee, adding milk to his.

"What?"

"This room. You did all this, Carrie?"

"Yep." I painted the tiles behind the sink and stenciled the wallpaper borders, I even laid the antique bricks I bought cheap at an estate sale. I was quite the craftswoman. "Well, not the counters. I found the slates, but a man cut and installed them for me. And the cabinets were already here, I just refinished them."

It was a great room, my favorite in the house. I could've made it bigger, knocked out a wall and extended into the pantry; that was even allowed under the strict rules of landmark ownership. But it was a 120-year-old house—who had big kitchens in its day? And there were only three of us when I was weighing the decision. And now only two.

Jess scuffed the toe of his shoe across the throw rug he was standing on. "And this?" He looked up and smiled, and raised his eyebrows, and rubbed the flat of his hand against his chest—a combination of gestures I knew very well. In different lights, from different angles, I could still see the boy in his man's face. I felt such tenderness sometimes. It was dangerous, it wasn't even true, but sometimes I felt that I knew Jess better than anyone, that I was the only one who could really see him. But that was only the power of nostalgia. And loneliness. The mind plays tricks.

"I'm afraid so," I said, abashed. SWEET HOME, the rug said, with the date, in green and gray yarn over a replica of my house's façade. "My first and last rug-hooking effort. Months, this took." And it was only four-feet square. Of all the crafts I'd ever taken up out of curiosity, interest, boredom, desperation, whatever—rug hooking was far and away the most tedious. The one that had made me feel the most ridiculous.

"You're an artist."

"No." I laughed. "A frustrated one, maybe. Stephen used to say I took it out on the house." But I was so pleased. It was as if Jess had plucked a hair-thin wire running through me and set it vibrating. I am such a fool.

He set his cup down and came around the kitchen table I'd put between us—we'd been talking across the length of the room. "I have a job for you."

"A what?"

"I could offer you a job."

I saw myself milking cows in his barn. I'd have laughed, but I felt deflated. Stupid, but I thought he might've come for something else. "What job?"

"I'm looking for an artist. To do something. Make something." He looked me over, head to toe. "You're perfect."

I flushed. If he was making fun of me, it was for the first time. "What, you need someone to—to—" I couldn't think of the name of it, the person who used to advertise mattresses in department stores by sleeping, sleeping in a big bed behind a plate glass window while people on the sidewalk stopped and stared. I saw it once in an old movie.

"You wouldn't make a lot of money." I sensed a trick, but the light in his eyes drew me anyway. "But you'd make more than Margaret Sachs is paying you."

"Who told you about that? Ruth," I answered myself. "Well, that's not saying much, believe me. Oh, Jess, I need a *real* job."

"This is a real job."

"What is it?"

"It's kind of a long story. Do you remember Eldon Pletcher?"

"No. Eldon? I remember Landy Pletcher."

"Eldon's Landy's father."

"Landy—you mean from school?" A boy two years ahead of Jess and me at Clayborne High. A shy, backward boy, I remembered; his father had farmed tobacco.

Jess nodded. "Well," he said, and rubbed a long index finger across his sideburn, deciding how to proceed. "Do you know about the Arkists?"

"The what?"

"No, you'd moved away by then. I'm surprised your mother never mentioned them, though. They—they're—" He scratched his head, smiling down at the floor. Such a man, I thought, with his deep voice and his rough hands, the weathered skin around his eyes. Stephen had lived in his head, but Jess lived in his body. I wasn't used to a man like him in my house. "Let's see," he said. "About twenty years ago—about the time you left—Eldon, Landy's father, started a religious group called the Arkists. Also known as the Sons of Noah. Small, mostly local. Well, not that small, they had a couple hundred souls in their heyday. You never heard about this?"

"No. When was their heyday?"

"I use the term loosely. Ten years ago? I'm not sure what they believe in besides the great flood, but probably the usual, what you'd expect. From a southern offshoot of Protestantism."

"They don't handle snakes?"

"No."

"Take multiple wives? Speak in tongues?"

"None of that." He laughed, but he really wanted to reassure me. "They're good people, not well educated but well meaning. Gentle. They don't preach that they're the one true faith."

"That could be why their heyday's over. Like the Shakers. No, wait, they died out because they wouldn't procreate."

"Right. Anyway. . ."

"Anyway. What's the job?"

"When Eldon had his religious conversion, he promised God he'd replicate the ark before he died."

"Replicate the ark?"

"To save the world from a second devastating flood, figuratively speaking. Not to mention his own immortal soul."

"Figuratively speaking?"

"In fact, if he breaks his promise, he believes he'll go straight to hell."

"He's telling you this?"

"Landy told me. He's my neighbor now—he bought the old Price farm next door about twelve, fifteen years ago. We're friends. We help each other out."

"I see."

"Where was I?"

"Eldon Pletcher's going to replicate Noah's Ark. Is he going to sail it?"

I was joking, but Jess said, "Yeah, on the Leap."

"You're kidding. What do I do, skipper it?"

"Ha."

I frowned. He looked so sheepish. "That was a joke," I said. "Right?"

"Right. Right, you don't have to skipper it."

I spread my hands, completely baffled. "Well, *what*?"

"Arks need animals. Figuratively. Eldon thinks God wouldn't mind if he stocked the ark with representations of His creatures somehow, pictures, models—he's not too clear on this, to tell you the truth."

"Who, God?"

"Eldon. But he wants them to look good, you know, he wants realism, and the problem is, there aren't any artists among what's left of the Arkists."

I started to laugh. "And this is where I come in?" Something caught my eye in the window over Jess's shoulder—the fender of my mother's Buick in the driveway. "Oh, no."

"Well, wait, think about it."

"No, I mean—"

"You could do it. You're an artist, Carrie, it's obvious." He waved his arm around my kitchen. "And I know it sounds crazy, it's completely absurd, but that's the beauty of it, isn't it?" Oh, I could never resist that reckless gleam in Jess's eye. "I don't know what he'd pay you. People say he's got money, but nobody knows for—"

"Jess," I said in warning.

The back door flew open and Ruth burst in, red-cheeked from the cold. Everything curves up when she smiles, mouth, eyes, cheeks, eyebrows. Oh, light of my life, apple of my eye. Love for my daughter swamps me at unexpected moments. I flounder in it, flailing for what I can't hold on to much longer. "Hey, Jess," she cried, "I saw your truck! Hi!"

"Ruth—I can't believe it. You *grew*."

Laughing, they stood in front of each other for an awkward few seconds, before finally exchanging a quick, shy hug. Their gladness surprised me—I wasn't sure what I thought of it. Half a dozen times since Stephen died, Ruth had asked me to drive out with her to see Jess, see the cows, his dogs and cats, all the fascinating features of a dairy farm. But I put her off because I was too tired, too weird, too something. I wasn't ready. She'd missed him, it was obvious, and that was my fault. Well, something else to be guilty of.

If Ruth was surprised to see Jess, my mother was floored. She did a double take in her ladies' luncheon finery, fur jacket over a navy wool suit, fur hat, medium-heeled pumps, navy handbag. Oh, Lord, and here came Birdie behind her, Mama's lifelong bridge partner and oldest friend; she'd been a sort of half-dotty aunt to me for as long as I could remember. All of a sudden the kitchen was teeming with women.

"Mama, you remember Jess Deeping," I said in a hostessy voice, thinking, *If she pretends she doesn't know him, I'll kill her*. But she said, "Why, of *course* I do," in her best southern accent, "you came to my son-in-law's funeral, I *so* appreciated that." Such an accomplished liar. Before Stephen's funeral, Mama had been delighted not to lay eyes on Jess Deeping for twenty-five years.

"And Birdie," I said, "Jess, this is Mrs. Costello, my mother's good friend." They said hello, how are you, nice to see you. And then, because the silence was expectant and I was jittery and everybody was staring at me, I blurted out the worst possible thing. "Jess came over to offer me a job."

"A job?" Birdie's faded blue eyes snapped with interest. She rubbed her hands together.

"Wow! What job?" Ruth demanded, crowding in.

My mother said nothing. She stared.

Jess looked hounded, disbelieving. The glance he sent me—*Carrie, what the hell?*—should've cowed me, but it didn't. For some reason it warmed me up. Us against them: just like old times. He closed his eyes for a second. And then with a pained, hopeless smile, he told everybody about Noah's Ark.

4

Good Help

I'll be seventy years old in the spring. I've been sixty-nine for nine months, and hardly enjoyed a minute of it. Sometimes I feel like I'm in a car speeding toward a boulder in the road somebody's chiseled into a giant 7–0. The scenery might be nice, but all I can see is those numbers, high and hard and coming up fast. I've got a one-track mind.

I must be bad off when George notices. "Dana," he said to me the other night, "is anything bothering you?" Well, that got my attention. That was like a blind man saying, "Did somebody turn the lights on?" I tried to remember what I'd just been doing that could've focused George's attention on me instead of his computer screen. Nothing—telling him to move his big feet so I could vacuum under his desk; fighting on the telephone with Birdie, who doesn't think I should run for president of the Clayborne Women's Club; slamming things around in the kitchen for the hell of it, just to make some noise. Calling Carrie twice in an hour with good advice. It must've been the accumulation, all four added up, because by themselves those aren't very remarkable. But imagine George noticing. As I say, it pulled me up.

He was sitting at his desk, working on the book he's been writing with a colleague for the last year and a half. It's about a poet from the 1700s named—well, I forget his name. Alexander Pope called him "Namby Pamby," so that's what I've been calling him. George is sorry he ever told me that. He swears they'll be done with the book by next May, which is about the time I'll be queen of England. When

George retired from the college two years ago, I thought our interesting new lives were about to start. We'd travel, maybe learn a foreign language together, take up some sedentary sport. Talk. Well, surprise, so far that hasn't worked out. He still spends all his time in his study with the door closed, reading, writing, and not talking to me. Carrie called one night about a month ago, teary and upset. "Mama, it's so quiet in this house. It's as if *everybody* died, not just Stephen." I didn't say it, but I thought, oh, honey, it's like that all the time at my house.

I pushed some papers to the side and sat down on the corner of George's desk, next to the computer so he had to look at me. "Is anything bothering me?" Already he looked sorry he'd asked. "My arthritis. My blood pressure medicine. My upcoming senility. Those are off the top of my head."

"Ha ha," he said, humoring me. He had his trifocals on top of his bald, freckled head. He's shrinking; these days when he drives, he needs a pillow to see over the steering wheel. I'm shrinking, too, but not as much as he is. He's two years younger than me, but he looks older. I hope.

"George," I said, "wouldn't you think at our age we'd know something?"

He turned his good ear toward me. "What's that?"

"When you were young, say when you were Ruth's age, didn't you think people as old as us knew something? Knew *something*? I sure did. But don't you feel like the whole thing's still the same mystery it was when you were fifteen?"

He just blinked at me. He's supposed to be the intellectual in the family. I married him partly for his brains, and look where it got me. "What's the trouble?" he said, but his eyes were drifting. He fidgeted when the screen saver came on, a reminder that time was passing.

What's the trouble. If I knew, I could fix it. "Oh, I just haven't felt like myself since the accident, I guess." That's what we call Stephen's death, "the accident."

George nodded solemnly. "We all miss him."

I nodded solemnly, too, but that wasn't it. I'm not sure anyone but Ruth really *misses* Stephen. That sounds terrible, I take it back—Carrie's a mess, sometimes I think she's never going to be her old self again. Well, me, then: as fond as I was of my son-in-law, as much as I approved of him for Carrie, I don't miss him, put it that way. Not that he wasn't a fine, decent, admirable man, good husband and father, all that. He was always standoffish, though, and now it seems to me he's just standing off a little farther.

"Do you remember if heart trouble ran in Stephen's family?" I asked. "Birdie told me I told *her* that's how his father died, but I stood her down and said that wasn't it at all. Do you have any such recollection?"

"Well, now, that rings a bell—"

"No, it was something else, it wasn't heart. Stephen's attack was a fluke, heart does *not* run in that family."

"Maybe so." He shrugged. He doesn't make associations the same way I do—one of our many differences. Stephen's death was Stephen's death; it didn't make George worry more about his prostate, or think about buying a plot at Hill Haven, or look at his old man's face in the mirror and ask it where his life's gone. Supposedly George lives a life of the mind, but it doesn't always seem to me to be his *own* mind.

He started drumming his fingers on the keyboard space bar. "Guess who was at Carrie's this afternoon," I said to keep his attention. "When I got there with Birdie and Ruth."

"Who?"

"Guess."

"I really couldn't say."

"Come on."

"Dana—"

"Okay. Jess Deeping."

He looked blank. Then, "Oh—that fellow, the one who's on the town council?"

"Yes, but—the one who used to be Carrie's boyfriend! In high school." God, men. "You remember, I know you do. You didn't care for him any more than I did."

"That boy? Really?" Hard to believe, but he was just now making the connection between childhood friend and Clayborne city councilman. "Well, he turned out all right, I guess. Did you and Carrie have a nice visit?" he asked politely, eyes drifting toward his computer screen.

"Get this, George." I leaned in closer. He frowned at my hip, which was encroaching on his papers. "Remember the Arkists?"

"The artists?"

"*Arkists.* The religious cult that started up around here years ago, the paper did a story. Those people who called themselves the Arkists? The Sons of Noah?"

"No."

"Oh, you do, too. The ringleader was that tobacco farmer, Pletcher, something Pletcher. Carrie went to school with the son."

"*Oh*, yes, yes, very, very vaguely. But it wasn't a cult, I don't believe, it was a sect. I thought they'd died out by now."

"Cult, sect—no, they didn't die out, and the old man's still alive. And the son not only owns the farm next door to Jess Deeping, he's also his very good *friend*."

"You don't say."

"And—follow me, now—this cult is all set to build an ark—an ark, I'm saying *ark*—and Jess Deeping wants Carrie to build the animals!"

"What?"

"A life-size ark! They want to sail it on the river for the glory of God! Can you believe it?"

No." He joined me in a wonderful laugh, our best in ages, we leaned back and rocked with it. "Why, that makes no sense at all."

"I know! You should've heard Jess Deeping trying to explain it."

"What did Carrie say?"

"She said no, of course." But not forcefully enough, if you ask me; she left room for hope, left the door open a crack. "I don't think so," she told Jess Deeping, and "I just can't imagine it. But I'm flattered you thought of me." Baloney. It wasn't flattering, it was frightening.

"She does need a job, though," I told George. "Soon, because she could lose that house."

"I still say she ought to sell it. Move someplace smaller."

"I know, but Ruth loves it. No, Carrie needs a good paying job, that's what she needs. She has to get out of that house, quit making those damn flower arrangements. Lord, they make me shiver, dried-up little things. They look like nests, they look like dead animals. If she'd gotten an education degree twenty years ago, none of this would be happening. She could've been teaching art at the middle school right now, maybe even the high school. *George*."

"Mm?"

"I've invited Brian Wright to dinner tomorrow night."

He looked up at that. "What for? Brian Wright? I thought Carrie and Ruth were coming tomorrow."

"He's thinking of hiring an assistant."

"Brian is? How do you know?"

"He told me—I ran into him at the bank. This'll be good, wait and see. Brian's on the rise."

George sniffed.

"He is, he's got gumption, he's making something of himself. Carrie could do a lot worse."

He looked alarmed.

"In a *boss*, she could do worse in an *employer*. That's all I'm talking about."

Suspicion narrowed his eyes for a second. But then he lost interest and turned full face to his computer screen. My time was up.

• • •

I served pot roast. I can make smarter, more glamorous meals—the other night I made chicken Monterey for the Becks, and a Peking duck last month for the academic dean and his wife. But Brian Wright is divorced, his wife got the kids, and he lives by himself, and something just told me a nice pot roast would be the thing. Warm and homey.

I thought the evening went well. Brian arrived first, and when Carrie saw him, there was just the tiniest nervous moment, but I don't think anyone noticed it but me. Well, and her. Thank God she looked all right for a change; she had on slacks and a sweater, perfectly nice, and her hair pulled back in a barrette, even a little makeup, hallelujah. Compared to the last time I saw her, she looked like Grace Kelly. She's forty-two, but she never looked it until Stephen died. And Ruth, bless her heart, I swear she gets cuter every day. She's going to be prettier than Carrie, I predict. She needs some poise and some of that nervous energy burned off, but one of these days, look out.

We had drinks in the living room, where it came up that Brian lifts weights. This I didn't know; he's fortyish, and I thought he was stocky, a touch overweight, but no, it's all muscle. Now I can see it—he's got those sloping shoulders bodybuilders have; his neck's as big around as my thigh. He made the room smaller, and not just with his physique. He's so full of energy and enthusiasm, a complete extrovert. He felt like a breath of fresh air on my sad, quiet family. He wears a buzz cut and a neat little goatee, of all things. Now I don't usually care for facial hair on a man, I think it's tacky, and no one should be allowed to wear a crew cut after he's ten. But somehow Brian Wright manages to carry these two fashion mistakes off. Maybe it's his size? You want to give the benefit of the doubt to somebody that big.

And eat? He gobbled up everything in front of him, and I kept the plates moving. No leftovers from this dinner. I know George doesn't like him, but he made an effort to talk and be sociable, and that helped smooth over the times Carrie clicked off. It happens all the time, she'll be pleasant and attentive one minute, lost in space the next. I'm so worried about her. I want to ask, "Honey, are you on drugs?" and I don't mean the kind doctors prescribe.

I was the one who finally brought up business. I waited till we finished eating and were having our second cups of coffee, still at the dining room table. "So, Brian," I said casually, "how are things at the Other School?"

"Great, just great, Mrs. Danziger, this is the best semester we've had. We've got twelve classes up and running right now, and about six more planned for winter term. We'll be going to four quarters starting in the spring."

"Why, that's wonderful, and in such a short time, too."

"Just about three years now." He smiled down, modest but proud, into the bottom of his rice pudding bowl. "I can't complain about growth, that's for sure. The whole thing took off like a rocket."

"Well, the town needed it," I said.

"It did," he agreed, winking at me. "It just didn't know it."

The Other School is one of those alternative, community-based "free" schools that do well in the big cities but aren't very common in towns as small as Clayborne. Except for the college, there's no higher or adult education in our three-county area. Brian saw an opportunity and started the school on a very small scale, practically in his spare time, while he was still working as the registrar at Remington. It grew faster than anybody imagined, and eventually he quit the registrar job to be a full-time entrepreneur. "He's crazy," George said, and plenty of people agreed with him, Carrie's husband included. "It won't fly and he'll lose his shirt," they said, but he didn't, and now the only question they were asking was why somebody hadn't thought of it sooner.

"It must keep you terribly busy," I said. "Tied to the office, no outside life to speak of. Unless, of course, you've got good help."

Carrie set her cup down and looked at me. I thought she'd have figured it out by now, but obviously the plot was just hitting her. She's not usually so slow.

Brian picked up instantly, such a clever boy—of course it helped that I'd already planted the seed in his mind at the bank. "Interesting you should say that, because as it happens I have been looking for some help. Not formally, I haven't advertised yet, just been keeping my eyes open." He looked straight at Carrie. "It's gotten too much for me. I've got a wonderful girl, but she's more clerical, you know, she follows directions. What I need is somebody who can make decisions, somebody *bright* who can talk to the instructors on their own level. Chris—that's my secretary—she's a sweetheart, I'd be lost without her, but now I really need somebody a cut above, you know what I mean." Above his goatee, his cheeks glowed pink with good health. "May I have a little more coffee?"

Carrie cleared her throat. I, her mother, heard amusement, resignation, skepticism, and curiosity, but I expect Brian just heard her clear her throat. "How interesting," she said dryly. "Tell us more."

"Well." He hitched his body around toward her, crossing one muscle-bound thigh over the other. "I'm looking for someone to take some of the load off, and that means dealing with advertisers, the day-to-day troubleshooting, making up the curriculum brochure—that's one of the big things, I want completely out from under that, and it's a big job. Somebody to interface one-on-one with our current instructors, and also help recruit more. I'd like somebody to brainstorm with me over new courses, new angles, trying to keep it fresh and alive. Because you gotta constantly refresh, you can't get stale in this business or you're dead. I subscribe to four newspapers, and I probably read eight more on-line, every day, day in and day out. *Got* to stay fresh. Thanks." He stopped talking to gulp his coffee.

I was getting excited myself—maybe he should give *me* the job. The Other School has courses like "Computers Don't Byte," "Your Backyard Vineyard," "A Closer Look at Van Gogh." They have them on weeknights in places like the Unitarian Church or the Elks Club, anyplace there's an empty room and a proprietor who'll let Brian borrow it. Carrie took a course in tole painting last summer; Birdie and I took one called "The Joys of Grandparenting." (George wouldn't go with me, of course, but it's just as well, because frankly that one was a boondoggle.) The fees are cheap, and the teachers get paid based on how many students enroll in their classes. I imagine overhead's practically nothing. My guess is, in a small, Clayborne-type way, Brian Wright's making a killing.

"It's still a risky business, I won't kid you." He pushed back from the table, wiped his mouth with his napkin, balled it up, and set it beside his plate. *So big.* His shoulders were so broad, I couldn't see the back of his chair. "I couldn't withstand a recession yet, for example. I mean, anything can happen. I'll be honest—anybody I hired would be taking the same chance I'm taking."

Well, I certainly admired his candor. Personally, I would love a job like that, all the riskiness and newness, everything not completely planned out yet. I glanced at Carrie, who was pressing her fingertips together and looking thoughtful.

"May I be excused, please?"

Poor Ruth, she was bored to tears. "Of course," I started to say, "why don't you and your grandfather go watch TV." While I start the dishes, and Carrie and Brian have a little private chat—was my thought. But before I could finish, Brian stood up and said he hated to go but he had an early day tomorrow, dinner was wonderful, thanks so much, etc., etc., good-bye.

People—mostly Birdie; sometimes Carrie—say I have no tact. This is not true. I happen to believe there's a time for tact and a time for action, and here was a perfect example. Tact was what got this business meeting started, and action would see it through to the end.

"'Bye, Brian, I'm so glad you could come, it was lovely seeing you. Carrie, could you get Brian's coat? Ruth honey, you go watch your program. George, can you help me in the kitchen?"

There. Everybody went where they were supposed to go. Except for George, who kept going, out the back door and into the yard to smoke his pipe. I didn't spy on them, but before I closed the kitchen door I saw Carrie and Brian huddled in the foyer, talking in earnest voices. He was leaning forward, she was leaning back.

"Why didn't you just tell me, Mama? It would've been nice to know he was coming, that's all."

"I don't see why, and this way you didn't have to worry. Think of it as a stress-free job interview. Wasn't that a lot nicer than going down to his office and answering questions?"

"But what if he didn't want to interview me? You made it impossible for him *not* to."

"No, no, he did want to, I figured that out in the bank. What you don't understand is that this all started with Brian, not me."

"Oh, sure."

"Well, so? What did he say? Are you going to take it?"

Carrie straightened up from the dishwasher, swatting her hair back over her shoulder. "We both said we'd think it over."

"Oh. But he did offer it to you, the job, formally?"

"Well, I guess. Sort of. He told me more about what I'd do."

"What would you do?"

"Well, write all the copy for the spring semester's course brochure, that sounds like the main thing. Help him recruit new sponsors and advertisers. Write up ads and figure out new places to put them. 'Editorial and administration,' he said."

"My goodness, that sounds exciting."

"You think so?"

"Oh, my, yes. You'll be in charge of everything, sounds like. What will *he* do?"

She smiled, loosening up, getting over her huff. "I guess it might be okay. It doesn't sound too hard, nothing I probably couldn't learn."

"Are you kidding? He's lucky to get you. Did you talk about money?"

"No. Oh—he said he was glad to know I'm good with computers. Mama, what in the world did you tell him?"

"Nothing. Just that the last time you worked, which was in Chicago three years ago, you had a very important administrative position in a busy high-tech office."

"I was a part-time assistant in the math department at Stephen's college."

"Isn't that what I just said?"

Oh, it was good to hear Carrie laugh! Ruth came in while we were still at it. She went to the sink, pushing her mother aside with her hip to get a glass of water. Carrie reached up to push a lock of hair out of her face, but she shrugged away, still drinking. "So are you taking that job, Mom?"

"I don't know, sweetie. We said we'd talk about it some more."

"You and Mr. *Wright*." She set the glass in the sink too hard. She looked disgusted, curling her lip in a very unattractive way.

Carrie frowned. "Don't you want me to take it?"

"God, Mom, I so don't care."

"Well, nothing's formal yet anyway. He may not even offer it to me."

"Oh, he'll offer it to you, don't worry. I bet you a million dollars."

"How do you know?"

"Are you kidding? God, it's so *obvious*. The guy is *hot* for you."

Carrie stared, then laughed. "Oh, that's funny. Boy, are you off base."

"Nuh uhh."

"Ruthie, what am I going to do with you?"

"Jeez, Mom, are you really that dense?"

I didn't care for this conversation. I interrupted it to ask Ruth, hoping to change her mood, "How's that boyfriend of yours? The one I met at the bus stop the other day."

"Mama," Carrie said.

"I don't have any boyfriend, Gram."

"You know," I said, "Gull, Herring—"

"If you're speaking of Raven, he is not my boyfriend."

"Well, that's a relief." I laughed, hoping she'd join me. "I wanted to say to him, 'Honey, where's your calendar, Halloween's *over.*'"

"*Mama.*"

"*What?*"

It was a cold, nasty day when I met this person, probably forty degrees and spitting rain, but all "Raven" had on was leather pants and a black fishnet top. *Fishnet.* He had white makeup all over his face, and black lipstick on his mouth, the sides curling up in a creepy smile—it gave me the willies. He'd dyed his hair black, you could tell by the inch-long light-brown roots, and he wore it hacked off short on one side and combed over long on the other, long and stringy and absolutely ridiculous, like Michael Jackson's hair, like Dracula's. I was dying to hear what he had to say for himself, so I smiled at him and held my arm out the car window until he had to come over. Well, it was like shaking hands with the undead. His black lips moved, so he must've said something, but what I could not say. Then he walked backward, into the crowd of kids at the bus stop, and before I knew it he was gone. Like Bela Lugosi turning into a bat.

Ruth said, "I'm watching something on TV," and started to leave.

"But I'm sure he's a lovely boy. Hey, how about some ice cream? Want me to bring you some?"

"No, thanks, Gram."

"We've got chocolate *and* vanilla."

"No, thanks," she called from the dining room.

I could hear football coming from the TV room. "Make Grampa turn on something you like!"

Carrie shook her head at me.

"What? What did I say? I shouldn't have said Halloween. Okay, all right, I shouldn't have—but have you *seen* that boy?"

"He's actually very nice."

"Sure. That's what they said about those two at Columbine."

She turned her back and started drying the glasses.

I let a little time go by. "Now, listen. I hope you know I'd never want to push you into anything, but— " This time her laugh wasn't as pleasant to the ears. A snort, it sounded like. I ignored it. "*But.* I'm thinking you should take Brian Wright up on his offer."

"Oh, God." Her shoulders slumped. "I don't know."

"You should, for a lot of reasons. One, it would save you the trouble of looking for something yourself." Which she's not in any shape to do anyway; she could hardly leave the house to buy groceries. "Two, it sounds like a nice job, very responsible, with plenty of room in the future for growth. Three, it would get you out of your slump, because you'd have to get out and be with people. Four, Brian would make a great boss. And five, you need the money."

"You're right," she said lifelessly, elbows on the counter, staring at her reflection in the black window. "You're right, you're right, you're right."

"And six," I said to lighten the mood, "nobody else has offered you a job except Jess Deeping. To build ark animals!"

"Why do you always call him Jess Deeping?"

"What?"

"You always say his last name. You never call him Jess—you never did."

"Really? I never noticed." Why was everybody mad at me tonight? "Anyway. I still can't get over that ark business. Wasn't that the funniest thing? Even your father had a good laugh. You building ark animals—now I've heard everything. What was he going to pay you for that?"

"I don't know, Mama, we never got that far."

"I guess not."

"Jess wouldn't have paid me anyway. The church would have."

"The *Arkists*. My Lord, it never ceases to amaze me what people will start up a religion over. Next we'll have the Sons of Jonah—the Whalists." Carrie eked out a smile. "I didn't know you and Jess Deeping—excuse me, *Jess*—were friends again. I was surprised to see him at Stephen's funeral, in fact." But not as surprised as I was to see him in Carrie's *kitchen*. What a jolt that was. I hadn't been going to bring this subject up at all, and here I was smack in the middle of it.

"Why wouldn't we be friends again? It's—I thought Ruth might've mentioned him to you."

"Why would Ruth mention Jess Deeping to me?"

"Because they—well, it started when we ran into him at the hardware store last, I don't know, last spring sometime." She finally turned around and leaned back against the counter. "Ruth liked him, and he had a lot of dogs wriggling around in the back of his pickup truck, so of course that cemented the bond. She had to do a paper for school on a local industry, and it was her idea to call Jess up and ask a million questions about dairy farming. And then"—she waved her arm vaguely—"it just, you know—"

"Cow stomachs," I recalled. "The science fair project."

"Right, more research. And so—well, anyway, that's it, end of story. Do these go in here or the dining room?"

"I have to say, I think it's just a little odd that this is the first time I'm hearing about all this."

"All what?"

"You know what I'm talking about."

"No, I don't. I really don't."

"Okay, never mind. The good glasses go in the mahogany cupboard in the dining room, please, top shelf. Thank you."

We stared at each other for a few seconds, but it felt like a lot longer. Were we fighting? We used to, years ago, then we quit—

Carrie put up a wall. I'd give anything for the closeness we used to have. But it's gone, and no matter what I do I can't get it back. I thought when she moved back to Clayborne after twenty years away, the pattern would change and we'd become friends again, the way we were—when? When she was about Ruth's age. That was the best time for us. The only time Carrie ever loved me as much as I love her.

What is it I do, I wonder. What's my fatal flaw? Every mother swears all she wants for her children is happiness, but in my case it's the truth. I love my daughter more than anyone else on this earth, even more than my granddaughter, but she won't let me in. She's like a shadow that moves whenever I move, I can't touch her. She pulls away, turns away, backs away. Did I raise a cold child? Or is it me? We're not even close enough to fight anymore.

"Dining room," Carrie said, and walked out with her hands full of wineglasses.

5

Who Is That American Girl?

I was walking home from school by myself because I missed the bus and Caitlin and Jamie, who I usually walk home with as far as Madison when that happens, had already left without me. I passed a store I've noticed before but never gone in. What caught my eye this time was a sign in the window that said TIRED ALL THE TIME?

I'm not, but my mom is. Also sad all the time—maybe they had something for that, too. Under the TIRED ALL THE TIME sign was a big pyramid of pill bottles, and another sign that said, "Clean, pure Nature's Turn Algae, grown wild in the glacier-fed lakes of Ontario, promotes energy, stamina, and mental clarity." I went inside.

Krystal's Mother Earth Palace and Natural Healing Salon, the store was called. They could also have called it Heat and Incense, which is what rushed out and hit me in the face before I could get the door closed. It was like walking into a furnace burning perfume logs. I unwrapped my muffler and unbuttoned my coat, nodding to the only other person in the store, a lady moving jars around on a shelf. "Need any help?" she asked over the plinking of dulcimer music. "No, thanks," I said, "I'm just looking."

Nature's Turn Algae cost $16.95 a bottle. Tough luck, Mom. Gram and Grampa gave me a big check for Christmas, but I still had to be careful about money. Who knew when I'd get more? I went over to the vitamin shelves, which covered two whole walls, thinking maybe some iron pills. Iron, iron . . . things weren't alphabetical here like they were at the drugstore. Did Mom have chronic fatigue? That would explain a lot. If so, she needed Fibro Malic or Aqua Flora. Or Protykin, a powerful antioxidant to fight the onslaught of free radicals, which wreak havoc by destroying cells and tissues. Okay, but what exactly is a free radical? I pictured it as this, like, boomerang-shaped sickle slicing through the air, invading you through your pores or your nose, maybe your food. Nobody's safe. Fibro Malic or not, something's always going to get you.

Wow, this store had pills for everything. Prostate problems, joint pain, thinning hair, trouble breathing, blotchy skin, hormonal imbalance. I have both of those last two. And I've been having a very slow heartbeat lately, sometimes I can't find my pulse at all. These easy-to-swallow soft gels could help; revolutionary studies revealed the amazing cardio-protectant effect of tocotrienols. Some products had typewritten testimonials taped to the shelf under them. I paused at one for a miraculous intestinal cleaner. Some guy, Clifford C. of Spaulding, VA, wrote, "I used it every day for a month, and I was amazed at how all the poisons and decaying matter just kept coming out." Message to Cliff: *Yuck*.

The incense smell was nice once you got used to it, a sort of lemon and cinnamon combination. It was coming from a pot on top of a woodstove at the back of the store. A bookshelf and a couple of soft, ratty-looking chairs closed the area off and made it look cozy, like somebody's very small living room. The books were what you'd expect, New Age stuff, herbal remedies, spiritual healing, 12-step programs. I ran my finger along the spines and pulled out *Live Well, Live Forever*. Snort. Yeah, right. I carried the book over to one of the chairs and sat down.

Well, whatever ailed you, this book could cure it. Acne, allergies, anemia, anger. Heel spurs, hemorrhoids, hiccups. Jealousy, jet lag. Phobias, poor body image, postnasal drip.

Heart disease, page 253.

Oh, man. All the things, all the tricks he could've tried, the safety measures he could've taken. He could've cut out meat, dairy, and processed foods. He could've taken chromium, magnesium, vitamins C and E, and selenium, he could've done yoga. Or meditated, he could've visualized himself swimming easily through the four clean chambers of his heart and out into the coronary arteries, shining a healing blue light on the artery walls as he swam, letting go of all troubling emotions. "Picture something worrisome to your heart such as anger, sadness, or injustice. Throw it over your left shoulder and let it go."

"That's a good book. On special, forty percent off because it's after Christmas." The woman who had been stocking shelves plopped down in the other chair, and immediately a fluffy white cat that for some reason I hadn't seen before jumped up in her lap. "What are you looking up?" She had a round, smiling face framed by a lot of streaky reddish hair, pleated in cornrows and tied with gold beads. And she had a low, gentle, husky voice that took the edge off her nosy question.

"Heart trouble."

"Have you got heart trouble?"

"No." I closed the book, kept pressing it along the spine, erasing the page I had turned to. "My dad. He had coronary heart disease caused by mild atherosclerosis, hypertension, and elevated blood cholesterol. He died." The woman nodded sadly. "He wasn't a type A, though. He wasn't overweight and he didn't smoke. He jogged every two days."

"What was his dosha?"

"Pardon me?"

"In Ayurveda, you can be either *pitta*, *vata*, or *kapha*. *Pittas* are passionate and fiery and hot-tempered, and interestingly, they often live in New England. *Vatas*, they're creative and romantic, usually have curly hair and dry skin, they can get spacey and very ungrounded when they're nervous. *Kaphas* are more phlegmatic, very calm and forgiving, large-eyed people who tend to gain weight. They're your couch potatoes. We've got all three in us, of course, but usually one predominates."

"Um, well, I guess he'd be mostly . . . What was the first one?"

"*Pitta*. Did he have red hair and freckles?"

"No."

"Blond?"

"Sort of. Light brown."

"There you go. Strong metabolisms and effective digestive systems, that's your *pittas*. It's a shame he didn't take arjuna. That's an herb that strengthens the heart muscle and promotes healing. I'm so sorry." She leaned forward, frowning in sympathy. "I just *know* it could've helped him."

I pressed the book to my chest and looked at the fire in the woodstove, murky orange behind the dirty glass window. I was standing by the stove in the Markuses' kitchen when I heard about my parents' accident. We were making fudge. Jamie, Caitlin, me, and Marianne Werner. It was about eleven-thirty at night, and we were arguing over whether to put in walnuts. The phone rang but stopped ringing before Jamie could answer. "My mom got it," she said, and went back to stirring the pot on the stove. About a minute later Mrs. Markus came in the kitchen with Mr. Markus. He had on his robe and pajamas, but she was still in her clothes. I thought we were making too much noise and she'd brought him with her to lay down the law. But they stood in the doorway and didn't say anything, so then I thought they'd come for some fudge. I kept waiting for Jamie to tell them it wasn't ready yet. Mr. Markus said, "Ruth?" I didn't even think he knew my name. As soon as he said it, I knew something awful had happened.

"Would you like some tea? By the way, I'm Krystal." The lady got up and went behind the counter, coming back with two ceramic mugs. "It's chrysanthemum today."

I said, "Well, um."

"Good for the capillaries."

"Really?"

"No question. Have you had headaches lately? Or insomnia?"

"Yeah. Yes, I have."

"This'll help. You'll find you see better, too."

"Wow. Thanks." I took the mug, which Krystal had filled from a copper pot at the back of the stove. "Mm," I said politely. "It's a little . . ."

"Bitter? Put some honey in. Here. I like it plain now, but it took some getting used to." The white cat jumped back up in her lap. Even over the hiss of the woodstove, I could hear it purring. Krystal had a pretty face, and she was a little overweight; she looked like Tracy Chapman, only white and older. Probably a *kapha*. What I couldn't figure out was how she could wear all those clothes in this hot, hot store. She had on a long brown wool skirt with a yellow turtleneck and a multicolored woven sort of tunic thing over that, plus beaded moccasins and long socks and a bright red and orange scarf around her waist, cinching in the tunic. Wasn't she boiling?

"I'm Ruth," I remembered to say. "Ruth Van Allen."

"Hi." She beamed, her face warm and friendly and bland. "It's quiet today. Not many customers."

"I guess you wouldn't need any help, then."

"Hm?"

I stared into my cup, amazed. "Guess you don't need anybody to work for you. After school for like three hours or something, three to six o'clock, and then weekends." I glanced up. Krystal didn't look embarrassed or disapproving or disgusted, she looked thoughtful. "I've been looking for a job ever since my father died." A little exaggeration; I'd been thinking about getting a job, but this was the first time I'd done anything about it. Mom getting hers pushed me into it.

"I could use somebody, actually." Krystal set her mug on the arm of her chair. She turned the limp-limbed cat over and cradled it like a baby, smiling into its blissed-out face. "I'm getting a certificate in naturopathic doctoring, and I need time to study. You're in high school?"

"A sophomore. I get out at quarter to three and I could be here by five after, every day except Monday and Thursday. Soccer practice."

"That would be good. Know anything about natural healing? Health foods? It's okay," she said when I didn't answer. "Mostly you'd be working with stock anyway, not customers. I could teach you."

As soon as she said "I could teach you," I wanted the job. I had to have it. I could learn everything: Ayurveda, vitamins, aromatherapy. It was all here, the secret was right in this room—and a few minutes ago I didn't even know there was a secret. Here was a way for me right now, I could get in early, not have to wait till I was twenty-one, twenty-five, thirty, to learn it.

"This would be so great," I said, trying not to bounce or yell or do anything stupid. "I'm very responsible. I have a Social Security number. I could work all day on Saturdays and Sundays."

"Well, I'm not open on Sundays."

"Oh." I blushed, hoping I hadn't offended her religious beliefs or something. "Do you want me to fill out a form or anything?"

She shrugged, still cradling the cat. "I don't know what it would be. A form? You could write down your phone number, I guess."

Mom was going to ask me a lot of questions. Like how much this job paid. But I didn't know how to ask without sounding rude. I decided to tell Mom the minimum wage, and if it turned out to be more, that would just be even better.

The bell above the door jingled, somebody came in. Krystal looked over but didn't get up. She was a very laid-back shopkeeper. I already loved that about her. "Well," I said, "I guess I should go home. Thank you for the tea, it was very good. When do you think you would like me to start? I mean . . ." I blushed again. "Is it for sure? Are we doing this?"

"Yeah! I have an excellent feeling about it, don't you?"

"I do! I really do."

"You know, I read auras, among other things. Yours is a sort of slate blue—today, anyway—and my cool greenish silver meshes perfectly. I know we're going to get along great. You're a . . ." She narrowed her eyes, studying me. "Aquarius—am I right?"

"Cancer."

"I knew it, it had to be one or the other. I'm Pisces, which is water, too. Ruth Van Allen, we're going to get along like two koi in a lily pond."

"Oh, wow." I hugged my arms, thrilled.

I woke up from a dream I have a lot these days, that I'm running for a train. It's nighttime and very foggy, rainy, and I hear the train whistle blow and I start running toward the tracks. I have on my black jeans and my army green V-neck sweater—this is very important for some reason, what I'm wearing, because it never changes—and I start running along beside the train, which is going faster and faster. I reach out and grab for the cold metal handle, and *whoosh*, pull myself up, and the train picks up speed. I just hang there, feeling the wet wind in my face—and that's the end. I have this dream *constantly*. Running in my black jeans and green sweater in the fog after a train.

Then I couldn't go back to sleep. I got up to get a drink, and heard the TV on downstairs.

"Mom? You still up? It's three-thirty."

"No, I'm not still up. I fell asleep, I just woke up."

I pretended to believe that. She stays up every night almost all night with the TV or the radio or the CD player on, and in the morning she pretends she's just woken up. Then she sleeps all day. She still hadn't gotten around to taking all the Christmas decorations down. Not that she put that many up this year.

"What are you watching?" I asked.

"Nothing. A movie."

I made her move over so I could sit next to her on the sofa. All the lights were out except for the TV. She was huddled under a chenille throw Gram got her for Christmas, wearing one of Dad's old gray Henley shirts and her nightgown. She looked terrible. "I can see that. What is it?"

"Why are you up? You should be in bed."

"I'll go in a sec."

"It's James Stewart in *Call Northside* 777. I thought it would be a Hitchcock, but it's not."

"Who's this guy?"

"He's in prison, he's been in for eleven years for killing a cop. James Stewart's a reporter who thinks he's innocent and is trying to get him out."

I love watching old movies with Mom. It's one of the best things we do together. That and going shopping and then having lunch in a restaurant. Although we haven't done that in a long time, but we used to. We'd almost always get ice cream instead of food, and she always made that seem exciting and nervy and forbidden. "We won't mention this to your father," she'd say in a low voice, ordering two double hot fudge sundaes, one with nuts and one without, and I'd say, "What he doesn't know won't hurt him." We'd laugh, and eat ice cream until our stomachs hurt.

It was a pretty good movie. James Stewart got Richard Conte out of prison at the last second by enlarging a photograph that showed the date on a newspaper, which proved he was innocent. In the very end, they showed Richard Conte getting out of jail and meeting his wife and son and her new husband. She'd divorced him but she still loved him, and she wasn't going back to him because now she had E. G. Marshall.

"Would you ever get married again?"

We both stared straight ahead at the TV. "I don't know, honey. I don't think so, I doubt it. I can't imagine it."

"What if you fell in love with somebody? You're not that old."

She made a face. "I feel old."

"No, but in ten years you could meet some guy and fall in love all over again. You could. It's possible."

She pulled her knees up under her nightgown, dropped her head, and ran her fingers through her hair, messing it up.

"I'm just saying it's possible," I said, touching her on the foot. She had on a pair of Dad's old woolly socks. She never used to wear his clothes like this when he was alive. "Right? You can't be sad forever. Nobody is, except in books. People start up again, they go on." I had been studying this, noticing. "Sonny Bono's wife started dating like nine months after he died. Remember? And after Diana's wreck, the princes went to parties and stuff, they showed pictures of them laughing and looking happy, and you'd never have thought they could do that from the way they were at the funeral. Remember?"

"Yep." She put her arm around me. I burrowed against her, liking her warmth and her flannel smell, even her dirty hair smell. "Tell me about your day."

"I already did. Oh, we saw a movie in World Cultures. It was on the Scottish Highlands, which are incredibly cold and barren, but really really beautiful, and they have more sheep there than people. I was thinking how cool it would be to live there."

"Why? If it's cold and bleak and nobody lives there."

"Because, it just would be. Nothing could happen to you because nobody would even know you were there. And the rent would be cheap."

In fact, I fell asleep tonight thinking about what it would be like to live in a stone cottage with a thatched roof on a hillside all by myself, just a black and white collie for company. I could be either a writer or a painter. People would talk about me, that

American girl who lives alone and doesn't speak to anyone. They'd observe me walking along the cliffs with my dog and the wind blowing out my hair and my black cape. "How lonely she must be," the natives would say, seeing my solitary figure. I'd have a walking stick. I'd speak with a hint of a brogue. Then a handsome, older man would move into the cottage on the neighboring cliff. He too would be an artist, but a tortured, unsuccessful one. I would become his muse. Because of me he would regain his ability to write haunting poetry. Together we would win the Pulitzer Prize, and in our acceptance speech he'd say that without me he would be nothing. We'd get a lot of money and live on the barren heath forever.

"I can't wait for my new job to start," I said. "When does yours?"

"Next week. Monday morning."

"So you better start getting ready, huh? Going to bed at eleven or so. Right? So you can get up in the morning." I gave her pantyhose and perfume for Christmas, and also a new digital alarm clock, so she's got no excuses.

"Good idea," she said.

"Mine starts tomorrow." It would've started sooner, but I had to get a work permit because I'm not sixteen.

"I know."

"It's so totally cool, Mom, it really is." She nodded and smiled, but she wasn't thrilled about it. But that was because she didn't get it; once she met Krystal and checked out the Mother Earth Palace and all the stuff there, she'd be cool with it. Who wouldn't? Caitlin was like, "Oh, wow, that is so weird," but in a good way, and Raven totally gets it, totally thinks it's an excellent choice. First thing, I have to look up sore throat in one of Krystal's books, because I've had one for two days. Low-grade and not bad enough to stay home, but this is how a lot of things start, including esophageal cancer. But it's probably not that. It's probably, like, a cold.

"So what are you going to wear on your first day?"

Mom laughed. "I have absolutely no idea. You think I'll have to get dressed up?"

"Just show your legs a lot, he'll like that. Mr. *Wright*."

"Ruth, what is this with you? Why don't you like Brian?"

"I just don't."

"But why?"

"He's a jerk. Do you like the way he looks at you?"

"The way he looks at me?"

"The way he does everything."

She shook her head, like I was speaking in some other language besides English. "Honey—Brian's okay, he's just a guy. He'll make a good boss but nothing else, you know? Know what I'm sayin'?" she tried for a joke. I hunched my shoulder and put it between our faces. "Listen," she said. "It's important for you to know that I'm not—playing the field or anything."

"Gee, Mom, you sure know some hip lingo."

"I'm just telling you, I'm not available. Nobody is taking your father's place. Nothing's going to change."

"Right."

"Is that agreement or sarcasm?"

"Did you know him before Dad died?"

"Yes, of course. Not well. We'd run into him at college functions."

"What was he like then?"

"He was fine—what do you mean?"

"Didn't you see his eyes that night at dinner? And before, when you were having drinks, how he swooped down on you?"

"Ruth, really—what are you talking about? Brian's friendly, he's personable, he likes people. He stands close when he talks to you, he—touches you sometimes, just to make contact. It doesn't mean anything. It's probably why he's good at his job, it's just the kind of person he is."

"Right. Like Bill Clinton." She laughed, so I laughed, too. I wanted to get off this subject anyway. "Where is the Other School, anyway?" I said. "If it's near the Mother Earth, we could go home together after work sometimes."

"Well, except I'll probably be finishing up about the time you're just starting."

"Yeah, I guess," I said. "Too bad."

She gave me a hug. I didn't know why until I figured out that she thought it was cool that I wanted to go home from work with her. She's so easy sometimes. "Listen, you," she said. "I am going to take your advice and clean up my act, start going to bed early, getting in shape. But you know that I'm really all right, don't you? You get that?"

"Sure," I said, "I know."

"*Really* all right. So don't worry about me."

"Okay. And you don't worry about me."

"No deal, I'm your mother, I get to do that full-time."

"Seriously, Mom, because I'm fine, too."

"I know you are."

"I *am*."

"I know."

Well, somebody was lying. I wondered if she knew it was both of us, and if she thought I believed her, and if she believed me. It didn't matter that much, though, not while we were huddled up together on the couch, her with her arms wound around my arm, me with my head on her shoulder. Watching Bob Dornan walk down a fancy staircase and explain why *Elephant Walk* was a classic and what Elizabeth Taylor was doing when they made it. Right here under Gram's soft blanket, we were safe. We had each other, we practically *were* each other, and it was like we were full. For tonight.

6

Sensible Meals at Appropriate Hours

At eighteen, I was thrilled to leave Clayborne for the big city—Washington, D.C. I went to school there, met Stephen, married, moved to Chicago, had Ruth. I thought I was through with small towns, and certainly through with the south. I never reckoned on Stephen's pleasant liberal arts college denying him tenure, a turn of fortune that effectively rendered him unemployable for any position his pride would let him accept. Except at Remington College, and there only because my father pulled strings.

When we moved back to Clayborne three years ago, I was filled with misgivings. Dread, make that. The things that drove me wild about my hometown were still there, and most of them could be summed up in the word *small*. But something happened to me during my twenty-year self-exile. Smallness didn't oppress me anymore—now I could even see advantages. Old age, I suppose.

It wasn't as if *nothing* had changed in Clayborne—shopping malls full of the usual chain stores had sprouted up where pretty farms used to be; we had new glass and metal office buildings, a few gentrified, brick-paved, gaslight-lined streets downtown where cars weren't allowed. The Leap River had a new four-lane bridge across it, and a "fitness trail" where the old towpath used to be. But the old college hot spots were in the same wooden two-story buildings on Remington Avenue they'd been in when I was a teenager; only the names had changed. Remington students wore different clothes, different hairstyles, but their faces still looked harried, carefree, snotty, scared, drugged out—same as they did in the sixties and the seventies. And the college still gave Clayborne whatever thin veneer of culture and sophistication it had. Without it, we'd have been just another sleepy Piedmont farm village with tenuous ties to the Confederacy and funky architecture. With it, we were a poor man's Charlottesville. A wannabe Chapel Hill.

My family always disdained the local paper, the *Morning Record*. Pop wouldn't read anything but the *New York Times* or, for slumming, the Richmond *Times-Dispatch*; Stephen didn't even know the *Morning Record* existed. But I liked it. When I was in town, I picked up a copy and read it with as much guilty pleasure as if it were the *National Enquirer*, which it certainly was not. At the *Record*, everything was newsworthy, the school lunch menus, hospital admissions by name—but not ailment, fortunately—minutes of meetings of the zoning board and the PTA, the record of deeds and transfers—they printed how much you paid for your house, how much you got for your farm. Fascinating reading. My favorite section was the police blotter, because there was hardly any crime—teen vandalism, some DUI's, a lot of college drunkenness, the tantalizing "lewd conduct," which usually turned out to be peeing in public. That was about it. "Hit and Run" meant somebody had banged into a mailbox and kept going. The commonest headline for traffic accidents was "No One Hurt."

After Chicago, it was like Oz. When I was a young girl the sleepiness of my town made me crazy, but now I liked it. And it wasn't *altogether* that middle age had turned me into a fossil, as my daughter claimed. It was also Ruth herself. Bad things could still happen—I knew that, I wasn't blind—but they weren't as likely. Simple as that. Here in Clayborne, Virginia, the law of dreadful probabilities was in my child's favor. Proximity to my mother, I often had to remind myself, was a small price to pay for peace of mind.

"Look, there's my first boyfriend," I said to Modean, my neighbor, on a chilly, sunny, Sunday afternoon in the middle of January.

We were sitting on a bench in Monroe Square, Clayborne's town center, and I was stalling, thinking of things to say so she wouldn't get up and make me start jogging again.

"Where?" She squinted her kind, nearsighted eyes, looking out across the concrete and grass at the mothers pushing baby strollers, the jostling students, the old men playing checkers. I pointed. "Oh, *him*. Mm, very handsome."

The Confederate Soldier had been standing in the center of Monroe Square since 1878—the plaque said so. He wasn't famous for anything in particular; Clayborne had sent plenty of sons off to the War between the States but, except for dying, none of them had done anything spectacular. He wasn't even on horseback; he was just a regular soldier, rifle over his left shoulder, right leg jutting out as he strode boldly north, toward trouble. "Such a crush I had on him. I even named him," I confessed to Modean.

"What?"

"Beauregard Rourke. Beau to me." Modean snickered. "I used to coast my bike around and around him and make up dreamy stories."

"Like?"

"Like . . . I was a beautiful spy from Philadelphia and he was my secret contact. And clandestine lover."

"How romantic."

"Already I'd figured out the beauty of a bronze boyfriend is that he has to be anything you want, and he can't change."

Modean said, "Carrie, how was your Christmas?" She'd asked me that question yesterday, when she and Dave got back from three weeks in Atlanta, where his folks live, and I'd said, "Fine! It went well, really, much better than I expected."

But now I told her the truth. "It was sad," I said, leaning over to rub a sore place on my heel through my sneaker. "Ruth was so sweet. She did everything she could think of to cheer me up. I did the same for her, so by one o'clock we were both exhausted and we hadn't even gone to my mother's yet."

"How was that?"

"Okay. Same as always, pretty much. My cousins were there, and Aunt Fan, my father's sister. You know my mother always takes over at things like that, the big family occasions. It's her show. Stephen—well, he tended to recede as much as he could. That was just how he coped."

She nodded. "Yeah, I know he was quiet in groups. Shy."

Shy? That was one way to look at it. "Well, he wasn't much of a participant in family events," I said. "He observed. If anything. I did the work and Stephen . . . attended."

"Oh, well. That's just how men are."

"Oh, I know," I said quickly, "they're all like that."

Modean, who saw nothing but good in everyone, was the last person in the world I could complain to about Stephen. Not that I wanted to complain about him. But I wanted to explain to someone why I hadn't missed him terribly over the holidays. I wanted to tell Modean how he could make himself invisible. He did his duty—strung the lights, wrote checks, bought the booze if we were having a party—then he disappeared. It was the same every year, and eventually I got used to doing everything myself. How could I miss him at my mother's house on Christmas day? His absence was noticeable, but not remarkable. Without him, Mama's show really did go on.

"We had an okay time in Atlanta," Modean was telling me. "Dave's dad has a drinking problem, I think I told you, but he stayed on good behavior because of the baby. But there was always that tension, you know, and not knowing. I worried a lot about Dave because he was worrying a lot about his father. So mostly I guess everybody just worried."

Modean was the most perfect friend I'd ever had. She was kind-hearted, happy, simple, direct, and together. I'd given up my cynical search for the crack—the secret drinking, the sudden religious proselytizing, the kleptomania. It wasn't there, and she was a paragon, with the saving grace of a sense of humor. Dave was a tall, reedy guy with bushy gray hair and a perpetually startled look, as if he couldn't believe the amazing turn his luck had taken. He was older, widowed for about fifteen years when he found Modean. And Harry was the perfect baby for these perfect parents. I considered it a point in my favor that I had never, even at my lowest, most miserable, self-pitying point, hated the lot of them.

Forcing me, with Ruth's complicity, to go jogging with her was the first mean thing Modean had ever done to me. "You need to get strong, Carrie, you have to build yourself back up. How do you expect to start working eight-hour days? You'll collapse at that office before lunchtime." All true, but I still hated it. When I was in better shape—before Stephen died—I used to jog with him every once in a while, but it never worked out very well. I only did it for the chance to spend time with him, and he preferred to run alone. Cross-purposes.

"Ready to go?" Modean jumped up and started doing stretching exercises. I mimicked her halfheartedly, stiff as a plank. She was ten years younger than me, but even at her age I was never that fit. She was small but strong, with frizzy blonde hair and fair skin, and blue eyes with blonde lashes. She looked like a baby bird. "Okay?" she said, and took off. I followed creakily. It was only eleven blocks from the square to our street, and she regularly ran ten times that without breaking a sweat. I was panting before we hit Jefferson Street.

"So are you all set for work?" She slowed for me, practically running in place. "What are you going to wear tomorrow?"

"Oh, gosh," I wheezed, "I don't know—there's only one other employee besides Brian—a woman—I think it's pretty casual."

"A pantsuit, maybe."

"That's what I was thinking."

"Heels?"

"For the first day."

"Yeah." She paused, thinking she was letting me catch my breath. "I have a new jacket. Got it in Atlanta. I think it would fit you, and it would be terrific with black slacks. It's just right for now, and it's really office-y. I don't even know why I got it, except that I liked it. You could wear it—you could even have it if you think it looks good. Because I really can't imagine where I'm going to wear it."

The only problem with Modean was that she was too good. I'd never had a friend with no edge or shadow at all, no dark spot, some pettiness, a flair for sarcasm, *something*. I was usually the good one—comparatively speaking—in my relationships with women, the one who gasped, "Oh, that's *terrible*," while stifling guilty laughter over the other's wicked observation or unkind gibe. But with Modean, I was the bad one. I worried that I wasn't up to it, that eventually we'd bore each other to death and drift apart. Well, I hoped not. Because I liked her so much.

The Other School was a two-room storefront on the north side, the rundown side, of Virginia Street. Its neighbor on the left was Dr. Jawaharlal, the chiropractor, and on the right, the Cobra Tae Kwon Do. Across the street the streaky showroom window of Coyle's Appliances was plastered with yellow, peeling, three-year-old GOING OUT OF BUSINESS signs. Clayborne didn't have a real slum or ghetto, at least not one compacted into a single small, identifiable section of town. If it had a disadvantaged commercial district, though, North Virginia Street was its epicenter.

"Well, hi!" Christine Fledergast said after I told her who I was. She jumped up from a desk behind a waist-high Formica counter that stretched the width of the narrow front room of the Other School. Behind her, a dark doorway opened to another office—Brian's, I assumed. Christine came around the counter with one arm stretched out, big smile of welcome on her long, exceptionally plain face. She was at least six feet tall, lanky and rawboned, with coarse blonde hair cut short and spiky; not fashionably spiky, more as if she'd cut it herself. "Hey, how are you, it's great to meet you! Brian's out of town—did he tell you?—he won't be back till tomorrow, so it's just going to be me showing you the ropes today—sorry about that. He'll tell you all the important stuff tomorrow."

Modest self-effacement, I'd find out soon, was typical of Chris Fledergast. By lunchtime I'd figured out who ran the office, and it wasn't Brian. If he needed somebody "bright" who could make decisions, she was right here. The miracle was that she didn't seem to resent me, even though I was going to be, in effect, her supervisor. But how could she not? She'd been Brian's right hand for three years. All my puny work background was in academia, the *fringes* of academia, miles away from a growing, dynamic place like the Other School. What was Brian thinking? What could he see in me that I couldn't see in myself?

"Brian's great to work for," Chris confided over tuna fish sandwiches at Creager's, the nearest lunch spot. "Whenever you need time off, you usually just have to ask. And for a small business he gives super benefits. He pays attention, he's appreciative, and he doesn't make you work any harder than he does."

"That's good to know," I said. Because my salary had been a big disappointment. Brian assured me it was temporary, after a few months he'd be able to pay me a wage "more in keeping with your worth." I wasn't sure what that meant, but it was nice to know I'd enjoy enlightened working conditions in return for the pittance he was paying me in the meantime.

Chris's husband, Oz, was a sales rep for a pharmaceutical company. "He travels a lot. He got back from a trip on Christmas Eve at ten o'clock at night, and he was gone again the day after. I didn't see him for a week! He's got no idea, no conception of what it's like trying to pull Christmas together for two kids by yourself."

She didn't wear a speck of makeup that I could see. She wore flat shoes, hunched her shoulders, and slumped. She was spectacularly unattractive in any conventional way, but I had liked her face the minute I saw it. All of a sudden she clapped her hand to the top of her head. "Oh God, Carrie, I'm sorry."

"Why? What?"

"Listen to me going on about Oz. Me and my big mouth. I always talk before I think."

"Oh, no, it's fine, don't worry."

"No, but it must've been just a *terrible* holiday for you. I can't even imagine it. Brian told me about your husband, how sudden it was. I'm so very, very sorry." Her hazel eyes filled with tears.

Oh, great. And me a sympathetic crier. I snickered wetly and handed over a Kleenex, taking one for myself. We blew our noses in unison.

Chris apologized—"This is all you need, I am so sorry, I cry at Alpo commercials"—and blushed. "Not that this is like an Alpo commercial, I mean, this is *much* more serious."

I had just taken a sip of my drink. When I choked, a fine mist of Pepsi sprayed out over my plate. Chris stared at me for a shocked second, then started to giggle, hesitantly at first, checking to make sure it was okay. Before long we were leaning back in our facing seats, braying at each other. She had a swooping, crazy-woman laugh; the sound of it tickled me so much, I kept on laughing. After a while I lost track of what we were laughing at, but part of it had to be relief over not having to be so damn careful with each other.

Fledergast was Oz's name; hers was really O'Donnell. I told her mine was Danziger. We told each other about our hobbies, my crafts and decorating, her creative writing classes. For some reason I found myself telling her about Jess and the Arkists. I was used to Ruth's and my mother's disdain, and Chris's delight took me by surprise. "What fun," she cried, "what a blast you'd have! You're not doing it?"

"When? When? I can't, I just haven't got time."

"God, I know. If I had time, I know what I'd be doing—writing books for kids."

"Really?"

"I've already written one—well, actually I wrote three when Andy was little. But now he's nine, I don't have the excuse that I'm writing them for him anymore. I miss it."

"Did you ever try to sell them?"

"Oh, no, no. Although they weren't terrible. But they weren't picture books so, you know, I doubt there'd've been much of a market anyway. But honestly, they weren't bad."

"I bet they were great."

"If only we didn't have to make money. You know?"

I laughed.

"Wouldn't it be a happier world? This job's fine, I'm not complaining, but what does it have to do with *us*? For Brian, it's the best job there could ever be, but that's because it's *his*. I'm jealous of him. I think people who have found their life's work are the luckiest people in the world. Join me in the chorus now . . ."

We laughed again, but she was right. It was a disheartening thought for the first day of my new job.

Three weeks later, Brian braced his hands against the edge of my desk, his weight-lifter shoulders hunched, head jutted, eyes intent. "We can go to four quarters by the beginning of next year. We can. Already we have too many classes per term for the amount of space we've got, or we will by next summer. Thanks to you, Carrie."

"Oh, no. That's not true, but thanks." I wasn't being modest. I'd made some contacts, phone calls, had conversations with Brian about new courses, nothing more. Crediting me with pulling off the expansion of the Other School by a full quarter was taking employee boosterism too far. But that was the kind of hype Brian excelled at. The amazing thing was that even when you knew he was doing it, it worked. I glanced past his shoulder at Chris, who winked at me.

"Yep, yep, don't tell me, I know who's making a change around here. New ideas, fresh air, that's what we needed. Got stale, got sleepy, can't let that happen. Like when you get tired driving—you want to get where you're going, you don't pull over and take a nap, no, you open a window, let the cold air blow in your face. That's you, Care, a breath of fresh air."

I laughed, flattered in spite of myself. Oh, he was so full of it.

But my new job wasn't as interesting as he'd made it sound. Or maybe it was me. Chris had been doing the work of two people, so my job was to take over half of her workload. Right now it was challenging, but I couldn't help wondering for how long.

I guessed it was worth it, though, toy salary and all, because I had to get up at seven every day, shower, put on lady clothes, leave the house. Eat sensible meals at appropriate hours. Nobody, not even Margaret Sachs, was sorry to see the end of the assembly line of miniature flower arrangements. As routine and horizonless as I could imagine Brian's job becoming, at least it had accomplished what my mother, guilt over Ruth, and fifty milligrams a day of Zoloft hadn't been able to: my return to the real world. Half of me might still be in the ether, zoned out and inattentive, mired in the old grief and guilt that a death in the family brings—*naturally*—but the other half was coping. It was a start.

Brian leaned in closer. With anyone else, a man especially, I'd have moved back, maintained the conventional distance, but I was getting used to his enthusiastic invasions of my space. "Summer term will tell the tale," he prophesied softly; I could smell the clove-flavored gum he chewed after he smoked a cigarette. "That's the key. If it's big, we'll know. That's the next corner we turn. Right? So are we on schedule? Did you get Lois Burkhart on board again? You have to nail her down, Care—"

"I did."

"—because those finance courses are big in the summer. After April fifteenth everybody wants to reform, turn over a new leaf.

They read the brochure in May, they can't wait to sign up for 'Debt-Free Living' or whatever it is."

"I got her."

"And Albert Meyer, I want him for day trading again, and he didn't reup. Call and get him on the bus. I was thinking we should beef up the touchy-feely stuff for summer, get more girls. I know, but it's *true*, you offer 'Relationships for the Millennium'—that's just off the top of my head—and you've got fifteen, twenty women ready to talk, and not a man among 'em. Am I right?"

"Probably."

"Right, so let's think about it, get somebody from social services or one of the university shrinks. 'Be Your Own Therapist'—how's that? 'Learning to Like Yourself.' Because we've got enough tech stuff, enough computer, Internet, and small business, we need to girly things up a little for summer. I know!" he exclaimed, laughing, throwing up his hands. "But you know what I mean! Okay, I'm a sexist pig, and now I'm getting out of here."

"Where are you going?"

"Got a meeting with Hal Wiley at the paper."

"About an ad?"

"An ad, sure, but I'm talking to him about putting the brochure in the *Record*. The whole summer schedule."

"Printing it? Oh," I said, "that would be great."

"No, not printing it. The whole thing, talking about an insert. Think of the distribution! And hell, it's a community service." He grinned, held his arms out wide. He looked like a fullback. "Heh? Think he'll go for it?"

We women exchanged glances. "I think," Chris said with conviction, "he won't know what hit him."

Part of my job involved editing course copy the instructors sent in, the short, hype-filled paragraph allocated to each class in the brochure. Most of them needed punching up, "sexying," Brian called it, especially the courses that sounded a little dry to begin with—"Amateur Radio Operating," "Problem Solving," "Autumn in the Herb Garden." Any course could be jazzed up to sound more interesting, though, and I was getting pretty good at it. Titles were my forte. Last year's "Basic Waltz, Fox-trot, and Jitterbug," for example, would be "Gotta Dance!" next term; the old "Writing Screenplays for TV and the Movies" would be "Move Over, Quentin Tarantino." And so forth.

Rarely did the course descriptions come to me too sexy already, but Lois Burkhart's were an exception. She was an assistant manager at the Farmers and Merchants Bank on the Square. She sent me her course copy by E-mail:

> *Carrie—Got yr. note re. curric. brochure. Took under advisement and toned down copy. Again. Herewith, 2nd revised blurb:*
>
> LIVE FREE OR DIE!
>
> Wolf at the door? In too deep? Debt and worry ruining your life? Cast off the shackles of forfeiture and dependence! Learn inside secrets of smart money management from a pro NOW, and never fear that ringing phone or doorbell—could it be a CREDITOR?—again. Not a scam, pyramid scheme, or investment trick! Spend less, save more—sounds simple, but is it? Learn how with Lois. Bring a calculator and an open mind, and never lose another night's sleep worrying about filthy lucre. Results guaranteed. Textbook (optional; $45) may be purchased in class from instructor.

"Hello, Lois Burkhart, how can I help you?"

"Lois, it's Carrie Van Allen."

"Carrie! Hey, how are you?" She had a bright, convivial voice, full of warmth and intimacy, like the TV voice-over for a women's hygiene product. "I was just thinking about you. Did you get my last E-mail?"

"Yes—well, I think it's the last. That's why I was calling."

"I nailed it this time, didn't I? You know, I didn't agree at first, frankly, in fact I thought you were being a little—well, ha ha! I'll just say a little *strict*. But I went over it again and now I can see it's better, so all's forgiven. You were right and I was wrong," she declared magnanimously.

Lois claimed we'd met before, that she remembered me perfectly. It was possible; I did have an account at her bank, although nine times out of ten I accessed it from the ATM and never entered the building. Say she was right and we knew each other—did that make it easier or harder to tell her that her copy was still a mess?

"Well, it's much better," I allowed cautiously, "much, much better, no question about that."

"I took out all the exclamation points. It made it more dignified, like you said. You were right about that."

"Well, um, not quite all. Did I say dignified? Also—"

"*Most*. You do want it to have *some* life."

"Definitely, absolutely. It should definitely have some life."

"So what's the problem?"

Why hadn't I done this by return E-mail? "Well, the guarantee." Just for starters. "How does that work, now, I mean, who would pay—"

"Oh, that's nothing, it's irrelevant."

"Well, but who—"

"Carrie, nobody's going to ask for their money back!" A hard, cackling laugh.

"It's just that usually we don't guarantee results, you know, I mean never, we couldn't, and besides—"

"Take it out, then. Go ahead. Just take it out."

"Well, I think maybe we'll have to."

"Do it. Anything else?" The feminine hygiene voice went clipped and businesslike. Still melodic, but now it was selling disaster insurance.

"Well, the, um, textbook sale." So much easier to talk about the little errors, easily expunged, than tackle the larger issue of the blurb's overall inanity. "And the mention of your name in the text, that 'Leave it to Lois.' You know, usually we like to give the impression that somebody else, somebody objective and impartial is actually writing these—"

"Wait a second. What exactly are you suggesting?"

"—is writing these little paragraphs—What?"

"You think I get a cut from the texts? A little kickback? Is that what you're suggesting?"

"No, no. No, of course not."

"Well, I don't. It's a courtesy, a convenience, but you can cut that right out, too. Take out anything you don't like and write it yourself."

"Wait, now. Lois, hold it, that's not what I'm saying. It's just a policy at the school that instructors never sell anything, nothing. It keeps everything—it just looks better, that's all. I'm sorry if that wasn't explained to you."

"Nothing needs to be explained to me. I've taught personal finance for two of the three years the Other School has been in business, long before you were a gleam in Brian Wright's eye. I have a bachelor of science degree in business and two-thirds of a master's in accounting. I am an assistant manager at the fifth largest bank in the Commonwealth of Virginia. I know how to do my job. Overworking perfectly good course descriptions in your little brochure is apparently your job."

"Oh, Lois."

"No one has ever had any trouble with my course copy before, by the way."

"No? Well, first time for—"

"I've improved it, is the only difference. The guarantee, the textbook offer—these are entrepreneurial enhancements. But I wouldn't expect you to appreciate that. You ask Brian to call me, will you do that?"

"Yes, if you—"

"And if I don't hear from him, I'll be calling him myself."

"Fine," I snapped. We hung up simultaneously. With my hand on the receiver, I remembered. "Oh, *no*."

"What?" Chris had stopped typing halfway through the conversation so she could listen. "What happened?"

"I forgot—Brian's got a loan out at that woman's bank."

"So? She's not a loan officer. What happened?"

"No, but—oh, God, I should've been nicer. But she was so rude at the end!"

"You didn't say anything, I heard you."

"I should've given in. Probably. Let her write whatever she wanted. But it's *drivel*."

"No, it is, and we can't let the curriculum go out like that. Brian will support you, you'll see."

"She's calling him."

"Let her."

"Oh, *damn*."

"Carrie, relax, we've had crazy teachers before, plenty of them. And Brian never backs down if something with the school is at stake. Once this gas station guy, he was supposed to teach 'Powder Puff Mechanics,' you know, to girls and women, and he was donating his whole garage on Sundays, when he was closed anyway, and the students were supposed to bring in their cars and get them overhauled or whatever as part of the course. Which was great, we expected a big response, maybe we'd make it year-round instead of just a summer class."

"What happened?

"So this *guy*, he decides he gets a free ad for his service station in the brochure, *plus* he wants to give out discount coupons for oil changes and lube jobs to all the students. And Brian said no, no advertising and no selling, no discounts, no nothing. Guy says screw you and won't teach the course, but Brian held firm and that was that."

"Huh. Is Lois a good teacher?"

She shrugged, made a face.

"She is, isn't she?"

"I don't know, I guess. I've heard she's okay."

"Oh, great."

"But it doesn't *matter*."

"I know, I'm just not used to this."

"What, fighting with people?"

"All of it. The last time I worked, I did research for professors. I looked things up and took notes. I usually communicated by memo."

"Yeah, but you're doing a great job. You're good with people, you are, Carrie. I know Brian's full of it sometimes, but you are just doing an *excellent* job, he's right about that."

I thanked her, really touched. Chris was such a generous person. But it bothered me that I didn't care enough. Deep down, her praise and Brian's didn't mean much to me.

I kept putting off calling Jess. Brian wanted him to teach fly-fishing again, as he had last year. I let the whole week go by, I didn't even know why. On Friday, with the weekend looming, I couldn't keep procrastinating.

I stared out at the cold, gray day through the plate glass window, thinking about a story Chris had told me about her son, Andy. He'd gotten in a fight at school last week. The class bully had called him a girl because he was small and he played the violin and the piano. Andy had gotten the worst of it, and Chris had to go for a parent-teacher conference on Monday.

Jess and I met thirty years ago over a fight on the same school playground. We were just starting sixth grade. He wasn't in my class, but I knew him by sight. In fact, I knew him a little better than the other kids who weren't in my class, because already he'd started to acquire a reputation for wildness. And eccentricity. He was a country rather than a town boy, a big and meaningful distinction in sixth grade; he kissed cows—I knew that for sure because it was major playground gossip. Yes, he *kissed cows*, the ones on his father's dairy farm, and he *admitted* it—unwisely, he must have realized in retrospect, but by then it was too late. (One of my vividest memories of our later, adolescent love affair was the night Jess talked me into kissing one myself. On the nose, between its dewy, wide-spaced, long-lashed eyes. "See, Carrie? She likes it." She had seemed to, she being a two-year-old brown and white Guernsey named Magnesia.) He rode the school bus and got off at the bottom of a muddy lane in the middle of nowhere, and the fact that his house was invisible from the road—sycamore trees and a rise in the lane obscured it—added to the mystery about him. Or the rap against him, the communal school sense that Jess wasn't exactly like everybody else. Which was all it took in Clayborne in those days—probably now, too—to isolate a child and make him Other.

The fight in the school yard wasn't about cow kissing, it was over Jess's mother, who was "crazy." This was news to me. I was on my way home when I happened upon Jess and Mason Beckett beating each other up. Three of Mason's friends stood around in a nasty, excited circle, screaming that Jess Deeping's mother was a loony, a nutcase, a psycho, Mason should kill him, kill him, rip his nuts off. But it was the other way around: Mason was on the bottom and losing, and until his buddies jumped in to save him, I thought Jess might kill *him*.

I was a tomboy, but I was small, and a girl, and there were four of them. All the same, I came close to leaping on top of the pile of flying elbows and fists and just seeing what happened. My instant allegiance to Jess's side wasn't a mystery: he was the outnumbered underdog, and Mason Beckett was a known jerk. Later we romanticized it, but at the time, coming to his aid seemed only natural.

Instead of piling on, I ran in the school building and got the first teacher I saw, elderly Mr. Thayer. He stopped the fight, which had gotten pretty bad—skinny, gangly Jess had blood all over him, and not just from Mason's nose. "He started it!" all the boys swore, and I, Mr. Thayer's only impartial witness, couldn't honestly confirm or deny it. But I knew *why* the fight had started, and even though it was scary to rat on four big, resentful boys, I didn't hesitate. "They were taunting." A new word; I'd learned it that year. It meant teasing, and it was specifically forbidden on the playground. "They called his mother crazy, they said she was in the loony bin, and they said he was crazy, too. They called his mother names."

Jess wouldn't look at me. Mr. Thayer had him by the shirt or he would have turned his back on me. I wanted him to look up, acknowledge me. Well, what I wanted was for him to thank me. But he stood with his head averted, wiping blood out of his yellow hair, and never looked at me once. A disappointment for me—almost a betrayal. I'd thought we were together now, a team. A pair.

Years went by and we never spoke. But I watched and noticed him, and I knew he noticed me. Once, sitting behind him at an assembly, I fixated on the back of his neck. If I cut my hair off, would my neck look that thin and fragile and nervous? Did girls have those two weedy tendons, sensitive cords that appeared and disappeared with the turning of the head? After that day, I paid special attention to the backs of boys' necks—in fact, I still do. Some were flat and uninteresting, some were short and muscular, barely there (like Brian's), some were long and reedy, giraffelike. I was always taken by the kind that had a shallow indentation between the two tendons. That little declivity, that gentle dent, was associated in my mind forever with callowness and pride and skittish bravado.

I found Jess's number in the Rolodex, although I already knew it, and punched in the digits carefully. On the fourth ring, his answering machine picked up.

"Hello. This is Jess Deeping," came his surprisingly stiff, formal voice; for a second I didn't recognize it. "Please leave a message when you hear the tone, and I'll call you back as soon as I can. Thank you."

I hung up.

I pictured him at his desk in his cluttered office, composing his message, reciting it into the machine, maybe trying it again, not satisfied the first time. He'd want it to be right; he'd want to sound cordial and serious. He'd think that was important.

His office was once the living room of his parents' house; the "parlor," his mother called it, he'd told me. We used to do homework on the sprung, Indian-bedspread-covered sofa, me at one end, Jess at the other. And there was a window seat in an alcove you couldn't see from the parlor door because it was in the corner. We'd sit there in the late afternoons, out of sight of sad, slow-moving Mr. Deeping if he happened to pass by. That's where Jess kissed me the first time, in that window seat on a rainy afternoon in the spring, and afterward we wrote each other's names on the fogged-up windowpanes. In those days the view was of a broad, shallow pasture against a blur of maples that obscured the flood plain and the river. Jess bought the long strip of land beyond the pasture a few years ago, cut down the trees, and built a dock on the river. He swam from it, fished for trout, and tied up his little boat, the *Cud.* His house hardly resembled the old stone farmhouse he grew up in, he'd added to and knocked out and renovated so many of the small, dim, low-ceilinged rooms. All that was left of the original was the parlor. His office.

I dialed his number again. Cleared my throat while his message played.

"Jess, this is Carrie, calling from the Other School. I don't know if you knew, but I'm working here now. Um, Brian was wondering if you'll be teaching fishing again next June. Would you call and leave a message, please, one way or the other? Any time over the weekend. Okay, thanks."

I almost hung up.

"And—I also wanted to say, I'm sorry, again, about the, um, ark animals, and how all that—went. My mother—oh, God. Well, you know. Anyway." Yes, I'm great with people. "Ruth misses you, she says hi. Wants to come see you one of these days. She's got an idea that she can drive around on your back roads by herself—I can't imagine who put that in her head. Well, okay. Be seeing you. Don't forget about the course. 'Bye, Jess."

I didn't know if I was hinting around for an invitation or not, I truly didn't. But he called the next day, Saturday, and invited Ruth and me to tea. Yes, tea. Thirty years later, he was still doing the unexpected.

7

Two of Everything

"Mom, this car is such a tool. You know what Connie Rosetta's father gave her for her sixteenth birthday? A brand-new Cabrio. In the school *colors*."

"What's a Cabrio?"

"*God*, Mom. It's a VW convertible."

"Oh."

"This is the dorkiest car in the whole town. Who would buy this car?" A Chevy Cavalier, crud colored, with nothing but a radio, not even a tape deck. Automatic, of course, so you couldn't downshift or rev it in neutral or anything. "Who bought it," I asked her, "you or Dad?"

"I guess we bought it together."

"*God*."

"Be careful on these curves, you're almost speeding. Are you watching your speedometer?"

"Yes, I'm watching. Hey, look, Jess got a new sign."

"Slow down."

"I *am*. Isn't it cool?" DEEPING FARMS, it said in white and gold on a green background, on a wooden plaque just inside the old stone gateposts. I steered the Chevy onto the gravel driveway, slowing to a crawl for Mom's sake. "Why is it 'Farms,' though? Doesn't he just have one farm?"

"He has another place out past Locust Dale, I think. Smaller. A tenant runs it."

"I didn't know that. Hey, whose car is that? It's not Mr. Green's."

"Who's Mr. Green?"

"Jess's hired man. Think he got a new car? Jess, I mean." Not new, I saw; used. A gray Ford Taurus almost as ugly as this one. God, I hoped it wasn't Jess's. But I also hoped there wasn't anybody else here. I wanted it to be just us three.

Except for the house, Jess's farm is really beautiful. Everything matches. All the barns have stone foundations, and they're all painted bright white with red trim. Even the silos are white with red tops. The fences are neat and straight, not falling down or rotting or rickety like you see on a lot of farms, and Jess even keeps the messiest places, like the muddy yard where the cows mill around waiting to be milked, as clean as he can by putting fresh straw down and also sometimes rotating them to an alternate waiting place while the other one dries out. When I first saw the farm, I couldn't get over how perfect it all looked, like a play farm, the kind little kids build with toys for their train set. There's shit and everything, I mean, it's definitely a real farm, but—like, even the cows are clean, they don't clump around with filthy butts from sitting in muck all the time. It must take a lot of extra work to keep your farm looking nice. Think how much easier it would be to let things slide. And tempting, too, because you'd probably get the same amount of milk out of the animals. Jess must have a lot of pride.

"You can turn around in the circle," Mom said. "Stop right here, this is good."

"I know, I am." I stopped, put the car in P, turned the key off, pulled up the hand brake. Before we could get out, we were surrounded by a pack of wild dogs.

Except they weren't really wild and there were only four of them. A stranger would've been scared, which I guess is the point. I got out and clapped my hands and Red, the oldest dog, came right up to me. Then Mouse, the little gray one. I had to get down on my knees to make Tracer come, she's the sheepdog mix, and old

Tough Guy never did—so far I've never even petted Tough Guy, he's too scared. Jess said he bit the UPS man once, but only because he accidentally kicked him.

"Hello!"

"Hi, Jess!" I jumped up, grinning, not sure what to do. He looked good, and really glad to see us. I felt like hugging him, but I didn't for some reason. Something about Mom. Like maybe she'd think it was disloyal to my dad or something.

"Glad you could come," he said, and started walking backward, toward one of the big stone and wood barns instead of his house. He had on brown corduroy pants, a regular blue shirt, and an old leather jacket, unzipped. And sneakers. He'd just combed his hair, you could tell by the comb tracks; he wears it straight back and kind of long, and it's just starting to recede in front. He's tall and on the skinny side, but I know he's strong because I've seen him lift a 120-pound calf like it was my book bag.

"Tracer knows a new trick," he said, still walking backward. "Want to see it?" Tracer's the smartest of the four dogs. When Jess found her she already knew how to shake hands, but he taught her how to turn it into a high five—it's so funny. He called her and she ran over and sat down in front of him. He stuck his hand out and made a gun with his index finger and his thumb and yelled, "Pow!"

Tracer dropped to her stomach, rolled over, and stuck all four feet in the air.

What a riot—Mom laughed almost as hard as I did. Then I tried it, and Tracer did it again, perfectly. "What a great dog! She's so smart."

"She's a genius."

"What else can she do?"

"Well, we're working on milking the cows," he said, not cracking a smile. We looked at him for a second, then burst out laughing. "Let's go in here first," he said, "unless you're starving. Are you?" We said no, not really. "Good, because there's someone I'd like you to meet."

I'd never been in this barn before. It was smaller than the main barns; I figured it was for tractors and machinery and big equipment. The red double doors were as high as garage doors. Jess hauled one open and we went in. Yeah, tractors and combines or whatever, big yellow vehicles sitting up on huge black wheels, blades and paddles and rusty metal teeth behind. It smelled like gas, sawdust, dead grass, and paint, and it was almost as cold inside as outside. Straight back, a light was on in the high, beamed ceiling, and I could see a man with his back to us hunched over a sawhorse, sawing wood.

Damn. I didn't know we had to socialize, I thought it would be just us. We started walking toward the man, and about halfway down the echoey plank floor, it hit me who he was and what he was doing: that Pletcher guy, making ark animals. Jess tricked us.

Sure enough, he said, "Carrie, you remember Landy, don't you?" and to me, "Ruth, this is Mr. Pletcher, my neighbor. Landy—Carrie Van Allen now, and her daughter, Ruth."

Landy, what kind of a name was that? He was short and slight and he smiled without showing his teeth. "Carrie? Well, I declare." He put his saw down and took off his old, stained John Deere cap. He had dull, straw-colored hair, thinning in back. He shook hands with Mom and she said, "Landy, it's been ages. How've you been? You look just the same." He must've always been ugly, then. I had to shake, too, and his hands were rough as sandpaper, with big knobby bumps on the knuckles, it felt like holding an old sock full of stones.

"Why, you do, too," he said, "I'd've known you anywhere," and turned red under his beard stubble. He had on work clothes, denim coveralls under a filthy beige windbreaker, and clunky, mud-caked boots. "How long have you been back home?"

"About three years now. We're living on Leap Street, Ruth and I. We—I lost my husband in August, I don't know if Jess told you."

"He surely did, and I was sorry as I could be." His face got even more crinkled and wrinkly. "I know how it is." How? How could he know how it is?

"Thanks," Mom said quickly. "Well, what's all this?"

As if we didn't know. Jess told us all about it that time he came over and tried to get Mom to take the crazy ark job. This guy's father, Eldon, used to be a tobacco farmer back in the 1970s, and he was fairly rich and also sort of a wild man, he played cards and drank a lot and ran around on his wife. Then he got stricken with lung cancer, which is pretty ironic, and on his deathbed he converted to religion because of a dream. He made God a promise, or more like a deal—if He would spare his life, he'd give up his sinful ways and start a new church based on the story of Noah. And to glorify the Lord he'd build an ark, fill it with animals, and sail it on the Leap River for forty days and forty nights. Well, sure enough, God spared his life, so he had to start a religion called the Arkists. But unfortunately for him, he never did get around to building the ark, and now he's dying again, this time for real because he's like eighty or something. So he got his son to say he'd do it for him because otherwise he'll go straight to hell, and the only problem is that Landy's bitten off more than he can chew because hardly any of the other Arkists are helping and time's running out, which is where Jess was hoping Mom would come in. I think all these people are totally nuts.

Landy started showing Mom his handiwork, which was pretty pitiful. "I've only done four so far," he said, dragging boards or something out from under another sawhorse, these flat wooden shapes painted brown, gray, and yellow. If you looked hard, you could tell the gray one was an elephant and the yellow one was a giraffe, but the two brown ones could've been anything.

"Bears, right?" I guessed.

His shoulders drooped. "This one is. That one's a kangaroo."

"Oh, yeah. Very nice," I said politely. "But don't you have to make two of everything?"

He ducked his head and rubbed the back of his neck and mumbled.

"Pardon?"

"Uh, that's under discussion. Hoping to get around that. Still debating."

"Landy, how's your father?" Mom asked.

"Not too well. Heart trouble. He's weakening every day."

"I'm so sorry. Is your mother still living?"

"Yes, she is. Yes, she is."

A man of few words. I looked around for something to do. This part of the barn was Jess's workshop, cluttered with tools and pieces of machinery and workbenches and different kinds of saws. Power saws, lots of them—so why was Landy using a handsaw? For that matter, why was he using Jess's barn, why not his own? He supposedly lived next door. "Are you also building the ark?" I asked.

"Ha," he said, and did the head ducking thing again. He was either really shy or not all there.

Jess said, "That's still on the drawing board," and he said it so straight and firm, so matter-of-fact or something, it was like, well, at least there's one completely sane person here. "In fact, it's *literally* on the drawing board. Come and look."

We went over to one of the workbenches, where there was a big sheet of drafting paper with a drawing of an ark on it. It had the pointy ends and the flat-roofed box on top like you always see in pictures of arks. I had a lunch box in third grade with an ark and all the animals on it, I don't know why, and it looked like that.

"Cool," I said. "How big is it?" I looked up to see Landy and Jess grinning. "What? What's funny?"

"That's something else that's still under debate," Jess said, and he and Landy started to laugh.

Landy had a big, dark gap between his two front teeth, which must be why he tried to smile with his lips closed. "My father would like it to be three hundred cubits long, fifty cubits wide, and thirty cubits high."

Mom said before I could, "What's a cubit?"

"The distance between the tip of the middle finger and the elbow," Jess said. "Biblically speaking."

"So what does that—"

"It comes out to about four hundred and fifty feet long, seventy-five feet wide, forty-five feet tall."

"Wow!" I said. "That's bigger than a football field!"

"Good heavens," Mom said.

Everybody looked depressed.

"So a cubit is your arm from here to here," I said, measuring mine. "What's that, twenty inches or so. Okay, but everybody's different. What if you took, like, an infant's arm and measured. It'd probably be about a fourth the size of a man's, but it would still be a cubit."

Everybody stared at me.

"Right? So you could still have the ark be three hundred cubits long, but instead of four hundred feet it would only be one hundred. Which is still huge. Does the Bible say whose arm you have to measure?"

You'd've thought I just invented the electric light bulb. Jess and Landy looked stunned and then hopeful. "You think?" "I don't know, what do you think?" Mom said, "Could you do that?" and Landy said, "I think so. I hope. He's very reasonable—when I explain, I think he'll say yes."

Yeah, that's Eldon, all right, Mr. Reasonable.

Landy said he'd like to ask Mom's advice about something if she wouldn't mind, she being an artist and all. That's when I knew he was shy, not mental: he'd hit her right in her weak spot. Oh, no, she said, she wouldn't mind at all, and pretty soon they were having a great time talking about plywood thicknesses and paint finishes.

Boring. "Any new calves?" I asked Jess.

"Twins. Want to see?"

"You bet." And we split.

• • •

Walking through the dirt farmyard toward the real barn, the huge one where most of the cows live in winter, I thought about how much I could say to Jess about this ark project. It looked like he was in on it, though, so I didn't want to hurt his feelings. I started with, "So is that guy going to do all the animals? *All* of them?"

"Probably not."

"Yeah, because wouldn't that be impossible? How many species are there, a thousand? No, more like a million. All the animals you never think of, the wombat, the weasel. The wolverine. Shrike." Jess was grinning, which encouraged me. "Wildebeest. Jackal. Dogs! Hey, if you do dogs, don't you have to do all the different breeds? Because, I mean, after the flood you wouldn't want to be stuck with nothing but, like, Dalmatians."

"True."

"Fish, you have to put in all the fish. All the shrimp and minnows and rockfish, tuna—whales—there's gotta be a million!"

"Don't forget reptiles."

"Yeah, two of all the snakes and lizards and everything. Don't forget the snail darters!" We both started laughing, and it was great, I felt grown up making fun of this adult thing, something adults had dreamed up and it turned out to be crazy. "It's nuts, isn't it?" I asked, just to be sure.

"It is completely nuts."

"I know! So why are you doing it?"

"Hell if I know. Haven't you ever done anything that didn't make any sense? Just because you wanted to?"

"Not that I can think of. Playing and make-believe, okay, but you're supposed to outgrow that, right?"

He just smiled, lifting up one crooked eyebrow at me. It had a scar in the middle, and he'd told me how he got it—when he was twelve a pony he owned named Dylan pulled a barbed-wire fence down on his head. Most of the time Jess looks like he's kidding you, because he smiles a lot and that crooked eyebrow looks funny and playful and in the know. But other times his eyes, which are very light gray, get dreamy and faraway, and then he looks to me like a sad man.

It was much warmer in the cow barn. Jess has about two hundred head of cattle, mostly females—that's what a cow is—and in January and February they live inside. He swears they don't mind it, not even staying in their stalls all day except for the two times, four in the afternoon and five in the morning, when they get milked. He calls them "girls." "Here come the girls," he says when they start plodding out of their barns and crowding around the milking parlor. They scared me the first time I got up close to a whole crowd of them in one place, but I didn't know how gentle they were. They all look the same to me, fat black and white Holsteins with sweet, vacant faces. But Jess actually knows who's who—or so he claims. And this I can hardly believe, but he *says* he knows their *names*. "Okay, who's that?" I'll say, pointing to some cow at random. "Cinnamon," he'll say if it's nearby, or "Can't tell," if it's in the distance. "Might be Tulip, can't see her off side." He could be pulling my leg, but I don't think so. I think he really knows all his cows by name.

"I can see how you could start to like them," I said, leaning beside him against the door to one of the birthing stalls and looking in at two sleeping calf twins. "They're nice. They don't have any . . ." I couldn't think of the word. "They could never plot to do something bad."

"Nope."

"They're simple. They have good souls."

"Except when they break your foot."

"God, that had to hurt. Which one did it?" Last summer Jess got stepped on in the field by a cow that wouldn't move, just stood on his foot until she broke it. He was on crutches for two months.

"That would be Crocus."

"You still have her?"

"'Course."

"Jess, can I pet the calves?"

"Sure."

But I stayed where I was, next to him with my foot braced on the bottom rail, arms folded over the top. The barn smell of cow, urine, manure, and feed is amazing, the first whiff almost knocks you over. Then you get used to it and it's not bad. That surprised me, the fact that all that cow shit and pee doesn't stink to high heaven. It stays in your nostrils for a while after you leave, but you don't really mind it. It's a fresh smell, dark and sweet, like old grass and earth. I almost like it.

"So," Jess said into the peaceful quiet, "how's it been going for you? How's school?" he added—that was in case I didn't want to talk about personal stuff.

"School's okay. I have this pretty cool English teacher, Mrs. Fitzgerald. We're reading some poetry. And she's making us keep journals."

"Who's your best friend?"

"Oh . . . Jamie, I guess. And there's this guy." He made an interested sound. "He's not my boyfriend or anything. His name's Raven. Gram thinks he's bizarre. Mom, too, but she doesn't say it, she's trying to be cool, but it's so obvious."

"What's bizarre about him?"

"You name it. No," I said, laughing, "he's not really, he just wears makeup and dresses like a vampire, it's no big deal." I laughed again, this time at Jess's face. I was *this* close to getting the giggles, which I thought I had finally outgrown. "He's very smart, he's probably the smartest kid in the class, he probably shouldn't even be in school. We just hang together sometimes. He gave me a book of poems. When my dad died. I like him, but it's not like this *grand passion* or anything."

I could see he was thinking it over, figuring out if he should say it or not. Finally he couldn't resist, but he kept his voice really casual. "He dresses like a vampire?"

I put my head down on my arms and snorted. Why was it so funny? Some sort of hysteria felt like it was right around the corner. "Sometimes, yeah. It's nothing, it's just a thing. An expression of his angst and disgust at the hollowness of the culture."

Something rubbed against my leg—I looked down and saw a skinny, dusty black cat. I petted it gingerly until it slunk off. "Which one was that?" I challenged Jess, and he said, "Blackie." I couldn't tell if he was kidding or not. "My dad was allergic to fur or dandruff or something, we could never have pets," I said, "not even a cat. Not that I would want a cat."

"I like cats."

"Yours are okay." He had about a dozen cats or kittens who lived outside, barn cats whose job was to catch mice. "But usually they're sneaky. Once I had a guinea pig for about two days, but Dad said I had to get rid of it. So then I got fish, some goldfish, but all they did was die. It was totally disgusting. I'd wake up in the morning and there would be my new goldfish stuck to the top of my dresser."

He leaned over to rub the pink nose of one of the calves, and I could smell his lemon aftershave. My dad used Old Spice, which is sweeter, more prickly on your nose than Jess's brand. "I was a little older than you," he said seriously, like he was starting a story, "when I lost my father. His name was Wayne. My mother was Ora."

"Wayne and Ora Deeping." They sounded so country.

"He was a small, slight guy, only about five foot five. He started to go bald when he was in his twenties."

"You sure don't take after him."

"Well, not that way. Other ways."

"How did he die?" How people die is the thing I want to know most these days.

"An accident. Threshing machine."

I didn't know what to say.

"I still miss him. It's been nineteen years. I think I stayed here because of him. Wanted to make a go of the place for him, and I guess I did."

"Yeah, sure. You're probably rich."

He laughed, which was a relief, because I didn't hear how rude that sounded until after I said it. "My dad worked harder than any man I ever knew. He taught me that—to love what you do, give everything to it. He was very quiet. He moved like this—" Jess straightened up very deliberately from petting the calf. "Slow as a turtle, so he wouldn't spook his cattle. It worked, too, you never saw such happy cows. His doc told him he had no blood pressure at all."

Death is so weird. Here I am with a dead father, and here's my friend Jess with a dead father and a dead mother. Everybody dies. Millions and millions of people are dead. All the people who ever lived since the beginning of time, since the beginning of the world, are now dead. I picture them as stacked on top of one another, like a gigantic pile of cordwood about a trillion miles high. How could God, if there is one, think this is a good plan? How can it be anything but horrible, the absolute worst?

"My dad's heart gave out," I said. Jess already knew that, but now I was telling him my story. "He was driving home with my mom on a Friday night. They'd just had dinner with my grandparents, but he wasn't drunk or anything. He leaned over against the door, and his heart just stopped. Maybe even before the car crashed. Before that he never had anything wrong with him, he never even got colds. Sometimes." I put my fingers on my lips and whispered. "Sometimes I think it would've been better if it had been her instead of him. And then—I'm glad it was him, because if it was her it would be even worse. And then I feel rotten because I know I'm making it all about me instead of my dad. Mom's still a wreck and there's nothing I can do, I can't fix it. I can't change anything, I can't do anything. I don't even get why he died. Why did he die? Does anybody know? Do priests know? Philosophers? You don't know, do you?"

Jess, of course, said no. The amazing thing was that I said all that, made that whole speech, without ever bursting into tears. That cheered me—a sign of growing up.

I started thinking: if anything ever happened to Mom, say she got a job in another city or something, I bet Jess would let me move in, live on the farm with him. He might think at first that I'd be a pest, but he'd soon change his mind. I could do the cooking and cleaning, I'd help out with the chores. At night we'd keep each other company around the kitchen table or, in the summers, out on the front porch. He's got a swing. Living all by himself, he has to be lonely. I'd be his right hand. Raven could come over sometimes, maybe he'd get a part-time job helping Jess out in the afternoons. I'm sure they'd like each other. They have more in common than meets the eye. Mom would come for visits on the weekends. She'd have her doubts at first, but then she'd see what a good job I was doing holding things together.

I heard a door slam and a car start up. When we went outside, Landy was driving away in his Ford Taurus and Mom was standing in the yard waving good-bye. I guessed they were buddies now. "Now who's starving?" Jess said, and we went in his house and had tea.

The house is not very farmlike, to say the least. It's modern and mostly brick, two stories painted white, and inside there's the living room, dining room, etc., etc., decorated just like some middle-class person's house in the suburbs. It's kind of a disappointment. The best rooms are the kitchen and the office, probably because they look like the only ones he uses. All the others are big, clean, empty, and sort of depressing.

Jess had the kitchen table set for three people, including blue-and-white-checked place mats and matching napkins, plates, cups, saucers, and a teapot. "Have a seat." He started heating a pot of milk on the stove.

"Can I help?" Mom asked. She looked pleased but kind of nervous.

"Nope. Like coffee cake?"

"Is that what that smell is? Oh, *man*." I really was starving all of a sudden. He took a loaf pan out of the oven and set it on the table. "Wow, did you make this yourself? Fantastic. Mom hardly ever bakes anymore."

"Go ahead, cut a piece. Eat. I've got sandwiches, too."

"No, we'll wait for you," Mom said.

"Go ahead."

"Okay," I said, "if you insist."

It was terrific, still warm from the oven, lots of brown sugar and cinnamon on the outside, silky cake on the inside. "Sour cream," Jess said when I asked him the secret. "How come you don't bake anymore?" he asked Mom.

"I know I should, but it's hard with just the two of us. And now that I'm working—"

"It's because she doesn't want to get fat," I explained. "She was moving in that direction, too, but lately the slide has been . . ." I couldn't think of the word.

"Decelerated," Mom said coolly. "Thank you."

"Thank *you*," I said when Jess filled my cup with hot cocoa and dropped a marshmallow on top. "Krystal doesn't eat sugar, but I do. I'll give it up someday, but I'm not ready yet."

"This is delicious, Jess, truly. I didn't know you were such a good cook."

"Thank you. Tea or coffee?"

"Tea, please. Thanks."

They were being sort of formal and stiff with each other. Friendly, but also really . . . alert. I said, "So did you all go to school together, you guys and Landy?"

They started to answer at the same time. She stopped and Jess said, "Landy's older, he was a few years ahead of us. He bought the farm next door about fifteen years ago, not long after his wife died. He's been a good neighbor. We help each other out."

"So the two of you were in the same class? You're the exact same age?" They nodded. "Landy looks a *lot* older than you guys. Maybe he had to stay back?"

"No, I don't think so. He has terrible arthritis in his hands, Jess."

"I know. That's why he can't use any of my power saws—I'm afraid he'll cut his arm off."

"He can't do all that work with a handsaw."

"No."

"What's he doing to do?"

He shook his head. After a minute he said, "I'm going to help him build the ark."

I almost choked on my hot chocolate. "Get out. No. You are, really?"

He smiled. Then he looked at Mom, who wasn't saying anything. "He's only got four months to do everything. He's not completely alone, some of the members of the congregation have been helping him out when they can. But they're old, and a lot of times—today, for example—they don't show up."

"He's not even a member of the congregation," Mom said. "I couldn't believe it when he told me that."

"No, he's a Methodist."

"Whoa," I said, "Landy's not an *Arkist*? Then how come he's doing this?"

"For his father. Because he promised."

"Wow. Wow. So he doesn't even believe in it." This just got stranger and stranger. "How come he only has four months?"

Jess looked funny, embarrassed or something. When he rubbed his cheeks with both hands, the raspy sound of his whiskers reminded me of my dad. "Well, according to Eldon, the Bible says the flood was in the six hundredth year of Noah's life, the second month, the seventeenth day. Apparently that comes out to the seventeenth of May."

"Well," Mom said, wiping her mouth with her napkin. "At least the weather should be nice."

"This is crazy," I reminded them. "Do you know how many animals there are? In the *world*?"

"Eldon had a dream, and in it there were *representations* of the animals," Mom said seriously. "So he doesn't have to make all of them. Luckily."

"Wow, *that's* a convenient dream. But he still has to make two of everything, which automatically doubles the—"

"I had an idea about that," she interrupted me. "I was thinking Landy could paint both sides of his plywood, not just one, each in slightly different colors—or even textures—so one side could represent the male and the other the female. So with his bears, one side could be brown, one side black—or lighter brown, darker brown, something like that. Male and female. You could even do"—she laughed—"different facial expressions on either side, ferocious and friendly, savage and sleepy—I don't know." She made a face. "Okay, I got carried away. But Landy thought it was a great idea."

I had a terrible suspicion. "You're going to start helping him, aren't you?"

"No. No, no. No, I can't, I already have a job."

"Not even on a consulting basis?" Jess said. "In an advisory capacity?" He was grinning, but I didn't think he was joking.

"Hey," I said, "did you know I got a job, too?"

"I did hear that. Who told me? Bonnie, must've been." Bonnie Driver, his former wife. I'm friends with Becky, her daughter; she's in my class. I had a lot of questions about Jess and his ex, but I couldn't see how to ask them. It sounded like they still talked to each other, didn't hate each other or anything. Becky's not Jess's daughter, she's Mr. Driver's, so they had to have gotten divorced at least fifteen years go, which is how old Becky is. Jess would've been about twenty-seven. When did he get married? Why did they split up?

"So do you want to hear about my new job?"

"Absolutely." He pushed his plate away and put his elbows on the table and his chin in his hands. Mom got up and started running water over the dirty dishes and puttering. "What's it called again? I've seen the store but I've never been inside."

"The Mother Earth Palace and Natural Healing Salon. It's far more than a health food store, we provide many other services."

"Such as."

"Well, for instance, we do biological terrain assessments. That's a saliva, blood, and urine test you can get to figure out your terrain, your baseline, biologically. We also do hair analysis, we do iridology, which is studying the eye, the iris, to see if you have a disease. Krystal does that, she's certified as an iridologist and also a reflexologist, and right now she's getting her craniosacral certificate."

"So you're liking this job."

"I love it. I'm learning so much. Krystal's letting me set up this aromatherapy, like, spa in the back of the store, where you can come in and lie down and smell soothing essences, which can change your whole outlook. This way you don't have to buy them all yourself, the different aromas, you can just take a treatment when you need it. You should try it."

"Krystal—she's the boss?"

"She owns it. You don't know her? Krystal Bukowski?"

"I don't think so."

"She's a native, I thought maybe you knew her. She's younger than you, though. She's great. She lives over the store in an apartment. She heats it with a woodstove. She's got three cats, and she has boyfriends who crash there sometimes. She's a vegetarian, but she's trying to be a vegan, which is not eating any animal products at all, not even milk, not even butter. She's teaching me to do transformational breath, because sometimes I can get really, like, hyper and it can calm you down, just breathing correctly. What I like about her is that she cuts through the crap, she goes right to the center of stuff, right to what's important, and it isn't school or studying or taking the college boards."

"No?"

"No, it's living in the moment. Living a gentle life that doesn't hurt anyone. It's moving along a spiritual path like a butterfly, disturbing nothing in creation, leaving no destruction in your wake. And treating God's universe with the utmost respect and love and delicacy."

Jess nodded thoughtfully. "Those are good goals. Can't argue with a single one."

"And of course it all starts with yourself, taking care of the body, which if you think about it is the only thing you have any control over anyway. Say, for example, you can take EDTA, which is a chelate, and it purifies your bloodstream of lead and mercury, which you probably have and don't even know. Oral chelation, this is called. I'm taking it, and I can feel a difference already in one month. So—there's all this stuff we can do, everybody should do. To keep ourselves well."

Wow, I was talking a lot. For some reason Jess touched me on my hand. I smiled, and he said, "It would be nice."

"What would?"

"If we could control things. Take a pill to make our lives work out."

I pulled my hand away. "That's not what I mean. I know we can't do that." Did he think I was stupid? "I'm just saying. There's something for everything if you know what it is. You should just come into the store sometime."

"I will."

"Because we have everything. You don't have to put up with all the stuff that happens to you. Take dry skin—which you have on your hands, I notice, along with damaged nails." He looked down at his hands. "And this is just a for instance, the first thing that comes to my mind. Okay, we have Miracle 2000, made of collagen protein and grape-seed extract, and this can prevent and repair aging skin, hair loss, and damaged nails while increasing strength, endurance, and joint flexibility. Many customers have given written testimonials. I'm not making this stuff up."

"No. No."

"I'm just saying we can take action. We don't have to be so passive."

"Want some more hot chocolate?"

"No, thank you. You can lose weight while you sleep—we've got Night Slim, a blend of chromium, lipotropics, and special amino acids that break down fats while you sleep. Okay, you wouldn't need that, but what about mucus? Did you know death begins in the colon?"

"Ruth," Mom said from the sink, "did you want to take the car for a very short drive?"

"By myself?" I scraped my chair getting up.

"Will this work, Jess? I don't want her on any public roads. Back roads only, and just on your property. And someplace where there aren't any ditches."

So I got to drive by myself! First time, and it was way cool even though the road was windy and bumpy so of course I couldn't speed or anything. But just being by myself made it worth it, nobody watching my every move, telling me to start slowing down, turn on my signal, do this, do that. God, I cannot *wait* to get my license. How can I hold out for seven more months before my real life starts?

But when I got back, something was up. Mom and Jess were on the front porch with their coats on, and before I could even get out of the car she came over and got in on the passenger side. "What's wrong?"

"Nothing. Say thank you to Jess, honey, and let's go. It's getting late, he's got cows to milk."

"Did you have a fight?"

"No, no, everything's fine."

No, it wasn't, she was upset about something. Jess came over and put his hands on the door on my side, leaning in the window. He looked sad, too. *I leave for fifteen minutes,* I thought, *and look what happens.* The dogs were circling the car, looking confused. "Well," I said. " 'Bye, Jess. Thanks, I had a really nice time."

"Me, too. Come back soon." He looked across at Mom.

"Jess—I'm sorry."

"For what, Carrie?"

She waved her fingers in the air, giving this gulping laugh. "Being a mess. All my fault. I'll see you—come on, Ruth."

"Okay, okay." The motor was still running. Jess stood straight and backed up. When he clapped his hands, all the dogs got away from the car and ran to him. I took off the emergency brake, shifted into D, and stepped on the accelerator. The car lurched forward with a screech—I jammed on the brake. Mom grabbed at the glove compartment. Whiplash.

I looked back at Jess, who was trying not to laugh. That made me laugh. Then Mom laughed! All of a sudden I felt giddy and happy, everything was so *great.* I almost gave Jess the finger! Instead I thumbed my nose, and he waved and sent me a big, tickled grin as we zoomed away.

"God, that was great, I had the best time."

"I did, too." Her nose was all stopped up; she sounded like she had a cold.

"So what happened?"

"Nothing happened.

"Come *on.*"

"Nothing, really, I just got sad for some reason."

"Did Jess say something?"

"*No.* Yes—he asked me how I was doing. That's all it took." She laughed again, but I saw her squirrel a tissue out of her coat pocket and wipe her face.

"Shit. Are you crying?"

"No, I'm not, and don't say shit to me."

"Sorry. Mom?"

"I'm fine, I'm fine." She flapped her hand. Then she buried her face in the Kleenex and stayed that way.

The country, the low hills and brown fields and whitish sky that had been pretty before, now they just looked cold and dead. I counted telephone poles, dotted yellow lines, bare trees. Shit, shit, shit, shit. I don't think this is ever going to end. Can grief last for a person's whole life? I thought she was better, I thought the job was helping. "I don't know what to do," I said under my breath, too soft for her to hear.

"Hey, Mom?"

She sat up and started fixing herself, blowing her nose, wiping her eyes. "What?"

I had my Walkman in the nylon duffel I'm using for a purse these days. I found it at the bottom after some one-handed fumbling. "Put the earphones on." Good, the tape was wound right, I saw. "It's the first song. Press 'play' and listen to the first song. Listen to the words."

"What is it?"

"Just listen. It's a song."

Jeez. It took her forever to figure out how the earplugs went in her ears, which button to press, how to work the volume. *It's not brain surgery,* I wanted to say, but smart talk right now would've hurt her feelings.

"Who is this?"

"It's Belle. She used to be with the Storm Sewer Troupers. This is her first solo album."

"Belle?"

"Shh, just listen."

"I can't hear the words."

"Turn it up higher."

More dorky fumbling, then finally I heard the high, tinny crash of music over the car's engine drone. The chorus is the best part.

I am water, I am stone.
Take my heart, I'll take you home.
You're not gone, I've got you here, love,
There's no such thing as good-bye.

And then the ghostly harmonies she does with herself, *Ah-eeeeee, oh don't go, oh-weeeeee, stay in my soul,* over and over in that achy voice that goes straight to your heart, right to the marrow of your bones. It gives me chilly bumps.

"It's about getting over the pain of losing somebody," I explained. "She's saying they're not really gone as long as you can remember them."

Mom nodded slowly. She had her eyes closed again, but now she was smiling. In fact, she looked like she was going to laugh.

Belle is so great. She's better than therapy.

8

THE DECENCY TO FEEL BAD

Stephen and I met in a bar. Not very romantic, but I was so intrigued by what I took for his tense, brooding aloneness, I freighted our first meeting with the dark romance of a Brontë novel. It was Washington, the summer of 1981. I was twenty-three, living in Logan Circle, beginning to despair that I would ever be an artist—prophetically, as it turned out. He was in graduate school at Georgetown; a math student. If I'd known that when I saw him in Rainy's, a hot, grungy tavern on M Street, I might not have found his melancholy so irresistible. I took him for an artist or a writer, for childish reasons: his intensity, the way he held his cigarette, the fact that he never spoke but wouldn't stop staring at me.

I was with women friends, my housemates in a roach-infested duplex on Fifteenth Street. The hot-eyed stares, eventually mutual, went on until I seized the initiative, something I wasn't accustomed to doing with men, particularly strange ones in bars. I didn't smoke, but I did drink; that night I drank enough chardonnay to make slipping a cigarette from my friend's pack of Winstons, taking it over to Stephen's barstool, and asking for a light seem, if not quite natural, inevitable.

I remember the first thing he said to me. "Can you get away?" Such thrilling directness. I loved the implication under it that we were fated, that we'd both just been waiting. We only went for coffee in a café up the street, but I'd have done more—probably anything he wanted. It was a long time before I understood that his heated concentration on me, his rapt, flattering regard, was as much an illusion as my cigarette.

I wonder if I tolerate Raven, Ruth's friend, because I know so well what attracts her to him. It's that same fascinating otherness, the romantic loner persona, that attracted me to Stephen—and before him, of course, to Jess. How clever women are at self-deception; we swallow whole the stories we've already told ourselves.

Stephen drew me as well because of the otherness of what he *knew*. He read books with titles like *P-Resolutions of Cyclic Quotient Singularities*, and I never understood a single thing he told me about them. I liked to hear him talk, even though he might as well have been explaining a concerto to a deaf woman. I ceded to him most of the power in our relationship because I thought he was a genius. I took his silences and abstraction for depth, evidence of realms of knowledge I could never enter, much less comprehend. And I was so restless in those days, easily sidetracked, unable to apply myself to my various art projects—no doubt because I didn't know what I was doing. I don't think he loved math more than I loved art, but he had intensity and focus and I didn't. I envied him.

He was a formal man, even a little straitlaced, and I found I enjoyed trying to seduce him in inappropriate places. I surprised him one afternoon in his carrel at the university library, and he started telling me about the formula or the problem he was working on. As usual it made no sense—but his attention to it, his absolute passion for it, excited me. Or maybe they made me jealous. I remember squeezing onto the edge of his desk, using his body and the carrel partitions for a shield, and unbuttoning my blouse, undoing my bra. He was angry, shocked, determined not to respond. But I made him. I could take him out of himself, and that made me feel strong—I got some of the power back that way, I thought. We made love standing up behind the stacks that day, and it wasn't the only time. I relished making Stephen lose control. I honestly thought it made us even.

I've been thinking about what sex was like later, after we were married. And what it means that I don't miss it very much now. I know a lot of me has gone dead inside, but it's more than that. Toward the end it was just sex, not much closeness, usually not even kissing. Toward the end? No, that's not true, it started earlier. When Ruth was little. So I don't miss it much. Or—no more than I ever did.

Something funny about Stephen. He always came up from behind to hold me or touch me. He would hardly ever put his arms around me from the front, kiss me on my mouth, my face. It was always from behind, pressing against my back, nuzzling my neck, my cheek. Sex was different—he could and did make love in the face-to-face position—but for everyday, standing-up, fully clothed affection, he literally couldn't face me.

I hadn't been lying to Ruth that afternoon at Jess's; I honestly wasn't sure what had set me off, made me red-eyed and teary again. The usual, I suppose: an excess of emotion and a loose cap on it, combined with too much sensitivity where Jess was concerned. I was like a garden hose shut off at the nozzle, and he was the hot sun: prolonged exposure caused ruptures.

I'd had such a nice time until then, drinking tea in his kitchen, half listening to Ruth's rambling monologues. Meeting shy, shambling Landy after so many years and remembering why I'd always been fond of him. Just being at Jess's farm in the winter quiet, everything fallow, gray, utterly still, smell of woodsmoke in the air. For once, with Jess, I felt relaxed, no forbidden attraction, no push-pull. No guilt.

Then Ruth went for a drive and left us by ourselves. I finished the dishes, and stared out the kitchen window at the white, hilly line of a fence in the distance. "Is it snowing?" I said, and Jess came over to stand beside me. I thought I'd seen snowflakes, but he said no, it was ash; Mr. Green was burning brush today behind one of the barns. We gazed out at the occasional drifting speck, hip to hip, not speaking until he said, "Remember the first time you talked to me, Carrie? A snowy day. Eleventh grade—remember?"

I said yes, I remembered, and it struck me that there was something we had never done together: we'd never reminisced. The circumstances of our separation had cut off the possibility of nostalgia, at least the mutual kind. The truth was, I longed to tell Jess what I remembered best, what had stayed with me all through the years, and to hear him say what had meant the most to him.

"I remember what you had on," he said, standing a little away from me on purpose—to make the conversation seem casual. "A red coat with a hood. Plaid hood. And boots—you made me think of folk songs. Spanish leather."

"I thought you were wild," I said. "I was afraid to speak to you. I'd heard so many stories." He smiled, but it was true; by eleventh grade, Jess was famous for climbing the Cherry Street water tower to impress a girl, for almost drowning trying to swim across the Leap River on a dare. The best story was that he'd read about an Indian healing ceremony for casting out devils, and performed it himself, *nude and in the rain*, for the benefit of his crazy mother. A wild boy.

"But you did speak to me," he said. "I remember what you said."

"Not much. As I recall." I recalled it perfectly. Over the Christmas holidays, his mother had died in a fire at Brookner's, the psychiatric facility in Culpeper where she'd been a resident off and on for years. I'd heard the news in homeroom, along with excited whispers that there were *suspicious circumstances*. Had she set the fire herself? Had she meant to burn the place down or just commit suicide? Overnight, Jess Deeping became an even more interesting character. His mother's sensational death seemed suitable somehow, in hindsight, maybe even predictable. It was so much the sort of thing people had come to expect from him.

The kids who knew him were gentle with him in a shy, awkward way, while the kids who didn't stared at him covertly, fascinated. I was one of the latter. I saw him waiting for his bus outside, by himself on a bench by the concrete walk that led to the school parking lot. Everyone else was either inside, crammed against the fogged-up glass doors in the vestibule, or huddled against the wind under the shallow eaves outside, puffing on forbidden cigarettes. Reserved, standoffish, especially around solitary boys I didn't know, I can't say what made me sidle away from my gaggle of laughing girlfriends and go outside to speak to Jess. His aloneness, I suppose. A sadness that hung around him like a coat. I went to him full of trepidation, breathless from my own daring, but with a vague sense that the inevitable was about to happen. I do remember that—it's not retrospective romanticizing. I really did think, crunching my way across the crusty snow in my new boots, *About time*.

He watched me come with a deepening frown; once he even looked over his shoulder to see what else, besides him, I could possibly be headed for. His hair and his shoulders and his thighs were all white from snow. He must be freezing, I thought, with nothing but a hooded sweatshirt, not even zipped up. I stopped in front of him. "Hi," we both said. He sat up straighter when it was clear I wasn't passing by, I meant to stay and speak to him. His sharp knees poked out under the worn denim of his jeans. In my sixteen years, I had never seen anything as male as Jess Deeping's long legs.

I'm sorry about your mother—that was my only message, the sole purpose for my nerve-stretching trek through the snow, but now I couldn't get the words out. My hand closed around a pack of gum in my coat pocket. I drew it out and offered it to him. Up close, his face wasn't as slick and handsome as I'd thought; I could see flaws, pimples on his chin, a patch of beard he'd missed shaving. One eyebrow arched slightly higher than the other, making him look skeptical or reckless. The nails of his big, dry, cold-reddened hands were chewed down to the quick. *Oh*, I thought, *he's not for me*, and I felt relieved and disappointed. *He's just a boy*. Then his mouth went wide in a sad, surprised smile, and that was it. A click in the brain. Yes.

"Thanks." Delicately, he pulled a silver stick of Wrigley's from the pack. He looked at it a moment, then slipped it in his sweatshirt pocket. These memories are so vivid to me. I feel the wet snow on my cheeks, I can almost smell spearmint.

A gust of wind rocked me. "It's cold," I said.

He looked away, beyond my shoulder. "Here comes your bus."

Damn, I thought, watching it lumber up the narrow lane to the turnaround. Under the dismay, my heart skipped—*he knows my bus number*. "I'm sorry you lost your mother," I said quickly. And Jess's eyes filled with tears. I was covered with embarrassment. I felt feverish, then freezing. I stared at my feet, sick with distress, in over my head.

"She didn't kill herself," he said. He didn't hide his face—crying didn't embarrass him at all. When tears spilled down his cheeks, he swiped them off with the heel of his hand.

"She didn't?"

"No. She didn't, she was better, she was almost ready to come home again. She was smoking a cigarette in bed."

"Oh."

"That's how it happened."

"Oh."

I glanced back at the knot of students queuing up to get on the bus, gauging how many more seconds I could stay before I had to make a run for it. "If my mother died . . ." But I couldn't imagine it. "I don't know, I don't know what I'd do."

He had a two-stage smile. The first was pained and gallant, a hero's grimace; it came an instant before the real, glad, natural smile. It made him look as if he knew the world was a sad and tricky place, but he was in love with it anyway. "You just do what you always do," he said. "Only it's not as good anymore."

"Yeah. God, Jess." Just saying his name made me dizzy. "I have to go now." He kept his face alert, animated, but I thought, as soon as I was gone, it would sink back into that sadness I'd startled him out of. I didn't want to go. The last two kids climbed into the school bus and disappeared. "I can't," I said, although he hadn't asked me anything, and ran.

A coward even then. *Why did you miss your bus?* my mother would have wanted to know, and already I had misgivings about explaining Jess, anything about Jess, to her. That was no shrewd instinct, no flash of clever intuition. More like grasping a simple law of physics or chemistry: oil and water don't mix.

"That was the second time you rescued me, Carrie," Jess said, and I smiled, recalling the first—the sixth grade playground brawl. "No one else would say anything to me about my mother. As if it had never happened, she'd never died. I thought you were brave."

"Me?" What a laugh. Jess was more than I could handle, I knew it in my bones even then. I was young, and I couldn't stop seeing him through my mother's eyes. He scared me. Fear and excitement, fear and wanting, fear and love—I twisted and swiveled and pivoted between them for the next two years. Then I lost my courage completely and ran away.

"Twice you saved me, Carrie, and you didn't even know me."

"Well, but that explains it. It was only *after* I knew you . . ." I swallowed. I'd started out playfully, and walked right into the truth. "That I turned into a chicken," I made myself finish.

I walked to the bench under the opposite window, put my knee on it, looked around his kitchen with ostentatious alertness. "Your house is so different now. You've changed it so much, I'd hardly know it. From the old days."

"I ruined it."

I smiled uncertainly. "That's a funny thing to say."

"It's true. It took a while, but I finally figured out why I did it. I'll tell you, but only if you promise not to laugh."

"What do you mean, Jess?"

"Promise?"

"No—yes. I won't laugh."

"I was trying to make it a house your mother wouldn't hate. I blamed you for giving in to her, but then, in a way, I did the same thing. I think it's turned out that your mother was stronger than both of us."

I could only stare at his pained, amused face. How like him to share the blame for my worst mistake.

"After my father died, and there was no more hope for you and me because we'd both married other people, I started changing my house. I didn't understand why until it was finished. One day I looked around and it hit me. I'd taken all the country out of it and made it a house Mrs. Danziger wouldn't be embarrassed to live in. Shit, Carrie, it's an awful-looking place, isn't it?"

I put my hand over my mouth.

"Don't you laugh," he warned, smiling the saddest smile. "My herd's three times the size of my father's. I lease farmland to tenants in Oakpark and Locust Dale. I'm prosperous and respectable, I'm a gentleman farmer. Hell, I'm on the town council. And I owe it all to your mother."

"Jess."

"I wanted to show her. Show you, too. And all I did was ruin *my* mother's pretty little farmhouse. Don't you think that's funny?" He came closer. "Hey, Carrie. Don't cry. I didn't tell you that to make you sad."

Where was the bitterness, why wasn't he angry? "Sorry—I cry at everything. Ruth's back," I whispered, hearing the car on the hill. "I don't know what to say to you. Give me some time, Jess. To think of something besides 'I'm sorry.' I'm so sick of telling you I'm sorry." I found my coat and went outside to meet Ruth.

What would I do with this new knowledge? He was right, it was funny. And so sad. I wished he hadn't told me—and yet I always knew it. In the car, Ruth thought I was weeping for Stephen. She tried her best to comfort me. The twin absurdities almost did me in: Jess spoiling his house for my mother's sake, me finding consolation in the lyrics of Belle, formerly of the Storm Sewer Troupers. Oh, my heart could melt with tenderness sometimes. Even when I was drowning, going down for the last time, the people I loved saved me from touching bottom. And lately, thin streaks of happiness had been scoring the dark at lengthy intervals, zigzag spurts of hope in the black sky, reminding me that I was getting better. I was.

This is what happened.

Ruth had just turned five, the, sweetest, brightest little girl, the reason for my life. For Stephen and me, the best was ending, if best meant the time for believing your life was a rising line, everything gradually improving, enlarging, like a stock market graphic in good times. My expectations had begun to diminish in the early years after Ruth was born, a time that coincided with Stephen's retreat, the start of his metamorphosis into the subdued, closed-off man he would be until he died. It's ironic that what attracted me in the beginning was what repelled me in the end, and that was no one's fault but mine. I profoundly misunderstood him. So—the best was over, but I didn't *know* it was over because I was living in it, I was in the distraught but hopeful stage, when repairing our married lives still seemed possible, if only because the alternative was unthinkable. Leave my baby fatherless? Not if I could help it. And I still had energy then, a sense of myself as an actor, a doer. A person who could change.

We'd left Washington the same year Ruth was born, moved to Chicago for Stephen's new teaching appointment. That he wasn't going to set the math world on fire, either as a theorist or a teacher, was another dawning downer around that time, and I didn't appreciate until too late how much his professional failures demoralized him. I should have, but I'd made another wrong presumption—

that wife and child were the main ingredients in a happy man's life. Not in Stephen's. But his childhood was awful, one loss after another; how could he not be a sad man, a careful, withholding, brittle man?

We'd been planning for weeks to go home for a long weekend—my home, Clayborne—to see my parents, and to go to my fifteen-year high school reunion. A day or two before, we had an argument. I don't remember what provoked it, just that it was worse than usual because for once Stephen participated in it. Whatever started it, soon enough we were blaming each other for our unhappiness, dredging up old resentments and unveiling new ones, saying hurtful things for no reason except that they were true. When it was over, it seemed that for a change a destination might have been reached, a place where the road might actually fork. We were barely speaking. He refused to go home with me—and that may have been his goal all along, it occurred to me later, since he hated that kind of thing, obligatory social occasions at which, as *husband of*, he was even more peripheral than he wanted to be. In the end Ruth and I went by ourselves, and stayed in my old room in my parents' house (now the guest room, all traces of young Carrie long since swept away during one of my mother's remodeling binges). Stephen had to go to a last-minute math conference, I told Mama, and she believed me.

They had the reunion at the Madison Hotel, downtown Clayborne's finest. What happened seems inevitable now, but at the time, every minute unfolded like a slow surprise, the revelation of a complicated secret. Jess and I hadn't kept in touch, no Christmas cards, no wedding congratulations; when he and Bonnie divorced, I wrote him a very short note saying I was sorry, but then I tore it up. We hadn't seen each other since the year after our high school graduation.

We shook hands cordially in a group of people shaking hands the same way. Chameleons, we were, blending right in. We did it so well, even *I* didn't suspect us. For half the night we did a dance of separating and coming together, parting and finding, until at last we just stayed put—for me, a matter of giving up pretending I wanted to be anywhere else.

It wasn't that we picked up where we'd left off, as if the intervening fifteen years had never happened. For one thing, Jess had changed. Obviously—he was thirty-three, not eighteen—but it was more than that. His house wasn't the only thing he'd toned down, I see now; he'd done it to himself, too—tried to. He'd moderated himself, conventionalized himself—those aren't the right words, I can't describe the new phenomenon of Jess. Anyway, the important thing is that it didn't matter, because it didn't work. I saw through his dark suit and paisley tie then, his side-parted hair and his sober, diffident manner, and I still do.

We talked. I told him everything I could about my life except that I wasn't happy. Which meant I had to leave out a lot. He did the same, scrupulously avoiding all but the most general references to his ex-wife. We never danced, never touched. We stayed to the end, through the toasts and jokes and speeches and prizes. He walked me to my car and we said good-bye. "'Bye, Jess." "Good night, Carrie." We touched hands, and he said, "Or you could come home with me," and I said, "All right," and we got in his car and drove to his house.

It was a soft June night, heat lightning in the distance, I remember, and no moon but a skyful of stars. If that matters. One looks for culprits in retrospect, villains to blame, even inanimate ones, anything to spread the blame around. When it was over, I remember wishing I'd had too much to drink so I could add alcohol to my litany of motivations. But no luck: I was sober and clear-headed, and everything I did was deliberate and on purpose. There. Mea culpa can't be any more ecumenical than that.

I hope I haven't passed any of this sexual guilt down to Ruth. I don't even know where it comes from. Litany, mea culpa, ecumenical—I'm not even a Catholic! And what about this—the only consolation I found in the aftermath of sleeping with Jess came from knowing that at least I hadn't enjoyed it. At least it wasn't a transcendent experience for either of us. The night ended in awkwardness and sorrow, and I suffered for it long after with regret and depression and guilt. My mother didn't teach me this, did she? I'm accustomed to blaming her for most of my flaws, in particular my failures of courage; but if she's in here, it's not as a towering moral figure. Maybe a social one. The goddess of snobbery, observing a tawdry one-nighter.

We never made it upstairs. Looking back, I wondered if Jess had been afraid from the beginning it wouldn't work, and had made love with me on the couch in his living room to give me less time to think. If so, that broke my heart, because it was so unlike him. Neither of us pretended we'd come to his house to talk. We were kissing before we were all the way through the door, deep, passionate kisses that felt like the past and present coming together, as if the years in between didn't exist. We hardly talked at all—how could we? Everything depended on no words being spoken. In the end, though, it was our guilty, unnatural silence that helped break the spell. I disengaged; went cold. It wasn't a return to sanity; more a gathering hopelessness, like a dark, dirty fog blearing a prospect that had been bright and sharp seconds ago. This couldn't work, it hurt too many people. The deeper we went, the more irredeemable it felt. I started to cry before it was over.

Jess stopped, put his clothes on, told me he would drive me back to my car. Before that, I have no idea what it meant to him. Did he like it, did he think we were good together? I don't think so. It was too full of shadows, and too frantic at the end. I remember the kissing more than the sex. I think my brain shut down when he came inside me, I think it was just too much. Too much. Now I can say it happened too soon, that I was still involved in my marriage, that by no means had I severed emotional ties to Stephen, that I wasn't ready for another man, even Jess, especially Jess. But at the time, it only felt like a calamity.

The rest is an embarrassing blur. I kept apologizing—he got quieter and quieter. I promised never to hurt him again—he said that wasn't possible. I cried some more. Understandably, he didn't want to prolong the conversation. He made me get out of his car and into mine, but I kept stalling. I wanted to comfort him and I wanted him to forgive me. Stupid, selfish, impossible.

For years I thought, *What a drip I was.* What a *drip.* I wished Jess had gotten angry, or *shown* it if he was angry, because at least that would've sharpened the squishy, drippy edges, given us something *meaty* to look back on, something to sink our teeth into. Really I wanted it all ways—for it not to have happened, for it to have happened and been wonderful, or for it to have happened and been awful, but with dignity. Instead I got the worst of all the possibilities.

I never told Stephen. He already knew about Jess; my "high school sweetheart," I'd called him, and once I'd gone so far as to say, "I guess I was in love with him." He took my casualness at face value, never questioned it or probed deeper. I would have. If Stephen had loved someone before me, I'd have wanted to know everything. What was she like, why did you like her, how did it end? His disinterest in the details of Jess was typical, though; one might even say emblematic.

On the airplane ride home, I made a decision to rededicate myself to making my marriage work. Something good might still come from the debacle with Jess, I reasoned, and besides, I owed it to Ruth—good as gold, chattering to herself as she turned the pages of a book, her feet sticking straight out in the patent leather Mary Janes her grandmother had bought her. The thought that I might have jeopardized my baby's safe, stable world froze me with horror. Anything, anything I had to do to keep the family together was worth it. No sinner ever embraced her penance more willingly.

I saw a therapist, who told me I was depressed and prescribed pills. I started to feel better. A time came, when Ruth was about eight, when Stephen made the supreme sacrifice and went with me to couples counseling. For four months, after which he declared our marriage "cured" and gave me an emerald ring for our anniversary. And that was the end of that.

Jess is still my one and only . . . what is the word . . . indiscretion. I hated it that I had been unfaithful, that I could never again claim fidelity and truthfulness as virtues of mine. But over the years my harsh judgment faded, as those things do, and I forgave myself, pretty much. Then all that was left was loss.

Deep down, though, I was always glad it was him. I've been drawn to other men from time to time, but I never gave in to the attraction. Self-serving, I know, but I do think, if you're going to cheat on your husband, you should at least have the decency to do it with a man you've loved all your life.

9

What Can You Do But Laugh?

If, God forbid, you had to go in a nursing home, Cedar Hill was probably as good as most. At least it was new; I could stop worrying about sticking George (or him sticking me) in Pacific Acres, the depressing, decaying, god-awful excuse for a rest home out on Route 15, Clayborne's best about forty years ago. Cedar Hill was like a funeral home—it looked a lot nicer than its neighbors. I guess they were trying for a luxurious estate look with all the gray stone and the wood shingles, but it didn't work. The wheelchair ramps gave it away, and the black rubber floor mats and the automatic sliding doors. And all that mulch—my Lord, to have the mulch concession at Cedar Hill. In six months you could retire and move to Florida.

Helen Mintz's room was on the third floor of A wing. Birdie and I signed in at the front desk as usual, where there was a new girl on who didn't recognize us. "Why would a pretty young girl like that want to work in a place like this?" Birdie said as we went down the two-wheelchair-wide, mauve-carpeted corridor.

"Why would anybody." I lowered my voice at the elevator bank, where four or five old ladies in wheelchairs or on walkers waited in silence. Like cows, I thought unkindly, patient and dumb. "Thank God *somebody* wants to," I said close to Birdie's ear. "I couldn't do it, I'm too mean. They're better than we are, Bird, that's all there is to it."

"Oh, yes," she agreed automatically. But come to think of it, Birdie would make a pretty good caretaker of the old and dotty, whose needs couldn't be that complicated—bathing, feeding, changing, medicating. I could see her doing all that with a lot of quick movements, a lot of wasted nervous energy. And all the time she did it, she'd never stop talking.

The elevator finally came. It took forever to get all the old ladies on board, and it was a miracle nobody's wheelchair got stuck on anybody else's, but there were a lot of close calls. I caught Birdie's eye after we finally got wedged in among all the canes and brittle hips and motorized chairs, and we had to look away. It's not the humor, it's the horror. I'm sorry, but what can you do but laugh?

Helen's door was ajar. "Yoo-hoo, anybody home?" No answer, but that didn't mean anything. Birdie pushed open the door to the tiny sitting room, overstuffed with furniture and reeking of air freshener. The TV was on without the sound. "Helen? Yoo-hoo!"

A weak voice from the bedroom, "Hello?"

We went in, and Birdie cried, "Hi! Well, don't you look smart!"

"Hey, Helen, how are you?" I said with a great big smile. "Good, he's not here," I muttered, stripping off my gloves and unbuttoning my coat. Hot, hot, it had to be eighty degrees in the room.

"Lord, yes," Birdie muttered back, and advanced on the bed to give Helen a hug. "Hi, honey, how you doing? You look so pretty! Is that a new peignoir? We always said pink was your color. You look wonderful, I bet you just got your hair done. It's nice, I like that shade of rinse."

I leaned over from the other side of the bed. "Hey, Helen, it's Dana."

"Dana." She blinked her thin-lashed eyes. Impossible to say if she knew me or not.

"Bird and I came to see you. It's been about three weeks since we were here last time, remember?"

"Why, I surely do, I surely do. How have you been?" She was nothing but a china doll, frail and brittle against the fat pillows behind her. The bluish hair was a wig, I saw up close, prissy marcel waves stacked on either side of a low part, freakish-looking above the spotty, deep-grooved, canvas brown that Helen's face has turned into.

She used to have long wavy chestnut hair, and she wore it down and loose until she turned fifty. Then, "I'm too old for long hair," she announced one day at bridge club, and the next week she came back with it all cut off. It looked so cute and young, one by one we all got ours cut off, too. Oh, Helen used to be the style setter at the bridge club. Such a lady. Just last fall, she'd've played hostess from her steel bed, or more likely her wheelchair, seeing to it that we had chairs and mints and cans of Coca-Cola, taking the lead in the gay conversation. Today Birdie and I found seats on our own, and all the talk started with us. All poor Helen could manage was, "Oh, is that right. Well, you don't *mean* it," with a sweet-faced smile.

Birdie plunged in with all her news, then all the news about everybody else she could think of. She forgot about Eunice. "Eunice had a hysterectomy," I mentioned when she paused to take a breath. Helen and Eunice Shavers had been bridge partners for thirty years—same as Birdie and me. "She said it didn't make a damn bit of difference, Henry's *still* not interested."

Birdie cackled. Helen smiled and nodded. "Oh, is that *right*."

"Dana's running for president of the women's club," Birdie informed her next. "Nobody can talk her out of it."

"Most people don't want to talk me out of it."

"Sensible people can't talk her out of it."

"Some people are just jealous."

"Some people choose to go blind and deaf so they can't see the handwriting on the wall. Pride goeth before a fall."

"Oh, dry up."

Helen smiled, eyes peacefully drifting back and forth between Birdie and me. I think she knew us then, just in that second. We had little spitting contests all the time, we were known for them at the bridge club. I think this one helped jog Helen's mind and we finally registered on her: *Oh, it's you two.*

She used to be sharp as a tack. She'd volunteer at the drop of a hat at the hospital, the cancer auction, hospice, the Red Cross. A real dynamo, even if it was just to get out of the house. Years ago the four of us, Helen, Eunice Shavers, Birdie, and I, went to Richmond for a couple of days, stayed at the Jefferson Hotel, went shopping, saw a show, a real ladies' weekend. Saturday night in the hotel bar, we were sitting around yakking, carrying on, enjoying ourselves. Feeling no pain. A man sidled up and started talking to Eunice by herself. Now Eunice is normally a levelheaded woman, but that night she was feeling even less pain than the rest of us. They carried on in private until it got late, time to go. She'll deny it to her dying day, but she was ready to go off with that man. "We're leaving," we kept telling her, but she wouldn't budge.

Helen saved the day. I can still see her herding that man away from Eunice, butting in between them like a sheepdog, chest out, chin up. He was a slick-looking character with silvery hair and a green cashmere sport coat; he sold golf equipment, I remember. He and Helen had words. We never knew what she said to him; afterward, she'd only say, "I called on his better instincts." But it did the trick—Mr. Green Jacket paid the tab for everybody, kissed Eunice on the hand, and said good night. And that was Helen for you, efficient as hell but always a lady. I always wished I had that combination.

Already she was slipping back into her own world. "Carrie's working for Brian Wright now," I told her in a loud voice. "You remember him, he runs that adult education program where we took the cooking class. You and Maxine Stubbs and I, about two years ago?"

"Yes, oh, yes."

"Doesn't pay much, but Brian's such a go-getter, I've got high hopes for Carrie's advancement. That job could take her anywhere. You know she lost her husband," I reminded Helen, who smiled and said, "Oh, is that *right*." "And Ruth's working at a health food store," I went on determinedly, "that Palace of something or other on Remington Avenue. Loves it. She's learning to drive. Worries Carrie to death. It all comes around, doesn't it? I was a nervous wreck when *she* was fifteen and learning. Ruth's fine, though, and at least she doesn't smoke."

"That you know of," Birdie said.

"That I know of."

Birdie's daughter's oldest boy, Jason, took dope and who knows what else before getting thrown out of his fancy prep school in Minneapolis, three or four years ago now. I guess he's straightened out since then, but Birdie was still touchy when it came to other people's grandchildren's wholesome accomplishments. I tried to be sensitive, but every once in a while I couldn't resist bragging about Ruth. The perfect teenager. How she turned out so well considering how permissive Carrie can be—well, that's a mystery. But a good one, so I don't examine it too closely. Wouldn't want to look a gift horse in the mouth.

Birdie said, "What do you hear from Raymond, Helen?"

"Oh, for the Lord's sake." I should've seen that coming, should've followed her train of thought and headed it off.

"What? What did I say? Oh." Birdie saw Helen's eyes fill with tears, and sent me a look of distress. Old fool. Anybody knew the surest way to make Helen cry was to mention her son Raymond's name. He lived in Florida now, Key West or one of those places where gays congregate; he never visited, and as far as I knew he never even called. Or if he did call, his poor mama was in no shape to remember it.

"Helen, honey?" Birdie got up and hovered over her, patting her fluttering hands. "There, now. There, now, sweetheart." The tears kept coming, but by now Helen probably didn't even know what she was crying about, she just knew she was sad. Dear God, I thought, give me the strength to kill myself. Don't let me get this way, I swear I'll blow my brains out first. Not a very Christian prayer, but I didn't mean it anyway. I used to say things like that all the time—"I'll swallow weed killer before I'll end up senile and in a diaper." Funny, though, the older you get, the more you lose interest in disposing of yourself. It ought to work the other way around.

"What the hell's going on here?"

Calvin Mintz filled the doorway with his wide, plaid-shirted bulk. A man that age ought to've started to shrink by now, but if Cal had lost an inch or a pound in the last twenty years, I couldn't see it. Old age hadn't sweetened his temper any, either. He looked mad as a bear.

"Why, hello, Calvin," Birdie chirped. "Helen's fine, she's just fine. Aren't you, honey? Look who's here to see you, it's Calvin."

Helen gave a tired smile, batting her eyes while Birdie wiped her cheeks with a hankie. I got up and gave Cal my side of the bed. He didn't touch or kiss his wife. He stood over her, a hulking man with a fleshy face and invisible lips, small eyes as dark and quick as Birdie's but much more purposeful. A mean face, I always thought. He came to see Helen every day, sat with her from morning to night. Such devotion. Such fidelity. What a shame he hadn't exhibited either one of those fine traits back when she was sharp enough to appreciate them. I despised him, or any man who was so bottled up, so *stunted* he could only be kind to his wife after she'd lost the capacity to recognize him.

"It's time for your arts and crafts class, Helen," he said in a voice that shocked me—so gentle and solicitous, I barely recognized it. "Two o'clock, up and at 'em, that's my girl." He stretched his arm back and snapped his thick fingers. "Oh!" Birdie peeped, realizing he wanted Helen's bathrobe from the foot of the bed. Bastard—that was more like it. She handed the robe to him and moved around to help, but he turned his back on her and fumbled

Helen's bony, listless arms into it by himself. It was like watching a father dress his little girl.

I looked around for the folded wheelchair and opened it without asking. Cal lifted Helen off the bed and set her in it carefully, straightening her robe where the collar had twisted. "Move," he said. I was in the way, I was blocking the path to the door, no question about it. His meanness helped me make a decision.

"We'll come with you," I said brightly, bending over to look Helen in the eyes. "Won't that be fun? Birdie and I'll come with you, honey. We'll *all* play."

"Play," Helen said with happy surprise. She beamed. "Let's all play."

Calvin actually swore. Foul, foul man. Birdie looked confused. I spun around and led the way out of the room.

Arts and crafts was exactly as pathetic and depressing as I'd thought it would be. *Kill me, Lord,* I prayed with new energy. *Put me out of my misery before it comes to this.* Eight old ladies, seven in wheelchairs and one sprightly gal on a walker, sat at card tables and learned how to make valentines out of red construction paper and doilies from an eighteen-year-old cheerleader. Well, she might've been twenty-two, but not a day older. And "learned" was stretching it. Debbie, the cheerleader, went around making all the ladies' valentines for them, leaning over their humped, arthritic shoulders with her strong, slender arms, crooning, "Isn't that pretty? Who's your valentine to? Bet you've got a lot of sweethearts, Margaret, don't you? Bet you're a real heartbreaker, aren't you?" And Margaret would giggle, or Nancy Jo would look vacant, Rebecca would click her dentures.

Calvin wouldn't let Debbie make Helen's valentine, of course, no, he had to do it for her, cutting heart shapes out of white lacy doilies and pasting them on bigger, blood-red paper heart shapes. It would've been touching, all that patience and gentleness, if you didn't know what was what. If you hadn't listened, off and on for the last thirty-five years, to a hundred stories about Calvin Mintz's neglect, coldness, and meanness. If he missed his wife, it was because there was nobody around the house to bully anymore. No sympathy from me. *Wallow in it, you SOB.* Calvin and his like, domineering, abusive men, bring out the worst in me.

It was a stupid idea, coming to arts and crafts. Helen didn't even know we were there. "Let's go, Bird," I said. I'd only wanted to yank Calvin's chain. Mission accomplished, I guessed, although it hadn't been very satisfying. "Bird?"

She looked up from the absorbing task of gluing half a dozen small red hearts on a big white lace heart. Her gray wool coat dwarfed her; she looked like a bag lady. She looked demented. "Thought I'd make one for Kenny." That was her youngest grandson. She winked—and the little chill that had begun to steal into my chest melted away. Just for a second—but no, Birdie was okay, she had her faculties, or as many as she ever had. And she was frequently the world's biggest pain in the you-know-what, but you couldn't not love her. I didn't like how she'd looked at that card table, though, squinting at her hearts, turning them around in her stiff fingers while she snipped them out with a pair of child's scissors. She fit in too well. She looked right at home.

Not me, I thought fiercely. I will *not.* Swear to God, I'll jump off the Leap River bridge first.

A cold February twilight was settling in; the color of the sky through the sliding glass doors to a brick-paved patio made me shiver. I hate winter. I hate the end of daylight savings time. Outside, gray geese were marching around a frozen man-made lake at the bottom of the sloping lawn. This place wouldn't be half bad in the summertime. At least you could get out. I watched a deer gallop across the lawn and skid to a stop not forty feet away. Pretty thing. A doe. It sniffed the air with its delicate snout, shivered, and bolted toward the patio.

That deer's coming right at me, I thought in a frozen part of my mind. *Of course it's not,* my rational side scoffed. *The hell it's not.* I had time to shout, "Look out!" and jerk an amazed Birdie out of her chair by her coat collar before everything went haywire.

Crash! The shock of seeing glass suddenly shatter and fly at you was nothing compared to the sight of an *animal* blundering in right behind. A big, brown, naked *animal* with a lolling tongue and white-rimmed eyes rolling in panic. It made noises—another shock; I thought deer were silent—harsh fluttery neighing sounds through its distended nostrils. It bolted in one direction, butting over a table, another table, crashing its antlerless head against a wall. Nobody was screaming except Birdie and Debbie, the cheerleader; the rest of us were petrified, struck dumb. When it veered toward Helen's chair, Calvin flung himself in front of her, arms spread wide, shielding her with his body.

Nobody was doing anything. I pushed Birdie away. "Baaaah!" I yelled. "Rawwwh!" The terrified deer skidded in front of me and jerked up on its hind legs. I shook my hands over my head. "Wraaah!" I kept shrieking while I went toward it in slow, fearful steps, trying to narrow the escape routes, herding it closer and closer to the broken door. Blood spotted its forehead and chest. It lunged again, overturning a folding chair, and I made a wild run straight at it. It pivoted clumsily—more blood on its dainty front legs—and smashed against the closed door to the hall.

Debbie stopped screaming and crept out of the corner, darting toward a metal floor lamp the deer had knocked over. She picked it up in both hands, like a lance. It had a cheap metal shade, open at the top; she pointed it headfirst at the deer, who was blowing its ribs in and out, panting, looking at—the lamp. I figured it out. Debbie thought she was stunning it by shining a light in its eyes.

Well, that was so stupid, it made me brave. I circled around the now motionless deer, moving toward a walker I could see under one of the still-standing card tables. When I got close enough, I bent over and grabbed it.

"Yah! Go! Go!" I stabbed the air with the walker. "Beat it!" Beside me, Debbie echoed, "Beat it!" and together we took jerky steps toward the deer until the floor lamp went out—she'd pulled the plug out of the socket. The animal looked confused, exhausted, swinging its head from side to side. "Wraaah!" I shouted again, and shook my walker. Suddenly it turned. In one enormous bound, it leapt through the shattered door, over the glass shards and the valentines, and streaked away, white tail flying surrender.

I stood there with my chest heaving and my heart pounding. From her crouch in the corner Birdie called, "Dana?" in a cracked voice. Everybody looked dazed. "Who's hurt?" Debbie said. "Anybody hurt?" A miracle—nobody was. A woman swathed in handmade shawls wept quietly while two other old ladies comforted her. "Okay, if everyone's okay, I'm going to call security," Debbie announced. "Okay? I'll be *right back*."

Calvin huddled over Helen, patting the hands she had gripped to the arms of her wheelchair. "Wasn't that a sight, Helen?" he said in a cheerful tone, as if we'd just witnessed something pleasantly exciting, a balloon launch or a shooting star. "That gave me a turn, I'll say. But we're okay now, aren't we. We're— "

"You made Raymond go hunting." Helen stretched her thin, cordy neck out accusingly, rheumy eyes blazing. "Remember? You made him go up to Bear Lake with you and that redneck friend, what was his name? Bobby Mahr. Ray was eleven years old and you called him a sissy because he didn't want to hunt."

Calvin stared at her stupidly, opening and closing his mouth.

"*Remember*?" she said impatiently.

"Yes."

"And *damn you* if you didn't make him shoot at a doe. He missed—but imagine making a boy like that shoot a deer. *Imagine* it." One balled fist smacked her padded wheelchair arm.

"Helen." Calvin put his hands on his knees and hung his head.

"Oh, my," quavered Birdie, realizing he was crying. I knew I should look away, but I couldn't.

Helen sat back. The piercing look faded; she stretched out a trembly hand and gave his bent, balding head one sad pat. "We lost him," she said. "That's when it started. Our baby. Where is he, Cal, is he dead?"

"No, no. No, he lives in Miami."

"But where is he? Where is he?"

"He's in Miami."

She wilted, just clicked off, a lightbulb going dark. Cal Mintz got a wrinkled handkerchief out of his back pocket and stuck his face in it.

On the drive home, all I wanted to do was brood, but Birdie never met a silence she couldn't fill. "Do anybody's children ever turn out right?" she wanted to know.

A dumb question I had no patience with. "Mine turned out fine," I said.

"Oh, I know ours aren't drug addicts or drunks or thieves or what-have-you. I'm saying, do anybody's children really care about them once they get grown?"

"What are you talking about? Of course they do."

"But not enough, Dana. Don't you feel that? It's not enough. All we do for them, what's it turn out to be for? I would've lain down and died for Mattie and Martha, I'd've done *anything* for them. My babies. And now look, they can't come see their own mother at Christmas. Me a widow, and I haven't seen my grandsons in eighteen months."

I wanted to say soothing, sympathetic things, but I'd seen Birdie with her children. She could not shut up, would not *listen* to them, and her incessant nervous chatter made them roll their eyes. She never stopped talking long enough to hear what their lives were like, so she had no idea in the world what kind of adults her own children had turned into. She exasperated them—they broke her heart.

What is it *I* do? Carrie only came back to Clayborne because she had to—Stephen's job. It's not that I talk too much, I don't think. Something else. The worst is that she wants to be close again, too, but neither of us can punch through the wall. It's sad and it's wrong, two people who ought to be the closest, a mother and her daughter.

I think daughters want too much, though. Carrie wants me to approve of every little thing she does. "Unconditional love," that's called. But what kind of a mother doesn't try to steer her child in the right direction when she sees her veering off the track? I don't even want credit for it—I just want tolerance and understanding and decent treatment.

"I don't even know why we have children," Birdie said. "I think it's because we get pregnant. Did you and George plan for Carrie?"

"No."

"No, most people don't. What do kids *do* for us?"

"Bird, you're just in a mood." I reached over and gave her skinny shoulder a pat.

"You think they'll make your life better," she said, "you think they'll make you happy."

You think they'll give your life meaning, I corrected to myself. And for a while it works, but then they grow up and leave you, and there's nobody left to soften the blow that there isn't any meaning. Not your husband, that's for sure.

"But happy families are only on TV," Birdie was saying. "In real life your kids can't wait to get away from you. It's so unfair." She sniffed and blinked her eyes fast. "Because all you ever wanted was a little love in return. And to try to make their lives happy."

And maybe you can't do both, it occurred to me. In fact, maybe the second one cancels out the first.

10

Arrested Development

Clayborne High School's parent-teacher conference day carried over into the evening, 7 to 9 P.M., for the convenience of the mothers and fathers who worked. A thoughtful accommodation, but I was running late before I started. My plan was to leave the Other School at the usual time, go home and grab a sandwich, change clothes if there was time, pick Ruth up at the health store at six-fifteen, drive her to her grandparents' house, where she was to have dinner, and make it to the school no later than seven—right on time so I could be finished in an hour and a half, pick Ruth up, go home, and collapse.

Nothing worked out. At noon, Brian realized he needed *today*, not tomorrow, the final autumn course offerings list, to include in a small business grant application that had to be postmarked by 6 P.M. We made it, just barely, but by then it was too late to go home. I'd missed lunch, so I stopped at Creager's for a quick bite, where I got the world's slowest, dimmest waitress and a case of indigestion. And a headache. By the time I double-parked in front of the Mother Earth Palace and Natural Healing Salon, where Ruth was supposed to be waiting *outside* but wasn't, it was already quarter to seven.

I'd met Krystal once before, not long after Ruth began to work for her. It was easy to see why Ruth liked her. She was young and hip, undemanding and laid-back; she said "fuck" with great casualness. But she was a kind of throwback, wasn't she? Or were hippies back in style now? Ruth's reaction to my tentative, extremely reluctant question concerning the possibility of dope smoked, or possibly even sold, on the premises was predictable. "*Jeez*, Mom. Like—*no*. God!"

"Hi, Krystal," I called, spying her in the cozy back area, slouched in an easy chair next to the humming woodstove. "Is Ruth here? I'm picking her up."

"Hi, Carrie." She had a low, husky voice, very soothing. She'd have made a good hypnotist. "Ruth? No, she left."

"She left?" I went closer to the stifling heat. "When?"

"Oh . . ." She peered at the fire through the glass door, as if a clock might be in there. "An hour ago? Well, at six, when we close. What time is it?"

"But she was supposed to wait for me. She left at six?"

"Yeah. Bummer. I guess she forgot." She smiled consolingly. She had dry, curly, reddish hair, flat around the front under a leather headband today, bushy and wild in back, an electrified halo.

"Do you know where she went? Did she go home?"

"I don't know. She didn't say, she just left, same as always." She picked up the white cat on her lap, gently set it on the floor, and stood up. "Problem?"

"Can I use your phone?"

"Sure."

Ruth wasn't at home. I got the machine and thought of leaving a sarcastic message, but Krystal was listening; it might embarrass Ruth. I called my mother.

"Hi, Mama. Ruth isn't there, is she?" She could've gotten mixed up, had one of her friends drive her over there.

"Ruth? No. Should she be? I thought you were bringing her. Is she driving? But she can't yet, she doesn't—"

"Long story—we've missed each other. I'll call you back, okay? As soon as I find out where she is."

"Do you think something's happened?"

"No, no, it's just a mix-up. I'll call you back. Don't worry."

Damn.

"Have you got a phone book?" I asked, and Krystal rummaged around and found one under a small counter covered with jars of Aloe-Dent, Astragalus, and Vitamol. What was Caitlin's last name? It was on the tip of my tongue. All Ruth's friends were on speed dial at home; I had no idea what their numbers were. Caitlin, Caitlin . . . I couldn't remember. Jamie, then; Jamie Markus.

She wasn't there. Mrs. Markus thought she might be over at Caitlin's, and gave me the number. Caitlin McReynolds.

Mrs. McReynolds said Caitlin was over at Becky Driver's. Jamie, too, but she wasn't sure about Ruth. I called the Drivers.

"Oh, hi, Mom."

"Why are you not here?"

"Where's here?"

My intense relief at finding her alive and unmolested evaporated very quickly. Underneath lay nothing but irritation. "I'm at Krystal's," I said through my teeth. "Where are you?"

"Oh, wow, I forgot. I'm supposed to go to Gram's, right?"

"Correct."

"Well, I forgot."

"Did you forget to come home, too?"

"No, because I knew you were going out."

"If you knew I was going out, how could you forget you were supposed to go to your grandmother's?"

"I don't know, I just *did*."

I pinched a white trail up and down the bridge of my nose. "I don't have time to pick you up now."

"That's okay, we were just about to eat anyway."

"I don't have time to call your grandmother and apologize, either. You'll have to do that."

"Oh, *man*."

"Ruth? I mean it."

"Okay, okay."

"As soon as we hang up. Now, how were you planning to get home?"

"Jamie'll drive me."

Jamie was sixteen, had been for about a month and a half. "No," I said, "I'll pick you up on my way home. About eight-thirty."

"No, Mom, come *on*. She can drive me, and anyway, eight-*thirty*? We won't even have our homework done by then."

"Oh, you went over to Becky's to do homework."

"Yes. I did! Partly. I *did*."

I was too tired to keep arguing. Stephen always said I gave in too easily, I was too lenient, I had no backbone. All true. I was probably ruining our daughter. The reason I was going to parent-teacher conference day in the first place was because Ruth's grades were sliding, and that was undoubtedly my fault, too. I felt like an invalid, an amputee, I had no control anymore, it was all slipping away.

"Make sure Jamie drives carefully, and I want you home by nine-thirty."

"Nine-thirty? *God*, Mom. Ten, come *on*. Jamie doesn't even have to be home till eleven."

"I very much doubt that."

"Ten, Mom."

"Nine-forty-five, and not a minute later. Hear me?"

"*Okay*."

"What are you going to do when we hang up?"

"Eat dinner?"

"Ruth—"

"Kidding, Mom, it's a joke. Remember jokes? Ha ha?"

"I'll see you at nine-forty-five. I imagine we'll have a lot to talk about."

That sobered her up. She said good-bye without making any more jokes.

"Do you take flaxseed?"

"What?"

"Flaxseed oil," Krystal said, shelving the phone book, "is very good for maintaining a healthy blood pressure. Comes in capsules. You want to take it with sage tea, a nerve tonic."

"Yes, that's—I'm sure that's a good idea. Would you happen to have any aspirin?"

She laughed gently. "No. Headache?"

"It's just starting. Tylenol?"

"Ah, Carrie. Belladonna, gelsemium, feverfew, wintergreen, willow bark, meadowsweet."

"Oh, I see."

"Autogenics, acupressure, aromatherapy, massage, juice therapy. These I can offer you."

"Ha-ha. But no Tylenol?"

"Are you familiar with Ayuveda? You could try a plain warm-water enema if you have a *vata* headache. Or rubbing the scalp and the soles of the feet with sesame oil, followed by a hot shower."

"Oh, thanks. I'll—"

"If it's a shooting, burning *pitta* headache, a sandalwood paste to the forehead and temples works wonders. For a *kapha* headache—does it feel worse when you bend over?—salt water in the nostrils is good."

"That's interesting. I'll certainly remember that. But now I'm so late, and I'm double-parked, I'd better run."

"Well, I wouldn't advise running. What you want to do right now, before it gets a foothold, is to imagine your headache is something else, say a leprechaun. Strike up a conversation with it. Make friends. Try a trade-off—you promise to eat better and get more sleep, your leprechaun promises to back off this time."

All this was said with a straight face and complete confidence. I searched for a twitch of the lip, a self-conscious twinkle in the eye, but in vain. Krystal Bukowski was the real deal.

"I'll do that. I'll try it in the car," I promised, and escaped.

What I tried in the car was speeding. On Cemetery Road, along the half-mile limbo section between residential and rural, where the houses ran out but the cornfields hadn't quite begun—suddenly a blue light flashed in the rearview mirror. Cop.

I slowed but didn't pull over—maybe it would pass, maybe it was after a criminal. I jolted in panic when the siren burst, *Wheep! Wheep!* No, it was me. It wanted *me*. My foot started to shake on the brake pedal and my hands turned clammy on the steering wheel. *Calm down*. I'd been speeding, not robbing a bank. But I was scared, and under the fear was fury, and over everything lay intense, skin-prickling frustration.

"Hello, Officer." I tried a bright, flirty voice. "Is there a problem?"

"Evening, ma'am. In a hurry tonight?" He wouldn't stand next to me, wouldn't come farther than my shoulder, I had to twist my neck to see him. A good tactic; it must deter the armed and hotheaded from shooting him in the face. "See your driver's license and registration, please." I fumbled them out of the glove compartment and handed them over. "Where you headed tonight, ma'am?"

"The high school. It's parent-teacher day." See? How wholesome and innocent?

"Uh-huh. Any reason you were going fifty-three in the thirty-five-mile-an-hour zone?"

I blanked. Should I tell the truth and say I was late? Deny everything? "Fifty-three?" I said wonderingly. "Are you sure?" I still couldn't see his face, but his voice sounded young and unsympathetic. "I never speed, honestly. It was an accident. I'm teaching my daughter to drive, I go *under* the limit usually."

"Ma'am, would you turn on your emergency blinkers, please?" I did, and he sauntered back to his patrol car and got in. I could hear him talking on his radio. I burst into tears.

What in the world was wrong with me? I wanted to sob and sob, not stop for days. It was crazy, I couldn't account for it. I barely had myself pulled together when he came back and handed me a pink ticket through the window.

"I'm going to give you a warning this time, Mrs. Van Allen."

"Oh, thank—" Mortifying tears flooded my face. "Sorry." I found a tissue and blotted my eyes. "Thank you. I'm—I'll—I won't do it again."

He finally leaned in the window, a little late now, but probably to see if I'd been drinking. I saw his face by the dashboard light. Young, yes; he was only a boy. "Better not, because next time, if it's me, I won't be so lenient."

"No, I know. I won't, don't worry."

"You don't want to mess up your good driving record."

"No."

"You want to set a good example for your daughter."

"I know. Yes."

"Okay, ma'am. You take it easy now."

"I will. Thank you, Officer"—I squinted at the badge on his chest—"Sherman."

He followed me all the way to the high school. I drove with exaggerated caution, five or six miles below the limit, careful to stay in the exact center of my lane. I didn't cry again, but I was still on some tricky kind of an edge. What a strange overreaction. Why such childish humiliation and rage? I couldn't remember feeling like this before, not over something so trivial. I looked normal, I wore pantsuits and worked at a computer, I could go for days at a time without crying. "Carrie's finally coming around," my mother was starting to tell her friends, and even Ruth didn't worry about me quite as much. But see how little it took to level me. Officer Sherman hadn't even given me a ticket!

My old school got a face-lift in about 1990, tinted windows and a new pink brick facade, even a tastefully harmonious addition. Now it looked about half its real age—thirty-five. But most of the interior changes were only cosmetic, and when I turned up for open house or one of Ruth's glee club concerts or science fairs, it was very much like stepping back in time. Because of the smell, always the same, always a humid, sweetish mix of chalk dust, mildew, wet wool, and sweat. As soon as I inhaled it, I was seventeen again, and a thousand ripe memories bombarded me. Like fruit falling out of a tree on my head.

No memories tonight, please. I wasn't myself; my poor head ached already, I was so tired, all I wanted to do was go home and pull up the covers. Besides, I was weak and vulnerable, and memories of high school always meant memories of Jess. I needed to focus on who I was, not who I used to be; I was an aging widow, here for her troubled teenage daughter. *Think of Ruth and getting home,* I advised myself, *Ruth and getting home.* That ought to squelch nostalgia.

There were long lines outside the classrooms of the teachers who taught Ruth's new worst subjects—biology, history, and amazingly, math. But that was some consolation, wasn't it, the fact that she wasn't alone? Maybe these teachers were incompetent, maybe lots of kids' grades were slipping.

But, no. Ms. Reedy, the biology teacher, and Mr. Von Bretzel, the history teacher, unfortunately struck me, in ten-minute interviews with each, as entirely capable; they were also sympathetic and understanding, and brought up the subject of Stephen's death even before I could. No scapegoating there. I'd been hoping—I realized it when I saw it wasn't going to work—to put all the blame for Ruth's troubles on the callousness and insensitivity of her teachers.

This must be what it's like waiting for the priest at confession, I thought, queued behind two other mothers outside Mr. Tambor's room. Did my companions feel as guilty as I did, as personally responsible for their children's academic shortcomings? But how could Ruth be failing algebra? There must be a mistake; math had always been her best subject. Now it was English, which made no sense at all. No, this had to be a mistake.

Eventually Mr. Tambor poked his head out the door. "Who's next, please?"

The blackboard across the front of the room was covered with formulas and equations; just the sight gave me a queasy feeling. Unlike Ruth, my worst subject had always been math. Plump, swarthy Mr. Tambor had a fringe of black hair ringing the back of his head and exactly three strands, very long, combed across the dome. How easy, I knew from experience, to make fun of a teacher who looked like that. But Mr. Tambor's brown doe eyes were kind, and when he smiled he looked like an Indian prophet, Meher Baba perhaps. I liked him immediately. Instead of sitting behind his metal desk, he gestured to a student desk in the front row, and took the one across from it only after making sure I was settled.

I introduced myself, and he said, "Ah, Ruth's mother," very sadly. "I am sorry for the loss of your husband."

"Thank you." He had a formal way of speaking, but surely I was imagining the eastern accent; he wasn't really *from* India. "I'm concerned about Ruth's math scores lately, Mr. Tambor. She's always been so good in math—she talks about majoring in it in college. I can't imagine what's happened," I said. Disingenuously. "I mean, to go from A's and A-minuses to a D-plus in three months—it's very worrisome."

"Yes. Yes, it is worrisome." He put his fingertips together thoughtfully, or maybe prayerfully. "Have you asked Ruth what might be the problem?"

"She says the class has gotten harder. She also admits she's not studying quite as hard."

Mr. Tambor pursed his lips. "Mr. Van Allen taught mathematics at the college," he observed.

"That's right, yes."

"Advanced courses, topology, numerical methods, number theory, so on."

"Yes."

"And Ruth was very close to her father?"

I'd seen the question coming, so it didn't surprise me. "Not really. Not as close as she always wanted to be." The fact that I had told this complete stranger the truth—that surprised me.

"Ah?" His lips made a small, fleshy circle. "She spoke of him in class sometimes. Always with great pride."

"Did she?" Oh, why was that so sad?

"But of course Ruth doesn't really have a mathematical mind. I wish it were otherwise—she's so very bright. But she won't study mathematics in college now. Clearly."

"She won't? Why not?"

He smiled and didn't answer.

"Why not? Are you saying she was only good in math to please her father? And now that he's gone—?"

"I believe so, yes. Don't you think?"

"I . . . Well, I have no idea." Yes, of course, it was obvious. Still, I resisted. I hated the thought of Ruth trying so hard to make Stephen notice her, even going against her own *nature* to get his love and attention.

"It's not so sad," Mr. Tambor said, leaning toward me, chubby shoulders straining against the seams of his cheap white shirt. "We'll help her. She'll make C's and B's, as she should. It'll be all right. Yes? Come. Everything will be fine."

I took the immaculate folded handkerchief he handed me, warm from his back pocket. Why be embarrassed? I'd already cried in front of a policeman tonight, why not Ruth's algebra teacher, too?

"Thank you," I told him, handing the handkerchief back after blotting my cheeks but thoughtfully not blowing my nose. "You're very nice. Now I know why Ruth's so fond of you."

He made a little bow of gratitude, palms together.

"Are you from India?" I asked. He'd lulled me into unwonted familiarity. "Or . . . Pakistan?"

Mr. Tambor looked amazed. "No, no. Italy."

"*Really*."

"Used to be Tamborini. We shortened it to Tambor when Uncle Guido was gunned down in the barbershop."

"No!"

"No." His smile stretched from ear to ear. "I come from Ahmadabad. That was a joke."

I laughed, and blushed, and decided I was in love.

I didn't recognize Bonnie Driver at first, probably because in the back of my mind I'd been thinking she was at home supervising three teenagers, including my daughter. She was walking down the hall ahead of me, and I thought, *That looks like Bonnie Driver's perky little butt*—you notice things like that on your ex-boyfriend's ex-wife. The swingy, chin-length hair looked familiar, too, but I didn't know it was Bonnie until she turned slightly and I saw her in profile. Long, intelligent nose, mild brown eyes, a friendly mouth—she was lovely, and a kind person, and everyone liked her. I liked her myself. Too bad she'd never liked me.

She turned around when I called to her. "Carrie—hi! Ruth said you'd be here. I left Dan at home with the girls, I ran right over as soon as we finished dinner. Don't you hate these nights? How are you?"

"I didn't know she was going to your house—I'm sorry if that was an inconvenience. We had a mix-up—"

"Oh, not at all, Ruth's wonderful, I love having her, so does Becky. So tell me, how is your new job?"

She was so nice. When Stephen died she sent me a sweet, gentle note that made me cry. We didn't even know each other—and yet we did. She was the kind of person who would send a gracious sympathy note to someone she didn't like simply because it was the decent thing to do.

"Oh, the job's all right. Well—not exactly what I was hoping for," I said, truthfully for some reason, "but it's okay. Pays the bills." Barely.

"Maybe it'll get better." She smiled encouragingly. "Sometimes you have to break a new job in."

It was possible she didn't really dislike me. Well, why would she? Certainly not because of jealousy over Jess. She won, after all; she married him, then she divorced him, all long after I was out of the picture. I always felt a certain coolness, though, under the friendliness, as if she were watching me, collecting data, reserving judgment. She *wanted* to like me, but she couldn't quite bring herself to do it. We fascinated each other. God knew we had a lot in common. Well, one thing.

"I hear Jess asked you to help him out with the ark." She smiled less naturally, not as amused as she wanted to appear. "Such a crazy thing, isn't it? Poor old Landy, he's the one I feel sorry for."

I'd forgotten she knew Landy—he'd have moved next door while she and Jess were still married. "Crazy," I agreed. "In a way, I wish I *could* help out."

"Oh, it just seems so strange to me, something you're better off staying away from. It could swallow you up if you weren't careful." The generic *you*, she was using; surely she didn't mean me personally. "And now that the whole thing is public knowledge, it's just going to get bigger. I really wouldn't want any part of it—but that's me."

"What do you mean, it's public knowledge?"

"Didn't you see the paper yesterday?"

"No. The *Record*?"

"Page one—Eldon Pletcher's promised to buy all new playground equipment for Point Park if they'll let him build the ark on the fishing piers, right on the water. And then sail it on the river for forty days. The city council's taking it up at the next meeting. I'm not kidding."

And Jess was on the council. "Wow," was all I could say.

We talked a little longer, about our daughters and their mutual friends, then used the excuse of teacher appointments to separate. "Good to see you," we said, and "Take care," but neither of us was hypocritical enough to say, "Call me," or "Let's get together." I didn't know why her marriage failed—Jess would probably have told me if I'd asked, but I wouldn't. As much as I'd have liked to know. But the fact of their marriage, or rather the fact that it ended, was what kept Bonnie and me at arm's length. Which must've meant—well, I didn't know what it meant. It *seemed* to mean that I was mixed up in it somehow, and I didn't know what to think about that. So I didn't think about it. Much.

Three mothers and a father were waiting in line to see Mrs. Fitzgerald, Ruth's English teacher. My heart sank; if I joined them, it would mean at least a half-hour wait, maybe longer. No, I decided, to hell with it, I was going home. Ruth was doing well in English—that's why I'd wanted to talk to Mrs. Fitzgerald in the first place, to hear some good news for a change. But now I was just too tired.

The way out of the building led past closed double doors to a staircase. *Locked* double doors now, I was sure, but in my day they were always left open. Foolishly—because the stairs went down to the janitor's room, the furnace room, and the infamous Utility Room, No. B–45. Also known as the Make-out Room. This many years later, I could still remember the muffled blast of boilers and water heaters through cinder block walls, the smells of oil and electricity and disinfectant, the dim, grainy light from one flickering fluorescent tube high up in the pipe-lined ceiling. Senior year, the winter months, I had met Jess down there every day at 12:35, for the precious fifteen-minute interval our lunch periods overlapped. We were never alone, other couples trysted in dark corners nearby, but for a public place the utility room had been remarkably intimate.

Since then I'd had a handful of lovers and a longtime husband, and with one or the other of them I imagined I'd done most if not everything that healthy, reasonably inventive people did in the sexual area. But kissing Jess was still my lifetime's most erotic memory, the touchstone, the baseline for all physical passion. Arrested development, I called it after we broke up. I tried to demystify the experience by talking about it to my college friends, describing it, laughing about it. "Up against the wall in this smelly utility closet, kissing and kissing till our mouths hurt! Oh God, it was so funny." A lie. And I even knew I was betraying him. No help for it, though, I'd had to save myself. I was young, stupid, myopic; too much self-knowledge would've been like shining white light in my eyes.

I was aroused, I realized, buttoning my coat, trying to remember what row I'd parked the car in. Ridiculous. But I was; my stomach felt tight and heavy, pulled down by gravity. It was the atmosphere, the circumstances, the power of setting. Well, if you were going to feel like a hormonal schoolgirl, what more logical place than your old high school?

Did Ruth feel like this? Disconcerting thought. Of course she did, she must. We talked about sex occasionally, the wisdom of waiting, the importance of protection, all that sort of thing. What we never talked about was how it was for women, what its place might be in our lives, not with any frankness. We never put sex in context. She was still too young, I told myself, but that was just a cop-out.

My mother was fairly open about sex, even when I was little—open as in willing to speak her mind, that is, not as in liberal or permissive. From the age of about six, the message I received was loud and clear: *don't*. Nice girls wait, cheap girls don't. *Tacky* girls don't—that was the thing. Because in Mama's book being *tacky* was as low as a human being could go. Better to be morally bankrupt, a pervert, better to be a serial killer than *tacky*. It was her strongest prejudice. In a sense, it defined her; it was the motive behind all her life's decisions, large and small.

Well, everybody needed a code, a model for right conduct. Not being tacky: in its way it was a standard, no worse than a lot of others for civilized human behavior. Its limitations—snobbery, intolerance, racism, classism—had driven me crazy for most of my life. It wasn't the philosophy, though, as much as the strength of my mother's belief in it and the power of her personality that had made me a confused, unwilling follower all through my childhood. I think it was the main reason—not the only one—that I never went all the way with Jess. As much as I loved him, as much as I wanted him. Amazing, in retrospect.

Or maybe not. No, probably not. You could only blame your mother for so much. I was the one who was intimidated by his passion for me, his wild, excessive ardor—so it seemed to me. Not giving in to him was the only way I knew to control him. Instinctively, I feared chaos if I gave in, some kind of annihilation.

Another way of saying I chickened out.

So many regrets. I shivered as the car heater blew cold air on my shins, slowing self-consciously at the spot where the policeman had pulled me over. Right . . . there. If I'd left work on time, if Ruth had been where she was supposed to be, if I'd left Krystal's a little later, a little earlier . . .

If only, if only. What if I'd married Jess? He'd asked me. Over Thanksgiving break, my freshman year of college. I almost said yes. He didn't bully me, he said he'd wait till I graduated, but then he wanted me to come back to Clayborne and live with him on the farm.

At first the prospect tantalized me. I loved his house, the land. Live there with Jess? Paradise. But by Christmas I had doubts. College was incredible, everything I'd expected and more, I could *feel* myself turning into the kind of person my childhood, my family—my mother—had been preparing me to be. Men who were going to be lawyers, artists, scientists, wanted to go out with me. I started letting them. Eventually, the idea of spending the rest of my life tending cows on a little farm in Virginia began to seem less and less plausible, until finally it seemed—outlandish.

So I'd told Jess no. We were growing apart, couldn't he see that? We didn't have as much in common anymore, we wanted different things. What pains me now, all this time afterward, is that I honestly didn't think it would hurt him—I thought surely he could see I was right, he must agree, it was so clear. What a shallow, self-involved little twit I was. And when I saw that I *had* hurt him—I offered to sleep with him! At last! What a magnanimous gesture; the perfect farewell present. Oh, that memory can still make me cringe. To Jess's credit and to my everlasting shock and shame, he refused. I didn't see him again for fifteen years.

I unlocked the front door to the dark, chilly house with a shuddery feeling, even a sense of dread. *I'm as empty as this hall. I'm as cold as this living room.* It was only a little after nine, Ruth wouldn't be home for at least half an hour. Sometimes loneliness felt like panic, a low, thudding sensation in the diaphragm. A drink? No, I might end up in tears. Again. But coffee would keep me awake. I hung my coat in the hall closet and went upstairs. Maybe a bath to soak the chill out of my bones. Maybe I was coming down with something.

The answering machine in the bedroom blinked a message. The tape took forever to rewind—that meant it was Mama. I lay down on the bed to listen.

"Hi, it's me," came her bossy, confident voice, booming over the silence. "I thought you'd be home by now. Give me a call when it suits. I've got an idea—I'll tell you about it when we speak." But no, she couldn't wait. "What do you think about a little getaway? Just the three of us, for a weekend someplace interesting." *The three of us*? Me, Mama, and Pop? How bizarre. "I think it would do us all good, I really do. End of the month, maybe, when it's a little warmer. We could go to Richmond, we could go to Washington, Baltimore, wherever we want. I know Ruth works on Saturdays, but surely she could take the day off one time."

Oh, *those* three. An all-girl getaway. Much less bizarre.

"'Course, the sale of colonic cleaning agents may fall through the floor, but homeopathy as we know it will survive." She chortled merrily. "Carrie, erase this tape immediately, hear me? All right, call me when you get in if it's not too late. Oh—Ruth called, by the way. A mix-up tonight, signals crossed. We missed her, but we understood. She is the sweetest child, I could just eat her alive. Let's go to Washington, don't you think she'd have more fun there? Okay, call me. Love you. 'Bye."

I pulled the blanket up over my legs and crossed my hands over my chest. An out-of-town weekend with Ruth and my mother—what a nice idea. Theoretically. Three generations of Danziger women, all at difficult ages and stages, on the loose in the nation's capital. It could be fun. It could be disastrous. It was one of those ideas that were so compelling and irrefutable *in the abstract*, as soon as you thought of them they were virtually inevitable. Destined. If only because all the arguments against them sounded neurotic.

I caught myself dozing. *Get up, get undressed*. I would. In one minute.

I was in the backseat of the family car, the blue Ford we had when I was in junior high. At first I thought Mama was driving, but now I could see it was Ruth. Trees and sky streamed past the open windows, vivid watercolor streaks, blue-green-blue-green-blue-green, and the pine wind blew in my face. "Don't go so fast," I warned, but Ruth paid no attention, didn't even turn her head. Then Stephen was beside me on the seat, his thigh grazing mine. I wanted Ruth to look around and see us, see that we were together. I called to her, but she had her headphones on, keeping time to some cool, silent beat, swaying her shoulders. I couldn't see Stephen's face or his upper body, just the leg of his old green corduroy trousers. I moved my hand on his thigh, studying the contour of my fingers, light on dark, and then it was Jess's leg.

He put his chin on my shoulder—my bare shoulder; all of a sudden I was naked—and kissed me under my chin. "Wait, now," I whispered. Even though my eyes were closed tight, I could see the dazzle of blue-green-blue-green flood past faster, faster. Ruth was driving too fast, something horrible was going to happen. Jess had me pressed down against the seat and our legs were tangled up, his covered with tickly blond hairs, I wanted to stroke along his thigh and ruffle the fine hair, just graze it with my palm. I opened my mouth to tell Ruth to slow down, and Jess slipped his tongue inside, and we made love until the wail of a siren turned my hot blood into icy slush.

Ruth was still speeding, but in slow motion. Jess didn't get it, he wouldn't cover up, wouldn't stop touching me, and I couldn't scream at him because Ruth would hear. Even though the car was still moving, Officer Sherman poked his head in the driver's window and handed Ruth a ticket. *Don't turn around*, I begged, *Oh, don't see us*, frantic, shoving at Jess's slick shoulders. Officer Sherman dissolved, changed into Mr. Tambor. "It's your fault," he said mournfully, wagging his finger in my face. "She is failing all her subjects. You have only yourself to blame."

"Mom?"

"Hey." I struggled up on my elbows, cleared my throat. "You're home. What time is it?" I put on a good-natured smile, in case any of the dream still showed.

"Ten-ish." She waved her hand vaguely. She had an ostentatious stack of books clutched to her chest. I patted the bed and she dropped down beside me, scattering books on the blanket. "Were you asleep? In your *clothes*?"

"No, no. Just thinking with my eyes closed." A joke of Stephen's. We smiled wanly. "Did you have fun at Becky's?"

"It was okay. I heard you saw her mom at school."

"Yes, we had a nice visit. What did she give you for dinner?"

"Some casserole. Then we had cake left over from Becky's little sister's birthday. She's twelve. It was pretty good."

Her arms were bare under her dun-colored short-sleeved sweater. Long, pale, child's arms, the curve of the wrist so tender and defenseless. "Aren't you cold?" I said, pinching the fold of skin at the back of her elbow.

"Yeah, it's freezing in here. So . . . did you just get home?" Casual yawn; bored examination of the line where the wall met the ceiling. My heart squeezed. Helpless love flooded me. *Don't change, don't do anything, don't get older.*

"I had talks with all your teachers except Mrs. Fitzgerald."

"Oh, shoot, Mom. She's the best one."

Shoot. How sweet we could be to each other. I'd been cleaning up my language for Ruth's sake for years, and now she was cleaning hers up for me. "We'll talk about it tomorrow," I said, "it's too late tonight. You look tired, I want you in bed. But I'll just tell you—nobody told me anything tonight I didn't already know."

She bowed her head, relieved.

"We will, however, be making some changes soon. In the studying department."

"Right, okay."

"Right, okay. I'm not kidding."

"I *know*."

I thought about what Mr. Tambor had said, that she probably wouldn't study math in college because Stephen was gone. She didn't have to try to please him anymore. I was different—I'd given up on my father when I was even younger than Ruth, about thirteen. (I could be fairly precise on the date; I uncovered it with the help of a very careful therapist in Chicago nine years ago.) I hadn't stopped loving him, but I gave up expecting fatherliness from him. But Ruth hadn't given up on Stephen yet. I had watched with a sick heart while she persisted, virtually up to the night of his death, in trying to get his attention and his love. That's what scared me the most about her, her puppylike constancy, her hopefulness. At fifteen, a wafer-thin coating of skepticism flavored her language these days, her rotten-teenager attitude, but underneath was a big, sweet smiley face. I counted the days before somebody's thoughtless, random cruelty—please God, don't let it be mine—erased it, killing her innocence.

"Go to bed, sweetie," I said. "Kiss me good night first." The red light on the answering machine reminded me. "Oh, Gram called. She wants us to go away for a weekend sometime. Just the three of us, to Richmond or D.C., someplace like that."

"God. I mean, too weird. So do we have to?"

"Don't you want to? I was thinking it would be fun." She made a face of incredulous revulsion. Did they practice in the mirror? Was there a course they took, "Contemptuous Expressions Sure to Hurt Your Mother's Feelings"? "Well," I said stiffly, "we'll talk about that later, too. Get ready for bed now, you look exhausted."

"I am, I'm really wiped. Can I stay home tomorrow?"

"No, you stayed home today."

"Yeah, but it was a holiday. I am really, really wrecked."

"Then you should've rested today."

"I wasn't tired today, I'm tired *now*."

"Go to bed, then."

"I could have mono for all you know. I could have chronic fatigue. I probably do have a liver dysfunction right now."

"Good night, Ruth."

"*Jeez.*" She snatched her books up, stormy-faced, and flounced out. In the hall she threw back, "Becky gets to stay home tomorrow."

"Oh, really? Now I'm beginning—"

She didn't hear. "Mrs. Driver has a lot more compassion than you," she finished cuttingly, before closing her bedroom door with just enough force to register anger and resentment but not enough to justify the punishment for slamming. She'd perfected the distinction. She had it down to an art.

I slumped against the pillow. Bonnie Driver had a lot more of a lot of things I didn't have. A nice bout of self-pity would've been very comforting right now. With Stephen gone, I ought to have felt *less* underappreciated than I used to. Nothing like a teenage daughter to keep you whittled down to size. No sustained highs allowed. I couldn't remember being hateful to my mother in any long-term, persistent way when I was a girl, although I probably had been. The difference was that Mama was tough and strong and thicker skinned, and when you hurt her, she didn't sulk or get depressed, she got mad.

An out-of-town weekend with Mama and Ruth. Well, maybe so. Maybe it was just what Ruth needed. She might learn important life lessons from her grandmother. Lessons her mother couldn't teach her in a million years.

11

Texas Two-Step

I could've called Landy and asked him about the article in the paper on Noah's Ark. He was the logical one; the ark was his project, after all. But I called Jess. I wanted to hear firsthand about the city council vote, I told myself. Ignoring the obvious fact that, since Landy would undoubtedly have been at the meeting, his account would've been firsthand, too.

Jess was out, as usual. Farmers didn't seem to spend much time in their houses. I left a message. He called back when I was on another line, trying to sign up an instructor in white-water rafting for the summer term. At about three in the afternoon, we finally connected.

"Hi—what's this I hear about playground equipment?" I asked, all business. "Now Pletcher's bribing the city council?"

"He thinks of it as an inducement. How are you, Carrie?"

"Do you think it'll work?"

"Well, the treasurer did some figuring last night, and came up with a little under thirty-nine thousand to replace everything at the park."

"Thirty-nine thousand *dollars*?"

"And that's not even top-of-the-line equipment. There's opposition to the ark on the council, no question, but I think, for that much money, a lot of aesthetic sensibilities are going to roll over."

"It wouldn't surprise me." Wait until my mother heard about this. Launching a fully stocked ark on the Leap even sounded tacky to *me*.

"Meanwhile, Carrie, Landy's animals are getting uglier every day."

"Sorry to hear that."

"The *Morning Record*'s sending a reporter out next week to take pictures. For a feature."

"Uh-oh."

"It's only a matter of time before Eldon and the Arkists all look ridiculous. Landy, too."

"Sorry," I said again. "Nothing I can do about it."

"You could come out and help us."

"Jess—how in the world did you get caught up in this?"

He sighed. "It started out so peacefully. Landy had a wood-working project—that's what he called it—and asked if he could use my band-saw. The next thing I knew, I was cutting out rhinoceroses."

"*You're* doing animals now?"

"Yes, and I don't have time, I've got an ark to build. The original was made out of gopher wood. Any idea where we could get some gopher wood?"

"Eighty-four Lumber?"

"Funny."

"When do you milk your cows?"

"I knew there was something I forgot to do."

I laughed. "This is all your own fault. You could've said no."

"I could've. But I like it. I like the idea."

"But it's so *crazy*."

"That's what I like about it."

I smiled to myself. That was the Jess I knew.

"And you need it, Carrie."

"*I* need it? Oh, I assure you, I don't need it."

"Okay, then, I need you." Quiet for a second. "Come over Saturday, will you? Bring Ruth."

"No, no, I can't. Anyway, Ruth has to work."

"Come by yourself."

"I can't, Jess, really."

"Think about it. Try to come."

"Andy's giving up violin," Chris Fledergast announced, coming to stand in front of my desk while she pulled on her coat and wound a wool scarf around her neck. "Maybe piano, too, but we're putting that decision off till summer."

I turned off my computer. How could it be five o'clock already? "Andy's giving up the violin? Why?"

"Because he hates it."

"Well, sure, but . . ."

"I know. Believe me, if it was up to me, this would not be happening." She jammed a maroon wool cap down so low on her head, it hid her eyebrows. So clumsy and gangly on the outside, so graceful inside, a genuinely gentle person. "It's all Oz's doing," she said, folding the ends of her muffler across her chest and buttoning her quilted coat over them.

"Oz doesn't want Andy to play the violin?"

"It's not that." She smiled at Brian when he came out of his office. "Telling Carrie—Andy's quitting violin, and maybe piano, too."

"How come?" Brian draped one muscular thigh over the corner of my desk and sat down.

"Oh, he hates to practice, he hates the recitals. He's starting to say he hates music."

"It's just a phase," Brian said. "What is he now, ten?"

"Nine. He says he wants to play baseball."

"And Oz is all for that," I guessed. I'd only seen Chris's husband once, when he'd dropped her off at work and come in for a second to meet me. He was nice, I'd liked him, but big and tough, a pretty macho guy—I could imagine him not minding much if his kid gave up piano.

"No, it's not that," Chris said. "It's not a guy thing, you know, not Oz wanting him to get tough or anything."

"Oh." So much for what I knew.

"He says Andy should be allowed to decide for himself." She scowled down, jabbing the side of one gloved hand into the spaces between the fingers of the other. "Oh, I don't know. I just think, how is he supposed to know what's good for him? He's nine, how could he know?"

"Yeah," Brian said, "but if he hates it."

"I know. I don't know. We argued and argued, Oz and me."

"I had to take piano," I said. "Took it for four years, and I can't play a single song." Not strictly true; I could play "Für Elise" and "Country Gardens."

"I always wanted to take piano," Brian said, "but my folks couldn't afford it. I'd've been good, too. Too late now."

"Andy's very musical, his teacher says he's got loads of talent. I say of *course* he wants to play baseball—he'd rather eat ice cream than spinach, too, but we don't let him. But Oz says he's old enough to make his own decisions, so."

"Well, I guess if he's supposed to play the violin—"

"He'll come back to it—that's what Oz says." Chris shook her head, worried. "We'll see."

I tried to think what I'd do if Ruth wanted to give up something she was good at—reading, say. No, bad example, because of course I'd have to discourage that. But—say she wanted to give up both her team sports, soccer and volleyball, and spend her time . . . drawing pictures of fashion models in designer clothes. Just for example. Would I allow that, even though she has no talent for drawing or design but she's excellent at soccer and volleyball?

I wasn't sure. Probably.

I knew who would violently disapprove of that decision, though. Mama. If she thought she knew what was good for you, you didn't have a prayer. She'd wear you down to a nub and you gave in.

"Chris," Brian said, "did you get that payroll spreadsheet printed out before you shut down?"

"In your in box."

"Great. You going home now?"

"Thought I would." She grinned at me, holding out her arms. *What does he think I'm doing in my coat?* We laughed at Brian behind his back sometimes, but in a nice way, tolerant and affectionate, the way women laugh at men they like. Brian took advantage of Chris, though. She was so smart, but she didn't push herself. She did whatever he told her, cleverly and efficiently, because loyalty and hard work were what she thought he'd hired her for. If he'd appreciated her, it would've been different, but he didn't. He took her for granted.

He cracked his knuckles, one of his boyish habits, swinging his leg back and forth against the side of the desk. "I need somebody to brainstorm with," he said, frowning. "You have to get right home?" he said to me.

"Um . . ."

"Because we could do it over dinner. An early one while we talk, if you're free. I need to get back to Carmichael on this Remington thing, and I'm not sure what to tell him."

Remington College recently made an interesting offer: in return for nothing except goodwill and community relations, the college would let Brian hold some Other School courses on campus, in free classrooms, mostly at night, and they'd even spring for on-campus ads to that effect, and include the school in the annual catalog under college-associated community services. I thought it sounded terrific, but Brian was being cautious.

"Well, I could," I realized. "Ruth's going over to a friend's house after work and she won't be home till late, so it's a good night for me."

"Great!" He bounded up from the desk, rattling my computer monitor. "I need ten minutes, then we can go. We'll take my car."

"Hey," Chris said when he had disappeared into his office. "He never invites me to dinner. Guess you have to be good-looking and single."

But she was kidding—I looked to make sure, and she was grinning.

"Too much air?" Brian touched a button discreetly hidden in the leather side panel of his Lincoln Continental, and the window went up without a sound. "I'm just saying it could muddy our image. Is it the Other School or is it Remington College? The distinction won't stay clear in some people's minds."

"Brian, where are we going?" We'd been driving in the country for twenty minutes.

"Great place, you'll see." He threw his right hand across the back of my seat, leaning back to steer with his left. "You're thinking what difference does it make if it's clear in their minds or not. Just as long as it gets us more enrollment."

"No, I'm not."

"I can see your point, too. I'm probably being too proprietary."

"No, I think it's a legitimate concern. One of the school's biggest assets is its independence. It's the *Other* School. Most people have a sense that it's alternative."

"Right, it's out there, it's a little on the edge. You put it on the college campus, it's just another post-secondary program. People think continuing education, adult education, associate degree, Other School. And that's wrong, that's not who we are at all." He smacked his hand against the steering wheel for emphasis. The smell of his cologne was strong at the office; in a closed car it was overwhelming. And the Lincoln was huge, but Brian's bulk made the front seat feel almost cozy.

"On the other hand," I said, "you can't ignore the benefits. The hassle factor—you'd never have to hustle for classroom space again—that's just one thing. Enrollment. I have no idea how much it would go up—"

"Plenty. You got kids sweating through poli sci, trigonometry, the history of the rococo period in Belgium in 1840—and they see a notice that next week there's this cheap night course on how to get laid on the first date and it's *right across the hall*—you got a big jump in enrollment."

"That's a joke, right?" With Brian, you could never be sure.

"I'm talking on that order. We'd definitely gear a lot of courses to attract the students, though, much more than we have been. That's common sense. You'd have to take advantage of what's practically a captive audience."

"But how to get laid on the first date, that's—"

"An example! Of course we wouldn't call it that." He gave my shoulder a playful jab. "I'd count on you to think up something tasteful—'Overcoming Shyness in Your Interpersonal Relationships,' something like that. Huh?" He laughed hard—he always laughed hard at his own jokes. "'Dispensing with Inappropriate Shame'—you like that? Ha ha ha ha!" He'd flicked on the turn signal. He was braking, pulling into the parking lot of a long, shingle-sided, neon-lit restaurant. "We're here," he announced, easing into a space between two shiny pickup trucks. "Ever been here before, Care?"

CACTUS FLATS, read the blinking green-and-yellow sign. Cocktails, beer, steaks and chops. Live entertainment Fri., Sat., Sun. "No," I said. "My first time."

"You'll love it. You like rib eye? Best in the Piedmont. It helps if you can stand country music."

Cactus Flats was an old-fashioned roadhouse, low and dusty, reeking of beer, big enough to maintain separate sections for its three primary activities—drinking, eating, and dancing. Brian wanted to "brainstorm" here? No live music tonight, a Thursday, but the jukebox was as loud as a band, and it never took breaks. After a while the twangy George Jones and George Strait and Vince Gill tunes got into my head. It was true that the older I got the more I could tolerate country music, and it wasn't to embarrass Ruth (as she claimed). I could hear the words and sing the melodies—was that asking too much? Lowbrow, Stephen used to tease me; you can take the girl out of the country, but you can't take Carrie out of Clayborne. He hadn't said it in a very nice way.

We sat in a booth along a knotty pine wall adorned with saddles, spurs, Stetsons, and longhorns. I felt sorry for the waitresses, who all wore tight jeans tucked into high-heeled cowboy boots. "Do you come here a lot?" I asked Brian over a peppy Patty Loveless song, something about only going halfway down. I had to shout my question again, not so much to be heard over the music as to attract Brian's attention. Because he was gone. As soon as he gave the waitress our drink order—a couple of Lone Stars, what else—he went into another world, appeared to get lost in the music and the . . . *ambience* wasn't the right word for Cactus Flats. The experience. He even sang along—I could hear his pitch-perfect falsetto just under Patty's. Sometimes I came upon Ruth in her Walkman headphones, wearing the same intense, absorbed, blissed-out expression and wailing along to the music of bands with names like Hole and Anthrax.

Brian grinned happily and either nodded to my question or continued to keep the beat with his head, I couldn't tell. When the beer came, he clicked his icy stein to mine with so much gusto, I was afraid we'd chip our glasses. "Isn't this great, Carrie? Isn't this the perfect place to unwind?"

I nodded, smiled back. Well, it was. It really was. But I wished I'd had a little notice; I could've unwound more efficiently if I'd known I was supposed to. But how amazing to see this new side of Brian I'd never suspected. He'd taken off his suit jacket and rolled up the sleeves of his shirt, loosened his tie. He looked younger, carefree, not nearly as intense as usual as he slouched against the wall, one foot drawn up on the seat, banging out the beat with his fist on the back of the wooden booth.

The music changed. All of a sudden he shouted, "Two-step!" grabbed my arm, and hauled me up and out of the booth. I tried to resist, but it was ridiculous, Olive Oyl fighting off Bruno. "I can't do this!" I yelled, trotting to keep up as he pulled me along, out onto a huge, nearly empty dance floor. "Brian, wait! I can't do this!"

"'Course you can." He dragged me up in a close clinch, one beefy arm clamped tight around my waist, the other holding my right hand down at my side. "All you do is walk backward. I walk forward, you walk back." He demonstrated by walking into me. When I stumbled he just picked me up, an inch off the floor, and kept walking. It was like dancing with a bear.

A big, sweaty, masculine bear. As the shock wore off and the mysteries of the two-step became clearer, I tried to figure out what I was feeling. How was this? Did I like being held against Brian's strong, hard, weight lifter's body? Yes and no. Impossible to say, the situation was too ambiguous; I couldn't separate the fact from the context. The context was that it was *Brian*'s body, Brian my colleague, Brian who signed my paycheck every two weeks. How could I know what I felt? Was this all good clean fun? Did he just want to get some exercise?

We were panting by the time the dance ended. He held my hand on the way back to the table, swinging it up and down with muscular exuberance. Oh, I thought, this is nothing. The directness, the lack of calculation, the *boisterousness* in the way he touched me—finally I realized he was just being Brian, friendly and bluff and fun loving. And I was an ass for worrying. I always made things too complicated.

The waitress came for our order. Brian was as forceful about rib eye as he was about the two-step, but in this case I didn't mind. "Just don't tell Ruth," I joked. "She's trying to turn me into a vegan."

"How are things going at home?" he asked, leaning in, elbows on the table. "How's Ruth getting along without her dad? It must be really tough on both of you."

"We miss him a lot. Sometimes I think it's getting easier, and then something happens and it's hard again. But we're doing all right. I don't know what I'd do without Ruth—she's my lifesaver."

"I'm sure she feels the same about you."

I made a dubious face. "Hard to say. You know kids."

"Oh, I know kids." His were nine and twelve, both boys. He saw them on weekends, alternating holidays, and a month every summer. "Craig wants to go to computer camp this summer—that's the latest."

"I thought it was basketball camp."

"That was last week. He's the opposite of Gordon, whose goal never changes."

"Uh-oh." Gordon, the twelve-year-old, wanted to play lead guitar in a heavy metal band. "I wonder who's harder to raise," I mused, "boys or girls."

"Boys," Brian said immediately, and told a story about the night Gordon set fire to his mattress by hiding the lit candle he wasn't supposed to be playing with under the bed. That reminded me of the time Ruth put so many newspapers in the fireplace she set the chimney on fire, then the roof. "If the neighbor hadn't seen the flames and called the fire department, we'd have lost the house."

"Oh, that's nothing," Brian said, and told about the time Craig and Gordon decided to "drive" the car by coasting it down the driveway and out into the busy street where, by a miracle, it came to a harmless stop on the grass median between two lanes of traffic. "You don't want to dance, do you?"

"What?"

"You looked funny. Lost in the music."

"Oh, no," I said, laughing, "go on, no, I'm listening."

No, I wasn't. I was listening to Neil Young sing "Helpless." It used to be my favorite song. I'd played it so often, my *Déjà vu* album got warped. Jess borrowed a friend's tape deck and recorded "Helpless" twenty-seven times, one after the other, on both sides of a blank tape, and gave it to me for my eighteenth birthday. To this day, it's the sweetest, funniest gift anyone's ever given me.

Over our steaks, Brian told me his life story. He grew up in eastern North Carolina, oldest of three kids, came to Clayborne to go to Remington, got a B.S. in business administration, married a local girl, and stayed on. For his first job—already an entrepreneur—he started an employment counseling and temp service. But in Clayborne there weren't enough people to counsel or find temporary jobs for, so that failed. Then Norma got pregnant and poor Brian had to settle down and find a real job—registrar at the college. He hated it. "I can't stand working for anybody except myself, is my problem. Don't have the patience. They don't go fast enough, they don't see far enough," he said feelingly, jabbing at a piece of meat with his fork. "When things get screwed up, I don't want to blame anybody but me."

"That's good to know."

"Not that I'm a control freak, at least I don't think so. You think I'm a control freak?"

"No." Yes.

"Yeah, because I don't think so. I pick good employees, tell them what I expect, and then I don't get involved in what's their responsibility. Right?"

"Right, boss."

"Right, because I don't need to. You're good at what you do, Carrie, I'm good at what I do. We make a team."

"And Chris is good at what she does, too."

"Sure." He toasted me with the last of his beer and signaled the waitress for another round.

"Not for me," I said.

"No? Sure? Well, this is my last. Never have more than two drinks when I'm out, not if I'm driving."

The second beer loosened him up enough to talk about his ex-wife. He never had before, not even to joke. I knew, because Chris had told me, that the split had been bitter, that they still only spoke when necessary, and that Brian deeply resented that Norma had gotten custody of the children. Now I got to hear what a bitch Norma was. Not that he ever used the word, but he didn't have to; a woman who was manipulative, shallow, childish, passive-aggressive, unreasonable, withholding, judgmental, and intellectually bankrupt was pretty much, by definition, a bitch.

I listened for as long as I could, then excused myself to go to the ladies' room. On the way, I used a pay phone in the corridor to call Ruth. She was at Jamie's, and this time I had the number with me.

"Mom," she said immediately, "where in the world *are* you?"

I'd gotten used to the noise; it took me a second to realize she could hear the music on the jukebox, currently a bluegrass tune, lots of fiddling and banjo picking. I laughed. "Oh, I'm someplace called Cactus Flats. It's a sort of roadhouse, it's—"

"Out on Route Twenty-nine? *That* place?"

"Have you been here?"

"No, but jeez, I've heard of it. What are you *doing* there?"

"Well, Brian wanted to talk business, and so—and it was time to eat anyway, so—we came here. He likes it, he's been before, I think he comes here regularly, in fact."

"Business?"

Trust Ruth to leap immediately on the only weak point in the explanation. "Yes, actually. We've been brainstorming about a new direction the school might take, or might not." In the car, en route, but that counted. "How are you doing? Get your homework done? I just wanted you to know where I am in case you get home before I do, although—"

"Well, good thing, because I'm just leaving."

"Oh, so early? Well, that is a—"

"It's not that early, Mom, it's eight o'clock. In fact it's *ten after*."

"Is it? Well, that's not so late. Okay, so you're going home now. Got your key? And you know the routine. Lock the doors, don't—"

"I *know*."

"Don't let Jamie drive off until she knows you're safe inside. Blink the porch light so she'll know."

"Mom, I know."

"Okay."

"So when are *you* coming home?"

"Very soon. We're ordering coffee."

"You've been drinking."

"What?"

"Haven't you. I can tell. I can tell by your voice."

"Ruth—" I'd have laughed, but she might think I was drunk. "Honey, I had one beer. About an hour ago."

"Yeah, right. What about *him*?"

"'Him'?"

"Are you on a date?"

"No, I am not on a date. I told you—"

"Right, you're brainstorming, it's a business dinner at Cactus Flats. That's a good one, Mom."

"Listen. I—we're talking about other things, it's true, and we had a drink before dinner, but that's it. We're not—"

"I totally don't care anyway."

"Fine, but this is not a date."

"Okay, fine."

"Ruth."

"But even if it is, I don't care."

"But it's not!"

"Okay."

I banged my forehead lightly against the black metal edge of the phone box. "We'll talk about this when I get home."

"I'll be asleep."

"Tomorrow, then."

"What for? According to you there's nothing to talk about. I gotta go, have a nice evening."

"Ruth—"

She hung up.

In the ladies' room, I leaned over the sink and looked myself in the eye. *Are you on a date?* I honestly didn't know. I touched up my lipstick self-consciously, thinking, I would do this anyway. I'd do this if I were with girlfriends, it doesn't mean anything.

As it turned out, we didn't leave Cactus Flats until after nine. It was open mike night, and Brian said we had to stay at least for the beginning. I worried about Ruth—her suspicions, not her safety—but he wheedled and prodded until I couldn't say no. And then I had to admit, open mike was a hoot. "I told you!" Brian crowed, clapping and whistling for a young man whose cover of a raunchy Hank Williams Jr. song brought down the house. "This is the next best thing to karaoke."

"That was fun," I said truthfully on the drive home. "I'm really glad we did that."

"Good. I thought you could use a night out."

"Thanks, Brian." I smiled at him warmly. It changed things, thinking he'd chosen a place like Cactus Flats for my sake. "That was nice of you."

"Well, sometimes we don't know we're stuck and need a change. We're in a rut."

"It's true."

"You lost Stephen, but you're alive. Gotta keep remembering that. It's not even good for Ruth to see you depressed all the time."

"No. Well . . . I wouldn't say I'm depressed all the time."

"You just need to get out more."

"Probably."

"Definitely. It's been six months."

Six months. That had a ring to it. *She went to a country-western dance hall, and her husband dead only five months*. That sounded callous; that was borderline despicable. But *six* months, now you were veering over into acceptable territory. You could go out to a roadhouse at six months and it sounded respectable. But with a man? Hmm. That muddied the water. But if the man was your boss, that was different, surely.

Who was I imagining the sound of these numbers *for*, though? Not myself, and not for my friends, who couldn't have cared less if I went out to dinner with a man, boss or not. It was for my mother. I was forty-two and I still had conversations in my head, mental dialogues, imaginary debates; in some I played myself and in some I played my mother. A form of self-censorship. Did all daughters do that? Did Ruth? Were we all second-guessing schizophrenics, bound from the start to be both the sound and the distorted echo, the main character in the story of our lives and also the critic? Mother Nature's system of checks and balances. Very efficient, and what it lost in spontaneity it made up for in prudent living. Being a mother and a daughter, I could see the pros as easily as the cons. Mama's emotional hold on me was tiresome and life sapping and unhealthy—mine on Ruth was caring, selfless, sensitive, and benign. That neither of those extremes could possibly be true was just, in my old age, beginning to dawn on me.

We picked up my car at the office, and Brian insisted on following me home. I intended to say good night at the door, or even on the sidewalk by the car, but he parked, got out, and came inside with me. I wasn't sure how that happened; one minute we were on the front porch, me rooting in my purse for the key, the next we were in the foyer and he was helping me take off my coat.

"Well," I said, "thanks again." The living room light was on, but no Ruth. She must be upstairs. "That was really fun. Just what I needed."

"This, too," he said, pulled me into his arms, and kissed me.

Well, that answered that. We *were* on a date.

"Brian . . ." He had a big, soft mouth, furry at the bottom—his goatee. He opened his lips and enveloped me, sucked me in. Behind closed eyes, I had a vision of a dark cave, deep and scary, damp inside. "Brian," I managed to say, "don't."

"Why not?"

Stuck for an answer, I hesitated. He took it as permission to lift me under the arms and pull me up against his chest. The bear maneuver again. He clamped one arm around me and used his other hand to rub the bare skin of my back, under my hiked-up sweater. He kept kissing me, mauling me with his lips, using his tongue. "Stop, stop it," I hissed. I wanted to yell, but I didn't want Ruth to hear. I stuck my chin in the air, out of his range. "Put me down. *Damn it.*" He had me in a vise, pressed back between his body and the front door. The expression on his face looked friendly and interested, excited but in a good way. Anticipatory. "Brian, stop it!" He put his hot mouth on my neck and sucked.

Was this really happening? It could be a joke—he was a kidder, a practical joker, especially with Chris, maybe this was some kind of a—

He wormed his heavy hand between us, got it on my left breast, and squeezed.

I turned into a woman with a lot of joints, especially elbows and knees. None of them did any damage—he was built like a safe—but they finally got his attention. He took his hands off and backed up.

For the first time since it started, my feet touched the floor. My heart was pounding; I felt shaky in the knees. I said, "Jesus, Brian," and wiped my mouth with the side of my hand.

He kept smoothing his palm down one lapel of his jacket, a habit when he wasn't sure of himself. "Bad timing, I see. Sorry, Care. Didn't know you weren't ready."

Weren't ready? To be assaulted? I got a hand on the door knob behind me and jerked the door open. "Good night." I stepped back, letting in the cold.

"No harm done, I hope. Right?" He grinned, friendly and hopeful. Just a big teddy bear. Doubt made me scowl at him. Could I be overreacting? No. But—it was only Brian. Not Jekyll and Hyde, just Brian. My vivid new image of him was already fading, bleeding into the old one, the jovial, easygoing, good-hearted guy, who brought raisin muffins to work because they were Chris's favorite. I just knew something extra about him now. Keep away from him.

"Maybe I gave you the wrong impression," I conceded with reluctance. "I'm not interested in a romantic relationship."

"It's too soon." He nodded understandingly.

"No—ever. I'm just not interested. Sorry." I'd have added more, softened the blow, blamed myself—the art of breaking up was coming back to me fast—but I was still so *angry*. Even "Sorry" came out through my teeth.

Something passed over his face too quickly to read. Anger? Hurt? But he said, "Okay," and grinned some more, buttoning his sport coat, poise regained. "I've got it. You don't have to hit me over the head twice."

I wanted to hit him over the head once. "It's late. Sorry for the misunderstanding."

"Oh, that's all right," he said, forgiving me. "Dating's a tricky business nowadays, huh? You know what we should do? A course on the war between the sexes. Heh?" I froze when he seized my upper arm and gave it a tight, cordial squeeze, passing me in the doorway. On the porch, he turned back. "Well, Care—"

"'Night," I said, and closed the door in his friendly face.

In bed, I went over it again, egged on by insomnia from the two cups of coffee I'd stupidly drunk after dinner. The only good thing about the way the evening ended was that Ruth hadn't witnessed it. I hoped. I'd tiptoed upstairs as soon as Brian left and peeked into her dark, silent room—silent except for soft snoring. Which she could've been faking. But I didn't think so. I prayed not. Literally: *God, please, please let her be really asleep*, bent low over the messy, cluttered bed, scrutinizing the slow rise and fall of the blanket on her shoulder. "Are you awake?" I whispered. Her delicate eyelids may have fluttered, but it was hard to tell in the dark. I put a soft kiss on her cheekbone. "Love you," I murmured, and slipped out.

Anyway, I consoled myself, the very worst that could've happened was that she was feigning sleep and she'd seen everything—why would that be so terrible? Embarrassing and undignified, yucky, all that, yes, but if she had *seen* it, then she'd know once and for all that I wasn't interested in Brian Wright. That should be a relief, not a trauma. In fact, maybe (looking on the brightest possible side) it had all happened for the best. A minor humiliation for Ruth's peace of mind—a good mother would gladly make that trade.

Small consolation at 2 A.M., when I was still tossing and turning. Where exactly had the evening gone wrong? Brian was a jerk, I made no excuses for him, but I must've done something, unconscious or not, to make him think behaving like a jerk might pay off. What, though? I'd never invited him in, so it wasn't that. Some body language maneuver, maybe, around the time he helped me take off my coat. Nothing came to mind, though, no accidental flash of skin or inadvertent intimate contact. No, it had to be that I was just irresistible. I drove men insane.

That moment of hesitation with Brian, that second when I couldn't answer his "Why not?" question—at least I knew what that was about. Curiosity. I'd wanted to experiment, find out what I was like with a man who wasn't Jess and wasn't Stephen. That was why it was so hard to make Brian the villain, even though he deserved to be—because off and on tonight, I'd been comparing him to the other men in my life. My two passions. What if Brian had taken my breath away? It might've changed everything. So my reasoning had gone.

Well, now I had the answer. Imagine making love with Brian—no, no, I didn't want to, it would be like sleeping with a Saint Bernard, a Great Dane, one of those breeds that slobbered on you.

Sleeping with Stephen had been like . . . like sleeping with a computer. A very solicitous, efficient computer, though, one that was programmed to satisfy. Physically. I'd had no legitimate complaints—as he'd often assured me. But somehow our sex life had become detached from our regular life. At the end it wasn't an extension of anything, not an expression of closeness or love, it was just itself. It bored me to tears. Literally.

I got up and took a sleeping pill. I still had a few left—the doctor prescribed them after Stephen died. I'd been hoarding them.

Settling in bed again, I finally thought of something funny. On the drive out to Cactus Flats, I'd come to a decision. Assuming the evening went well, I'd decided to screw up my nerve and do something I'd been putting off for too long. Ask Brian for a raise.

12

Actively Growing Before Your Eyes

"Wanna go somewhere?" Raven slid to the floor with his back against the locker next to mine and crouched there, dangling his hands between his knees. He had on skin-tight black pants, a white poet shirt, and black leather lace-up boots. He looked depressed. What else is new.

"You mean, like, the cafeteria?" It was eleven-thirty, lunchtime. I rummaged around in my locker, exchanging my math book for my English book, getting out a new notebook.

"Someplace that's not here."

"Oh." I looked down at the top of his head. The whole left side was dyed sparkly metallic red today. I liked it better than last week's yellowish green. He had new piercings, too; his left ear looked like the side of a spiral notebook. "Okay," I said, "I guess so. You driving?"

He nodded slowly, staring at his fingers.

"I've got an algebra test fifth period," I felt silly mentioning.

He lifted his head slowly, slowly, until it banged on the locker behind him. Slowly his heavy-lidded eyes met mine. "An . . . algebra . . . test?"

"But it's no big deal, I don't mind cutting. So where do you want to go?"

In the graveyard with Raven. It sounded like a song. Or a Clue game—Raven, in the graveyard, with a joint. We were smoking the joint before we ate lunch because Raven said that was the only way to make the food we'd snuck out of the cafeteria for our picnic edible. But it was Friday, hamburgers and french fries day, my fave before I became a vegetarian, so I didn't really have to smoke to be hungry. I took a few hits to be sociable, though, and so Raven wouldn't have to toke alone. And so I wouldn't look like a dork.

"This is so totally weird."

He took a long time to stop staring at the clouds, roll his head sideways, and look at me. "What's weird?"

"Getting stoned here. Right next to his grave. I mean, what do you think he'd say?"

"He wouldn't say anything. He's dead."

"Yeah." I lay down on my back beside Raven and put my hands behind my head. "Yeah. He's dead."

You could look at the piece of sky in your vision, just that section, and block out everything except your mind and it. Like meditating. So there was nothing in the universe except your eyes and the blank blue and the white clouds. You could even take away the space between, you could be *in* the sky. "Are you being the sky?" I asked Raven, who didn't answer. "Are you, like, up there? I can't even feel the ground under me."

After a long time, he said in a croaky, marijuana voice, "I'm not doing that. I'm doing the clouds. That one." He pointed. "It's a guy with no head. He's been executed. He was a mass murderer, he killed . . . all the algebra teachers."

I snorted. "No, it's a wheelbarrow. And that one's a horse. See the head? See there, the mane?"

"It's not a horse, it's a hatchet. An ax. The one that cut off the murderer's head."

"No, it's a horse. It's coming to save the murderer, who's not dead. He's innocent, it was a frame-up."

"He's got no head."

"No, he's in cahoots with the executioner, it just looks like there's no head, it's a trick."

Raven sighed and shut his eyes. He hardly ever smiles. I used to try to make him, but it was like trying to crack up the guard at Buckingham Palace. "I read this thing in the paper," he said with his eyes closed. "A family, mother, father, two little boys, they were driving home from a trip in an old junky van, the two little boys asleep in the back. They get home, it's late at night, and the parents start carrying the kids into the house. And then they realize the kids aren't asleep, they're dead. They both asphyxiated from carbon monoxide poisoning."

"Oh, God."

"There isn't any God. That proves it."

"Oh, God. I don't know."

"You don't want to see. Nobody does."

I sat up and wrapped my arms around my calves. The dead grass was still damp from yesterday's rain; I could feel it through the coat I was sitting on. It wasn't cold here, the hill behind us blocked the wind. "My mom's never had anyone die on her before, as old as she is. You can get to be forty, even fifty, and if you're lucky no one dies."

"My aunt died."

"But that can never happen to me. For the rest of my life, I'll be a person whose father died when she was young."

Raven lifted his arms and made a square frame with his hands to look at the sky through. The sleeves of his shirt fell back, showing how white and skinny his arms were. "She had one of those aluminum caskets. Like a space capsule. They guaranteed it for twenty years, but who's checking? It's been three years now, the lining's bound to be shot. Dark blue velvet. It's gotta be wet and moldy and rotten. Anyway, nothing's left but her dress, so what's the difference?"

"Bones. She'd still have bones."

"They put her in a red suit, put a lot of makeup on her face. Like she was going to a party." He sat up to relight what was left of the joint. He sucked in a lungful and passed me the roach. "Want the rest?" he said in a strangled voice.

I shook my head. "I put a note in my dad's casket. At the wake. I just slipped it in next to his shoulder."

"What'd it say?"

"Oh, you know. Good-bye and all that." How much I loved him, how much I would miss him. Stuff I couldn't say to him when he was living.

Raven took a few more little puffs on the joint, which was about a millimeter long, and stabbed it out in the grass. "That fence reminds me," he said, lying back down. I glanced over at the spiky wrought iron fence that ran down to the lane separating this high, hilly part of the cemetery from the lower part. "There was this guy who was drunk and slid off a roof and landed on a fence post. It went right through him. Vertically. It went from his groin up through his whole body, it stopped an inch from his heart. He was standing on his feet with a stake inside him."

"Did he die?"

"No, he just stood there, moaning and crying. People thought he was drunk, as usual, so nobody helped him. A couple of hours went by. Then he died."

I rested my cheek on my knees. "Is that really true?"

"Sure."

"How do you hear things like that?"

"How do you not?" He rolled to his side. "So do you want to eat now?"

Everything was cold and greasy and nothing had enough salt. He ate all the french fries and most of my hamburger. I nibbled on an apple while I weeded my father's grave, pulling back the grass from around his bronze plaque. This wasn't the kind of graveyard that had headstones, just plaques, flush to the ground to make it easier to mow the grass, I guessed. In the car, Raven said, "Let's go to the graveyard," but he'd meant the old one, the nice one on

Hickory Street. I said, "Let's go to Hill Haven—that's the one on the way to Culpeper." He hadn't wanted to come here and I didn't blame him, it wasn't spooky or atmospheric or anything, it was more like a golf course, but when I told him it was where my father was buried, he said okay.

"It's not like I care about my algebra test," I said, kneeling on my coat, wiping my hands on my jeans. "I don't care if I flunk algebra."

"Al-ge-bra. What is it for? What does it mean?"

"It's nothing."

"It's nothing." Raven smoked clove cigarettes, which are like ten times worse for you than tobacco. He took one out of his pocket and lit it, blowing smoke rings at the sky. "Everything is nothing."

"So you're really flunking English this semester?"

"Sadly."

"But you're so good at it. You could get A's without doing anything."

He opened one eye to look up at me. "Fuck all," he said softly. "Fuck all, Ruth. Fuck it all."

"Oh, well," I said quickly, trying to erase that. No one knows what happens to you, anything is possible, so it was possible my father could hear us. That's stupid, I know, but still. You shouldn't say "fuck" while you're sitting by your father's grave, maybe sitting right on top of him for all you know, depending on which direction his coffin faced in relation to his plaque. For the same reason, I wasn't telling Raven about Mom's date with Brian Wright. Because if Dad heard that, it would kill him.

"You know how much meaning there is in getting an A in English?" Raven said. He made slow designs in the air with the smoke from his cigarette. His black-painted fingernails were chewed so short, it looked like his fingers were bleeding.

"None?" I guessed.

"There's no meaning in anything. It's all nothing. This is how we end up. I'm lying here now. In a little while I'll be lying here six feet deeper. That's the extent of the significance of our precious lives. For a few years we breathe, then we don't."

"What about reincarnation?" Krystal was heavily into that, channeling and past lives and regression therapy.

He looked at me pityingly. "That's the most obvious example of wishful thinking I know of. Even more than 'God.'"

"But don't you think there's *something,* some being or some outside force that's like a consciousness, like energy or electricity or something?"

"Why?"

"Because."

"Because you want there to be."

"Yeah! But also, how else could the world have been created, I mean, what makes it keep going?"

"Chemistry. Oxygen, hydrogen, carbon di—"

"But don't you just feel there's something that's more than us, a divine something or other, I don't know what, but—"

"There was this woman in New Jersey, she kept her daughter in a cabinet under the sink."

"No, but—"

"From the time she was one year old, this little kid had to live in a cupboard with a padlock on it. When they finally found her, she was like fourteen, and her bones had atrophied and her body was bent over double permanently, her backbone had grown into a curve, she could never stand up."

"Oh, stop."

"Tell me about the divine force who thought that one up. This is the God for me."

"I'm not saying there's not—"

"You know how many people have been slaughtered in the Balkans so far?"

"No, I know, I just—"

"Or Algeria? Or Rwanda, or Ireland, or Cambodia? How many women raped, how many children murdered? Usually in the name of religion?"

I hid my head between my knees and pressed in hard against my temples.

"This is not the Garden of Eden. We're worse than beasts, animals would never do what we do. We're monsters. There was this guy in northern California, he kidnapped a woman and chained her up in his basement. First he cut off one of her arms, and then after that healed, he cut off . . . Ruth? Hey. What's up, what are you doing? Are you crying?"

I couldn't talk.

"Hey, come on, it's okay." He gave my arm a soft, unsure pat. "Don't do that, okay? Everything's all right."

"No, it's not, everything blows, everything's horrible." I dug a wadded-up Kleenex out of my jeans and wiped my nose, keeping my head down. So totally embarrassing.

"Everything's not horrible. Come on, it's almost spring, we'll be out of school in three months. That doesn't blow."

"Everybody just dies, you're right, so what's the point? It's all so stupid." And that wasn't even why I was crying. "My dad, he—he—" I started hiccuping, crying in those short, gaspy inhales like a baby.

Raven put his arm around me. I got my breath back and rested my head on his shoulder. He felt bony and tough through his shirt, like a boy, not a man. The white powder on his face was streaky where I'd wet his cheek with tears. He wore an ankh on a black velvet ribbon around his neck. I touched it with my fingertips, instead of touching him.

"There could be reincarnation," he said after a while. "Nobody knows, I mean, *knows*. Anything is possible."

I nodded gratefully.

"There could even be a God. Shit. There could be a heaven."

He was so sweet, I started crying again—just tears, no sobbing. "No, I don't think there is. But I don't even care. It's not that I want him to be in heaven, I just want him not to be dead. I can't believe I'll never see him again. He was alive—and now he's *dead*?"

Raven held me and rocked me, and then—it was just like in a movie—he kissed me. Except he missed my mouth and got me on the side, mostly cheek. I turned my head, thinking, *Okay, let's do this, I'll freak out later*, and our lips met. His were still black from his lipstick. I opened my eyes to see what he was doing. His eyes were open, too, but when he saw me looking at him he closed them. He had his hands on my shoulders and he was moving them down, pretty soon he would be touching my breasts. I decided to let him. Once Barry Levine touched the side of the right one while we were dancing. I pretended not to notice, and never danced with him again. This would be the first time I really let anybody. That the person was Raven—no, I'd figure that out later, if I thought about it now it would ruin it.

So then we kissed using our tongues, which I'd done once before, but this was better. I worried that I might have bad breath, because Raven did, because of the pot and the clove cigarette, but I didn't mind. At first I didn't even know he was touching me, he did it so lightly. I felt dizzy with my eyes closed; I didn't realize I was slowly falling over backward until my shoulder blades hit the ground. It was scary and exciting, lying on my back with Raven practically on top of me. Except for where he'd sprayed it red, his hair was much softer and cleaner than it looked, and on the other side, where he'd shaved it almost bald, it was nice to run my fingers over the soft, short bristles and hear the whiskery sound. Shouldn't we talk, say something to each other? I couldn't think of anything that wouldn't sound stupid, but the silence, except for our hard breathing, was weird.

He put his hand under my sweater and my blouse, and I stopped thinking. Then I realized I wasn't thinking, then I forgot again. Then I remembered. *I'm making out on my father's grave.* I sat up so quickly, I hit Raven in the nose with my forehead. We both said, "Ow," and leaned over, holding our faces. "Sorry," I said, "I'm really sorry. I can't do this here. I forgot where I was. God! Is that blood?"

I'd given him a bloody nose. He stood up and walked a little ways away, keeping his back to me, hunching his shoulders. He looked just like Raven, slight and tall and gloomy. And to think we'd just been kissing. It was like a dream. I thought about him sometimes, had some fantasies about us being a couple, but more like . . . more like an old married couple that didn't have sex anymore. Or like a nun and a priest who were best friends. One day last fall he wore a skirt to school—just for first period, before they sent him home. He said it was a gesture, we should all challenge gender stereotypes, androgyny was the only sex role that didn't exploit people. But after that some kids thought he was gay or something. I hadn't known what to think. Well, I guess I did now.

"Is it really bleeding?" I scrambled up and went to him. He half turned around to say no, but it was. All I had was my wadded-up Kleenex. I passed it over his shoulder. "I'm really, really sorry. I just, all of a sudden, you know. Remembered."

"We could go over there," he said nasally, pointing to some trees.

"Um, well. I guess I should get back."

"Okay."

"Because I've got that test."

"Whatever."

"But that was . . ." I went blank. I turned away and started gathering up our stuff, pretending I hadn't said anything. How could anyone finish that sentence? Who would be stupid enough to start that sentence? "That was nice"? "That was fun"? "Thanks for feeling me up, let's do it again sometime"? I often think my life would be a lot easier if I were a mute.

Raven's car is an old Plymouth station wagon he spray-painted black to look like a hearse. The vanity license tag says CDVRS RUS, which hardly anyone gets unless they know him. The inside smells like decaying leather, old bananas, and smoke. He always drives slowly and carefully, not like every other kid I know who can drive. I kept sneaking looks at him, trying to figure out how he was feeling. I hoped he wasn't hurt or mad at me. I'd have apologized more, but I didn't necessarily want him to think I wanted to start up again right away or anything—like bloodying his nose was the only thing stopping us from some hot and heavy love affair. But I didn't really think he thought that anyway.

"Hey, you know my friend Jess? The guy I told you about, the ark guy? Jess Deeping? That's his road—if you turn right there, that goes to his farm." Raven nodded but didn't slow down. "Turn! Turn, okay?" The car slowed; we turned in at the gravel drive between the gateposts. "I just—I was thinking we could say hi, is that okay? He's probably not even there. Look, those are his cows, that's all his land, that whole hill. Isn't it pretty? Some of it's on the river, too." Raven kept his eyes on the lane and didn't look around. "We don't have to stay if you don't want to. We can just say hi." We rounded the last corner and the house came into view, then the barns. Raven probably thought farms were hokey or retro or exploitive or something, but I thought Jess's was beautiful. "That's Mr. Green, the hired man," I said, pointing. "Look, he's painting. He's painting that barn red again, and it doesn't even need it. Isn't this place pretty?"

The dogs were swarming the car, barking and growling, pretending they were fierce. "There's Tracer! Hi, girl!" As soon as Raven stopped, I jumped out of the car and dropped to my knees on the gravel. The dogs backed away, still barking, but I called them by their names and gradually they sidled over, all but Tough Guy, and started sniffing my hands, my clothes. "Hey, Mouse, hey, Red. Hi, guys, did you miss me?"

I stood up when I realized Raven wasn't getting out of the car, which was still idling. Mr. Green came over, wiping his hands on a paint-spattered cloth.

"Hey," he said, "how you doing?" He shoved the rag in the pocket of his dirty coveralls and squinted, trying to see who was in the driver's seat of the Plymouth. Mr. Green was an old man, maybe sixty, with a chubby, cracked brown face. He never had much to say, but he smiled a lot, showing two gold front teeth. "Come to see Jess, eh?"

"Yeah," I said, smiling back. "Is he here?"

"Up at the house. Go on in if you want."

"Thanks. How've you been?" I asked politely.

"Good, you?"

"Fine, thank you."

Mr. Green touched his temple with his finger and went back to his painting.

I leaned in the window on my side. Raven was slouched in his seat, lighting a cigarette. His hair hid the side of his face. "So, um . . ."

"Listen, can you get a ride back with this guy?"

I stood back. "Yeah, I guess. You don't want to come in?"

"I've got some things to do."

"Oh." I should go with him. I should go back to school. I was going to get in trouble. Plus I was ditching Raven for no reason, plus Jess probably didn't need company in the middle of the day. "Okay," I said. "Well, see you."

"Yeah."

"Hey."

"What?"

"Are you mad at me?"

"No."

"Sure?"

"Yeah."

"Okay." I didn't move, though, so he had to look at me. He has pretty eyes, light blue with dark, curly lashes. I used my willpower to make him smile. I did—I stared into his eyes with my feminine charm and *made* him smile at me. "See you."

"Yeah. See you."

He waited a second and then very slowly drove away.

Well, that was okay. This day could've been one of the kind that make you squirm at night when you're trying to fall asleep, I mean it could so *easily* have made it onto my Most Embarrassing Moments list, but I fixed it. There at the end I took control somehow, I'm not sure exactly how, and I saved it. So I hope I've got it down in my genetic code or something now for future reference, a DNA memory, because that kind of girl power is definitely going to come in handy again.

Jess's front door was closed but not locked. I went right in. I was about to yell "Yoo hoo" or something when I heard his voice coming from the direction of his office. I went through the living room nobody ever uses, past the kitchen, the dining room. I stuck my head in the door to his study. He was sitting behind his desk, talking on the telephone.

When he saw me, he looked amazed. And glad! He stood up, but he couldn't get off the phone; he waved, gestured to a chair, but he had to keep talking. "So this is an IPO? Sure, I'm interested, but I'd need a prospectus. No. So there's no revenue yet? They're still losing money?" He laughed. "Sounds like my kind of—no, send me the prospectus, I can't tell you until I see it. Okay. Okay. No, I agree with you. That's what I'm saying, I want to look at the internationals. Listen, I'll have to get back to you—" He smiled across at me apologetically. "Good, send it, that's great. Right, and we'll talk next week. So. Yeah. Okay, Bob. Thanks. 'Bye."

He hung up. "Hi," he said, coming around his desk and sitting on the edge in front of me. "Look at you. How'd you get here? Everything okay?" He had on holey jeans and an old green sweater and muddy, ancient-looking work boots, and he looked good, he looked really real. I grinned at him, very glad I'd come, even if I was interrupting his workday.

"Everything's fine," I said, "I just came to say hi—a friend dropped me off. Um . . . can you drive me to work at Krystal's in about an hour and a half?"

He put his head back and looked at me over his nose. "This is a school holiday, is it?"

"Yeah. Teacher training day. In-service."

He lifted one eyebrow. He folded his arms.

"Okay, I'm cutting." I laughed, sparkling my eyes at him. "You won't tell Mom, will you?" I knew he wouldn't, he was too nice. And I was too cute—I could tell I was getting to him.

"Depends. You do this often?" He wasn't smiling back.

"No. Really, I don't, in fact I never do. Really!" It was true, practically. "Just—today it was so nice out, and this friend said let's have a picnic, and so we did." Good; that could sound like a group of kids, not just me and one guy. I smiled winningly, shrugged my shoulders, spread my hands. "Didn't you ever cut class when you were in school?"

"Irrelevant." He shook his head, but I'd made him smile. "I ought to tell Carrie," he said darkly. "If you do it again, I will."

"Never again." I put my hand on my heart.

"You want a soda?"

"Okay."

I followed him out to the kitchen, where he got down a bag of pretzels and opened a Coke. "I've still got some phone calls to make," he said. "Can you take care of yourself for a little while?"

"Sure, go ahead, don't worry about me. You won't even know I'm here."

He looked amused and doubtful, but he didn't say anything. We went back to his office, and I sat on the sofa on the other side of the room from his desk, so he couldn't hear me crunching pretzels while he talked on the phone. He called somebody named Bill to order fish liver oil and TMR, whatever that is, and he called somebody else, I guessed the vet, to talk about some poor cow's inflamed uterus and whether he should give it antibiotics, electrolytes, or dextrose and estrogens. He called two different places for estimates on belts and pumps and vacuum regulators for his milking machines.

I watched him while he talked, thinking how efficient he was but still nice to people. You can learn a lot about somebody by listening to their side of a phone conversation. My mom's formal with strangers, almost too polite sometimes, to the point of sounding cold. Sometimes my dad was rude, especially to salesmen or people asking for charitable contributions. Jess had a soothing voice, even and low; I couldn't imagine him ever yelling at anybody. He was kind of a mystery to me, though. Even though he seemed so peaceful and easygoing, I was sure there was a lot going on inside of him. Would I want a man like him if I were older? A man who felt things a lot, didn't just think things? Jess is quiet, but I think he would tell me anything at all, anything I wanted to know, if I just knew the right questions to ask.

I got up and walked around the room. All the bookshelves were crammed with Holstein journals, Holstein sale catalogs, record books, a million books about dairy farming. On a cork board by the door were photos of cows wearing ribbons. I didn't want to disturb Jess, but I could see that behind his desk were the interesting pictures, ones with people in them, so I sidled around behind his chair, being as quiet as I could, and checked them out.

Wow, he looked exactly like his mother. Ora—I remembered the name. She had a big cloud of shiny light brown hair she wore up in an old-fashioned bun, but otherwise she didn't look old-fashioned at all. She was beautiful, very tall and slender, with big dark eyes and a soft mouth. She was laughing in the picture, standing by a rose trellis in a pretty housedress, and holding out her hand—she had long white arms—as if asking somebody if she could help. Jess, probably; if he'd taken this picture, he'd have been a little boy. I could see his face in the mother's face so clearly, the same long eyelashes and sharp-sided nose, but most of all the same expression in their eyes. Hard to describe—because they *weren't* really sad, were they? But that's how Ora looked, and it was how Jess looked sometimes, like he knew about something painful and heavy, it would make you cry if he told you what it was.

There was a picture of his father, too, a snapshot of him taken in this room, sitting at the same desk where Jess was sitting now. He looked much older than his wife, and smaller; he was a little, serious-looking man with frown lines between his eyes and smile lines around his lips. He looked worried and kind.

The best was a photograph of the whole family, Jess in the middle with his arms around his parents' waists, grinning into the camera. He was so skinny! He couldn't have been more than sixteen, and his long, streaky, rock star hair was much lighter than now. I'd have known it was him anywhere, but he looked so *different*, loose and crazy or something, reckless. I stared and stared, trying to see the man I knew in the boy's features. His mother wasn't laughing in this picture; she was looking at Jess, and her pretty profile was vague and wistful. They weren't at home, they were standing in front of a modern brick building with aluminum windows. Daffodils bloomed between two bushes—maybe it was Easter. Jess's father had on a suit that didn't quite fit him.

Now they were both dead and Jess lived all by himself. Did he get lonely? He had Mr. Green and some other hired men, but they didn't seem like much company. He had all his cows, which he knew by name (he said). He had friends, probably, and an ex-wife but no kids, and he was a member of the city council. Did he have girlfriends? Maybe I'd ask him.

"Going to the bathroom," I mouthed, and he nodded and pointed and kept talking. I went out and down the hall and into the bathroom next to the kitchen.

Jess had left the toilet seat up. Well, why not? Mom used to scold Dad about that all the time, but I could never figure out why it was the man's job any more than the woman's. Jess lived alone, though, so the whole thing wasn't even an issue.

After I peed, I stared at my face in the mirror, especially my lips. How many times would I be kissed in my whole life? So far, about four times, but today was by far the most serious. I'd only done it once with tongues before. Too weird. But I might get used to it. Caitlin did it all the time, or so she claimed. In fact, Caitlin was probably sleeping with Donny Hartman, her boyfriend since ninth grade, but I didn't know for sure. Jamie knew, but she'd sworn not to tell, and I could only get hints out of her.

I stuck out my tongue, examining the little pink bumps on it. It wasn't disgusting because it was mine, but the thought of Raven's tongue, that was different. Tongues. Who'd invented that? Who was the first person to put his tongue in somebody else's mouth and decide that was a good deal? And what did the person whose mouth he'd put it in think the first time? It was like—pesto or something. Who could ever have thought grinding up *leaves* and putting them on *spaghetti* would be a good idea?

Breasts, too—what was the huge deal there? I pulled up my blouse and studied mine in my bra, a 32-A. Caitlin was a 34-A; Jamie didn't even need a bra but she wore one anyway, she wouldn't say what size. My breasts were coming in okay, I guessed; I wasn't obsessed about it like some girls. Leslie Weber, for instance, who stared down at her own chest all the time. She sat across from me in English, and that's all she did, stared at her own breasts, like they were actively growing before her eyes.

"Boys will want to touch you there," Mom said to me once, in the most horrible, the most excruciating conversation we ever had. It wasn't the sex talk—we'd already had that when I was about eight. This was the date talk, brought on by Brad Donnelly asking me out to the movies last summer, just the two of us, not in a group. Big deal. Just because Brad was a junior, Mom decided it was time to talk about date behavior and condoms and AIDS and syphilis and breasts and French-kissing. *Gross.* Like I didn't already know all that. She actually used the word *fondle.* It was like an out-of-body experience, and me thinking, *Is this really happening? Is my mother really saying this?* The horrible part wasn't that she thought what she was saying might actually apply to my life; that was kind of flattering. The horrible part was thinking about how she knew all that stuff—she knew it because she'd done it herself. Which is obvious, but still creepy and revolting and bizarro.

I heard Jess walk by the door, heard water running in the kitchen, and guessed he was finished with his phone calls. It was funny to think of him being a businessman, not just a guy who milked cows and went fishing and taught funny tricks to his dogs. I remember being surprised to see him in a suit and tie and all at my dad's funeral. Like, because he was a farmer all he could ever wear was denim and flannel. Silly. I had a grass stain on the shoulder of my blouse, I saw. I was saving up thinking about Raven for later, though. I combed my hair with my fingers and went to find Jess.

We went outside and walked down to the river, to the dock that went out from the bank along the rough shore, which was half trees, half grass. The dock was high enough so you could sit on the edge with your legs hanging over and not get your feet wet. Except in spring after a hard rain; then the river flooded and the dock disappeared until the water receded. Jess was an expert fly fisherman, but here from the dock he just did what he called coarse fishing, using worms and what-have-you to catch chub and perch and roach fish. Last summer he taught me how to bait a hook with wasp grubs, how to cast a float rod, how to reel in a big fat carp. Maybe someday he'd take me fly-fishing.

We sat on the end of the dock and talked about fish for a while, and how we wished spring would hurry up because we were sick of winter. He must've thought I had something to tell him, that I'd come by for a particular reason, because pretty soon he said, "Everything okay?" and looked out over the water instead of at me, in case I felt shy about talking.

I really hadn't come for a reason, not that I knew of, it had just been a while since I'd seen him and we were driving right by his lane. Spur of the moment. Still, what popped out of my mouth was, "Everything's great, except my mom had a date last night. Can you believe that? My dad's been gone for half a year, and she goes out with this *body*builder."

Jess watched a buzzard flying high up in the sky and didn't say anything.

"Of course she says it wasn't a date, it was business, because the guy's her boss, but since when do you do business at night in a saloon?"

Jess still didn't jump in and sympathize, so I said, "Not that I care who she sees, it's none of my business, for all I care she can go out with every guy in Clayborne. I just don't think she should lie about it. And I don't think it's such a hot idea to date your boss anyway. Especially this guy, who's a total jerk. I mean, he wears a goatee." I bumped Jess with my elbow, trying to get a rise out of him. "A *goatee*. Plus he's got no neck."

Finally he grimaced. "You're talking about Brian Wright."

"Yeah. So do you know him?"

"Slightly. I do a course for the school."

"Oh, yeah. Fishing," I remembered. "So what do you think of him?"

"I don't know him well enough to think anything."

I hadn't expected him to get all discreet on me. Now I wished I hadn't even told him. "It's no big deal, I really don't care what she does."

"Maybe it wasn't a date," he said after a while. "Have you and Carrie talked about it?"

"I don't have to talk about it. She calls me from a nightclub, she's drinking, she's with a guy. I call that a date. Oh, and she gets home after *I* do. I pretended I was asleep—I didn't even *want* to talk to her." Jess started to say something. "Not that I care," I said again quickly, "it's her life, she can do whatever she wants. But I just . . ." I looked away downstream, where the river bent and the sycamore trees leaned over on both sides. From this angle, it almost looked like they touched in the middle. "She told me no one could take Dad's place—that's exactly what she said, 'Nobody's taking his place.' She said she wasn't available."

"Ruth."

"What? You don't have to defend her."

"I'm not."

"I know everything you're going to say. I'm being selfish, she's allowed to have some fun, what she said wasn't really a promise—I know all that. I just don't like it." I leaned out over my knees to stare down at the brownish green current, thinking I always talked too much around Jess and wondering why that was. He couldn't be a father figure because he wasn't anything like my father, and he wasn't exactly a friend because I didn't know that much about him. "Do you have a girlfriend?" I asked him.

"What?" he said, even though he'd heard.

"Are you going out with anybody?"

"No. Not right now."

He looked very uncomfortable, which cheered me up for some reason. "Hey, Jess, did you know Becky Driver's in my class? I met her mother—I had dinner at their house." He nodded pleasantly. "She's nice, Mrs. Driver," I said leadingly. "I mean, she's *really* nice."

"She is nice."

"Becky's not yours, though, right?"

"That's right."

"So . . ." What happened? How come your marriage didn't work out? You couldn't ask questions like that straight out, you had to beat around the bush.

I was trying to think of a subtle approach when Jess said, "Do you have a boyfriend?"

"Ha." Good one. Touché. We grinned at each other. "Well," I said, "there's this one guy. Raven."

"The vampire."

I laughed—he remembered! "Yeah. I'm not sure if he's my *boy*friend," I said, making a face. What a stupid word. "He's the one who dropped me off here."

"Ah. So you were playing hooky together."

"Just today, just this once. Honestly, this is not my practice, I mean, it's not my lifestyle." I decided to tell him. "We went to my dad's grave. We had sort of a picnic. It was nice. I mean, it was respectful and everything." If you didn't count smoking dope and kissing and making out. "I keep thinking, you know, if only he hadn't died. What it would be like. Or if he had to die, if only he'd lived for five more years, say. I think if I'd been, like, twenty, we could've been much closer. Sometimes I think he was waiting for me to grow up to be really friends. Now—he'll never know how I turned out," I managed to say before I started crying. Shit. I turned my head away, put my cheek on my knees, so Jess couldn't see.

He put his arm around me. I thought he would try to cheer me up, tell me my father had loved me very much, blah blah, but he just said, "It's sad," and it went right through me.

"It is," I said gladly, "it's so *sad*. I think trying not to be sad is worse than being sad."

"I do, too."

"So I'm glad I went to his grave." I sat up. "I don't think my mom goes. I don't know, she might. We went together at Christmas and on January ninth, his birthday. If she does go, she doesn't leave flowers, because there weren't any."

"I think she's trying to be strong for you. Trying to do the right thing, be what she thinks you need her to be. I think she's feeling all the things you feel about your father, missing him, and wishing there had been more time. One thing I'm sure of—you're the center of her life."

"Then why'd she go out on a date?" I laughed, to make it sound more like a joke. Less whiny.

He looked pained. "Why did you?" was all he could come up with.

"It's not the same, he was my *father*, not my *husband*. He would've wanted me to have a boyfriend. He wouldn't have wanted her to."

"Maybe you should talk to her about it."

"No. *No.* I don't want to hear her stupid explanations. *God.* She's so *embarrassing*."

"Embarrassing?" Jess gave me a crooked smile. "When I was your age," he said, "fifteen or so." He leaned back on his elbows and stared at his belt buckle. "You saw my mother's picture?"

"In the house? Yeah," I said, "she was really pretty."

"She was schizophrenic."

"Oh." I swallowed.

"It didn't start until I was about ten. Before that, she was fine. But she had a miscarriage, and after that everything changed."

"God. I'm really sorry."

"When she'd get bad, she'd have to go away, go in the hospital. My father and I were close, but we were lost, like orphans when she was gone. Then she'd come home, and I'd drive her crazy by not leaving her alone. I couldn't get enough of her. I was always trying to cure her, with presents and things I'd make for her, food, spells. Tricks." He laughed. "Sometimes it seemed to work, whatever it was—some drink I'd concoct, a special, particular prayer. But not for long. And nothing ever worked twice."

This was bad, but something worse was coming. I already sort of knew what it was.

"She did a lot of crazy things. She'd get lost, wander off and lose herself. We'd have to call the cops. One day we were in Belk's, buying me some clothes for school. It was the end of the summer. She'd been fine for months, her old self, but it was starting again. I could always tell. She was odd in the store, saying things that didn't make sense. She kept complaining that she was hot, burning up, why didn't they turn on the air-conditioning. I was afraid she'd complain to the saleslady, and I didn't want to be around if she did. I wandered off, into a different area of the department. Far enough away so I could pretend nothing was happening."

"Oh, God, Jess."

"I heard a commotion. Raised voices. You could feel it in the air—shock. Somebody called security over the PA. I didn't want to, but I had to go see." He reached out and touched me on the arm with the lightest pat, a reassurance, and he gave me a tickled, helpless smile. "She'd taken off her clothes. Every stitch. She was naked as a jaybird in the men's sweater department at Belk's."

I moved my hand far enough from my mouth to whisper, "What did you do?"

"Ran away."

"No."

"Yeah. But only to the elevator. If it had come immediately, I'd have gotten on and gone down and outside and away—I'd have run away. But it took forever. So."

"You had to go back."

"I've always been ashamed for that, how close I came to leaving her. I had this fierce love for her, I loved her more than anybody else. But she . . ."

"Embarrassed you."

He smiled.

I blushed. But I didn't feel lectured to or guilty or caught in the act in some sin. No question, he'd made his point, but not only was he not rubbing it in, he was helping take the sting out by admitting that once he'd done the same thing, only worse. With better cause, okay, but still.

God! Imagine having a crazy person for a mother. Really crazy, like certifiable, not just weird or irritatingly nuts like Mom. It really put things in perspective.

"That's awful," I said, and I put one finger on the sleeve of Jess's sweater. It was the first time I'd ever comforted *him* for anything. "That's so sad. She looks so beautiful in the picture. I think you look like her. Do you believe in heaven? She could be watching down on you. I'm sure she's very proud of you, you know, how you've turned out and all. *God*."

"What?"

"That's what people have been saying to me," I realized. "You know, old people, mostly—that my dad's probably still with me, he's proud of me, yadda yadda. Does that comfort you? Because it *never* comforts me. But now I at least get why they say it."

"Why?"

"Well, to be nice. To be kind, to show that you care and you wish the person didn't hurt."

"Yes."

"So that's something. Isn't it? It might be a crock, but the person saying it means well."

"I think it's something. I think it's all we get."

We lay on our backs and watched clouds and sky and birds go by, peaceful as two old, old pals. I almost told him about Raven, that's how comfortable I felt. I might have, but then he sat up and said, "Four o'clock."

"How can you tell?"

"Listen."

"I don't hear anything."

"Listen."

"Oh. Cows." They were mooing way off in the distance. "You have to milk them now?"

"Pretty soon. Mr. Green will start."

I scrambled up from the dock. "I didn't know it was so late," I said, matching Jess's long strides up the hill. "Guess you sort of blew off your afternoon, huh?" He just smiled at me, and I felt fine. "Hey, Jess. Can we take the pickup truck?"

"Sure, if you want."

"And, Jess?"

"Hm?"

"Can I drive?"

"Got your learner's permit with you?"

"Yes."

"Okay, then."

"Yay!" I clapped my hands, did a little dance. Jess's pickup was a stick shift, the most fun of all to drive. "And, Jess?"

"*What*?"

I laughed. "Can we take Tracer? Can we put her in the middle between us? I've always wanted to do that, drive in a pickup truck with a dog and, you know. A guy."

He shook his head. "The cowgirl look."

"I guess."

"Amazing. I thought you were into vampires."

"Well, I am."

"Or health food and vitamins."

"Them, too."

"You're a very versatile person."

"Thanks."

Versatile. I was very versatile. Cool. And here I thought I was just confused.

13

Ballroom Dancer

"Never mind, Dana, you wouldn't have had that much fun anyway. The women's club is full of poops, nothing like our day. You're better off without 'em."

"I'm *not upset*." I'd told Birdie that three times since we got in the car. "It's nothing. I'm not losing one wink of sleep over this, believe you me."

"Well, I should hope not. Because that would be a waste of perfectly good energy. How come your house is so dark?"

"What? Oh, he forgot to turn on the porch light again. I swear, it's like living with a mole."

"You sure he's in there?"

"He's there. He's either working in his office or watching TV in the den. Want to come in?" I invited without much enthusiasm. "Cup of coffee before you go home?"

"Oh, my, no, a cup of coffee would keep me up all night."

"Decaf, I meant."

"Rain check?"

"Sure."

"Unless you want me to. Unless you want to talk."

"I don't want to talk," I said, laughing, "I want to *sleep*. I'm perfectly fine, Bird, this means very little to me."

"Oh, I know that."

"I won't even think about it tomorrow."

"Of course you won't. You're too smart for them, that's the problem. They didn't know a good thing when they saw it."

"Thanks. Thanks for the ride."

"I'll call you tomorrow. Want to go to a movie or something? There's a sale—"

"Can't tomorrow. Maybe next week." Birdie's sympathy was starting to grate on me. Much better if she'd just say, "I told you so," and get it over with.

"'Night, Dana," she called. "Really, don't give it another thought, it's not worth your—"

"Drive carefully," I said, and slammed the door.

The house wasn't just dark, it was cold. More like living with a bear than a mole, some heavy, lumbering animal that hibernates, I thought, going around turning on lights in the living room, the kitchen, turning up the thermostat. Canned laughter sounded from the den. George has two passions, if you can call them that: his book and old TV shows. The older the better; he even buys them on tape from 800 numbers, old episodes of *Lassie, Bonanza, 77 Sunset Strip, The Loretta Young Show*. I don't know what to make of that. Was life so much better for him in the 1950s than it is now? Was there some *tone* then, something he responded to, some flavor or style that he's nostalgic for now? I wonder what it is. I would really love to know. But when I ask him, "Why do you like that old stuff?" all he ever says is, "It's amusing."

Tonight it was *I Love Lucy*. I walked into the den just as Lucy was opening her big mouth wide and crying, "*Waaaah*," because Rickie wouldn't take her on a vacation. George looked up at me and smiled with fond, laughing eyes—I smiled back before I realized it wasn't me making him so happy and appreciative. Should I have tried to be more like that? A silly, wacky, zany kind of woman? Was that what he'd wanted?

"You're back," he said, hitching over to make room for me on the couch.

Where did I go?—I almost asked, to test him. But I was blue enough tonight; if he flunked the test, I'd feel even worse. "From the women's club," I said instead, helpfully. "Election night."

A commercial came on, and he muted the sound with the remote control. "How did that go?"

"I lost."

"Oh, dear." He blinked sympathetically through the middle bar of his trifocals. He looked pretty natty in tweed trousers and the blue crew neck sweater Carrie gave him two Christmases ago. He had dandruff on his shoulders, though, and a yellowish stain on his chest, maybe dried orange juice. And he smelled like his pipe. We were a fairly handsome couple in our day, I've got pictures to prove it, but we've turned into the kind of people you don't look at twice. Which one of us will end up at Cedar Hill first? I wonder that too much lately. It's awfully easy to imagine me visiting George in a room like Helen's. Wheeling him down to arts and crafts, bending over his stooped shoulder, showing him how to make pot holders.

"Yep," I said, "the new president of the Clayborne Women's Club is Vera Holland. Who's seventeen years old."

"Really?"

"Or twenty-seven, what's the difference. A younger woman. Her platform was 'diversity.' Translation, let's all go out and recruit more of her tacky friends."

"Tsk." His eyes flicked briefly to the TV. A shampoo commercial.

"I didn't even want the damn job, I just didn't want her to have it." Well now, that wasn't true. "Oh, I sort of wanted it. Shake things up. I wanted to feel, you know . . . active." Alive, rather. "Anybody can belong to a club, that doesn't mean anything. What it was—I think I felt like testing myself before it's too late."

I felt a little breathless from the frankness of that. Showing much of myself to George, revealing my deeper feelings—I quit that years ago, it didn't pay off. A one-sided exercise that usually just left me feeling foolish. Not that *not* telling him things has gotten me anywhere, either. It's pretty much a lose-lose.

"Well," he said.

"Well. Well, what?"

"Well . . . maybe it's for the best. Lot of work you don't need."

"Yeah, maybe." I stood up. "And my life's so rich and full already. I don't know what I was thinking." I scooped up my coat and my purse.

"Dana."

"What?"

"I'm sure you'd have made an excellent president."

"I don't know if I would have or not, but it would've been nice to win. I really did want to win."

He shrugged, shook his head. Pursed his lips, blinked his eyes. Body language attempts at commiseration. *Words, George, I want words.* On TV, Fred and Ethel came into Lucy's apartment. Fred talked out of the side of his mouth, deadpan, and Ethel rolled her eyes.

"Well," I said, "let me get out of your way."

"I'll be up in two seconds," George called. Gales of laughter followed me up the stairs.

It was even colder on the second floor than the first. Undressing in front of my closet, I heard the flick of light switches downstairs, then the clump of George's shoes on the steps, slow and heavy, reluctant sounding. As good as his word, even though it was a little early for him. Did he feel sorry for me? To hell with that. But in the glimpse I got of him passing behind as I bent over to take off my hose, he just looked tired.

Ghastly sight, me in the bathroom mirror. Since 1979, I've been asking George to replace the fluorescent tube over the sink with a regular one, a tungsten bulb. He's never going to do it. I complain to Carrie and she says, "Well, if you can make yourself look halfway human in *that* light, just think how beautiful you must look in the real world." Nice logic, but it doesn't work anymore. Not for the last, oh, twenty years.

I brushed my teeth, brushed my hair. Which is thinning. Took my blood pressure pill. Hunched toward the mirror, I pulled down the collar of my nightgown to study the new lines on my neck. Turkey neck. Turkey jowls. This is a nightly ritual I really ought to discontinue. It's funny, but I'm getting more vain the older I get instead of less. No, *vain* isn't the right word. *Aghast.* That's it.

Would George want to make love with me if I looked prettier? Lost twenty pounds? Doubtful. Truthfully, I can't see him getting excited about sleeping with Sophia Loren. Maybe June Allyson; he's always liked her. Too bad for him he married a woman more like Ethel Merman. Joan Crawford. A coarse brunette, not a perky bone in her body.

He looked up briefly from his newspaper when I slid into bed beside him. "Tired?" he asked.

"Why, do I look tired?"

He shrugged and went back to his paper.

"Well, one thing I accomplished tonight anyway," I said, interrupting him on purpose.

"What's that?"

"I made a motion to start a petition drive to halt this ark-building foolishness, and it passed."

"You mean—the ark on the river?"

"No, the ark on I-95." I really was in a bad mood. "Yes, the ark on the river."

"Why would you do that?"

"Why! That's public property, George, people tie up boats to that dock."

"Oh, but not very many, I don't think."

"Well, what about the stupidity factor?"

"Ah."

"And separation of church and state? I'll tell you what happened—Jess Deeping railroaded that vote through the council before anybody knew what was happening. What if the national news gets a hold of this story? It's like—Charles Kuralt finding some lunatic in Idaho building a shrine to the Blessed Virgin out of bottle caps."

"He did?"

"No, I'm saying—we'll all look ridiculous. It'll be an eyesore, a public nuisance, we just can't have it."

He took off his glasses and started polishing them with the edge of the sheet. "What about Carrie?"

"What about her?"

"Isn't she interested in this? I thought she was—"

"That's just boredom, that's another one of her artsy-craftsy projects. Carrie needs to concentrate on her real job, not ally herself with this fundamentalist religious claptrap. Of all the crazy things! And wouldn't you know Jess Deeping's right in the thick of it? If that isn't typical. Blood tells."

"What are you talking about?"

"His mother. She was insane, don't you remember?"

"No."

"Well, she was, she died in an institution, and he's a chip off the old block."

He shook his head, *not* sympathetically, and rattled the pages of his newspaper. Conversation over.

That's typical, too. Ignore a problem by pretending it doesn't exist. Carrie probably wasn't going to appreciate my petition motion, either. She might even question my motives. Sure as shooting, she'd never *thank* me for it. The petition might not do any good anyway, it might be too late. Talk about an end run. Jess Deeping should be ashamed of himself. Maybe I'll write a letter to the editor.

"You know what Birdie said?"

George sighed. "What?"

"She said I just wanted to be president so I could boss people around."

He looked up at that. I waited for him to scoff, but he just looked at me.

"She said it as a joke, but I didn't appreciate it."

"No . . ."

"You think I'm bossy?"

"Absolutely not, dear." He ducked his bald head, shooting me a glance under his eyebrows. He had a hopeful twinkle in his eye. I laughed. And he laughed, and it was a good few seconds.

He folded his paper and put it away, turned out his bedside lamp. He falls asleep every night on his right side, facing away from me; after about forty minutes, he turns over on his back and snores. He started getting his covers just so, pushing the sheet out at the bottom so his feet weren't constricted—every morning I tuck it back in.

"George?"

"Hm?"

"Nothing. Never mind." A feeling came over me, a squeezing sensation, like a vise, something hopeful pushing up from below, something else old and knowing pushing down from above. "What do you think about taking ballroom dancing?"

He turned his head, craned it over his shoulder. Stared.

"Friday nights, out at the Ramada Inn. Six weeks, and it starts next week. We could have dinner first—a night out for us. Just something to look forward to."

"Well. Hm." He frowned hard. "The only thing is, Friday's the night I've been meeting with Albert on the book. I gather it's the only time he can do it."

"Friday is the only night of the whole week he can meet you? Friday night?"

"Well, that's what he says."

"Fine, never mind."

"Sorry. It would've been fun," he lied. "Maybe next year."

"That's a good idea." I reached for the novel on my table. "Let's wait till we're even older."

"Dana."

"Maybe next year they'll offer ballroom wheelchair dancing." I slapped open the book, found my place from last night. "Quit." I was so mad. I twitched his hand off my hip and turned over. "I'm trying to read."

He sighed like a martyr, rustled the covers, settled on his right side. "Night."

I met George when I was eighteen, working in the customer service department at Willie's Auto Repair. My first job. I did typing and filing and greeting the customers. I don't know where I thought this job would take me—nowhere, I suppose; we just got married in those days, we didn't have careers, not girls from my background anyway. One day George brought in his old rattletrap Plymouth and I waited on him, filling out the little form we had, getting his name and address, writing down what was wrong with his car. He had on an argyle sweater, I remember as if it was yesterday. College boy. I flirted with him because he was sweet and shy, but I'd never have made a play for him. I knew my place. When he asked if he could call me sometime, I almost said no. I thought he didn't know the rules, that, being from Richmond, he must somehow not be aware that Remington boys didn't ask out Clayborne girls. Not with good intentions, anyway.

He took me to an orchestra recital on campus on a Friday night. If he'd been Casanova, if he'd been Don Juan, he couldn't have come up with a more seductive date. I was thrilled out of my mind, and I was absolutely terrified. That very night I set my cap for him. *I want this*, I thought. To be with people who talked softly and said things that were just out of my reach. *Maybe I can learn this*, I thought. Campus—oh, just the word made me dizzy. *Campus*. It meant peace and quiet and safety. Most of all, it meant respectability.

It was easy to make him fall in love with me. I was pretty then, and I just pretended he was the center of the world, I cut out of my mind everything but George, I turned all the wattage on and blinded him. Nowadays I suppose I'd have had to sleep with him, but back then it was enough to make him want me. He's still the only man I've ever been with. He says I'm the only woman, but that's as may be. I don't question that too closely. The only one in many, many years, though, *that* I wouldn't doubt.

I think the reason I wanted to be president of the women's club was to see, before I'm a hundred and it really is too late, if my disguise worked. I come from backward people. My father was a drunk. I carry on like I belong in this house, this town, like faculty parties don't faze me, but I never know for sure if people are on to me. The fact that I lost the election to Vera Holland doesn't prove anything, unfortunately. All it confirms is that I'm over the hill.

I wonder if I shouldn't have married somebody like Calvin Mintz, poor Helen's husband. More in my class. Which one of us is meaner, Cal or me? Which one of us would've won? At least it would've been interesting. If we'd survived.

When I thought I could sleep, I turned out the light and settled on my side, facing away from George. Our rumps bumped. I scooted away an inch, still mad; I didn't want him touching me.

Here's how morbid I am lately—I think about waking up in the middle of the night and finding him stiff and cold in the bed beside me. I'm afraid to touch him. I call either Carrie or 911, I'm not sure which. Carrie, I guess, then *she* can call 911. The paramedics come. They knock at the door, blue and white lights flashing around the yard, the street, and I show them upstairs in my bathrobe and slippers. They do things . . . the fantasy gets less real there. The way a dream can start off hard-edged and then get vague, finally tapering off into nonsense. I never imagine any of the emergency people saying, "He's dead, ma'am." No. It never comes to that.

Time is turning me into somebody I can hardly believe in, I can't seem to make real. *Old lady.* Do other people who are old *feel* old? I always thought they did, they must, but here I am turning seventy any day now and I'm no smarter, no wiser, no happier, no more satisfied or fulfilled or content or enlightened than I was at forty. In fact, less.

I could live to a hundred, I thought, shutting my eyes against the moonlight seeping in around the curtain. Willard Scott could say my name on TV. Who knew, George could live to ninety-eight in the other wing of the nursing home. The *Morning Record* could run a picture in the Lifestyles section of us shriveled up in our wheelchairs, holding each other's knobby hand, cutting a sheet cake.

Foolishness. Why would I want to stretch out marriage to George for thirty more years? Didn't the last fifty teach me anything?

I don't believe in hopelessness, it goes against my raising. But the trouble with hope is it springs eternal. Crazy old ladies think miracles can still happen. George turned over in his sleep and butted his knee up against my rear end. The warmth felt good, so I stayed still, didn't poke him to move. See? He's good for something. That's hopeful.

14

ELEPHANT DAY

Alla prima. In painting it meant *at once,* applying all your pigments in one sitting, not layering them on over time. Van Gogh probably painted *Bedroom at Arles alla prima,* they say. The advantage over a more painstaking, considered approach was supposed to be excitement, intensity, fluidity. I must be doing very exciting work these days, that's all I can say. It was good to have an arty foreign word for it, too, *alla prima.* So much nicer than *slapdash.*

Wet otter fur. How did you paint wet otter fur? If I were using oils or acrylics on a good stretched canvas, I would start with a neutral base of ultramarine, Payne's gray, maybe raw umber, some titanium white. If I could afford it I'd use a Richeson no. 10, series 9050 brush, laying in the basic darks and lights first, trying to imagine the otter's body as a landscape, skin, muscle, and bone as hills, valleys, and ridges. I'd compose him in an appropriate setting, maybe climbing onto a log after a dip in a stream. The elements in the composition would provide perspective and proportion; we'd know how big the otter was by the size of the objects around him. He'd be gray, basically, but not drab because I'd put him behind autumn leaves (raw sienna, vermilion, Venetian red, Van Dyck brown) and in front of the wet fallen stump (burnt sienna, ultramarine, lamp black). I'd switch to a Richeson no. 3 brush, series 9000, for the fine work, the detailing and refining of his fur, whiskers, eyes, eyelashes, toenails.

I wasn't doing any of that. I was using a midgrade True Value exterior semigloss ($20.99 a gallon), in a grayish brown shade called "Farewell." I was laying it on with a three-inch nylon and polyester brush over what I hoped was an otter-shaped cutout from a four-by-eight sheet of three-quarter-inch polystyrene foam insulation. It was a handicap.

But not an insurmountable one. And I wasn't working completely *alla prima*, anyway: after the gray latex dried, I'd add white and black highlights with a small red sable round brush, my one indulgence, to enhance the sharp, sideways V shapes I'd decided clumped wet otter fur looked like. The trick was lifting up on the brush quickly when you got to the end of the hair shaft; otherwise the point wasn't fine enough. If I had time, I'd redo his eye with acrylics; I'd have liked to roughen the edge of his pupil, lighten the bottom of his iris with Turner's yellow and some more white. Because I'd decided the light would be coming from directly overhead.

I wouldn't have time, though. God gave Noah 120 years to build the ark, and He threw in the animals for nothing. Eldon Pletcher had given Landy, who gave Jess, who gave me and my "helpers," about three months to stock a three-story ark with, if you included fish, reptiles, and insects, approximately seventy-eight separate animal species.

Landy said pinning the old man down to seventy-eight wasn't easy, and I could believe it. At first some of his choices struck me as arbitrary. He'd insisted on the antelope but not the caribou, for example; wolf but not coyote; moose but not elk; mole but not shrew. Leopard but not puma, dog but not dingo, donkey but not mule—and so on. It made sense when you thought about it: between similar animals, he had consistently chosen the one that was either more immediately recognizable or else more—likable, for lack of a better word. People liked mice, they didn't like rats.

I approved of Eldon's list, on the whole. I was especially looking forward to making a chimpanzee. And an octopus—that would be a mechanical as well as artistic challenge. Landy was going to ask his father if I could have a little discretion with add-ons, because I loved slow, lumbering animals, and his list didn't include possum or manatee. But even if he said yes, I wouldn't have time.

It wasn't altogether a bad thing, the absurd May seventeenth deadline we had no chance of meeting. It allowed no time for second-guessing. My left brain, if there was such a thing, had been all but silenced; by necessity, I was going on uninhibited instinct. I'd never worked that way before. I was like a newspaper reporter who had to finish the story in time for the early edition. It was faster, obviously, but was it any good? I didn't know—I was afraid to hope—I thought it might be. But either way, I was having the time of my life.

The job was seducing me, in spite of all the restrictions and eccentric conditions Eldon had attached to it. It was swallowing me up the way a boa constrictor swallowed a rabbit. (I had been reading up on boa constrictors; Eldon wanted them to represent the snake category—the recognizability factor again.) When I worked, I almost sank into a trance. Not like the miniature flower arrangements trance—that was like sinking into a coma, and this was more like being hypnotized. I was aware of my surroundings, the chilliness of the space, the mooing of a cow outside, the oil, gasoline, and dead grass smells, the hum overhead of the fluorescent lights Jess had hung, along with an inadequate propane heater on the wall, when the barn became the official ark animal assembly area. But nothing distracted me, nothing got between me and what I was working on. It was as if I bled into the paint, and the paint bled into the surface and the surface bled into the object—in this case an otter. Extraordinary! It was the boon, the prize, it was the best part of making art. I used to feel it, but I barely remembered it. I never thought I'd get it back.

Landy broke my concentration, saying, "Sorry I got to go so early today." I jumped. The smooth line of my brush took a hitch upward, like a lie detector printout catching somebody in a whopper. "Oh—'scuse me—I thought you heard me!"

I laughed. We'd been working in Jess's barn since lunchtime, and even though our work areas were fairly close together, I often forgot Landy was there. It wasn't just my own absorption: he was such a quiet man, content to work indefinitely without saying a word.

"Good," he said, leaning over, peering down at my otter. "Looks just like one."

"I haven't finished the fur. Is he too gray? Think he needs more brown?"

"Hmm, could be."

"I'm using these photos and those drawings." I pointed to my otter reference materials, wildlife calendars and a couple of naturalists' journals. "Yes, more brown, I think. Otherwise he looks like a baby seal."

"No, no, he doesn't look anything like a seal."

I believed him, and let that particular worry go. Landy was my trusty, most reliable critic. He was always polite, but he never lied: if my pig cutout looked like an armadillo, he found a nice way to tell me.

"Are you going to see your father?" I asked.

He nodded. "Sorry I got to go so early, and so much still to do, but this is when he likes me to come."

"Don't worry about it." Eldon was in the hospital again, for chest pains and fluid on his lungs. "How's he doing?"

"Better. They say he can probably go home in a coupla days. Tuesday, they're saying."

"I'm so glad. He's a tough old guy." I hadn't met him yet, but that seemed safe to say.

"I got done six sets of wheels, I set 'em right over there. Sorry it's no more." He stretched his hands out and flexed his knobby, arthritic fingers. "Not such a good day today."

"It's the cold." I wore fingerless gloves when I worked, but Landy wouldn't, said they made him clumsy.

He buttoned his plaid jacket to the chin and jammed on his dirty orange hunter's cap. "Did two sets for the elephant, like you said. Front and back." He'd spent the afternoon attaching wheels to heavy wooden bases sawn from four-by-fours, because Eldon wanted to roll the animals onto the ark via a ramp. He could *just see it*, he said.

"Great. Think the brakes will hold?" I asked. We bought wheel sets with little foot-activated brakes; ridiculously expensive, but we got a deal by buying in bulk.

"I reckon. What're you doing after you finish coloring that otter?"

"Oh, I'm going to have some fun," I told him. "Today is elephant day."

His eyes crinkled almost shut when he grinned. "Wish I could stay and see that. You're having a pretty good time, huh?"

"I guess I am."

"Why'd you decide to help out? This sure ain't nothing to do with you, Carrie."

People kept asking me that; I ought to have had a better answer by now. "It crept up on me," was the best I could do. "I didn't think it would get this far. I thought I'd pitch in once or twice, help get things started."

He laughed his shy, wheezing laugh. "That's what happened to me! Hell, same with Jess, too. Pushovers is what we are. Are you sorry?"

"No. But ask me if I'm *tired*."

"Hoo, don't I know it! Say, the Finches told me they can come back one night next week, and then again next Saturday. If that's any help to you."

I hummed, noncommittal. The Finches, two elderly Arkist sisters, both spinsters, sincerely wanted to help me, but they were hopeless—on so many levels, it would've been mean to list them. Color blindness was one, though; another was decrepitude. But the worst was that they had *ideas*; they made *suggestions*. I hadn't known how proprietary I was getting until last week when Miss Sara Finch said the cow should be a Brown Swiss and Miss Edna Finch agreed with her. No, no, no. No. The cow was a black-and-white Holstein. Period. This was not a democracy.

"Just wish I could pay you somehow," Landy mumbled with his head down. "Here it is a Sunday, you could be home spending time with your fam—your daughter. Wish I could pay you back some way, that's all."

It really bothered him, I knew because he said it so often. "Maybe you can, Landy. When things settle down, maybe you can help me with a couple of projects around my house. Things I can't do by myself."

He beamed. "I'd be glad to do that, I'd be pleased. Anything I could do, it would be my pleasure. We'll count on it."

"Good."

No one knew, not even Landy, how much money old Eldon had socked away. He had to have some, or he wouldn't have made his playground equipment offer. (Would he? That was a thought. What if he were pulling one over on the whole town? I wondered if Jess had considered that. I'd ask him.) In any case, Landy wanted the ark effort to be as frugal as possible, because he said it was draining away his mother's inheritance. His, too—but he honestly didn't seem to consider that. He said he didn't want the old man's obsession to impoverish his mother once his father was gone. That was why I was using the cheapest good paint the hardware store sold, and slapping it on polystyrene instead of wood. It was why Landy and Jess, whose combined boatbuilding expertise wouldn't have covered a matchbook, were designing a 119-foot ark in their spare time, with only Arkist help and no professional guidance. I couldn't figure out whether Eldon was crazy like a fox or just crazy.

I said good-bye to Landy and turned my mind to elephants.

Everybody liked them, everybody was soft on them. To my generation they were what dinosaurs had been to Ruth's. But kids outgrew dinosaurs—nobody outgrew elephants. Well, ivory merchants, presumably, but nobody with a soul. There was something about elephants, and I wanted to try to capture it. Their sweetness and shuffling intelligence, their persistence and indefatigability. Honesty.

Like all the animals, I was doing this one life-size—a small elephant, granted, but life-size. The him-her, two-sided idea seemed to be working, although I hadn't succeeded yet at crafting two different *poses* on either side of the cutout silhouettes; I'd only been able to vary the two genders of the same animal with color. But I'd keep trying. I worked with four-by-eight insulation sheets, and until now that had been more than adequate; in fact I often got two small animals, both sides, out of a single sheet. It wouldn't be enough for an elephant, though, so I'd hot glued two sheets together, width-wise, edge-to-edge, then glued two more sheets, one on each side, across the seam to strengthen the joint, and finally glued four two-by-eight half sheets, top and bottom on each side, to fill in the gap. Now I had an eight-foot square of foam two and a half inches thick. Later I'd cut out ears, trunk, and tail, and glue them on separately for added dimension.

It was Chris's brilliant idea to use the polystyrene sheets. In a past life, she designed stage sets for amateur theatrical productions. Plywood, she pointed out, was heavier, more expensive, harder to work with, and buckled when wet. Polystyrene sheets glued together beautifully, cut with a craft knife instead of a band saw, and took latex paint like a dream. Chris only knew Landy from what I'd told her about him, but it tickled her to think how much money her suggestion had already saved him.

I usually drew the basic outline of an animal with the foam sheet flat on the floor, but that wouldn't work with an elephant; too big. Unless I crawled around on my hands and knees, but then I'd probably puncture the foam, which was strong but not indestructible. I stacked my eight-by-eight sheet against the wall, looking around for a box to stand on to reach the top. After dozens of practice drawings, I'd decided on a foreshortened three-quarter profile, so he'd be mostly head, trunk, and massive left flank, facing forward and fixing us with one small, kind, wrinkled eye. I wasn't drawing freehand, I was transposing proportional sections from grid to grid, final drawing to foam sheet.

Feet. Consider the function, I learned a million years ago in art school. The function of an elephant's feet was to hold up several thousand pounds of elephant. Big, round, platform feet at the ends of massive shapeless leathery legs, skin sagging down in bags around what would be ankles on another animal. Great folds of skin at the backs of the shoulders, too, wattlelike, and I hoped that was realistic—would an elephant that small have skin that wrinkled? Well, he was a little old elephant. He was born small. His parents were small and he was a chip off the old block. That's my story and I'm sticking to it.

The trunk was almost five feet long, curving in at the bottom, toward the dainty mouth. He was an Indian elephant, so his back was the highest point, higher than the shoulders, and arched slightly. The ears were big but not gigantic, not the flapping, sail-like ears on an African elephant—who, sadly, wouldn't be boarding the ark. Exclusions like that really gave me pause. I felt sorry about my choice of the grizzly bear, for instance (again, on recognizability grounds), over the black, brown, silver-tip, Kodiak, sloth, sun, Atlas, and spectacled bears. I liked to think old man Pletcher was, too, when he'd picked the walrus but not the seal, and when he'd decided to let the shark represent the entire fish kingdom. *Poor goldfish, poor salmon,* I hoped he thought; *poor speckled trout.*

Well, the rough draft silhouette wasn't bad. Flipping it over, I could see it would transpose well for the female. I'd make her a lighter gray, although it would mean buying another quart of paint; maybe True Value's "Smoky Moss"—the chip looked about right. Head wasn't flat enough on top, I saw. But the muscle in the middle of his forehead, the one that picked up his heavy trunk, I'd gotten that just right. And I liked one ear in and one ear out, but did it look like I'd just made a mistake? I loved the side view of his hip, round and bulging, a mass of moving muscle; clearly he'd just thrown his weight onto his left back leg and was about to pick up his right front. I'd nailed it.

It was when I was shading in the parallel horizontal lines on his trunk, making what amounted to a contour map, trying to show how the light struck the ridges and threw shadow into the hollows, that I had a brainstorm. I could do more than shade and highlight, *I could etch.* I figured it out by accident when I put too much pressure on my drawing pencil and cut into the foam. What if I *inscribed* the deepest wrinkly hollows on his trunk and face, those sad crevasses around his ancient eyes, and then painted dark paint into the etched parts and a second, lighter layer over the top? Texture! It would work, I was almost sure it would. However nicely I painted them, the problem of flatness, of having the animals resemble moving vertical platforms, stage sets on wheels, had plagued me since the beginning. This wasn't the complete answer—already the shortcomings were starting to occur to me—but it was a start. A really good start. I felt lit up inside, full of fresh energy. I'd experiment on scrap foam first, of course. With a pen? Knife? I'd try a craft knife with a new blade. I wanted more than a shallow indentation, I wanted real crags, dramatic black fissures. But without shredding the foam. And how well would gray latex cover black?

Stiff fingers and an ache in the small of my back woke me up from another trance. I'd forgotten my watch, but the edge of an early moon shone through the dusty, high-set barn windows. Late.

I stuffed the mess Landy and I had made, all the foam and wood cuttings, into plastic garbage bags, cleaned up my paints, tidied up the work area. I couldn't leave without looking at what I'd done this afternoon—the finishing touches on a jackrabbit, a nearly complete otter, and a rough drawing of an elephant. Not bad. Not half bad. But, my God, there were *so many more*. Landy needed more help, I could never do all these animals by myself in my spare time. Nobody seemed to be looking that fact squarely in the face.

I'd been hoping Jess would come down by now and talk to me, see what I was up to. I guessed he was still busy with milking. I turned off the heater, turned out the lights, closed the big barn doors. Blinked around in the chilly twilight like a mole. Moles might or might not blink, though; their eyes were approximately the size of pinheads, and since they spent their whole lives underground, probably all they could distinguish was strong light from darkness. I had to do a mole soon; I'd been reading up.

The hum of the milking machine drew me across the bumpy yard to the open, light-filled doors of the milking parlor. Inside, cows stood eight on a side, on two raised platforms over a shallow pit, where Jess and his helpers, Mr. Green and two neighborhood boys, went from cow to cow hooking up milking apparatus. I could never get over how docile cows were, how they plodded into their individual stalls on their own, stopped, and patiently stood until it was their turn to be milked. Why didn't they ever stampede? Jess had laughed when I'd asked him that. "They're peaceable by nature," he'd said, "and anyway, milking's what they like best. After food."

I stood just inside the doorway, enjoying the warmth, watching the mechanical but still earthy process of cow milking. Jess, in rubber boots and rubber gloves, washed the udder of an all-black Holstein with paper towels and disinfectant, then squirted a little milk out of each teat by hand. As he attached the rubber-lined suction cups, the milking machine made four soft, distinct sucking sounds. I glanced at the cow's broad black face, expecting bliss, but it didn't appear to change.

They were almost finished, I could tell from the urine and manure sights and smells. When they first started, it was neat as a pin in the milking parlor; then slowly everything went to hell. When it was over, they hosed it down, every surface, and soon everything was clean and neat again. What a job.

What a life! It wasn't one I'd ever envisioned for my wild, romantic boy, even though it was the only one Jess ever really wanted. At least, that I knew of. He told me something once: he said he hoped he was a mixture of his mother and his father, some of each, but not all of either. It made me wonder if he was afraid of his mother's illness. Maybe the hard physical work, the quiet cycles, the slow, unsurprising routine of Jess's days were a totem for him, a hedge against—craziness. If so, I didn't know what I thought about that. It was working, but was it sad? Was it funny? The problem was, I didn't know if Jess was happy or not. I couldn't tell—he'd turned into a mystery to me. Something else I never expected.

Mr. Green pressed a button in the tile wall of the pit, a metal gate slid open, and a line of milked cows clopped out of the parlor and off to an outdoor pen, where troughs of hay silage waited for them. Another gate opened; a new line of cows plodded in. Jess looked up and saw me. His whole face changed. Gladdened.

He couldn't be a mystery, I knew too much about him. He had a crescent-shaped scar on his right shoulder blade; he got it leaning into a truck engine when the hood slipped and fell on his back. He was thirteen; it was his father's '62 Ford pickup. He taught himself to play the guitar when he was fourteen. His favorite musician had been James Taylor. When we were sixteen, he showed me how to press my forehead into a cow's soft, bulging side and milk her with firm, gentle, rhythmic pulls, squirt, squirt, squirt, squirt. "Don't let your hair tickle her skin, Carrie, she's real sensitive, she can feel everything." The lanky boy with the long, strong fingers gave me my first grown-up lesson in sensuality when he taught me to milk that cow. Yes, he did, and in respectful treatment of the opposite sex. I wanted him to touch me with the same sureness and solicitude as he touched those big bovine ladies, great heavy flaunters of their own femaleness. That milking cows had a sexual component shouldn't have come as any great surprise, but in my adulthood I wrote it off as adolescent hormones in tumult. Now I saw I was wrong. It wasn't a function of age, but of susceptibility.

He stripped off his gloves, calling over something to Mr. Green, who glanced up and waved to me. He was a nice man, Mr. Green, but he was getting old. He wanted to retire and go live with his daughter in North Carolina, and Jess kept talking him out of it. Selfishly—he was the first to admit it. Mr. Green thought building an ark was the funniest thing he'd ever heard of in his life.

"Hey," Jess said. He had an endless stockpile of scruffy clothes. Cow tending was filthy work; why would he dress up? It was always a bit of a shock, though, the first time I saw him in his work clothes. Compared to his city councilman clothes, that is, or his man-about-town clothes. He led a double life. Tonight it was stained khakis torn at the knees, a frayed shirt, a dingy gray cardigan sweater, and a shapeless windbreaker with a broken zipper and both pockets ripped off. "Hey," I said, and we went outside and leaned against the side of the building, gazing off at the livid, streaky sky. "Smells like spring," Jess said, and I inhaled, but all I could smell was cow. "Come in the house," he said, "have some coffee or something—have a drink."

"I can't, have to go home. What time is it?"

"About six."

"I told Ruth I'd be home by six."

"What's she up to today?"

"Studying for a French test at a friend's."

"I thought she might come over with you. Since it's Sunday."

"She didn't want to," I admitted. "She thinks this is so crazy, Jess, she thinks we're all nuts." This morning she'd informed me, with much scorn and derision, "*God*, Mom, you are getting so *weird*." I said, "Oh, really? You're going to be ten times weirder than I am." "No *way*. How do you figure?" "No one's stopping you," I said, thinking of my mother. "No one's holding you back."

Jess smiled in sympathy. "I know it, we embarrass the hell out of her. How can you blame her?" I loved it that he liked Ruth, and not just because of me. "So what did you do today?" he asked.

"The elephant—the drawing for it. Oh, Jess, I think it's really going to be good."

"Let's see. Show me."

"No, I can't, I have to go." Neither of us moved, though. "What do you think Eldon would say if the tiger was flying through the air? Not standing or walking, but *pouncing*." I had a picture of it I couldn't get out of my head—all four big-pawed legs of the tiger straining forward, the muscular tail flying up and back, toothy mouth wide open, ears flat, and the whole thing at about a seventy-degree angle. A huge, open-air leap.

"How would it stay up?"

"Dowels coming up from the wooden base—from a distance you wouldn't see them. I'm only talking about eight or ten feet off the ground. But do you think it sounds too . . . predatory?"

"I think it sounds terrific. He might not, though."

"Well, he said he wanted realism. He doesn't want cartoons or smiling faces, he doesn't want to anthropomorphize the animals at all—he said that." That's when I said I'd help—when I found out Eldon and I shared the same ark aesthetic.

"True," said Jess, "but he might not want people to think too hard about what the tiger's going to eat on the ark for forty days." He licked his lips. "Tasty chickens, handsome gazelles. Tender, juicy rabbits."

"I never thought of that. Rats—which I don't have to do, luckily. Oh, Jess, you should *see* the elephant."

"Show me."

"I can't. Anyway, you're still working."

"No, we're done."

"You're not, you have all the washing up to do." After the milking came the cleaning, another half hour of washing, rinsing, and scouring until the milking parlor gleamed and the cooling room shone. Then all the record keeping; Jess had to keep track of how many gallons of milk every cow gave at every milking. "I don't see how you can build an ark with all the other work you've got to do," I said. "Oh God."

"What?"

"That sounded like my mother."

"Well, she'd have a point. I'll have to hire another man to help with the milking until this ark's finished." He rubbed his eyes, and I saw how tired he was. "I know it's only a platform, but it still has to float, and I'm not a boatbuilder."

"You'll figure it out. It's basically a raft, right?" He and Landy had explained the latest design they'd come up with. "With a sort of faux hull and two fake stories on top?"

"In theory. It still has to float," he repeated ominously. "And take a man's weight so we can load it with animals."

"I was thinking," I said. "Are you doing portholes?"

"Portholes?"

"You could do fake portholes, just painted circles—but I could paint faces looking out of them. It would be a way to get more animals on board."

"More animals on board."

There weren't many people I could say this to. Maybe only Jess. "Isn't it sad to you that the coyote doesn't get to go? Or the cougar? Or the crow or the penguin—these guys all have to die in the flood. They're going to be extinct. I'm just concerned about the differentiation of species, that's all, the proliferation—whatever it's called."

He kept his head down, but I could see his lips curve when he smiled. It made me smile. I was leaning against the milk parlor, pressing my palms to the wood siding, watching my breath condense in the air. Jess picked up one of my hands. I looked at his face as he stared down at my palm, still smiling, moving his thumb across the soft calluses I was getting at the base of my ring and middle fingers. It felt right to touch him, not shocking at all. Like walking through the snow in new leather boots. *About time.*

But then, just as I thought he would lift my hand and put a kiss on it, I took it away. Took it back. *Mine, you can't have it.*

We shoved our empty hands into our coat pockets and went quiet. What did I want? What the hell did I want? Some things never changed, and my endless capacity to disappoint Jess was one.

"Ruth says you're seeing Brian now."

That took a second to process. "No, I'm not. Ruth told you that? It's not true."

"Okay," he said neutrally.

"We went out to dinner. Believe me, I'm not seeing Brian."

"All right."

"When did she tell you that?"

"Couple of weeks ago."

I'd kill her. As soon as I got home. I'd begun to put that night out of my head. At work, Brian acted as if nothing had happened. I'd tried to copy his obliviousness—it seemed the only way we could work together—but I wasn't as good at it as he was. I wanted to confide in Chris, but I couldn't. She liked him, she'd known him longer, she'd be loyal to him; I couldn't disillusion her to make myself feel better. So, like Brian, I was pretending nothing had happened.

Jess watched me. "I can't come again until Wednesday," I told him. "But then I can get off work early, be here by four or so. Is that okay?"

"Yes."

"Will you be here?"

"Either here or at the Point."

"Okay, then." I hugged my arms, cold all of a sudden. "Well, I better go, let you get back to work. Oh—I can't come next weekend, either. Not at all."

He nodded slowly, as if he'd expected that.

"I want to, I wish I could, but I can't."

"Doesn't matter."

"We're going to Washington. My mother and Ruth and I. For the weekend."

"Ah."

"Yes, it should be interesting." I took a few steps backward, toward my car. But he didn't follow, so I stopped. "Girls together. I just hope we don't kill one another."

"How's your mother's petition going?"

I winced. Sore subject. Mama got her women's club to start a petition drive against the ark on the grounds that public property can't be used for religious purposes. "What do you think Eldon thinks about all the publicity the Arkists are getting?" I asked Jess instead of answering.

"Does your mother know you come here, Carrie?"

"Not—yes—well, no—" I stopped, rueful and defensive. "She knows I want to help."

He smiled.

"I'll tell her tonight," I said recklessly. "I have to call her anyway about the weekend. I'll make a *point* of mentioning it. That I come here as often as I can—which isn't that often anyway."

"Why?"

"Why what?"

"Why tell her?"

I lifted my arms and let them drop. "Why did you ask me?"

"No reason. Curious."

We stared at each other, me anxious, him amused. Maybe; I really couldn't tell what Jess's smile meant, I just knew I didn't like it.

"I'm not afraid of what my mother thinks. I'm not eighteen, you know." Just saying it made me feel like a child.

He said, “That’s good”—but now there was nothing he could say that didn’t sound like tolerance or sarcasm or condescension. Or baiting. He knew it, too. He kept smiling.

“Oh, good-bye. I’m leaving.”

“’Night,” he called as I strode away. “I’ll be here on Wednesday, Carrie. I’ll make a *point* of it.”

Oh, now he was mocking me? I got in my car with jerky, frustrated movements, and drove too fast down his rough, stony driveway. Why was it any of his business what I’d told my mother? And why was I angry? I didn’t know, but it felt good. Inappropriate, unwarranted, and fine. It felt like just the ticket. I hoped he was mad, too. *About time.*

We’d been through a lot together, but the one thing we’d never been with each other was angry. Why was that? In twelfth grade, when I wouldn’t sleep with him, he was understanding and I was guilty. When I wouldn’t marry him, he was sad and I was guilty. When we were together after the reunion and I let him down again, he was numb and I was guilty.

I hated this pattern. I’d have enjoyed a good fight, a yelling match, maybe some pushing and shoving. “You hurt me!” he could say, and I could shout back, “I know! How do you think that makes me feel!”

I wasn’t myself anymore. I felt as if I were on a drug; a good drug for once, but still a new and unfamiliar one. I couldn’t stand confrontation, I’d never liked mixing it up with people—but I would really have enjoyed starting a fight with Jess. I thought that was a good sign. It might mean we’d turned a corner.

Either that or I’d entered the perimenopause.

15

Blah Blah, etc., etc.

Spring's here. Mom let me skip school on Friday, and the three of us, me, her, and Gram, drove up to D.C. for the weekend. I got to drive, but only as far as Gainesville, because after that comes I-66 and then—gasp!—the Beltway, and God knows I'd have killed us all if I'd been the one driving on—faint!—the Beltway. So Mom and I had to switch around in the front seat while Gram ran into the ladies' room at the Exxon and peed for like the fourth time since we left home. I wonder if she's got something wrong with her, but she says no, she's always like this.

It was fun driving up, actually. I've done a lot of stuff with my mom and my grandmother before, but this was the first time I ever felt like I was one of them, not a little girl among the grown-ups. Like we were three women going on an adventure together. Part of it was because Gram said things in the car she usually waits until I'm not around to say, things I don't even necessarily want to hear, like how this trip was the longest time she'd been away from home in two years because Grampa never wants to go anywhere. And how what she thought would be their nice retirement, traveling around and doing things together, etc., etc., was apparently just a dream and is never going to happen. She didn't laugh or make it a joke, either, the way she usually does. Her voice got high and thin, and nobody said anything for a long time, and then I heard her blow her nose, and that was the end of that.

Mom looked miserable. I wonder what she'd have said if I hadn't been there. I mean, it was her own father Gram was dissing.

It's true Grampa can be sort of a drag, and I can see how being married to him would bring you down sometimes, especially if you wanted somebody who'd talk to you. But I never liked it when Mom used to say bad things about Dad. She didn't do it very often (and now she never does, just the opposite, I never even knew she liked him so much), and even then it was only little things, like how he left his beard hairs in the sink or he was too negative or he didn't try hard enough to be sociable to their friends. I hated it, though, and I'd leave the room when she started, I'd never stick around and sympathize, even if I could see her point. I didn't know who I was supposed to be being loyal to, her or him. When they'd fight, I'd get scared and think, what if this argument keeps going and going and doesn't stop, what if it goes on to its natural conclusion and they decide they don't like each other and split up? So I'd always leave, get the hell out, and try to think about something else. When I'd come back things would be okay again, silent but okay. She'd be depressed and he'd be in his office with the door closed, but at least the fight would be over.

So anyway, the trip up was pretty nice, especially when I was driving, and the hotel we checked into was incredible. It was on Massachusetts Avenue, and you could look down and see Dupont Circle from our eighth-floor windows. We had a suite; Mom and I were sleeping in the king-size bed in the bedroom and Gram got the pull-out sofa bed in the parlor. I hoped she didn't snore.

We spent all Friday afternoon looking at artwork. We took the subway to the Mall and went to the National Gallery. First we went to the East Building, which is all modern art, then the West Building, which is old art. I like both, but Mom prefers the modern and Gram only likes classical. My favorite of everything I saw was this special exhibit in the East Building by Monet, who is my favorite painter, who did gorgeous pictures of gardens, wheat fields, seascapes, and of course water lilies. He painted his wife, Camille, too. The info in the brochure said he cheated on her and had a child with some other man's wife two years before Camille died. After you find out something like that, it's hard to know how to feel about the person you used to like. For a while, like ten minutes, I didn't care for Monet's paintings as much as before, but then I got over it. "Artistic license," Gram said. "Men will be men." I wonder if Grampa ever cheated on her. I doubt it, not with a person, anyway. Maybe with a book.

Now that Mom thinks she's an artist again, she's gotten kind of obnoxious. We were looking at this painting by Monet called *The Highway Bridge at Argenteuil*, which is basically a river with a sailboat on the left and a bridge on the right. Well, imagine my surprise when she says to me and Gram, but loud enough for anybody else around to hear, that the dominant link between the four basic forms is the bridge, and isn't it neat the way the sailboat's mast joins the water, the sky, and the far shore, so your eye glides effortlessly—she really said "effortlessly"—across the canvas and into the depth of the picture and back to the surface, a constant interplay of lines and forms. She actually said "interplay."

So I said, "You know, saying 'form' is kind of like having an English accent, it makes people automatically think you're smart. Right, Mom? As soon as you say 'form,' you sound like you know what you're talking about, when really it doesn't mean anything. Thing, it means thing—why don't you just say the *thing* in the picture, why do you have to say *form*?"

She looked surprised. I must've sounded a little hostile. She started to push my bangs out of my face, but I backed out of reach. I *hate* when she does that. She said, "Well, but form is really more like a relationship than a thing. It's what *organizes* things. It dictates the content, like a sonnet or a ballet or—a rock-and-roll song." Oh, thank you for coming down to my level. "Form is really things in relation to other things, and art is the search for form. Which, if you think about it, is another way of saying it's a search for yourself. Art makes form out of chaos—or it finds form *in* chaos. What art is, is making form out of formlessness—"

I walked away.

But then when we were in the West Building looking at these gorgeous Turner seascapes, I couldn't help myself. I said, thinking this would get her—should've known—"I don't get why people paint at all anymore anyway. I mean, what's the point after they invented the camera, you know? Why bother?"

She tried to look really patient and like that wasn't the stupidest thing she'd ever heard. "Well, but think about it. If fifty people painted the same landscape, you'd get fifty different landscapes—or nudes, or vases. You don't paint to make a replica of the thing you're painting—"

"Sure you do."

"No, you don't, you paint it to share the special way you see it with the rest of the world. It's an *expression*."

"Of yourself."

"Yes."

"That sounds pretty egotistical."

"Self-expression? No, it's natural, it's—it's imperative, it's what we—"

"I think it's pretty selfish. Look what *I* painted, look how I made this building so abstract you can't even tell it's a building, stupid you." Meanwhile, I didn't really believe any of this, I just sort of couldn't stop.

"There's nothing selfish about self-expression," she says, starting to get impatient. "If anything, art brings you closer to other people. When you're painting—or whatever, writing a song—there's a feeling you get that you're part of things. You belong, you participate. It's like—it's almost like euphoria. It's the opposite of being alone. Rollo May says creativity brings us relief from our alienation, and I think it's true—I know for me it's—"

"So when you're making a giant squid out of Styrofoam in Jess's barn for the crazy people, you're, like, ecstatic? That's way cool, Mom, it's really great that you're not lonely when you're painting aardvarks, that's just a real relief to me personally." And I walked off to look at the Courbets by myself. I don't even know why I was so mad, I just was.

After the museum, we went back to the hotel to change clothes, then we had dinner early in a café in Foggy Bottom so we could be near the Kennedy Center when our play started. Gram picked it, and it probably sounded like a nice play for us in the one-sentence review they do every other Sunday in the *Times Dispatch*. It probably said something like, "A mother and her daughter discover the true meaning of family in this heartfelt drama of pain and redemption." They just forgot to mention the heartfelt drama is set in Bosnia and the mother and daughter discover the true meaning of family when the mother shoots the daughter so the evil soldiers can't rape and mutilate her. God! We walked out like zombies! Everybody did! And if there was any redemption, I must've blinked and missed it, because all I saw was the pain.

In the cab on the way home, Mom goes, "Well, *that* was cheerful," and Gram gets huffy, pretending she'd liked it and saying life isn't *The Sound of Music* all the time and once in a while it's good to see how lucky we are compared to people in other lands, blah blah, etc., etc. There was this horrible scene in the play when they were starving and they had to eat a rat, an actual RAT (!!), and so I said to Gram, "Yes, and I myself have a much deeper appreciation for Mom's cooking now." Mom let out this snort, and Gram tried not to laugh, but she couldn't help it, and pretty soon we were snickering in this sort of guilty, embarrassed, but really gleeful way about the very worst things that happened in the play. I was worried the cab driver would think we were fiends or morons or something, but he never looked at us.

Then I couldn't sleep. Mom stayed up late talking to Gram in the parlor. So much for being one of the grown-ups. No, I couldn't stay up and watch Conan O'Brien. No, we couldn't order room service, no, I couldn't eat the macadamia nuts in the honor bar.

No, we couldn't buy a futon, no, I couldn't have a leather jacket, no, we couldn't go to Georgetown tomorrow. That's the only place I really wanted to go, but no, we can't go there. There's no subway stop, plus nowadays it's full of riffraff.

This would've been such a great trip if only I'd gone with anybody besides my mother and my grandmother.

I was wrong—what a day Saturday turned out to be! First thing, Mom got a call from her old college pal who lives in Maryland, finally returning *her* call and saying yes, she could have lunch with her today, how about at the Lord & Taylor in Chevy Chase. So we three spent the morning shopping at Filene's Basement on Connecticut Avenue (I got two pairs of leggings, this really cool sweater, blue with one red stripe across the front, I wore it right out of the store, and some underwear), and then Mom left to go meet her friend. Now it's just me and Gram. The plan was to walk around downtown, have lunch someplace, maybe get in the tour line at the White House, see Lafayette Square, see the Corcoran, etc., etc. Like, boring boring boring, but you do it because you're with your grandmother and everything is her treat.

So we're sitting on a bench on K Street, getting organized, getting our bearings, and Gram goes, "Do you really want to go to Georgetown?" I'm like totally crazed, but I say very coolly, "Oh, I don't know, I guess it's pretty far. I don't even know how we'd get there. You don't want to go, do you?" Gram can be strict and kind of scary sometimes. She scowls, looks me right in the eye, and goes, "Ruth. Do you or do you not want to go to Georgetown with me. Right now." I swallow and say, "Oh, Gram, that would be so great." She stands up, sticks her arm out, a cab screeches over, and off we go to Georgetown!

It is the coolest place! If I can't go to school there, I would very much like to live there. Over a shop or a gallery. I could live on the second or third floor over one of the really funky art galleries and get a job. I'd wear Steve Maddens and a long black skirt and a black sweater. The gallery would have high white or beige walls and be quiet as a library, and I would explain the paintings to good-looking rich people, earn huge commissions, and live in a loft and take lovers. This is a daydream, but it's not impossible.

So, Georgetown. We had to walk pretty slowly because Gram had on the wrong shoes and the brick sidewalks are rough and uneven. She says, before we even get out of the cab, "Put your purse strap around your neck and hold it tight at all times," like every other person we see is definitely a mugger. It's so ridiculous, I am *never* going to be like that when I get old, suspicious and distrustful and always scared, I'd rather get robbed than go through life with that attitude. Mostly we just walked around M Street and Wisconsin Avenue, looking at the people and the stores. The thing about Georgetown is that at first it's almost depressing, you're like, I'll never be this cool, I'll never be this rich, I'll never be rich enough to be this cool. You're embarrassed by yourself. But then that starts to wear off and you get used to it or something and it's not so bad, although still you have this, like, yearning inside, you're wishing so hard you belonged and you know you don't. Sometimes I feel like my head will blow up if I don't grow up soon, if I don't get out of this life soon. This awful life, which is like being in prison or locked in a little dark room and nothing's happening, NOTHING, except that I'm ridiculous and everybody is laughing at me, or they would be if they could see inside my head.

Anyway. We went in a store that sells nothing but kites. We went in a store that sells nothing but maps. Clayborne is so lame. God. We have a few cute shops near the college, like the Book Stop and Pearl's Jewels and the candle store, but compared to Georgetown they're just cheap imitations. I really think I need a leather coat. Black or brown, I can't decide. Black. (Krystal wouldn't like it, though, she won't even wear leather shoes, she won't even drink milk or eat cottage cheese because it comes from a cow.) We went in a store that sells nothing but hats, and Gram said I could get one. So I got a cloche hat! I didn't even know I wanted one until I saw it. It's beige ("granite," according to the saleslady) and made of soft, soft wool and it's really me, everyone agreed. Although how that can be I don't know because it's very sophisticated. It makes me look much older, like nineteen or twenty, especially if I wear my sunglasses. I LOVE IT. No one in Clayborne has a hat like this, but that goes without saying.

We were in a restaurant called the Purple Dog having lunch (grilled pita goat cheese pizza for me, turkey sandwich for Gram) and there was this lady in the booth across from us. By herself. About twenty-eight, I guessed, no older. She had long shiny black hair pulled back in a barrette, down to about her shoulder blades, just straight back, no bangs or anything. She had small silver cluster earrings and a ring, a thin silver band, on the middle finger of her left hand, and no other jewelry. She had on gray slacks, like boot pants, and a black sweater, maybe cashmere. Black two-inch platform shoes, not leather but the stretch fabric kind. She'd already eaten, so she was just having coffee. And she was reading a book, but I couldn't see the title. A paperback with a really tasteful cover, not like a romance or anything. Once she pulled her sweater sleeve up, and I saw her bracelet tattoo. Tiny, just little blue links exactly like a delicate chain bracelet, all the way around her wrist. And when she got up, she put on a cloak, not a coat, with this graceful, floppy hood in back, and she had no purse, she just took money out of her pocket to pay.

She left. Gram said, "What's wrong with you?" and I said, "Nothing," but I don't know, I had this feeling. Worse than just how pathetic my life is, worse than, Here I am in this totally cool restaurant in Georgetown with my grandmother. It was like, Well, I might as well be dead. I'll never have what I want because I don't even know what I want. I look out at the people walking by on the sidewalk and think, Am I like her? Her? Who am I like and when will I know? When will I grow into myself? Ever? I love my new hat, but it's just not enough. If I had everything the black-haired lady has, it wouldn't be enough either. You have to know who you are on the inside before you can start decorating yourself, and in my case, there's nobody home, just ghosts going, "Hello? Anything happening?" Nobody can even see me.

"How's that boy you like? That Raven," Gram said deliberately—trying to make up for the time she called him Herring. "Is he still in the picture?"

"He's just a friend, Gram, I never said I *liked* him." I didn't mention he got suspended for three days last week for bringing his bull snake, Rocky Horror, to school. He said it was to show that the vast pet kingdom is wider than servile and obsequious dogs and cats, but I think it was just to scare girls.

"Oh, I see." She looked like she didn't believe me. Well, I don't know if I was telling the truth or not, because I haven't figured out what I think of Raven. I think if he's ever going to he should've asked me out on a regular date by now. Does he think I go around kissing guys in graveyards all the time? Ever since it happened he's been acting like it didn't. Fine by me, it's not like the earth moved or anything, I mean, big effing deal. I just think it's stupid to pretend something didn't happen when it did. It hurts people's feelings. It makes people feel like they don't exist.

"Want dessert?" Gram said. I hemmed and hawed a while, "Oh, I don't know, do you?" until she called the waitress over and told her we'd have two mousse fudge brownie cakes with vanilla ice cream and one cup of coffee.

I studied Gram, trying to look at her through the eyes of a stranger. Like, did she look like my faculty advisor? I could be a Georgetown student and she could be my art history teacher or my Victorian lit professor. She was trying to get to know me better because I exhibited much promise in one so young. She didn't have lunch on a Saturday with students very often, in fact never, but she was making an exception in my case. She wanted me to cowrite an important scholarly article with her, and she was trying to charm me because she was afraid I might transfer to a superior department at Columbia University.

If it weren't for her clothes, which are always too dressy and colorful and prissy, too Clayborne Women's Club, Gram really could look like a college professor. She wears her gray hair pulled back in a loose bun, no part, no bangs, but it's not as bad as it sounds, in fact it suits her. She's getting saggy in the face, but she's still pretty. Well, "handsome," that's a better word; she reminds me of a picture I saw at the museum by somebody, maybe Picasso, of Gertrude Stein, only Gram is thinner and grayer. But she still has that sort of rock solidness or something, like she can't be moved. And she's still got really good legs. She always says all three of us Danziger women, her, Mom, and me, have the same great legs. It's sort of a family saying.

She signaled the waitress for our check. "Your mother tells me she's been spending a little time over at Jess Deeping's," she said.

"A *little*. She's over there constantly."

"Is that right. How often?"

"At least one night a week, and always one weekend day, half day, I guess, morning or afternoon." It didn't sound like that much when I said it. It felt like much more.

Gram pursed her lips and shook her head. "Ridiculous."

"I know, it's so ridiculous!"

"I don't know what she's thinking."

"I know! It was okay when she was making the stupid flower arrangements, at least she was home, but now she's *never* home."

"It's irresponsible." She blotted her lips with her napkin and said casually, "Has she had any more evenings out with Brian?"

"No, Gram." We agreed on everything about the ark, how dumb and embarrassing it was, but we didn't agree on Mr. Wright. When I told her Mom went out on a date with him, she was *glad*. I couldn't believe it!

"Does she talk about him? What does she say?"

"Nothing, Gram, she doesn't say anything. She used to, but not anymore." Not since their date. She's probably in love with him and doesn't want me to know. Nah, but there must be some reason she hardly says his name anymore. "She likes Chris a lot," I said. "They're getting to be pretty good friends."

"Mm," Gram said, not interested.

I switched back to the subject we were together on. "I just don't get these animals, you know? There's so many things Mom could be doing around the house. Like the downstairs powder room, she's been saying forever that that's the next project, and after that, redoing the side porch. Doesn't charity begin at home?"

Gram laughed, as if I'd said something funny—like I was a child and I'd said something inappropriate but almost grown-up. Well, *doesn't* charity begin at home? I don't think it's unreasonable to expect your widowed mother to stay herself for a decent length of time, her same *old* self. That seems like common sense to me, regular human decency. You don't rock the boat, you don't go out and change your whole life, no, you try to provide stability for your loved ones. I.e., me.

So what did Mom do that afternoon while she was out with her old college pal? She got her hair cut! It looked okay, it looked pretty good, actually, after I got over the shock of how short it was, but I couldn't help wondering if she'd done it for Mr. Wright. I'm not saying she has to be single the rest of her life. She's not that old. I don't mind if she gets married again someday, like five or ten years from now or so. Everybody needs companionship, and anyway, by then I'll be long gone.

That night we had dinner in a Vietnamese restaurant near the hotel. I thought it would be a good time to ask Gram what everybody in our family died of. You have to put that down on medical forms when you go to the doctor, for one thing, plus it's just good to know your genetic predispositions. Krystal says heredity is way overrated, and I'm sure that's true. Still, you should know what's behind you so you can be prepared for what might be ahead of you.

Turns out we're riddled with diseases and conditions, especially on the Danziger side. On the Van Allen side, Dad's father had a heart attack, which was news to me, but his mother was killed in a car accident when he was eight, so only one disease there, and afterward he went to live with his grandparents, who were old even then, and they died of old age when he was about twenty. So that side's not too bad. But Mom's side, God, they had everything. Gram's father, my Great Grandfather O'Hara, who I never met, had diabetes and cirrhosis of the liver, Grandmother O'Hara had a stroke, Gram's brother Ralph had phlebitis, glaucoma, gout, and sciatica, and she thinks he died of blood poisoning, and her brother Walter had eczema and an ulcer and died of pneumonia. Meanwhile my grandfather's father had prostate cancer and his mother had lung cancer from smoking since she was thirteen. His brother, my great uncle Edgar, had epilepsy and a stroke, and his sister Fan is still alive but she has anemia and cataracts.

God! I mean, it's a wonder the ones who are left have the nerve to go outside! Right now I myself have a sore knee, for example, plus I have motes in my eyes. (Not always; sometimes.) I'm not saying it's rheumatoid arthritis, and I'm not saying it's macular degeneration. But it could be, it's certainly possible, and I just think it pays to be aware and take precautions. Sometimes my heart beats too slowly, I can hardly feel my pulse, it's like it's disappearing. Do I do nothing? No. Do I do something? Yes, I take arjuna, 500 milligrams two times a day—Krystal gives me a discount—and I do the "thumb walk" every night on the ball of my left foot, which is the reflex point for heart disease. So at least I have some peace of mind. Because you can be going along thinking all's well, that little cough is just a cold, and *whammo*, turns out your immune system's breaking down. You've got AIDS, you've got leukemia, you've got

Lou Gehrig's disease. My dad—he felt fine until all of a sudden. Because he had no idea. He wasn't thinking. We can control a lot of things with our minds, but first we have to *know*. That's the trick. We have to be aware.

So that's what I'm doing, just trying to be aware of everything. Like, sometimes a little muscle under my eye twitches. It could be an early sign of a brain tumor, or it could be Parkinson's. Or it could be nothing. Time will tell. The important thing is that I know about it, it can't sneak up on me. Because I am vigilant.

16

So Much for Candor

"Your daughter wants a tattoo."

"I know. Is she asleep?"

"Just about." Mama closed the outer of the two doors to the bedroom and padded over in her bedroom slippers. "With her eyes open. What does she write in that journal? I went to kiss her good night, and she covered it up like it was the atom bomb formula."

What was it I said the other day that had gotten such a disgusted rise out of Ruth? I couldn't remember; some outdated expression, though, like "atom bomb formula." Her scorn had known no bounds. I'd felt her hate—there was really no other word. It hurt me, probably too much. I knew, I really did understand that for Ruth right now I was the target, the designated punching bag, if only because there was no one else for her to hit out at. But it still hurt. Had I given my mother pain like that? I must have. Not in the same way, I didn't think, not with such undisguised callousness. I'd hidden my adolescent contempt more cleverly than Ruth did. More charitably? Probably just more fearfully.

Mama groaned under her breath and lowered herself onto the sofa, putting her feet up on the coffee table. "She wants a silver ring and a cloak, too, she's decided. She wants to start drinking coffee. When did you start drinking coffee?"

"I don't remember. College, I think. She loves her new hat—thank you for buying that for her, Mama."

"She looks adorable in it. You're going to have trouble with this tattoo thing, though." She leaned over to massage the toes of her right foot. "She's even trying to get me on her side. Fat chance. Of all the tacky fads!"

"I just want her to get through high school without having anything pierced, burned, or branded."

"Lots of luck. See if there's some juice in the refrigerator, will you? I don't know why, but I feel weakish."

"You shouldn't have let her run you around like that," I said guiltily. I found a bottle of orange juice and poured it in a glass. "Here. Want some peanuts?"

"She didn't run me around, not one bit. She was an absolute angel. Carrie, I can't get over your hair. I guess it suits you, but it's so *different*."

"I know." I leaned over to see myself in the mirror behind the couch. "I don't know why I did it—I wasn't planning on it. Pure impulse."

"And with a complete unknown, that's what gets me. You could've been scalped!"

I could've been. But Mr. Harold had done right by me—I hoped. "I'm too old for long hair," I'd told him, hoping he would disagree. He had, but only politely, then he'd proceeded to whack off my hair—which I'd been wearing in a braid down my back—to about collar length. "Volume," he kept saying, "you need more volume. More spatial extension." Now I couldn't stop looking at myself. I felt naked and fascinating. Voluminous.

"What possessed you? I didn't even know you were thinking about cutting it."

"Do you hate it?"

"No, it's cute. Really. Makes you look young."

That's what Ruth had said, only with a suspicious glint in her eye. "I guess it was seeing Barbara today," I told Mama, sitting down again, putting my feet up next to hers. "She's even older than I am, half a year or something, but she looks terrific. You should see her."

"Have I ever met Barbara?"

"She came home with me in junior year for spring break. Blonde hair, really attractive? She had a boyfriend who called late every night—"

"Oh, I remember. He was a law student at Georgetown. Did she marry him?"

"No."

"Too bad."

"She married a doctor."

"Well, that's good."

"But they split up. *Then* she married a lawyer."

"Oh." Doctors and lawyers were good; divorce was bad. Mama tapped her lips, in a quandary.

"Now she has three kids and a rich husband, a house in Chevy Chase, and a cleaning lady. And a golf habit."

"You envy her."

"Well, not the golf habit. Maybe the cleaning lady." I laughed, but she just looked at me. "Well, sure, Mama, in a way. Her husband's alive. Her youngest child is four and a half, so he still needs her. He even still *likes* her."

She patted me on the hand. "You're still in mourning for Stephen, that's all that's wrong with your life. Things will get better, it just takes time. It does, I can't help it if that's a cliché. And you've got a good job now, interesting work, new friends."

"I know, I'm all right—I didn't mean to sound like I'm miserable. I'm not."

"You still have to go through the process, that's all. You can't skip steps when you're grieving, much as you might like to."

Odd advice coming from Mama, even if she'd just read it in a women's magazine. What was her motive in telling me I wasn't through grieving for Stephen? "Ruth said something that struck me the other day," I said deliberately. "She said that life without her father isn't that different from the way it was before we lost him."

"Oh, I can't believe she meant that. Not that way. What did you say?"

"I don't remember. Maybe I didn't say anything."

"Well, it isn't true, of course."

"It is, though." For once, I wasn't going to let her tell me what my life was like. "It is, in a way. Our family—Stephen was the shadowy one. He was barely there, Mama. The *family* was Ruth and me, we were the—the noisiest or something. We did everything and he . . . observed and critiqued. That's it. He observed and critiqued."

"Oh, but he loved both of you very much."

"Well." Something else it was time to set straight. "He loved us as much as he could."

"Yes. Yes, he did." She set her glass down with a sharp click.

"It's true, I miss him sometimes, I feel forsaken and hurt and lonely, but—the thing is, Mama, I felt that way before I lost him."

She stood up. "Everybody's lonely," she said shortly, and walked out of the room.

Well, well, so much for candor. Press the wrong button and your frank mother-daughter conversation flew out the window. And yet I was *sure* one of the reasons she'd suggested this weekend was so that we could talk, really try to be close again. I wanted it, too, but my expectations were more modest. I knew my mother: she wanted our old, easy friendship back, but only on her terms. She wanted everything to be the way it was twenty-five years ago. When I was her best friend. Before I went away to college and got all those ideas that didn't agree with hers. The good old days.

Barbara had talked a lot about her mother this afternoon. I remembered Mrs. Cavanaugh well, a vivacious, red-haired widow, wild about golf, youthful, full of life. At twenty, I was envious because Barbara's mother was so young and cool. "I've lost my best friend," she told me today, teary-eyed over the second glass of wine. "I miss her every day, Carrie. I could tell her things I couldn't tell anyone else in the world." I could hardly imagine it. "Not that she didn't drive me absolutely crazy," she said, "in fact, nobody did it better. The funny part is, I'm getting more like her every day. Isn't that a good joke? If we live long enough, we turn into the person who gave us the most grief, the one we tried so hard to separate from. I just think that's hilarious."

Oh, yeah, delicious, hilarious irony. While we shuddered in horror, we drew closer and closer to the object of our revulsion, finally fated to understand her. To *be* her. The punishment and the reward all in one.

The toilet flushed; water ran. Mama came out of the bathroom and crossed the room to where her suitcase lay open on the floor beside the sofa. She squatted over it and pulled out her nightgown.

I started to get up. "I didn't think it was so late. You're probably exhau—"

"Stay, sit, sit, I'm not tired. I just want to get out of this dress."

I'd forgotten her trick of taking off or putting on clothes without showing any skin. The dress was unzipped and pulled off the shoulders, bra modestly removed with the back turned, flannel nightgown donned over the head, then dress, half-slip, girdle, and stockings pulled down from underneath. The brief flash of my mother's pale, fleshy back, soft and sagging where it used to be firm, gave me a tender, hollow feeling. Protective. I didn't want life to teach her any more hard lessons. If it meant she was happy, I wanted her to stay exactly as willful, overbearing, and controlling as she was right now. How long would that resolve last, though? Another five minutes?

She sat down beside me, opened a jar of cold cream—Jergens; the flowery scent smelled as old as time—and began to smear it over her cheeks. "I'm not so sure I should've told Ruth about her great-grandfather," she said.

I knew what she meant, but I said, "Told her what about her great-grandfather? Which one?"

"My father."

"Oh—you mean about the cirrhosis?"

"She probably can't make the connection now, but she will eventually. Between liver disease and alcoholism," she explained, a little testily, when I continued to look blank. "You know your grandfather was a drunk."

"Well." I did and I didn't. Mama had never said it like that before: *a drunk*. But I had speculated. I'd known something wasn't right about Grampa O'Hara—whom we never went to see, although he only lived an hour away in Nelson County. On a farm. Some sort of tenant farm, apparently, that she could never mention, and so she rarely did, without a visible tremor of disgust. The fact that she was saying these things now put me on the alert.

"And he wasn't the only one. Ralph drank, too, and Walter was heading that way before he died."

"I didn't know that. Did I ever meet Uncle Ralph?"

"You were too little to remember. We only took you out there to see them once." The way she said *them*—it was the way she always spoke of her family, coldly, unsympathetically. "I couldn't wait to get out of that house."

"You left when you were eighteen." I knew this story. She'd gotten a job at an auto repair shop on Ridge Street in Clayborne. Pop was a student at Remington. They courted for two years, and married each other a week after he got his part-time instructor appointment.

"Seventeen. I've always said eighteen. Doesn't sound as tacky." She took a wad of clean tissues out of her robe pocket and began to wipe cold cream off her face. Softening, wrinkling old face, skin drooping at the strong jaws. She didn't look as sure of everything as she used to. The thing I disliked most about my mother was her bossiness, but if she lost that, who would she be? A diminished woman, not a new one. I didn't want that. I didn't know what I wanted.

"Seventeen?" I laughed. "You never told me that."

"I never told you my father and my brothers were moonshiners, either. And if you ever tell that to another living soul, I'll skin you alive."

"Mama!"

"Hush, you'll wake up Ruth."

I stared. "Moonshiners," I said in a thrilled whisper.

"Not even good ones. They drank up most of the product before they could sell it. We were dirt poor. I hated everything about my life. Nobody abused me—nothing like that, that's not what I mean. But they were nasty, loud, dirty men, wild men, and my mama just took it. She had about as much backbone as a crawfish. I got out. I got out and made something of myself."

I almost smiled, amazing as these revelations were. She didn't look very fierce in the old pink quilted robe, her face stripped of makeup. She didn't look very self-made. What she looked like—I'd have died before telling her—was the woman in old photographs of Grandma O'Hara.

"What do you mean, they were wild men?"

"Not abusive," she said again, "not in a physical way. They yelled all the time, drunk or sober. Everything revolved around them, they were the kings and my mama was their servant. So was I till I got out. I can tell you I never looked back."

"So you came to the big city, and Pop swept you off your feet."

"Swept me off my feet." She snorted. She closed the cold cream jar, wiped her hands with the last tissue, set everything aside on the coffee table. "I wanted a man who couldn't hurt me or change me. I wanted marriage because I thought it would keep me safe, but the last thing I wanted in a husband was gumption."

Gumption? She hadn't said anything I didn't know, but still, I felt defensive on Pop's behalf. "So you never really loved him?" I wanted a hot, stinging denial—I didn't care if it was true or not.

"I admired him. I loved it that he wasn't a country boy. He was a scholar—*that* swept me off my feet. He was probably poorer than

I was in those days, but he always wore a suit and a tie. You could never, ever understand what that meant to me."

"So you never—"

"I *learned* to love him. Your father is a fine man, he has plenty of good qualities, he most certainly does. A solid marriage comes along when both parties know what they want and aren't blinded by—" She waved her hand dismissively. "Extraneous things."

"Like what?"

"Unimportant details. Things that don't last."

Excitement, sex, chemistry, good looks—was that what she meant? What if she meant love? And I had an idea what this conversation was really about. Jess.

"You said you were lonely," she went on, fastening the top button of her robe. "I'm saying I just don't think it's that rare, that remarkable. Everybody's lonely. A man can't make you happy."

"I know that."

"You have to make your own happiness after you've picked as wisely as you can. You have to weigh things like compatibility, good blood, having the same goals—"

"Good blood?"

"Nobody has a perfect marriage, honey. Yours and Stephen's was as good as most."

"How do you know?"

"I observed. And mother knows best," she said, laughing quickly, making it a joke. "Never forget that."

I smiled back grimly. "Did you know I used to see a therapist when we lived in Chicago?" Of course she didn't know, I'd never told her. "One time he said to me, 'All my women clients come to me to talk about Mommy. But do you know, after a while it almost always turns out she's not the problem. It's Daddy.'"

We watched each other.

"About a year ago, Ruth said something. Just a casual remark, but it struck me. Stephen was in his study with the door closed—as usual. She wanted to tell him something, show him something, I don't remember anymore, and she was complaining to me because he wasn't available. She called him 'the Invisible Man.' And I remembered—that's what I used to call Pop when I was a kid. To myself. I'd seen the movie, I guess, and that's what I started to call him. The Invisible Man."

Mama shook her head slowly. "No, no, I don't see that. Stephen was nothing like George, if that's what you're getting at."

It was exactly what I was getting at. "I didn't think so, either." But then I saw them standing outside that night Stephen died, and it was like a puzzle coming together, the last piece in place. *Click.* "It's true, Mama. I married my father." How clever of me. From two different men, I got the identical oblivion and inattention, the same ironic, distanced, fastidious, cerebral frame of mind. A depressing insight, but it wasn't brand-new. Saying it to my mother gave it an unwelcome freshness, though, like a bad smell that hadn't had time to grow stale.

"No," she scoffed. "No, no. I mean, why *would* you?"

"Well, maybe . . . to get it right. That's why they *say* we do these things. You know, repeat the experience that didn't satisfy you in your childhood, try to make it work in adulthood."

"No, I don't think so. They're both academics, that's all. That's as far as it goes. Stephen had opinions, for heaven's sake. He had likes and dislikes, he had *ideas*. George . . ." She heaved a sigh and didn't finish—to my relief. I'd heard enough from her about my father's shortcomings for one night.

"Stephen had a temper," I conceded. "He did like to have his way." So did Pop, but he got his by quiet, passive means that were probably even more infuriating. "You know, we didn't really know each other that well when we married. Ten months. He was a scholar, of course, very smart, dedicated, very ambitious—like Pop." I whispered, "I think it's true, Mama. I think I married my father."

She looked as if she didn't know whether to laugh or cry.

"I think," I said, "I spent the first half of my marriage trying to fix it, and the second half trying to be happy in spite of knowing it was broken. Just trying to make the best of things. Do you remember that time I called you in the middle of the night? From Chicago, when Ruth was little? I started to tell you—oh, a little of what was wrong, and you said—well, I don't remember, but after that—" Yes, I did, I remembered perfectly; she'd basically told me to suck it in, get over myself, welcome to real life. "After that, I pretty much gave up trying to change things between Stephen and me. And now that he's gone, I worry that I was wrong. Maybe I should've done more, maybe I shouldn't have given up so easily. Do you remember that night?" I asked when she kept silent.

"I remember you were drinking." She pressed her lips together tightly. "I don't take drinking talk seriously."

Had I been drinking? It wasn't impossible. But—"I wasn't *drunk*, for heaven's sake. I wasn't!"

She shrugged: *Who's to say?* "Well, Carrie, I did not know you were that unhappy," she said disapprovingly. "I truly did not."

"I wasn't," I said, determined to be honest, although I wasn't sure why anymore. The intimacy we'd both wanted from this frank talk seemed to elude us more the longer it went on. "Or if I was, I didn't know it. I think I spent a lot of time in a daze, frankly, not happy, not unhappy. Sleepwalking."

I looked away, blindsided by longing, a sudden surge of possibility. *I could call Jess. I could dial his number and hear his voice. I could call him right now.*

"Sleepwalking," my mother repeated in a flat tone. "All I can say is, you could've done much worse. If Stephen was a little like George, why is that such a bad thing?"

"It's not—"

"One thing I know, life's too short to sleep through." She stood and started snatching up the tissues she'd thrown on the coffee table.

"I agree with you, I'm—"

"Maybe you'd better wake up and smell the coffee. You had a good husband, you've got a beautiful child—really a very privileged life in many ways. I hope you're not thinking of throwing it away for something that's not worthy of you. Count your blessings, that's what you should do. Get up, Carrie, I need to pull this sofa bed out."

"Mama, what are we talking about?" I said, not moving. "What am I throwing away? What's not worthy of me?"

"You've got a good job now, and you're lucky to have it. You've got a boss who's steady and safe, and he's interested in you. What's funny about that?"

"Nothing."

Oh, I was dying to tell her how steady and safe my boss was. I'd kept it from her for a jumble of lousy reasons—embarrassment, a need to keep her from being disillusioned, uncertainty over her reaction—she might not believe me, or she might find Brian and slug him. Telling her now seemed nasty, though; the timing was just too perfect.

She didn't like my smile, which must've looked more like a smirk. "So Brian Wright is not good enough for you? You're not interested in a man with prospects?"

"A man who wears a suit and tie, you mean."

"*What's wrong with that?*"

"Not a thing. You want to talk about this, Mama?"

She flushed. "What do you mean? We are talking. I'll tell you what I want—you to get up so I can make my bed and go to sleep. I'm tired, I'm an old lady."

"I take it that's a no." I was as angry as she was. I stood up, because I was used to obeying, but I wasn't finished. "I don't like the things you've been saying about the Arkists," I said, pulling the coffee table out of the way. She stopped throwing cushions off the couch and stared at me. "Why are you doing it? You can be opposed to the project, that's up to you, but why do you have to take the lead in it, Mama? You didn't have to start a committee, you didn't have to write a letter to the damn editor."

"Why shouldn't I? I'm a member of the community, I can voice my opinion."

"You know why. Because this *means* something to me."

She clucked her tongue and went back to work. "Foolishness. Your own daughter says you're neglecting her. And for what? *Ark animals*," she said in a harsh, sneering voice; if Ruth hadn't been in the next room, she'd have yelled it. "In a barn, with a farmer. *Two* farmers."

"Well, now we're getting to it. It's got nothing to do with civic duty or church and state or good taste or—what was it?—small-town aesthetics. I should've cut it out of the paper, because you really outdid yourself."

"I didn't write it, the committee did."

"But it's your committee."

"I don't understand your attitude."

"I'm explaining it to you."

"Not now you're not, I'm going to bed. Honestly, Carrie, I'm tired."

I looked at her across the low, beige-blanketed sofa bed, weighing the pros and cons of prolonging the argument. I wasn't used to picking fights with my mother, but I was even less used to her retreating from them. It seemed perverse, upside-down, and I had that impulse again to protect her. Anyway, we had a ritual: she decided what we fought about, I mollified her until I couldn't stand it, we argued, she won or I backed off, and it was over. Comfortable as an old sweater. Look where it had gotten us.

She turned away first, went to the closet to get down extra pillows. "So, tomorrow. Would Ruth hate it if we went to the Botanic Gardens after the National Cathedral? I'd like to go, but not if it's going to bore her to tears."

She was good at this. A timely change of subject, along with a subtle reminder of who was the host on this trip, who were the guests. Gracious guests humored generous hosts; they didn't start family fights at one in the morning.

Message received, Mama. We kissed cheeks, said good night, and retired to our separate camps.

I took a shower to calm down, get the argument out of my head. *In a barn with a farmer* kept ringing in my ears. After a little while the harshness my mother had given the phrase faded, though, and a gentler connotation took its place. I missed my farmer. Missed his barn. I put on my nightgown and stared in the foggy mirror at my new, alarmingly short hair, and wondered if Jess would like it. Men liked long hair on women—I'd always heard that. What if I'd made a terrible mistake?

He touched my hair the last time we were together. Wednesday afternoon, in the ark barn. I took half a day off from work and went to Jess's to paint animals. Landy wasn't there, he'd had to leave early to go see his father.

After he left, Jess didn't talk. He wasn't haughty or cold, he just didn't say anything. On the Sunday before, he'd held my hand, but three days later he wouldn't speak to me. Not that I blamed him—I'd pulled away, spoiling the natural progression. The unspoken natural progression. I think we both knew we were drawing closer—but slowly, slowly, and on my terms, of course. At my pace.

"Come and look at this, tell me if the ears look funny," I said in the dim, drafty barn, standing back from my almost-finished elephant. My masterpiece, I considered it in secret. Jess put down his drill and came to stand next to me. "No, they look fine." "Sure?" "Yes." He started to go back to his wheels.

"I'm sorry about the other day," I said quickly. "Getting defensive about my mother—God, that was stupid." I trusted him to know what I was really apologizing for. "I don't even know why I was mad. I thought I wanted to fight with you. But I don't, that's not what I want."

His eyelashes came down, shuttering his expression. My long, messy braid—gone now—lay on my shoulder, and Jess lifted his hand and stroked it with his fingers. What I felt was the slight weight of his wrist on my collarbone, strong as a burn. Through my jacket, two sweaters, and a T-shirt. "What do you want, Carrie?"

Oh, just everything. I wanted him, mostly, but I was still afraid of him. I wanted to honor my husband's memory. I wanted my mother to approve of me.

"If I told you," I said, making my voice playful, "would you give it to me? Everything I wanted?"

"No." He slid his fingers inside my collar and stroked my skin. "But I'd try."

I had to close my eyes. "I don't know anyone like you," I whispered, "I never have. I need some more time." I looked at him, half afraid I would regret my words, but he nodded. "I'm not running away this time, I swear. But I'm standing still. Please, Jess—you do, too. Wait. Because it would be so easy . . ."

"So easy to . . ."

"Go too fast."

He bent his head and put his face next to mine. "When you make up your mind, let me know it in words." The whisper of his breath on my ear made my skin tingle. "Write it on a big sign, Carrie. Hit me over the head with it. Because I don't want to miss it."

I think he kissed me then, but the quick, warm pressure on my cheek was so fleeting I couldn't be sure. He was smiling when he pulled away. He went back to screwing wheels onto wooden bases, but only for a few more minutes, and then he went off to milk cows. Leaving me in a flutter. I couldn't even finish my elephant.

I could call him now, I thought again. Dial his number and hear his sleepy voice. And say what? "I miss you. Don't give up on me. I'm sorry it's taking so long." He deserved that. But didn't he already know it? If not, I'd been miscalculating for weeks. Months.

"Let me know it in words," he'd said. Well, I would. I would. As soon as the time came.

Ruth had left the lamp on on my side of the king-size bed. She lay fast asleep on her back, one hand in a fist by her head, the other open on her rib cage. Under the thin blanket the slight curve of her breasts, small but definite, rose and fell, rose and fell with her silent breathing. Sometimes I hardly recognized her with her new, stranger's body. She didn't even smell the same. *Who are you?* I went around wanting to ask. If I had the power to stop it right now, stop time this minute, would I? Yes, in a heartbeat. But in a little while, I'd regret it.

Who would she finally choose, I wondered, settling in beside her gingerly, trying not to wake her—neither of us was used to a bedmate these days. Would she choose a man like her father, or a man as unlike him as she could find? Once I'd had that choice. God, God, I hoped for once the whole issue skipped a generation. If only we could go back to arranged marriages, or ban the institution entirely until people turned thirty. Forty. Thank God Ruth didn't have a regular boyfriend yet; she still dated in crowds. The only familiar, recurring face was Raven's, and I couldn't work up much worry about him. Which undoubtedly meant he was the one to worry about.

I leaned over to kiss the air above her cheek. She smacked her lips and turned over, carrying most of the sheet under her arm.

If we could just build cages around them. Big Plexiglas boxes on wheels that they could move about in, really be quite comfortable inside, but never get out of. Involuntary safety. Ruth getting her driver's license next summer was bad enough; the thought of her going away to college in two years was so awful, I couldn't even think about it. I couldn't—I pushed it out of my mind. I had a bit of a knife phobia, couldn't bear thinking about blades, so of course sometimes my nerves played perverse tricks and sent images to the brain of knives, razors, etc., etc.—a minor torture. Same thing with

Ruth and college: my nerves attacked me with random nightmare pictures of dormitories, libraries, caps and gowns. I shook myself and pushed them away. Horrible.

I turned out the lamp, tried to get comfortable. Couldn't sleep in hotels. Twenty years from now, would Ruth and I go away for weekends and tell each other secrets? Would she see me as the kind of mother she could bear to confide things in? But then again, I didn't really want her to have any problems she needed to confide. Mistakes, regrets, defeats, lost opportunities—I wanted her to miss out on them, breeze right by them through some incredible stroke of good fortune. Ruth's life had to be perfect.

I turned over on my side, drawing my knees up and cupping my hands under my chin: my comfort position. And prepared to be terribly disappointed.

17

PARTY OF ONE

People were leaving and it wasn't even eight o' clock.

"Old fuddy-duddies!" I called my friends to their faces, pretending I was kidding, but I wasn't. And it was a perfect night, mellow and almost warm, the prettiest sunset going down over the garage roof, bats starting to flicker in the purple sky. It was the first night of daylight saving time, which in my book is a cause for celebration in itself. "George," I yelled across the patio, "make me another whiskey sour!"

I headed inside to get the portable stereo. Music, that's what this party needed. Where the hell was Carrie? Should've been here two hours ago. Birdie was putting dirty glasses in the dishwasher. "Leave that," I ordered, reaching past her to unplug the boom box on top of the refrigerator. "Quit and come outside, right this minute."

She flapped her hands. "I just want to put these away before they get broken."

"At this party? Not a chance." I slung my arm around Birdie's waist and muscled her out of the kitchen. "I want people to *dance*. I've got a new tape, all songs from the fifties." It hit me. "My God, Bird—fifty years ago today, I was twenty years old."

"I was seventeen," she smirked—she never misses a chance to rub it in that she's younger. "Oh, I don't think anybody's going to dance, Dana. Golly, nobody's still here but the Hoopers and the Dodges."

And the Dodges were leaving. "No!" I cried, sticking my arms out to bar the way across the patio. "You can't leave yet, you *can't*.

Why do you have to go?" I heard the pretend-desperate note in my voice and wondered if I was getting drunk. Well, if not, it wasn't for lack of trying.

"Sorry, I know," Sylvia said, making a heartbroken face. She linked arms with silent, morose Harvey and leaned against him. "Tomorrow's an early day for us. Susie and Earl are coming, bringing their kids." She rolled her eyes, to say it was all too much, children and grandchildren, but what a good sport she was. Sylvia's a faculty wife, like me; the only reason we were friends at all was because our husbands taught in the same department for thirty years. We saw a lot of each other at faculty do's, we were always cordial, we got up to the exact same level of conversational intimacy—and retreated every time. Nothing in common. "Thanks *so* much for having us," she said, kissing me on both cheeks, "and happy *birthday*."

"Happy birthday," old sourpuss Harvey echoed. Hard to believe, but he had even less to say for himself than George. "G'night."

"Hell with 'em," I muttered, flopping down in the Adirondack chair George had put my new drink on. "Make one for Birdie," I called to him across the lawn. "Where do you s'pose Carrie is, Bird?"

"Oh, no, I don't need another thing, I'm—"

"And put some alcohol in it! Swear to God, that man cannot make a drink. Fifty-one years of marriage, and he's yet to make a good one. It's the ice-booze ratio that stumps him. What is so hard about that, would you tell me?"

"Why don't you make your own?"

"Because it's his job. I do everything else, he's not getting out of that one." I took a sip of whiskey sour. "Ek. Too much sour." I set it down to let the ice melt a while. "Nobody drinks anymore anyway, everybody's so goddamn old. We used to have *fun* at parties, didn't we?"

"We surely did. Wild parties."

"They *were* wild. Nobody went home at eight o'clock, that's for sure. My God. 'Course, that was before all the alcoholics died or went on the wagon."

Birdie yawned behind her hand.

I remembered the music. "I'm putting on that tape," I decided, and got up. I'd worn a long red dress, thinking it would be more festive than slacks. I tripped on the hem as I crossed the patio on the way to the electrical plug on the screen porch, had to grab the picnic table to keep my balance. "Damn shoes," I muttered, kicking them off. One flew up and landed on the table, and I left it there. After a little fumbling, I got the boom box plugged in and the right tape in.

Somebody had turned the volume up too high; "Come On-a My House" came out like a police siren. Birdie shrieked; George and the Hoopers turned around with irritable, alarmed faces. Where the hell was the volume knob? I found it, turned it down. Birdie took her hands off her ears.

"Dance with me," I said, pulling her up. She had on slacks, she could be the man. She was so scrawny and brittle, though, it felt more like dancing with a child.

"Oh, Dana, I don't want to dance!"

"You have to, it's my birthday. I'm gonna give you ca-handy," I sang, stumbling through a fox-trot step. Maybe this was a jitterbug. "When was the last time you danced? I can't even remember. Margaret Whiteman's girl's wedding, I think. I mean with a man." I spun Birdie into a turn. "You know what?"

"What?" Her cheeks flushed; she breathed with her mouth open. No stamina.

"It's very possible this is the last time you and I will ever dance. I'm talking about for the rest of our *lives*. Think about that, Bird."

"Honey, you're just drunk." She quit dancing, wouldn't be moved. "Come on and sit down, I'll make you a cup of coffee." Her face crinkled with sympathy, and I pushed her away.

"I'm not drunk, and I'm not feeling sorry for myself. Make me a cup of coffee and I'll pour it down your dress."

"There, you just proved my point." Wounded, she crossed to her chair and sat. "Pour it down my dress. Oh, sure. Somebody I know is going to have a big headache tomorrow."

The most vulgar phrase came into my head, the kind my generation wasn't allowed to say. Carrie's was; Ruth's used it so often it didn't mean anything anymore. Shocking, how much I wanted to say it to Birdie, wipe that prissy look off her face. "Shit," I said instead, but she's heard that from me plenty of times; it only made her squeeze her lips together harder.

The Hoopers had to go, big day tomorrow, something about a chess tournament in Richmond and Edward was in the finals; I tuned out, didn't hear the details. Like the Dodges, Edward was a colleague of George's and Esther was a fake friend of mine. We saw each other at faculty parties but nowhere else, because there just wasn't enough to hang a real friendship on. "Thanks so much for coming," I told Esther as we hugged, thinking it was funny, ha-ha, that the Hoopers were the last to go and the Dodges were second to last, and I didn't give a damn about any of them.

"Where are *my* friends?" I said after the Hoopers were out of earshot. "Are they all dead? Besides you," I added when Birdie looked hurt. "I mean, of course, besides you." I dropped down on the arm of her chair and squeezed her skinny far shoulder. "Don't you think it's funny that George's friends stayed the longest at my birthday party? *His* stuffy old friends?"

"You had friends here, Roberta and Don, Kathryn, Binnie, the Strouds. They just had to go home."

"That's what I mean. How come *my* friends are worse party poopers than *his*?"

Birdie didn't know. George heard, but didn't look up from whatever he was doing to the grill, shaking out the charred briquettes or something. Doris Day began singing, "Once I had a secret love," and I sang along. "What movie is this from? Is it that one with James Cagney? I loved that movie. She wore the most gorgeous clothes."

"I love Doris Day," said Birdie. "She's saving the animals now, you know. She's such a lovely woman."

"She wore a fur stole in that movie. I wanted one just like it in the worst way. George was making nothing in those days, so of course it was out of the question. But *oh,* I wanted me a fur stole."

"I always wanted blonde hair," Birdie said.

"I wanted to be short and petite."

"I wanted to wear it in a ducktail, but Chester said it would look cheap."

I took a swallow of my drink, which was now perfect. "Too bad there's no such thing as reincarnation. Too bad this is it. That is one damn shame."

"Oh, I think there is reincarnation. I believe we come back again and again, until we get it right."

"No, we don't. That's ridiculous. They plant us and we rot, that's it."

"Oh, no, I don't think so." Birdie folded her hands and turned her face away. Old fool. A big rush of affection flooded me, though, rinsing away the irritation. Birdie's like an old song you've heard so many times it annoys you—"Harbor Lights," say, or "Some Enchanted Evening." But it's still a good song, and sometimes, when somebody sings it just right, you remember why it's a standard and you like it all over again.

"Well, you could be right," I said magnanimously. "Nobody knows, that's for sure, not till they're dead anyway, so what's the difference. You want to believe you come back as a cat, honey, be my guest."

The back screen door snapped open. "A cat! Gram, are you coming back as a cat?"

"*There* you are. Finally!" I got up and held my arms out. Ruth came and hugged me. She felt so good, young and squirmy and alive, I didn't want to let go. "Where've you been? This party's over, and it was a bust to begin with. You could've livened it up. Mm *mmm*, you look good enough to eat. Where've you been?"

"We got tied up," Carrie said from behind a gigantic pink azalea plant in her arms. "Where is everybody? Ruth, get this—" But she got the screen door open with her foot and scuttled through sideways before it could slam shut. "Happy birthday." She sounded relieved, a chore off her list, as she plunked the heavy azalea down on the table.

"Oh, how pretty," Birdie said, getting up to give Ruth a shy squeeze. "Dana, isn't it beautiful?"

"I picked it out," Ruth said. "Mom wanted a white one."

"White? No, no," I said, "pink's much better. Why, it's just gorgeous, and I know exactly where I'm going to put it."

"I was thinking for nighttime," Carrie said. "You know how white shows up at night in the garden." She fluffed her hair off the back of her neck. She looked hot, tired, and distracted. I can always tell when her happy face is a mask, because she can't smile naturally, her mouth just won't soften. "Anyway, happy birthday, Mama." Even her arms felt stiff, and her kiss on the cheek didn't have any zip, no energy. "Sorry we missed your party. I thought people would still be here," she said softly, and broke away. "Hey, Pop, I didn't see you." She hugged George, then stood back so Ruth could hug him, too. "How are you? You look mighty spiffy tonight."

George smiled down self-consciously at his sweater and his wrinkled linen trousers. He did look unusually snazzy, but only because Carrie had found the outfit in the Eddie Bauer catalog and given it to him for his birthday. Last year—when she had money. "Thanks." He winked at her.

"Like my dress?" I said, getting Ruth's attention when I couldn't get Carrie's. "Too young for me, I know."

"Oh, no, Gram, it's great, it's really nice."

"Nah, old ladies shouldn't wear red. Makes us look like madams." Ruth giggled. "Sit, everybody sit. George, put that plant on the ground so we can see each other. Are you starving? Carrie, have a drink—I'm having another. There's still plenty of food—" Birdie was already heading for the kitchen to get it. I let her; I was the party girl. "George, get Ruth a Coke or something. What do you want, honey, a Sprite, some ice tea, we've got lemonade all made. Carrie, you want a whiskey sour?"

No, she didn't want anything, and she wasn't hungry—she called out to Birdie not to bring her anything. And they couldn't stay long because Ruth had a soccer game early tomorrow, they'd just come by to give me my present and wish me happy birthday. I couldn't believe it! No way were they getting away like that! I kept after Carrie and kept after her, and finally she broke down and said she'd have a beer. "Well, I should think so," I huffed. "It's my birthday, damn it, I'm seventy years old and you can damn well have a drink to toast me."

That made her lift her eyebrows, but she finally smiled naturally. "How many of those have you had?"

"Not enough." I reached for Ruth's arm and squeezed it. "You do what I say, now, not what I do, you hear?"

"Yes, Gram."

"And I'm saying to you, never drink."

"Yes, Gram." She and her mother exchanged tickled glances, but I didn't care. I'd cheered everybody up. Maybe this was going to be a party after all.

"So," I said. "Why are you so late, what held you up? We grilled salmon, we had vegetable kabobs, Birdie made a cake. What happened?" I repeated when Carrie didn't answer, just looked uncomfortable.

"Oh, we just . . . couldn't get organized, and then something came up, and I didn't think you'd mind, you'd have so many other people here."

Ruth was practically bouncing in her chair. "She got fired," she said quickly, then hunched her shoulders.

"What?"

"You what? You got *fired?*"

Carrie sent Ruth a black stare under the hand she was massaging her forehead with. "Yeah," she said tiredly. "Yes, I got fired."

"*Why?*"

Ruth said, "Because she wouldn't do it with Mr. Wright! Ha—Mr. Jerk Face!" Carrie rolled her head back and shut her eyes.

"Is this true? No, I can't believe it."

"It's true, Mama."

"So we went to her office and got all her stuff, that's why we're late. Chris came down—Mrs. Fledergast—and they had to talk and talk."

George said disbelievingly, "Brian Wright?"

"Yes, Pop, Brian Wright." Carrie opened her eyes and looked at him coldly.

"When they went out on their date," Ruth piped up again, "Mom wouldn't kiss him good night, so he waited a while so it wouldn't look bad and then he fired her!"

"It wasn't a date. I told you, it was not a *date*."

"He did it yesterday afternoon. He said not to come in Monday, but he'll pay her for two weeks. What a dirtbag!"

"My lord," Birdie declared, setting a plate of food in front of Ruth. "I think you should sue him."

"That's what *I* say," Ruth said.

"For sexual harassment," Birdie said.

"I'm not suing anybody," Carrie said, as if she'd been saying it a lot.

"Well, I don't see why not. He shouldn't be able to get away with that."

"I don't understand," I finally got out. "How do you know—why do you think—" I couldn't think of the simplest words.

"*Retaliation.*" That was it. "What makes you think—Well, first of all, what's that about a kiss good night?"

"We can talk about it later," Carrie snapped, eyeing Ruth.

"Oh, for Pete's sake," Ruth exploded, "what do you think I am, Mom, eight? Here's what happened. She wouldn't kiss him good night—"

"Well—it was a little more than that," Carrie said, and we all ogled her. "But less than what you're thinking," she added with a laugh. "Something in between—the details aren't important." That's what she thought. "The point is, I know it's why he fired me." When I shook my head, she glared at me. "I was good at my job, Mama, there was no other reason. You can ask Chris if you don't believe me."

"I believe you." I hated it, but I believed her. I'd had ideas about Brian Wright. I'd discovered him; a diamond in the rough, I thought. I was going to use him to make my daughter happy. I felt like throwing up. "Low-down son of a bitch. If he was here right now I'd kick him in the—crotch."

Carrie clasped her hands together and held them to her chin. "Mama, I love you. You're so predictable." Whatever that meant.

Birdie said, "What are you going to do?"

Carrie shrugged, but she avoided my eyes and I knew the answer. She was going to go to Jess Deeping's and make ark animals. Full-time.

Nothing to do then but have another drink.

"Okay," Carrie said, "that's enough of that, can we please talk about something else?" She looked tired and angry and upset, but not very depressed. For somebody who'd just had her livelihood yanked out from under her, she looked pretty damn chipper. She took the beer her father handed her and lifted it in a toast. "Here's to you, Mama. Many more."

I could hardly even smile. I knew the beginning of the end when I saw it.

Birdie started talking about spring coming and wasn't the weather wonderful and how lucky we were to be outside this early in the season. George never brought me my new drink, so I got up to make it myself. In the process I tipped the table, just a minor jolt, but Carrie had to say, "Are you all right?"

"I'm fine, I'm fine. Don't I look fine?"

And I was in love with Ruth. I perched on the arm of her chair and petted her pretty, curly hair out of her face, stroked the back of her neck, hugged her and pressed the side of her face to my bosom. "I could just eat you up, I could just eat you alive." She even smelled good, sweaty and sweet and real. I buried my nose in her hair and inhaled.

"Dana, for the Lord's sake," Birdie said, "leave that child be."

"Won't. She's too sweet." I gave her a wet, smacking kiss on the temple, and she dropped her eyes, embarrassed. A second later she rubbed her knuckle across her cheekbone.

Across the table, George caught my eye and frowned. He glanced at my drink, glanced at me, back at the drink. Who the hell was he, Carry Nation? "Well, excuse me," I said, "but today I arrived at my eighth decade and I'm entitled to drown my sorrows. What are you, Ruth honey, seventeen?"

"Fifteen, Gram."

"That's right, I knew that. Wait'll you get my age and then see what you've got to look forward to."

"Mama," said Carrie, "you've got plenty to look forward to."

"What? Name something. Life is not such a rosy prospect at seventy, let me tell you. What's something good that can happen to you? Something really good? Nothing, that's what. Your joints hurt a little worse every morning. Bladder control—maybe you'll get to wear a diaper like June Allyson. Then your mind goes, you can't remember diddly-squat. Look at Helen Mintz—she's a vegetable."

"No, she is not," Birdie said, shocked.

"Or maybe you have a stroke. Maybe it's your heart, your arteries, or lung cancer or breast cancer, maybe you get your colon removed."

"Jeez," Ruth said, snickering, "you sound like Raven."

"Ruth's ghoul friend," Carrie explained to Birdie.

"Her what? Girlfriend?"

"I'm telling you, it's not a pretty picture, wait'll you get my age and you'll see. What do you think I'm going to do, take up a new career now? Suddenly start watercoloring? Beekeeping? It's *over*."

"Mama, for heaven's sake."

"Jeez, Gram, you're not a *hundred*."

"Drama queen," Birdie said smugly.

George shoved his chair back and muttered something, patting his pocket.

"Where're you going?"

"Just have a smoke. Right back. 'Scuse . . ." he trailed off vaguely, shuffling away in the direction of the garage.

I sat back. "And there you are, aren't you. There—you—are." I toasted his shadowy retreating back, but my drink tasted bitter. "Don't think you can get old *with* somebody, either," I said, wagging my finger in Ruth's face, "just 'cause you're married to him. Don't make *that* mistake."

"Mama," Carrie said sharply.

"I don't care, needs to be said."

"No, it doesn't."

"Be careful who you pick, Ruth honey. They look good when you're young, they act right, you think you'll never be lonely again, but they fade away. You don't even know it till they're gone, and then it's too late. You married a ghost. Right, Carrie? You're the one who—"

Carrie stood. "All right, we have to go. Kiss your grandmother and come on, Ruth, it's getting late."

I didn't move except to blink fast. I let the shock wear off while I went back over what I'd said. Well, let 'em leave. I meant every word, I didn't take back one. When Carrie touched cheeks with me and said, "Good night, Mama. Happy birthday," I didn't say anything back, just sat there stone-faced and unrepentant. By God, you're allowed to tell the truth on your birthday.

"'Night, Mrs. Costello," Carrie told Birdie.

"'Night, sweetheart. You take care." I didn't look, but I didn't have to—all kinds of secret looks were going on over my head. Carrie said something about going out the back way to say good night to her father. Fine, have a party out there for all I care. Have a love-in.

Then I waited for Birdie to start in. It wouldn't take long; silence is her worst enemy. "Well?" I said when she actually kept her mouth shut. "No words from you for the *drama queen*?"

She stood up slowly, using the table for support. "You've had too many of those whiskey sours, so it's no use talking to you."

"Good."

"But I'll say this."

"Here we go."

"My Chester was no angel, and there were some things about him I've never even told *you*. But I most certainly would never have told them to my children. I didn't try to get sympathy for myself by running down Matt and Martha's father in front of them."

"Well, aren't you just wonderful."

"No, I'm not wonderful. I just know there are rules. And drinking too much and feeling sorry for yourself because you're seventy doesn't give you permission to break them. A child doesn't need to know her father's a failure, no matter how old she is. That's just common decency."

"That's just crap. A mother and child are the closest two people in the world. If you can't tell your own flesh and blood what your life is like, what's the point of anything? I didn't cross any line."

"Yes, you did and you know it. Using Ruth as an excuse, too. 'Be careful who you pick, Ruth honey,'" she mimicked. "You ought to be ashamed of yourself."

"Oh, go home."

"I am."

"When?"

"When I finish my say. You have problems with George, then you should tell them to a therapist or a marriage counselor." I snorted. "Reverend Thomasson, then."

I reached for Carrie's half-finished glass of beer. "Oh, say, that's what I'll do, Bird, I'll go visit the pastor. What a wonderful idea, and so like me, just the kind of thing I'd do. Boy, you sure do know me well." Sarcasm's lost on Birdie unless you hit her over the head with it. "I thought you were leaving."

"Okay, don't, then, just stay home and fester." Leaning forward, she said earnestly, "I'm sorry, but you're getting sourer all the time, and I'm not the only one who's saying so. I just—I just think you could use some help, and not from your own daughter, who's got enough problems of her own."

"Thank you." Warm beer stuck in my throat; I almost spit it back in the glass. "Don't slam the door on your way out."

Birdie sighed. She came around the table, smiling and frowning. "You're the hardest friend I have. I love you, Dana, but you sure are a pain in the neck sometimes. Happy birthday, honey."

I pulled back when she leaned down to kiss me, but she kept coming and got me with a hard one on the cheek. I said, "Hmph," and didn't smile. "Maybe you should write an advice column, get paid for all that wisdom. You could call yourself Miss Buttinsky."

She laughed on her way across the patio. She had on a too-summery print dress, pink on white. The white glowed in the murky twilight—Carrie was right about that. "I take it back, you're not a pain in the neck," she called from the doorway. "You're a pain in the *ass*."

Oh, naughty, naughty, coming from Birdie that was like cursing the Lord. But she'd hissed "ass" in a stage whisper, like a little girl, so the effect was spoiled. She did slam the screen door, though.

I stared around vacantly, listening to the night sounds, trying to figure out what I was feeling. Guilty? Mad? Both. But mostly tired, tired in my mind, too tired to sort out who was right and who was wrong. It just didn't matter. Tomorrow I might wake up sorry and embarrassed for committing a family faux pas and driving my loved ones away, but tonight all I could dredge up was sullenness.

The moon was exactly half full. Chilly, sweet air. Turned earth and fertilizer, a real spring smell. It made me nostalgic for a time I couldn't remember, maybe hadn't even lived. I got up and went to find George.

The streetlight in the alley filtered through the budding branches of the locust tree behind the garage, dappling his bald head as it swayed slightly—he was sitting on one of the swings of the rusty old swing set we put out here years ago, then never called anybody to take away. He had his back to me, his head tilted sideways, resting against the chain. His stooped shoulders looked dreamy; he was watching the smoke from his pipe drift up into the tree branches, musing over something, at peace. I felt keyed up just looking at him, out of sorts, ungainly somehow. He heard me and pivoted, twisting the swing chains over his head. "'Lo," he called, wary.

I strolled over, hands in the pockets of my red dress, watching where I put my feet. Lot of roots around here. If I tripped on one, he'd say I was drunk.

"Hey," I said, and squeezed into the other swing. "I'm leaving all those dishes till morning."

"That's dirty—you're going to get your dress dirty."

"Don't care."

He glanced at me, trying to figure out what mood I was in now. The streetlight reflected off his glasses, dazzling me; I couldn't see his eyes. Presently he said, "Isn't that something now, about Carrie."

"Crazy. Of all things."

"I've known Brian since he was the registrar at Remington. Never liked him, but I never would've guessed at anything like this. Not in a million years." He shook his head, baffled. "Maybe she *should* sue him."

"Suing's tacky. Goddamn sonofabitch." I meant it, but I regretted saying it. He doesn't complain, but George hates it when I swear. But that's how reckless and mad I was feeling. And foolish. Tricked, and old, and hornswoggled. I felt like one of those old ladies you read about who get their life savings swindled away on the telephone by some smooth-talking con artist.

"Carrie will have to find another job now, I guess. She can always help me with my research. I've told her that before. Not forever, but in the interim."

"I don't think she wants to," I said dully.

His pipe went out and he relit it, making the bowl glow. "No, I don't believe so," he said with a wistful, flickering smile. I looked at him curiously. He pulled on his pipe and stared off at nothing.

An owl hooted; not the homey hoo-hoo one, but the one that sounds like somebody gasping or hissing, that eerie, raspy sound that prickles the hair on your arms. I concentrated on the friendlier sound of the traffic in the distance, and the familiar, semihysterical barking of Maisie, the neighbor's dog.

"You think we're like George and Martha?"

"George and Martha?"

"You know, *Who's Afraid of Virginia Woolf*. The old married couple were George and Martha. He was a college professor." She was the college president's daughter, though, so that's where the parallel broke down. I married my George to get out of an old life, but I never learned how to fit into the new one.

George grunted.

"They hated each other," I said. "But they loved each other, too." I let that hang, let the words float in the silence like an invitation. An advance.

George said nothing.

Such a sadness came over me. "Oh, God, what's going to happen?"

He scooted his swing a little closer to mine. Lightly, he patted the side of my thigh.

I picked up his hand and studied it in the meager light. Veiny old hand, wrinkled old hand. Yellow nails that smelled like nicotine. I wanted to lay my cheek against it, but it looked so foreign, like a machine, a device, not quite flesh; the longer I stared at it, the less it even looked like a hand.

I set it on my knee. "Have you been happy?"

"What do you mean?"

"On a scale of one to ten, how would you rate the happiness of your life, George?"

"Oh." He laughed.

"No, I mean it. What would you say? What's your answer?"

He sighed. "Seven."

"Really? Me, too. And here I thought we had nothing in common." We smiled, not looking at each other. We rested our temples against the cool, rusty chains of our side-by-side swings. If we sidled a tiny bit closer, we'd touch.

"Tonight I'm a four, though, George. I'm not doing so hot tonight."

"You had a little too much to drink."

"Maybe. But . . . I wanted something. Some feeling. I don't like this getting old business." I gave a mock shudder. "Hard to believe we used to *celebrate* our birthdays."

He gave my leg a pat and took his hand back to rub the side of his stiff neck. He lit his pipe again.

I didn't even *want* him to talk to me. I outgrew that long ago, the way a child outgrows expecting her stuffed dog to talk back. I just wanted . . . something. Tonight. Some kind of a connection.

"George."

"Hm?"

"You know, you don't have to smoke outside. You can smoke in the house if you want to. I don't mind anymore."

He nodded, looking thoughtful. "I think I'll keep it out here," he said slowly. "It's not so bad. I've gotten used to it."

Down the alley, somebody's garage door groaned before it slammed shut, *crack*, metal on concrete. A nice, final sound. I got up. "Butt hurts. I'm going in."

"I'll be in in a minute."

"Okay."

"Happy birthday," he called.

"Thanks."

I went in the empty house by myself. Something I've done a million times before, but tonight it felt like practicing for the future.

18

Good, Good

"Careful, watch his head. Look out for the door!"

"I got it, I got it. He's fine." The tinge of exasperation in Mr. Green's voice was what clued me in to the possibility that I was being a pain in the ass. Nobody was more even-tempered than Mr. Green.

"I can probably get the rest," I told him, "I just needed you for the big ones. Well—if you could help me with the polar bear, that would be great. Then go, you must have a thousand things to do."

Good humor restored, Mr. Green stood back to admire his placement of the giraffe, eleven and a half feet tall, against the sunny side of the ark barn. We were moving the animals outside so Eldon Pletcher could look at them in natural light. Landy and Jess were taking him to the river this morning to see the almost-finished ark; then he was coming here to check out the animals. He'd be here any minute.

"Looks good," Mr. Green said. High praise—he thought the whole ark project was ridiculous. But he regularly attended a church called the Solemn Brethren of the Bleeding Lamb, so I wasn't sure where he got off. I told him that to his face—we had very lively debates; arguments, really. He liked to play devil's advocate even more than I did.

"Do you think Mr. Pletcher will like them?" I asked, eyeing my colorful animal lineup against the wall.

"Oh, sure." I must've looked dubious, because he added kindly, "I bet he'll be real pleased. You don't have a thing to worry about." He gave me a bracing pat on the back, and I realized I was twisting my hands together. "Which one do you like best?" he asked.

"Me?" I liked them all. I loved them all. Which wasn't to say I wouldn't have loved a chance to do every one of them over again. "I don't know, which one do you?"

He glanced over the double rows of cutout kangaroo, cheetah, porcupine, llama, panda, ferret, goat. "What's that one?" he asked, pointing.

Uh-oh. "Can't you tell?"

He scrunched up his leathery face, peering. "Anteater?"

"Yes!" Relief. "That's your favorite?"

"No, this is. I think. This here donkey."

"Really? How come?"

"'Cause of his face. Looks like one we had when I was a kid, name of Larry. Patient as the day is long. Something about the eyes," he said, going closer. "Just something restful in his eyes. How many more you got to do before D day?"

Mr. Green called our May seventeenth launch D day. "Not too many. I really think we're going to make it. If nothing goes wrong." Like Eldon Pletcher telling me to start over.

"Good thing you got fired, eh?"

He thought he was being funny, but that was something I said to myself about three times a day. Thank you so much, Brian, for turning out to be an ass.

"So you can haul out the rest of the stuff, you think? I'll get on with some chores if you don't need me." He touched his cap.

"Go—thank you. I'm not taking them all out anyway, just some. And Jess can help me put them back. You'll never have to touch another animal again."

He laughed and called back, "You mean until D day!"

We would rent a moving van on the day of the sailing to transport the animals to the river; Mr. Green would help roll them out to the dock, up the ramp, and onto the ark. My job was arranging them around the railings on the first and second decks, for maximum visibility. A simple task, you might think, tall in back, small in front. But a museum curator couldn't have taken her assignment more seriously than I did. After all the work we'd done, I wanted the display to be perfect.

We expected a crowd, but no one could predict how big it might be. The ark story had been picked up in papers as far away as Charlotte and Baltimore. Reporters had called me for interviews. They'd called Jess, too, and of course Landy. I'd gotten Eldon's approval and finally done one, on the Remington College radio station. The only sticky moment came when the interviewer, a perky junior named Marcy, asked me if I considered myself a creationist. I went into an explanation about the purity of self-expression and how the art I was doing was apolitical and not religious in itself—and Marcy interrupted to ask, "So you'd say what you're doing is art?" with an unflattering inflection. I folded and said, well, not fine art, but certainly graphic art, yes, I did believe I was making a kind of illustrative art, and people were free to call it anything they liked.

She must've thought she was getting us back on surer ground when she switched to the topic of how essentially silly it all was, the idea of a modern-day ark. Of course I agreed with her—and yet I heard myself getting defensive on Eldon's behalf, and especially Landy's. I told her about how, just last year, a team of deep-sea explorers found an ancient, undisturbed beach on the floor of the Black Sea, and geologists from Columbia University were pretty sure it was the proof that a sudden, catastrophic flood had occurred about seven thousand years ago. Noah's flood. Marcy said, "Huh," politely but knowingly, and wrapped up.

It felt strange to be so firmly and obviously on the wrong side of a public controversy. Or at any rate, the side I would never have taken under any circumstances except these surpassingly peculiar ones. I wasn't a very effective spokesperson for the religious right. A fact about myself I could truthfully say I'd never expected to regret.

Jess, on the other hand, was relishing all the odd, skewed ambiguities of the situation, the strange-bedfellows syndrome, he called it. Sailing an ark was a phenomenon, he said, a wonder, a spectacle, something you did because you could. I should try harder not to put people into categories, he recommended. "Is Landy a good friend? Is his father dying? Are we hurting anyone?" And the most compelling question: "Is this making you feel better?"

If not for the opposition of my immediate family, I could answer yes to that without misgivings. Ruth's ridicule had hardened to hostility, though, and my mother was still fomenting resistance on the grounds of good taste. In spite of their unhappiness with me, I was, for some reason, happy when I was doing the work. I hadn't had time to ask myself why—I hadn't had time to do anything but make animals! And maybe that was the answer. Maybe it was that simple.

At least my mother couldn't throw irresponsibility in my face. Eldon had come through—he was paying me almost as much as Brian had at the Other School. Ruth pointed out that my hours were twice as long, but that was a gross exaggeration. I said if something excited and consumed and invigorated you, how could it be a bad deal? She didn't see it that way. So I muzzled my enthusiasm and tried to hide my long hours from her, leaving for Jess's after she went to school, getting home just before she did from Krystal's. Come to think of it, that was the same way I used to try to hide from her how much I was sleeping after Stephen died. I could see this wasn't healthy, but I didn't have *time* to fix it. If I'd had *time* I would've insisted on mutual frankness, I would've scheduled long, nonconfrontational truth sessions, tried harder to explain myself, made compromises. In less than three weeks the ark would sail, the flap would die down, and life would go back to normal. Surely Ruth and I could safely misunderstand each other for three more weeks. And I was planning on a big emotional letdown at the end—that ought to cheer her up.

Around noon, Landy drove up in a huge white station wagon I'd never seen before. Barking dogs immediately swarmed it. Jess and Landy got out on opposite sides and opened the two passenger doors. On Landy's side, a tall, round, white-haired woman in a violet sundress climbed out and looked around, shading her eyes from the sun. On his way around, Landy opened the rear door and took out a folding wheelchair. Jess told his dogs to stop barking. I was surprised when he, not Landy, leaned inside the car and lifted an old man out, holding him in his arms like a child, and gently settled him in the opened wheelchair. It was the woman, Mrs. Pletcher—Viola—who pushed him across the stony driveway and the uneven dirt path toward the barn Jess pointed to. Toward me, as well: I waited in the grassy shade of a tree, directly in their path. It seemed more suitable to greet them there for some reason, lower key, simpler—I don't know. Less as if I were Jess's hostess.

Landy made the introductions, calling his father "Reverend." Mrs. Pletcher and I shook hands, hers rough and strong, and I saw where Landy got his bashful smile. "Reverend Pletcher," I said, bending toward the old gentleman. "I've been looking forward to meeting you."

He had a mouth like a turtle's, the thin lips meeting in a point at the center. When he smiled, large, astonishingly white false teeth glittered and gleamed. "Carrie," he said very softly. I was ready to take my hand back, chagrined when he wouldn't shake it, but at last he unclasped his tight-skinned, discolored fingers from one another and slowly reached his right hand toward mine. His was cool and smooth, fragile feeling, thin as a swatch of twigs. We shook very gently.

I'd been expecting someone coarser, an old wreck of a man, making a deal with death years after he'd replaced degeneracy with fanaticism. Not this pale, parchment-skinned, straight-backed gentleman with soft eyes. It seemed his illness had burned away everything nonessential and left just the core of his dignity and his big, obsessed heart. Looking into the pain and patience in his face, I had an idea why Landy was bound to him, and to his last great folly.

I wasn't what he'd expected, either. "Thought you'd be old," he told me. He rolled one hand over weakly, thumb up, indicating Landy. "Like him." Father and son smiled, to my relief. It was a joke.

"Oh, you put 'em outside," Landy said, catching sight of a reindeer's rump sticking out past the side of the barn.

"Some of them," I said, "not all. I was thinking you might like to see them in the light. The way they'll look on the day."

The skin of Eldon's skull shone pinkish, only a fringe of white hair left at the back. Mrs. Pletcher leaned over him. "Ready to go and look?" He nodded, and I realized as she pushed him away what the light in his eyes and the quick clutch of his hands on the armrests meant. Excitement.

At first I couldn't stand near him, I had to wander off a little, like a film director who has to smoke in the lobby while his movie premieres. Jess came and got me. His knowing look did something to me. He took a light hold of my wrists and tugged. "Come on over. Talk to him. You want him mixing up the wombat and the yak?" I made a face, pretending I was insulted. He moved his hands up my arms, put his thumbs in the hollows of my elbows. "Come and get your reward, Carrie."

"How do you know he'll like them? What if he hates them?"

"Find out."

But I just wanted to stay there with Jess's hands on my arms. Over his shoulder, I saw all three Pletchers stop in front of the high, lunging tiger. The reverend looked almost preppy, more like a retired professor than a tobacco farmer in a cardigan sweater, pressed khaki slacks, and huge blue running shoes. I imagined him meeting my father, having a conversation with him. They would probably like each other.

Mrs. Pletcher rolled him on to the next animal. "Okay," I said, and Jess let go of my arms. Nothing to do then but go hear the verdict.

Reverend Pletcher was smiling—I hoped that meant he liked the prairie dog, not that he was laughing at it. It was only visible from the waist up, if a prairie dog had a waist, its head and paws sticking up over the lip of a brown-painted papier-mâché burrow. "Good," he said. And at the kangaroo, he said, "Good," again, and I showed him the baby in the pouch on the mother's side. "I can paint it out if you think three wouldn't be allowed," I said. "Nothing to it, I can fix it in two seconds. I just wasn't sure. You know, biblically speaking."

He pursed his turtle lips. "Mother?" he said after a minute or two of thoughtful gazing.

"She'd smuggle it on," Mrs. Pletcher said immediately. "If the Lord chose her and she had a little baby, she'd hide it. Just like that."

"Yes . . . but . . ."

"The Lord would know, of course. But He'd turn a blind eye."

Eldon smiled, and that was it. Kangaroo was in.

"Good," he said in front of the moose cutout, the skunk. "Good," he said of the lynx and the ferret. For a preacher, he was a man of very few words. I was spoiled now, greedy for more than "Good." He put his hand out to pet the owl. I'd made him out of store-bought turkey feathers hot glued to sculpted urethane foam, with black phone cable taped to L-shaped coat hanger pieces for his legs, a whittled wooden beak, eyes painted on flat oval stones I found in Jess's driveway. "Good," Reverend Pletcher said, his hand lingering. "It's very . . ." His head wobbled on his cordy neck. He closed his eyes. His wife stroked his shoulder soothingly. "Okay?" she said, and he smacked his lips and nodded.

Oh, he was so weak. I hadn't known. Landy sent me a bracing smile behind his father's back, and I shook off the shock, realizing I must've looked stricken. After that I became morbidly conscious of time passing, of the heat, the sun, the fact that Eldon wore no hat. Why didn't he have a hat? I wanted to cup my hands over his unprotected head, shade him. I hated it whenever his wheelchair hit a bump and jostled him. When he'd looked at all the animals outside, I said, "There are more in the barn, but maybe you've seen enough. It's cool in there, though. Whatever you like."

"Oh," he said, "all." I think it was his teeth that made him sound as if he had something, a lozenge, a Life Saver, on his tongue; they were way too big for his mouth.

"Are you thirsty?" it occurred to me to ask.

"Thirsty?" Mrs. Pletcher echoed, leaning over his shoulder. I started to leave, run for the house for a glass of water, but "We have some here," she said, and took a plastic bottle, the kind cyclists carried on their bikes, from a clip holder at the back of the wheelchair. Eldon covered her hands with his while she held the flexible plastic straw to his lips. After every swallow he said, "Ahh," sweetly appreciative, like a baby.

By the time we finished touring the barn, he was pale and perspiring and no longer erect in his chair, his narrow chest caved in, shoulders curving. "I think we better go," said Mrs. Pletcher, who looked tired, too. She didn't protest when Landy took her place and pushed his father's wheelchair back to the car.

Again, Jess was the one who lifted him up and carefully put him in the backseat of the station wagon. I waited to say good-bye, but when Jess straightened up, he said, "He'd like to talk to you, Carrie." I went closer. The old man smiled up at me, patting the seat on his other side. I walked around the car and got in the backseat beside him.

"First," he said, and paused for breath. The skin around his nose and mouth was a pearly blue-white, nearly transparent. "Good job. I'm so happy."

"Thank you. Thank you."

"You have no faith?"

Landy must have told him. It was true, but I answered, "No religion," to save his feelings.

"Why'd you do it?"

"Why did I make the animals?"

"Not for money."

"No. Well—that helped. I'm not sure why I did it. But I wanted to, from the beginning, as soon as Jess told me. It never seemed crazy to me."

He nodded—as if he knew that about me already. "Know what it means?"

"The ark? I think I do."

"Tell me."

I'd rather he'd have told me. "Rebirth," I plunged in. "Starting over from scratch. Being saved—being chosen." I wasn't going to get into the matter of the destruction of the earth for its sin and corruption; that was his department. "I think it's a symbol of rejuvenation. A new beginning, everything pure and clean."

"New life."

"Yes."

He sighed shallowly and relaxed against the seat, hands going limp at his sides. "That's what I thought."

I blinked at him, realizing it hadn't been a test, but a question. And my fumbling answer had reassured him. "How many more?" he asked.

"How many more do I have to do? About six. We'll make it," I said confidently.

"One thing. The cow."

"The cow? It's wrong?" My pretty Holstein?

"If you have time. For me."

"What? Anything."

"I've always . . . liked a Guernsey. But only if there's time."

"You mean—in addition?" He nodded. "I can do it. Okay, a Guernsey, yes, absolutely. Spotted brown, smaller than a Holstein. I like them, too."

"Pretty faces, I always thought. Had one. When I was a boy." I thought of Mr. Green's donkey. Larry.

"I'll start it right away," I said.

He gave a tickled laugh and twinkled his eyes, charming me. "No. Save it for last."

"Okay. But I'll have time, I promise. I'll make time."

He lifted his frail arms and put them around my neck.

I was so surprised, it was a second or two before I could hug him back. He smelled clean and powdery, like an infant, but under the scratchy sweater his body felt as brittle as an armful of sticks. Every time I thought we would let go, we didn't. I kissed his cheek, trying not to cry, and he kissed mine. We drew away. His grip on my hands was amazingly strong. I said, "See you on the seventeenth," and he smiled.

I waited for him to say *God bless you*, I wanted him to say it. Landy opened the driver's door and started to climb in—no more privacy. *I* was the one who whispered "God bless you" in a panic—and I'd never said it before in my life, not to anyone who hadn't just sneezed. The look on his face was surprised, amused, and triumphant. *Gotcha*, it said, but with love.

Jess couldn't stop for lunch. "You go ahead, Carrie, make something for yourself, but I have to get to work."

"I'll make your lunch," I offered, "and bring it to you. Where will you be?"

"In the small barn. Doing nasty things. If you could just leave me a sandwich on the counter, that would be great."

Nasty things? Like what, castrating a bull? One could only speculate. I made him two sandwiches, one turkey and one cheese, and put them in a paper bag with an apple, a banana, and four cookies. I found a Thermos in the cupboard and filled it with ice water. It was radically uncool to bring your lunch to school, according to Ruth, so I hadn't gone through this packing ritual since Chicago. I noticed I hadn't missed it.

Nasty things, indeed. At first I wasn't even sure what Jess was doing. In the smallest barn, he and Mr. Green had a cow, probably a heifer because she was small, in a sort of double yoke, front and back, and they were—I really couldn't tell. Something to do with reproduction or elimination, or quite possibly both.

"Here's your sandwich," I said, putting the bag on the straw-strewn floor. Two cats zipped over to investigate; I picked it up and set it on top of a post. "Mr. Green, I didn't bring you anything."

"Already ate," he said, closing the top of a smoking metal tank at his feet. "Thanks anyway. Liquid nitrogen," he explained—I must've looked curious. "Keeps your bull sperm frozen."

"Oh, I see. So you're doing, um, you're impregnating her?"

"Yup."

"Ah. And yet . . ." I could've sworn Jess had one of his long-gloved arms up the poor cow's *rear end*.

Mr. Green caught his eye and winked, then handed him a long, thin tube with a rubber bulb on the end. "Ready," Mr. Green said, and took hold of the cow's tail so it had to quit swatting Jess in the chest with it. Quickly but carefully, Jess inserted the tube into what I assumed was the cow's vagina, while he did something with his impaled hand; his shoulder moved subtly and his face took on an even more concentrated look. Slowly he squeezed the rubber bulb. Then everything came out, tube, arm, and cow from her bonds. Jess led her into a stall and she went docilely enough, but I couldn't help thinking her heifer face looked indignant.

"I just have one question," I said faintly. "What is the point, um . . . why do you have to use *two* hands?"

Mr. Green, who seemed to be enjoying himself, said, "You got to go in the other way first to get aholt of her cervix. Got to grab it just right through the rectal wall and tip it. Jess here is a expert."

"Is he." How interesting. "So now . . . is she pregnant?"

"We won't know for a few weeks," Jess said, frowning as he wrote something on a clipboard.

"This is her first time," Mr. Green offered, "so she might not settle."

"Did she ever meet the father of her child?" I asked.

"Nope. S'pose to be a sweet little Angus. You want to breed a new girl to a little guy her first time out, so her calf'll be small. We'll just see now, Sophie, won't we? We'll just see what happens." Mr. Green reached over the rail and slapped Sophie affectionately on the behind. "Who's next?"

"Two-forty-one," Jess said. "Carlene."

"Carlene!" He went off to get her. I'd never seen Mr. Green so animated before. Either he really liked artificially inseminating cows or he was having some fun at my expense.

"You look a little green," Jess noted while he thawed a tube of something, presumably bull semen, in a pail of ice water.

"Me? Oh no, I'm fine."

"Going to stick around a while, then?"

"Well, I probably should get to work. Eldon says he wants a Guernsey."

"I heard." We smiled at each other.

"Did he like the ark, Jess?"

"He did. Very, very much."

"He loved the animals, too."

"I know."

Mr. Green came back with Carlene, who was huge, definitely not a new girl. I made a short speech about how much work I had to do in the other barn, and escaped.

But I couldn't concentrate. I leafed through my cow calendars and cow books, looking for just the right Guernsey, then remembered what Eldon had said about waiting till the end. Good idea: I might've had enough of cows for one day. But I couldn't keep my mind on my wild boar cutout, either. I felt restless and keyed up. I caught myself pacing. I wanted to be sad about Eldon and happy about the ark project *with* someone, and there wasn't anyone. Plus I wasn't dressed right, I felt awkward and hampered in the straight skirt I'd worn for the Pletchers' visit. And it was *beautiful* outside, the most perfect spring afternoon. What I really wanted was to be with Jess, and he had his arm up a cow's butt.

Hopeless. Finally I gave up and went outside. If I couldn't work, I should just go home. I could clean the house, which was an absolute wreck; I could make Ruth a real meal for a change, not a slapped-together casserole or last-minute microwaved leftovers. I could go visit my mother. I'd been avoiding her, because she didn't like me much these days. She was mad at me for something I hadn't even done yet.

Yet?

I went for a walk. One of Jess's dogs followed me, Tracer, the smart one. We took the dirt lane that zigzagged uphill for half a mile and deadended in a high, empty meadow. Wild apple trees bloomed in a tangle along the edge; I found one with a smooth trunk and a rockless, rootless base and sat down under it. Below me, a deep-cut creek, blue-brown with the sky's reflection, meandered between Jess's farm and Landy's, forming the boundary in some places. A tributary of the Leap, it came close to drying up in the hot summer, but today it almost overflowed its steep-sided banks. Cows, nearly indistinguishable from boulders at this distance, sprawled under a cover of early willows arched over the creek like chartreuse awnings. Birds chirped, bees buzzed, grasshoppers hopped. Tracer ran off and left me for a more interesting adventure in the meadow. Was I prejudiced or was Jess's farm prettier than Landy's? Landy's stony fields didn't slope as gracefully. His cows didn't look as contented. Even the color of Jess's fields was sweeter, a mellower yellow-green: gold ochre and chrome oxide. Jess had the Italy of farms, I decided. Landy had the Ukraine.

Everything was Jess today, I couldn't get him off my mind. Burgeoning, bursting, swelling, stirring spring didn't help, either. Ruth had taught me a meditation of Krystal's involving the repetition of the phrase "Who am I?" on slow, calming exhales. You were supposed to answer, *I'm a woman,* or *I'm a mother,* then contemplate those responses in a deeply relaxed, nonjudgmental way. When I'd tried it, I'd gotten stuck on *I'm tired,* and *I'm late. I'm wasting valuable time here.* Still, it might be worth a second try, to calm my mind. Get Jess out of it. I slumped lower on my tree trunk, closed my eyes, clasping my hands lightly over my diaphragm. Breathe in, breathe out. *Who am I? Who the hell am I?*

I fell asleep.

Only for a few minutes, but long enough to wake up cranky from a confusing dream about thrashing palm fronds in a rain forest or a jungle. I stood up and brushed the dirt and grass off my skirt, rolled the crick out of my neck. Might as well go home.

I went in Jess's house first for a glass of water. In the kitchen, fresh coffee perked in the machine on the counter. I walked out to the hall and listened, and presently I heard Jess's voice coming from his office. I poured myself half a cup of coffee and drank it while I waited for him, staring out the kitchen window. He needed to pay attention to his flower garden if he wanted his perennials to grow higher than his weeds this year. Me, too; my garden at home looked like the seediest corner of a vacant lot. But at least we would get an ark launched, and that's what counted.

Tired of waiting, I poured another cup of coffee and carried it down the hall to his study. He was sitting on the edge of his desk, talking on the phone to someone about fertilizer—I assumed; I heard "nitrogen content" and "percent potassium." He smiled at me when I handed him his coffee. I stood in front of him. We looked into each other's eyes while he said, "Yes, but I need it now, I can't wait till the end of next week. Well, that would be great. If you can—right. I'd appreciate it." He still had on his barn clothes, but his face and hair were damp, shirtsleeves rolled over his elbows, as if he'd just had a wash. I smelled soap, hay, cow, coffee. What would he do, I wondered, if I put my hand on his jaw, or touched his neck? Pulled on his ear?

I kept my hands to myself. But when I sat down on the arm of the easy chair in front of the desk, I crossed my bare legs slowly to see if he'd look at them. He did.

After he hung up, he sipped coffee for a while without talking. I couldn't decide if it was a comfortable silence or not. "What's up?" he said eventually. "I thought you were working."

"Couldn't seem to make any headway. Restless, I don't know why. What are you doing?"

"Phone calls. Business."

"You have a strange job," I said.

"Do I?"

"Maybe not. Part of it's earthy, part of it's not."

"Most of it is."

"I'm sad, Jess," I said. "I didn't know I'd like Eldon so much."

"I know."

"He's so frail. What if he can't make it to the seventeenth? Poor Landy."

He bowed his head and nodded, rubbing the heel of his hand down the long muscle in his thigh. "They'll sail the ark anyway, Landy says. No matter what happens."

"I'm glad." But what if Eldon thought his salvation depended on sailing it while he was alive? What if he was convinced that, by not fulfilling his promise to God on time, he'd doomed himself? "Good people are too hard on themselves," I said.

Jess smiled. "Sometimes. Landy says his father's got a lot to repent."

I resisted that. I didn't want to imagine Eldon as a great sinner, a man who could do damage to his family out of selfishness or thoughtlessness, or worse. Not that sweet old man.

Jess looked at the clock on his desk.

"How's Sophie?" I asked, to keep him.

"Resting comfortably."

"Do you ever breed them the natural way?"

"Sometimes. Landy's got a bull stud who's sire to about forty of my herd, one way or another."

"He told me he can't stand to ship his cattle." *Ship*; that was a euphemism for sending them to market—which was a euphemism for butchering. "I remember how you used to hate it, too. Do you still?"

"Yes."

"But you do it."

"Sure. Well. Mostly. If you don't count Martha."

"Martha?"

"She's twenty-six."

"No!"

"She quit giving milk about thirteen years ago, but I couldn't ship her. Would've been like killing my elderly aunt."

"So you put her out to pasture. Did I ever meet Martha?"

"I don't remember. She wasn't famous then, she was just a cow."

"How long can they live?"

"Twenty-eight, thirty. That's if you treat 'em like goddesses." He picked up his cup, set it down when he remembered it was empty.

"Want some more coffee? I'll get it."

He crossed his arms, looked at me curiously. "What's behind this urge to take care of me today?"

"Sorry. Didn't mean to hover." I stood up, a little hurt. I wanted him to say, "No, I like it," or something, but he just looked at me. "What time do you have to start milking?" I asked.

"Four. Same as every day."

The clock said 2:20. How did you make a move on a man you'd said *no* to so many times, he'd quit asking? *No* had become our theme song; over the years we'd learned to dance to it with a certain amount of grace. How could I tell Jess now, out of the blue, that I wanted a new song?

I couldn't, of course. You had to lead up to something like that slowly; you dropped girlish hints; you flirted. You changed the temperature gradually, so nobody's system went into shock.

"What if you had an emergency right now," I said. "So you couldn't do your phone calls or your business. Would anything terrible happen?"

"No. Why?"

"I don't know, I just thought—maybe you needed to relax." My God, I sounded like a call girl. This was completely wrong; I pushed the whole idea out of my head and changed tacks. "Sometime when you're not busy, would you like to go out to dinner? With me?"

What was he thinking? The outline of him seemed to get sharper, better defined, more distinct from the desk and the wall behind him, like a bas relief. He steepled his fingers in front of his face, hiding his mouth and nose. "Yes."

"Good. Then sometime we should do that."

I was on my feet, I had delivered my exit line. But instead of leaving I said, "Do you miss being married? Not—I don't mean do you miss Bonnie, but do you miss having someone? To be with?"

"Yes."

"I always wondered what broke you up."

"You know what broke us up."

"I do? No, I don't."

"Carrie, what's going on?"

"Hmm?"

"Why did you bring me lunch? Coffee. Why did you show me your legs?"

I blushed. I considered getting huffy—*I have no idea what you're talking about*—but I said, "I don't know what's going on," truthfully. I was full of wanting him, I was bursting out of my skin with it, and I had no idea how to tell him.

"Are you . . . lonely? Is that what this is about?" He said it *kindly*.

"'Is that what this is about?'" I repeated, laughing. Now I *was* insulted. "Does the widow need a little consoling, you mean? The answer's no." I moved away. "I'm not lonely, not at all. But thanks for asking. As a matter of fact, I can't remember when I've been less lonely. I really don't need a thing."

I stopped at the door to the hall, keeping my back to him. "Oh God, I'm just so bad at this."

"What?"

"No practice, that's the problem."

"Bad at what?" He sounded baffled. But hopeful.

"Telling you I'm ready," I said, turning around. "But I'm not lonely, honestly, not anymore—I don't know why. I don't need you, I just want you. There—you said to say it in words." But now I'd panicked myself. I was afraid he'd touch me, afraid he wouldn't.

He did neither.

"*Did you just look at your watch?*"

He laughed, a glad, real sound. "Sorry." Still laughing, he came and put his arms around me. Kissed me. Held me, pressed me against the wall, put his hands on me. Happy ending.

Was it like high school, the dark, electric-smelling utility room? Maybe; because I thought of it, I made the association. And there was a familiarity in the feel of him that I wasn't prepared for, I thought everything would be new, strange. Molecularly speaking, doesn't the human body change completely every—so many years? I didn't expect our bodies to recognize each other. "It's the same, isn't it?" I said between long, deepening kisses, but he said, "No, it's completely different." So I don't know.

A little later, I caught him sneaking another glance at his watch, behind my shoulder. "Look, if I'm keeping you from something . . ."

"I have to make a call. Two seconds."

He left me to call and ask if a Mr. Turnbull could come to the farm tomorrow afternoon instead of today, same time. He must've said yes, because Jess thanked him profusely.

"Who was that?"

"A.I. tech."

Artificial insemination technician. "And his name is Turnbull?" Everything was so funny. We laughed our way up the stairs and into Jess's room, and I was so relieved when it wasn't his old bedroom, the one I used to do my homework in. Glad too when it wasn't his parents' big, gloomy room, still cluttered with dark, old-fashioned furniture. Jess's room was the old sleeping porch at the back of the house; he'd enclosed it and added wide, ceiling-high windows. I could see a silver ribbon of the Leap through tree leaves at the bottom of the long, grassy flood plain.

"This room isn't ugly," I said, feigning surprise, glancing around at the plain oak dressers, the sturdy bed—unmade; manly navy sheets in a tangle—both bedside tables covered with magazines and books. "What went wrong?"

"Hmm. Guess I thought your mother would never come up here."

We took off each other's clothes like brand-new lovers, smiling and reverent, practically glowing from gladness. Underneath the excitement, it felt like coming home. I don't know why I wasn't more self-conscious, why I wasn't paralyzed with nerves. The familiarity again, I think. Not a sense that this had happened before; more a feeling that it should have. I did mind that my naked body was twelve years older than the last time Jess had seen it. But he didn't. He told me I was beautiful, so fervently that I believed him. How it was to be with him came back to me quickly, and the best was the way he could make me feel that nothing I did was wrong or clumsy or tentative or silly. With Jess I was lovely, I was a pretty fish gliding through water, all certainty and grace.

He was what I knew he would be, passionate and tender, undisguised. Lost. "I promise not to leave in the middle this time," I whispered to him—in the middle. Questionable timing for a joke, but if we were both remembering our last time together, I thought, we might as well speak of it. Dig it up and disarm it.

It took him a moment to react at all; I could actually see his eyes clear, shift from absent to present, and I remembered that that absorption, that mindless departure into the nothing of sensation was one of the things that had frightened me away from him so long ago. I was a girl then, I couldn't lose myself the way Jess could—that was a goal to spend your life chasing. At least I wasn't afraid of it anymore.

"I wouldn't let you this time," he said, poised above me, his hair backlit, a coppery halo. "That's been the problem, me letting you go." He didn't smile; he wasn't joking. Could that be true, could it really be that simple—the "problem"? I wanted to talk to him almost as much as I wanted to make love to him. And then I wanted to paint him.

In patches of nostalgia, I remembered what it was like to lie in bed with a man, the thrill of someone else's ceiling, a different scent on the pillow, another slant of light from unfamiliar windows. My mind drifted to old lovers—not to Stephen, but men I knew before I knew him. No one in particular; just the sensation of newness, excitement, what it was like to be naked for the first time with a naked man, the lawless, liberating feel of skin on skin, the sense of boundless physical possibility.

It was like that with Jess, and then it was more. Everything between us multiplied, compounded, like mirrors reflecting us in the present, and then an infinite number of diminishing images of our past. We had now, and we had everything that had happened before between us. The most extraordinary combination. Exactly the same and completely different—we were both right.

Afterward, I lay with my head on his chest, listening to his heart beat, feeling his hand in my hair. Our heavy, wordless silence felt right for a time, the only appropriate response to what had just happened. But I was impatient. I wanted answers to all the tantalizing whys—why did he love me, why did he like sleeping with me, why did he pick me and no one else. And how could he want me again after the last time, after *all* the other times I'd disappointed him?

"If it only rains every twelve years, you don't curse it when it finally comes," he said. "You curse the drought."

An analogy. My farmer, my cow herder, my dairyman made a metaphor about *me*. I sank in deeper, seeded in love, planted. "But why did you ever even *like* me?" I was recalling the eighteen-year-old virgin, the overachiever, mama's girl.

He said the nicest things—that I was brave, I had a loving heart, I was kind to him, I liked him even though I didn't understand him. "Caution" ruled me in the end—that was the word he used, *caution*—but by then it was too late, he said, he already loved me.

"It's not wrong to want to please everybody, Carrie. It doesn't work, but it doesn't make you a bad person."

No, just a weak one. But the last thing I wanted to talk to Jess about right now was my mother.

"I always knew you loved me," I said. "It was a secret I tried to hide from myself, but I couldn't, I kept it with me all through the years. I can't imagine my life now without it. Such a gift."

I wanted to know about his wife, but I wouldn't ask. In fact, I wanted to hear about *all* the women in his life, and I wanted him to place me among them. I would've liked a chart, frankly, a detailed graph of the hierarchy of all Jess's women, with me at the tip-top. Not because I was that needy and insecure—I just felt like celebrating. Doing a dance on top of the pyramid.

"Remember when you told me I needed to do the ark animals? And I didn't believe you. You said, 'You *need* this,' and I just laughed. How could you have known that, Jess? Because it's true,"

I felt comfortable telling him, "I did need it, and it *saved* me. All I had before was Ruth to be alive for. The same way . . ." The same way my mother only had me to be alive for. God help her.

"People are like sheepdogs," he said, but his straight face crumpled when I raised up on my elbow to gape at him. "It's true. A sheepdog isn't happy unless he's herding. That's his one and only job, that's his work. You weren't doing your job, but now you are and you feel better. That's why you're here with me right now."

"But what is my job? Making giraffes?"

"Making something. Maybe it doesn't matter what."

"Yeah. No," I realized, "it does matter. It can't be just for me—it has to be more than stenciling wallpaper or refinishing the furniture." Hooking rugs. Shudder. "But I don't know what, and when this is over I don't know what I'll do."

"You'll find out."

"What happened to me? I lost my artist's eye, I forgot how to see. Once—I did a self-portrait out of all the numbers that defined me, my Social Security number, telephone, address, my birth date. For nothing, just for myself. I used to do collages, I did contour drawings, conceptual art, I did rubbings of textures, like—sidewalks and tree bark, bricks. I tried to paint an emotion. I made *connections* between things, I could see sculptures in tree limbs, I could see Renaissance Madonnas in fruit, I could *see*. But then I lost it, I went to sleep. I never thought I'd get it back."

"Your sheep."

"My herd. I got my work back." I moved over him, began to kiss him passionately. "I'm not saying I'm any good—that's a different subject." I wanted him, but I couldn't stop talking. "But I know what I'm supposed to do now. In general, not specifically. Jess, Jess. You are so . . . mmm. Do you have other girlfriends? Do you like my hair short? You've never said."

Well, we'd talk later. Those were reminders; I stuck them in like stick-on notes before Jess shut me up by kissing me back. We made love again, slowly, and so sweetly it made me cry. And it worked this time, and it didn't remind me of anything.

Then it was time to go. "Four o'clock, you have to milk cows." This was going to be a challenging affair, I could see. A daytime affair. "At least it's spring," I said, watching him dress. God, he was good to look at. "Warm. I'm looking forward to a lot of outdoor trysts. Rolls in the hay." I tried a lewd wink, not difficult considering I was flat on my back where he'd left me, naked and uncovered.

"I like your hair," he said, pulling his T-shirt over his head. He looked different to me, more substantial or something. His whole body was real now, not a rumor.

"You never mentioned it. So naturally I assumed you hated it."

"I didn't know what I was allowed to say. I couldn't tell what the new rules were."

"You didn't used to have any rules."

"I changed." He smiled.

"Is that my fault? Do you blame me?"

"I used to. Now I try not to blame anyone for anything about myself."

A model I should try to follow more often. "Anyway," I said, privately defensive, "I don't think you've changed that much. It's more that you've adapted. Really. You're not your house, Jess."

"It doesn't matter. Everybody changes."

But he was sadder, quieter, he'd grown more discreet. I knew some who would say he had room for a little discretion, that curbing his impulsive ways was just part of growing up. I didn't agree with them, now or twenty years ago. Jess had changed because of me—that wasn't ego, it was the truth. But I couldn't despair, even if part of him was lost, because under it all, older, wiser, sadder, gentler, stronger, he really was still Jess. Still mine.

"I might fall asleep," I said, stretching, showing off. What a long time it had been since I'd felt any sexual power at all. You didn't know what you'd missed until you got it back.

"Not for long." His socks had holes in the heels. He pulled on his work boots and tied the laces in knots instead of bows because they were both broken. He needed taking care of! This just got better and better.

"Not for long?"

"Just a catnap."

"Why, are you kicking me out? Got another girl coming at five?"

"Heh heh." He leaned over me. He put his hand on my stomach. His whiskers felt prickly on the skin between my breasts. "Got you coming at five, play your cards right."

"Oh, you're coming back," I said, thrilled. And already the puns were starting, the lovely, corny sex jokes. I could've died from happiness.

"I've got to talk to Mr. Green for a few minutes, get the boys started with the milking. Don't you go away."

"Don't you worry." I sat up when he turned to look at me from the doorway. "Mr. Green's going to know, isn't he?"

"Probably, unless I make something up. Want me to?"

"No, I don't care. Not at all. But . . ."

"Other people."

"Some other people. Ruth. Especially." No need to mention my mother; she was a given.

"Will she hate this?"

"I honestly don't know. Ruth loves you, Jess, but I don't think she's ready for this."

"She's loyal to Stephen."

"Yes. Very. More than that, though. It's a funny age," I tried to explain. "She's using you to grow up. Sometimes you're her father, sometimes you're her friend. And sometimes, more than a friend."

"I know that. I've tried to be careful."

Of course he knew that. I wanted to tell him then that I loved him. The feeling was on me, strong as a flood. What was the barrier? Habit, I decided, listening to the fall of his footsteps on the stairs, the opening and closing of a door. Habit and caution. Jess wasn't the only one who had grown discreet in his old age. But our lives had taken a turn, and by some miracle we were back at the tricky place that had confounded us—me—years ago. Only an idiot would pass up a second chance.

19

Not That I Care

We're supposed to be keeping journals for English. Mrs. Fitzgerald says to write in them every day, preferably first thing in the morning before our censoring brains wake up, so what we say will be freer, like an extension of our dreaming selves, or failing that, right before going to sleep because sometimes the tired mind is as uninhibited as the just-awake one, so it's the same thing.

Yeah, right. I don't have time to eat breakfast in the morning, much less jot down Deep Thoughts, and at night I might get two sentences down before I fall asleep. I think I've got sleeping sickness. It's like the opposite of insomnia. What is that, somnia? I'll ask Krystal. Anyway, I do like writing in my journal, but the only time I can fit it in—and we have to show Mrs. Fitzgerald, she goes down the rows on Fridays to see how our notebooks are filling up; she doesn't read what we've written but she looks to see if there are pages with words on them—so I guess you *could* copy the newspaper or a book or something into your notebook to fool her, but I don't know anybody who's doing that—the only time I can fit it in is when I'm in class. So instead of paying attention in math, say, or biology, I'm writing in my journal, and Mr. Tambor and Ms. Reedy just think I'm taking notes. It's cool.

What's hard about writing in a journal is always having in the back of your mind the thought that somebody besides you is reading it. (Which could happen—Brad Leavitt left his journal on the bus and Linda Morrissy, a sophomore, found it and brought it to Mrs. Fitzgerald the next day, who gave it back to Brad. So that's a minimum of two people who could've read Brad's journal, not to mention potentially Linda Morrissy's entire family and all her friends, plus Mrs. Fitzgerald's friends and her husband and her college student son, and all her son's friends. *Time*, we see, is the only limiting factor.) Anyway, Mrs. Fitzgerald says the only way to get over feeling self-conscious is to write down some embarrassing things about yourself. Don't embellish them, don't let yourself come off as the hero or the innocent victim, just spit it out, something really stupid you did or said, and don't censor it. (But then really make sure you don't leave your notebook on the bus.)

I've been practicing that. The hard part is deciding what to pick among all the humiliating possibilities. So much to choose from. Once I wrote, "I used to stand in front of the bathroom mirror with the door open and pretend the laughter and applause from a program on TV downstairs was for me. I was a famous, beloved performer, and everybody in the audience clapped and laughed uproariously just at my facial expressions, they were so hilarious. I practiced looking surprised and humble during long bursts of applause."

That's the kind of thing that gets you warmed up. You get over being paranoid about confessing something like that, and then you can start writing the real stuff. Like, "I hate my mother. Who's not even my mother anymore, she's turned into some completely different person. It's like the aliens snatched her, implanted a chip in her brain, and sent her back down, and now she's just impersonating herself. She's doing a really shitty job, too."

School sucks. Caitlin is definitely making it with Donny Hartman now, so she and Jamie have, like, circled the wagons and I'm not allowed in, like it's too huge a deal to be a three-way secret. Meanwhile, I am so not interested. I've always known they were better friends with each other than with me. But when I first moved here from Chicago they were having one of their breaks from each other and I got to know Jamie first, then Caitlin after they made up. So I was always the third wheel, which was okay until now, when I'm not much of a wheel at all. I'm getting to be pretty good friends with Becky Driver, but even she has people she's known about a hundred years longer than me.

Raven at least is talking to me again. Except what he's talking to me about is suicide, so that's not too cheerful. Not *his* suicide, just in general, I mean, I'm not worried he'll jump off a bridge or anything. We went to the movies once, but I don't know if it was a date because I just met him at the theater on a Friday after work and we sat with a bunch of other kids from school. We held hands while we watched, but then Mark Terry and Sharon Waxman drove me home because they live nearer. Figure that one out. Not that I care.

So school is a wasteland and even work is sort of boring these days—and *then*, then I get home at six-thirty after a long, hard day and I'm tired and hungry and maybe in the mood for a couple of laughs and some chitchat, a little human contact, not much but some, you know, to keep up the pretense that in my house there still lives an actual family—but what do I get? Nada, because there's nobody home. The house feels shut up, like nobody lives there—I told Mom we should rent it out to crackheads during the day, that way we'd at least get some money from it, and they wouldn't leave it any messier than it already is. All she can say is, "It's temporary." Everything is supposedly going back to normal in one week, when the stupid ark sails.

I wish it was tomorrow. It's getting worse, it's *all* she can talk about—should the horse be a palomino or a regular reddish brown one, wouldn't it be neat if it rained on the seventeenth, should Jess paint the ark white or a color or not at all, and on and on, like I'm somebody who cares. She didn't like it when I told her the first thing Noah did when he landed on land—this is in the Bible—was to get out, build an altar, and sacrifice some animals. Too bad for that species! Instant extinction! She keeps saying she's almost finished, but she gets home later and later every night, and she's so *weird*, either really quiet and off in her own little world or else laughing and talking like she's high, and trying to make *me* happy by telling dumb jokes or tickling me or saying let's go get ice cream—and that's almost worse because it's, like, nothing to do with me, I'm just the one who happens to be there, and whatever mood she's in I'm the one it gets inflicted on.

What if I died? What if the house caught on fire when I was in it and she was out? What if I was asleep and she was the only one who could've saved me, but she was over at Jess's making aardvarks? When she came home she'd turn into our street, wondering what all the fire engines were doing there, why all the flashing lights, who the ambulance was for. The closer she got to our house, the scareder she'd get. And then she'd see it—the stretcher with the body on it in the front yard, the sheet pulled up over the face. The cops would try to hold her back, but she'd break free and throw herself on top of it. "My baby!" I'd have died of smoke inhalation, not burns, so my face would still look nice. In fact I would look very peaceful and beautiful. Mom would completely break down. She'd be ruined.

Sometimes I go over to Modean's after work and play with the baby. It's better than starting my homework or trying to figure out what's for dinner when Mom hasn't left me a clue. Modean always talks to me, asks me about school and work, how my life's going. She bought an aromatherapy kit at Krystal's, and once she let me do an essential oils treatment on her. She said it was great, she wants to do it again sometime. She's a really great mother. Harry's going to grow up without any hang-ups at all, he'll be like the poster child for good parenting. Unlike me, the poster child for neglect.

I call up Gram sometimes and we talk about how stupid the ark is. She's definitely on my side. "Is your mother home yet?" she says, and I'll say, "No," and she goes, "I'm coming over there right now and making your dinner. It's seven o'clock!" But Mom always strolls in around then, so Gram never actually comes over, at least not so far. I wish she would. Wouldn't Mom be embarrassed?

If I just had my driver's license, this wouldn't be happening. It wouldn't feel like solitary confinement around here because I could get out anytime I wanted, like being in prison but with the door open. I told Gram it's like time stopped and I'll *never* get older than fifteen and three-quarters. She said wait till I'm her age and see what I think about time.

What I should do is report Mom. She's starting to get famous, ha-ha, in Clayborne because of the ark; they did a front-page story on her and Jess in the *Morning Record*, and also a feature in the Richmond paper, about how wonderfully zany and nutty it is that they're doing this and what inspired them and blah blah, it was like *gag me*, I could hardly read the articles. So what I should do is call up child welfare and turn her in for neglect. Then you'd have some headlines! "Ark Lady Cruel to Latch-Key Daughter." "Ark Artist Implores Court to Keep Child, But Loses." They'd put me with a kind, loving foster family. She wouldn't even be allowed to visit. No—she could visit, but only an hour a week, and she'd spend the whole time crying. I'd be nice to her, but then it would be time to go back to my foster family. She'd promise to reform and be the best mother ever, but the court would say I had to stay with the foster family until I was eighteen. Then it would be time for college. She'd have missed the best years of my life, and she'd have only herself to blame.

That's better than the house-fire fantasy. It's more grown-up, plus I'm alive at the end. I think I'll put it in my journal.

20

Giveaway Intimacies

Chris called while I was baby-sitting for Harry at my house on Saturday afternoon.

"Carrie, hi! How are you?"

"I'm so glad you called," I said, shifting the baby to my other hip and getting a better grip on the phone. "I've been wanting to call you for weeks." I heard relief in her big, braying laugh, and knew I'd said just the right thing. "In fact I was going to call you today or tomorrow, Chris, I really was—"

"Oh, sure."

"No, I was! Because the crunch is finally over and I've got some time to breathe. It's been so crazy, honestly, you can't believe how hectic."

"No, I do believe it. I've been reading about you in the paper."

"Oh, God."

"You're a famous person."

"Famous lunatic. Anyway, it's all over but the sailing, and that's the day after tomorrow."

"Yep, and we'll be there, the whole family."

"You're kidding."

"Absolutely not! We wouldn't miss it for the world."

That was my worst fear and my secret hope, that lots of people would turn out for the launch at Point Park on Monday: an actual crowd. "Well, I'll look for you among the hordes," I joked—sarcastic humor was good for warding off disappointment.

"You sound great, Carrie. You sound a lot better than the last time we talked."

"Do I? Well, I'm feeling pretty good, to tell you the truth."

"I'm glad, that's a relief, because I still feel awful about what happened."

The baby grabbed a fistful of my hair. To distract him, I found his training cup on the counter, still half full of orange juice. "Why should *you* feel bad?"

"I just do. I feel like Betty Currie." We laughed, and it was like old times. "I really miss you," Chris said. "It's dull at work all by myself. I guess it was dull before you came, but I didn't notice."

"I miss you, too."

"God, Carrie. I look at him now. I believe everything you told me, I truly do, and yet—when I look at him, I still can't picture it. I can't believe he'd do such a thing. But I *do* believe it, that's not what I—"

"No, I know exactly what you mean. I couldn't believe it either, the whole time it was happening."

I didn't mean the night Brian mauled me in my front hall, I meant the day he called me into his office and fired me. He did it on a Friday, and he waited till late, after Chris had gone home. I couldn't understand what he was saying at first, I thought it was a joke. I laughed. Then I stopped laughing. "You're serious," I said, staring at him in utter disbelief. "You're firing me." He said, "I don't want to. I *wish* I could keep you," rubbing his hands together with fake boyish nervousness. His forehead was pink and wrinkled with worry, eyes brimming sympathy. *This is the hardest thing I've ever done*, he tried to say with his face, and for half a minute I believed it, actually thought there was some truth in his halting explanation—that I wasn't working out, he really needed somebody with more *personal initiative*, somebody he wouldn't have to give any direction to at all. But when he spread his hands and said, "Almost like a partner, an equal," the truth hit, and I knew he was lying.

"First of all, you don't pay me enough to be a partner," I said—since then I've thought of a dozen much more scathing ways I could've put that. "Brian, why don't you just admit it. This is about that night, isn't it?"

"What night?" The blankness, the absolute incomprehension! I wanted to scream at him, but I knew I'd only feel more humiliated afterward, and he'd still win. All I could do was insult him, inadequately—"You are a complete joke!"—and storm out of his office.

"What *is* it with men?" Chris wailed. "How could he be so stupid, and then be so *mean* about it?"

"But he's never done anything with you, never tried—"

"Never, nothing. Oz asked me that, too, of course, but there's never been anything, not even a hint."

"It's weird."

"It's *weird*. And it's not even so bad that he *tried*, as rotten as that is, it's that he got rid of you afterward! I can't get over that. I'd quit if I could, but I can't."

"No, you can't quit, that wouldn't make any sense."

"That's what Oz says, but I tell you, I feel like it. I'm seeing Brian in a whole new light. I can't trust him anymore, and it changes everything."

"Chris, I'm sorry."

"It's not your fault. If I had something else lined up, you know? Another job to go to. But right now we really need the money, and I feel like I'm stuck."

Harry threw his cup on the floor and shrieked in my ear.

"Modean had to go out, so I've got Harry for a couple of hours. As you can tell, it's lunchtime."

"Oh, okay. Well, see you Monday, then. At the launch."

"You're really coming?"

"Of course!"

"What a pal."

"Listen, now that you're unemployed again, you want to have lunch or something? I could meet you. Away from the office—so you'd never have to see *him*."

"I'd love it. How about next week?"

We made the arrangements, and after we hung up I thought, *There*. One good thing had come out of the Other School—my friendship with Chris. Even Brian couldn't ruin that.

"Where'll it be, big guy, your place or mine? Yours," I decided, eyeing my just-cleaned kitchen floor. If I fed the baby here, I'd have to wash it again afterward. "Want to go home?"

"Mama?"

"No, Mama's not home yet, she'll be home *soon*. Let's go eat lunch!"

"Lunts!"

In Modean's kitchen, I set Harry in his high chair and gave him half a banana to eat while I heated his SpaghettiOs in the microwave. He was a lazy, sweet-natured baby, and so funny, just his facial expressions cracked me up. Spending the afternoon with him was like watching cartoons or the Marx Brothers; you got lost in deep play. "Handsome boy," I cooed, setting his bowl in front of him. I gave him his spoon, too, but only as a courtesy; he ate everything with his fingers. "Want me to feed you?" I offered, waving the spoon. No. His bib was the plastic kind with a food-catcher at the bottom; by meal's end, it was half full of spaghetti, and the other half was on his head. "Did you eat *anything*?" He laughed at me, banging his cup on the table in time with his bouncing legs. He could speak in sentences, long ones, you could even detect the punctuation. You just couldn't get the words. I couldn't; Modean swore she understood everything.

I cleaned him up at the kitchen sink, got a pudding pop from the freezer, and carried him out to the front yard. Should I put sunscreen on him? We'd stay under the maple tree by the porch; surely the dappled shade would be okay for half an hour. I couldn't remember constantly worrying about sunscreen for Ruth when she was an infant, but maybe I did. What different babies they were. There sat Harry on the grass like a Buddha, quietly absorbed in picking apart a dandelion. If I'd turned my back on Ruth at that age, she'd have been three doors down the street by now, staggering along in that cute, drunken, hand-fluttering walk that made you laugh until you realized she was going, she was *gone*.

Harry said, "B-bb-bbbb," which gave me the idea of blowing bubbles—possibly his intent in the first place, you never knew. I carried him inside, found the bottle of bubble liquid in his toy box in the family room, carried him back out to the porch steps. Ruth used to love bubbles. Me, too. Harry let me go first. I blew a perfect stream of airy, iridescent globes, so pretty, gone in seconds, like fireworks. "Bbbbb," the baby said, and I put my cheek next to his soft one and said, "Bbbbb" with a little more air, and we blew a big floating bubble that didn't pop until a grass blade speared it, *poof*.

A car slowed in front of my house and started to park. Not a car, a truck. Jess's pickup. I couldn't see him through the wavy, sun-streaked windshield, but he saw me—he backed up forty feet and parked in front of Modean's house instead of mine. I hadn't seen him in three days.

"Tuck," the baby said. He sat between my legs, leaning back against my chest, pointing. I should get up, but some other kind of weight besides Harry's was keeping me where I was. Jess had on white tennis shoes, maybe running shoes. Was he a jogger? I hadn't known. The jogging farmer. Black jeans and a blue T-shirt, and he was striding toward me, swinging his arms, Jess. Coming up the walk, and Harry stopped pointing and scooted back, amazed. Jess came right up to us and squatted beside my left leg. I could see a place on his jaw where he'd cut himself shaving, and for some reason it made me weak. I rested my chin on the top of Harry's head. Jess smiled his slow, two-stage smile. "Hi," he said. "Who's this?"

"This is Harry. That's Jess," I said softly in the baby's ear. Harry could be skittish with strangers. "Can you say 'hi, Jess'?"

"Tuck," Harry said.

"He likes your truck."

"Tuck!"

So then we had to get up and go over to Jess's truck and look at it and touch it, and Jess let Harry sit in the front seat and play with the steering wheel. I wondered how we looked together. Could people tell we were lovers? I had to remind myself to keep my distance, not lean into him or absentmindedly stick my fingers inside his waistband or in his back pocket—giveaway intimacies I already took for granted. "I missed you," I murmured, surreptitiously brushing his hip with the back of my hand. "I wanted to come see you today, but my neighbor called and asked me to sit for Harry. I couldn't say no." Especially since Modean had been so good about watching out for Ruth while I was up to my eyes in ark animals.

"I haven't been home all day," Jess said. "Missed you, too. Can we go somewhere and kiss?"

I laughed, weak again. "Maybe. What have you been doing?"

"Last-minute things at the river. Guess what I dreamed last night."

"What?"

"The ark sank."

"Oh, no."

"Broke in half and went straight down."

"Like the *Titanic*. Did the animals float?" He laughed at me. "Well, did they?"

"I don't know, I woke up." He took Harry's hand off the gear shift for the third time. "The portholes are perfect."

"Really? Do they show up?" Eldon let me paint extra animal faces on three-foot round plywood shapes Jess cut out for me on his band saw. I hadn't seen them on the ark yet. "Did you put them on all three levels or just around the bottom?"

"All three. The chimpanzees look great hanging off the lower deck. That was a great idea."

"Maybe I'll drive over this afternoon and look. I know, I said I wouldn't, but I can't stand it." The way I made myself stop putting finishing touches on the animals, which were still in Jess's barn, was to take all the paint cans and brushes over to Landy's and store them in his basement. The end. It's over.

"What have you been up to?" Jess asked.

"A million things, all the things I've been putting off since this started. Yesterday I cleaned my house, and it took *all day*. I've been calling people, reminding them I exist. And trying to think about a job, but that's not working—I can't see past Monday. Will you be glad when it's over, or sorry?"

"Both."

"Me, too."

Harry was getting more aggressive; he wanted to take off the hand brake. "It's time for his nap," I told Jess, scooping the baby up. "Come inside with me. You don't have to go right away, do you?" Harry gave a bitter wail. His roly-poly body became all muscle, all of it straining to crawl over my shoulder, fat arms outstretched and beseeching, "Tuck! Tuck!"

Hugs, apple juice, and more bubbles calmed him down. I put him on the floor and let him play with the pots and pans in "his" cabinet (all the others were padlocked) while I heated water for his bottle. "Modean should be home any sec, but I'll put him down first—" Jess turned me around and pulled me into a long, hot kiss. "Oh, I really missed you," I said, holding tight, "I didn't know I would this much."

"You're the only thing in my head. You were before, but that was nothing."

"Can you stay? When Modean comes, we could go to my house."

"Where's Ruth?"

"At Krystal's—she works all day on Saturdays." We kissed again—but it scared Harry for some reason, so we had to stop.

Modean came home. We three chatted in the kitchen for a while. Once she felt comfortable, Modean could talk, and she liked Jess; she'd told me so even before I'd started bringing his name up, so I could talk about him to someone—one of the frustrations of a secret love affair, I'd discovered. Precious minutes ticked by in the kitchen, and eventually Jess said, "Well, Carrie, we should probably go see about that flying squirrel."

Modean didn't even blink. "Oh, okay, see you guys. Thanks again, Carrie," she called, waving to us as we walked across the driveway, trying to look purposeful. That was easy.

Lovemaking was different now. Orgasms with Jess—not at first, but lately—felt as if they were in the exact center of me. As if, before, they all were slightly askew, off middle, but now they were exactly where they were supposed to be. Could that possibly be literally true? Probably not. More likely my body was trying to tell me something. It was making an analogy.

I kept a picture of Stephen on the far bedside table, Jess's side of the bed. He had it propped on his chest when I came back from the bathroom. The photo flattered Stephen, made him look loose and fun loving, shading his eyes from the full sun, his teeth showing in a tight, rare grin. Jess lifted his eyes from the picture to me, and I waited for what he would say. He lay with the sheet twisted between his legs, rumpled and rangy, at ease with everything, and I thought how different they were, the two men in my life. Once Ruth came home from a visit with Jess, talking about who she'd rather marry, a man who felt things or a man who thought things. An oversimplified distinction, but I knew whom she was comparing. Women wanted both, of course, but we were usually drawn toward one more than the other. My mother chose a thinking man because she thought he would be safer. And I guess he was.

I lay down beside Jess. He put the picture back and took my hand without saying anything. I talked more than he did. I had with Stephen, too, but that was different. Jess's silences were safe, intriguing, not indifferent, never dangerous. He was like a—a thermometer, something with mercury in it; my symbol for him in my mind was a tall blue column, upright, running the length of him, and all for me. Jess was true-blue.

"You never ask me about Stephen," I said, draping an arm across his stomach.

"Tell me anything you want."

"Don't you want to know anything?"

He thought. "Me being here—what's it like? I've got my head on his pillow."

"I know. I know, I've been feeling guilty because I don't feel guilty. Enough. I didn't wait long enough, most people would say. In a way, I've been unfaithful to Stephen twice. With you. Once when he was alive, and now."

Jess brushed the back of my hand across his lips, watching me.

"Do you want to know why I married him? One reason?" He nodded, but he didn't have the same compulsion that I had to confess, thrash out, make sense of. "I knew what I'd be getting into. He'd be a college professor, and that was certainly a life I understood, but with Stephen I'd really belong, I'd be his equal." Not like my mother, who had never belonged. "I would be an artist and he'd be a genius. And we'd have perfect children."

"And that's why you loved him?"

"That's why I married him. I fell in love with him because I thought he was someone else. Or maybe he *was* someone else and he changed. Or I changed."

"Who did you think he was?"

"Somebody like you. But safer." This was a hard confession. "I was twenty-three when we met, living in Washington, trying to be an artist. Failing. I'd run completely out of money, and I was down to two choices, get a job or go back to school. The end of my life, I thought. And either one meant caving in to my mother, who always said I should get an education degree and teach art in the public schools. Stephen and I weren't dating anyone but each other, but it wasn't that serious yet. When he finally understood my predicament and what it meant to me, he said—he said, 'Come live with me, and be my love.' In those very words. I guess it sounds silly, but it meant the world to me. His first and his last poetic utterance. He was offering to save me, and he had no motive except generosity. I thought he was like that. I thought . . . I didn't know that this was . . . uncharacteristic. So I fell in love with him."

"And then?"

"Oh . . . we moved in together, but it didn't save me. We fell into marriage, too quickly, and then Ruth was born, and life turned very practical. No more poetry, no more art. Crafts—for money, I started making wreaths and selling them, wreaths for all occasions. Then I made wreath *kits*, and they did pretty well until I got sick of them. Literally. My first depressive period. Is this much, much more than you ever wanted to know?"

"I don't think we can save each other," Jess said.

"No. But—you don't think you saved me?" He smiled. "No, I know," I said, "but it *feels* that way to me."

He began to put his tongue in the spaces between my fingers. "If I didn't exist, if I disappeared, you'd be all right."

"Oh, no." I kept saying no, but it occurred to me that I had changed, and that I would be stronger if I lost Jess than I had been when I lost Stephen. Where was the sense in that? "The sheepdog factor," I realized. "You're saying it's the work. Well, I don't know. I still think it's you." I rubbed against him, pressing kisses on his throat, under his ear. Two months of ark building had made his hands even more rough and jagged, and I liked the feel of them coasting over my skin, pinkening it, arousing me. "Let's not talk about our spouses anymore, not for a while. Let's have a moratorium."

"Okay."

"Don't sound so reluctant." We began to make love again. Slowly this time, not so frantic. At the moment when I began to shudder and spiral up, Jess paused, and I heard it, too—a familiar sound. The squeak of a footstep on the staircase.

I twisted up, fast as a snake, and raced to the closed door, which had no lock. "Hello?" Ruth called from the hall.

"Don't come in." The door knob turned. "Ruth, don't open the door."

"Why? Mom? Who's there?"

My bathrobe lay on the floor at the foot of the bed, but I was afraid to move. Jess rolled off the bed, snatched up the robe, and threw it at me. "I'm coming out," I said, shoving my arms inside the sleeves, yanking at the belt. He'd gone around to the other side of the bed, invisible from the door. I tried to smile—*Sorry—can you believe this?*—but it came out a grimace. He pushed his hair back with his hands, baring his teeth in comical sympathy, and just for a second it calmed me. Just for a second I wasn't sorry. I opened the door.

Ruth looked white and ill. "Are you all right?" In a reflex, I put out my hand, but she flinched away, out of reach.

"Who is it?" she whispered. Fear made her sharp features stiff, like carved wax. Oh, Jesus—she thought it was Stephen. I could see it in the frightened, irrational longing in her eyes.

"Sweetheart," I said, "let's go in your room."

"Who is it?"

"It's Jess."

Incomprehension. Then a split second of relief—oh, *Jess*, well, then—and finally, understanding.

My chest hurt. "Oh, baby." I saw clearly and for the first time that I'd picked the most heartless thing, the worst way to hurt her. She backed up, her mouth open but no words coming out. I followed because I thought she was bolting for the stairs, but she dashed past them and into her room, slamming the door in my face.

Jess, half-dressed, took me by my ice-cold hands and pulled me back into the bedroom. I could hardly feel his arms around me. "Let me stay," he said, but I said no, go, he had to go. He hugged me tighter, even when I tried to push him away. In spite of myself a little warmth began to seep in. I rested my head on his shoulder. "What have I done? I don't mean that, I'm not sorry—but if you'd seen her face—oh God, Jess, I don't think I can fix this. You have to go, please, I can't talk to her, I can't do anything until you leave."

But after he was gone, it was worse. What if this was unmendable? My fingers were shaky when I tried to button my blouse; I put a sweater on over it, I put my shoes on—trying to look *dressed*, I realized. I was afraid to look in the mirror. *Stop*, I thought, but I could feel it coming on, the old contempt for myself. No, a B-movie situation, that's all this was. I'd explain everything to Ruth and—it would break her heart. But she'd recover, and afterward at least there would be no more secrets. But that was a good outcome for *me*: what about this dreadful situation could ever be good for *her*?

I found her doubled up on her bed, arms folded around her stomach. "Are you sick?" When I touched her shoulder she scuttled away, sitting up, pushing back against the headboard. Her eyes looked black in her pale, pinched, merciless face.

"How long has it been going on?"

"I'm so sorry you had to find out that way. I was going—"

"I'll bet. How long have you been screwing him?"

"Stop it. Stop it."

"What, you don't like my language? Hey, I'm really really sorry, I deeply apologize." Her shoulders were jerking in spasms. "How long have you been having sexual intercourse with Jess Deeping?"

"I want to tell you. I would have, but not yet. Because—"

"Because you were ashamed."

"Because I knew it would hurt you."

"Because it's shameful."

"Ruth—I've loved him my whole life—"

I saw how wrong that was as soon as I said it. She recoiled, jumped off the bed. "So did you—did you do it with him while Daddy was still alive?"

"No." But I didn't answer quickly enough.

"You did. God! God!"

"It's not like that—I wasn't having an affair with Jess. I loved your father, you know I did."

"Then how come you're so happy now that he's dead? Anyway, you're lying, I can tell."

"Ruth—"

"You deserve each other. I hate both of you, I can't stand you."

"*Wait*. Hold it!" She hung in the doorway, radiating insolence and loathing, except that her eyes were swimming. "Don't walk out when I'm talking to you. Come back here."

"No. Talk to me from there."

But what could I say? I didn't know any words that could fix this, and I couldn't stop internalizing her disgust. I'd lost sight of my side of the argument, I could only see hers.

"Did you cheat on him or not? Just tell me that, Mom, just say one honest thing. Did you?"

I let too much time go by again. "Once." She winced. "And it was a long time ago."

"A *long time ago?*"

"I don't know how to explain this to you! Anything, anything I say will hurt you. If only you were—"

"That's right! So don't say anything, okay? I don't want to hear a word from you."

I hadn't seen her bottom lip quiver since she was ten years old. It happened when she was trying not to cry. "Darling, please listen to me. If you were older—"

"I'm not too young to know what you are. A slut! Keep away from me, okay? Maybe we'll talk when I'm older. Like five years from now!"

She ran out of the room. My heart stopped—I thought she would fall on the stairs, her loud, banging footsteps sounded so clumsy. I waited for the front door to slam. Instead, a moment later, the kitchen door slammed. Was she going next door? I hoped so—although I hadn't wanted Modean to know about Jess yet. Too bad: exposure was a price we sluts had to pay.

In my room, I stood over the rumpled bed and wrung my hands. The scene of the crime. How could we have been so careless? What kind of a mother did such a thing, took such a risk in her own house? And why was it so easy to feel guilty about my own happiness? Who taught me that, my mother? But she'd been the convenient scapegoat all my life. This time I knew it was me, just me.

I wandered from room to room, unable to settle; in the kitchen, I peeked through the blinds, searching for a sign of Ruth next door. Should I go over there? She might not even be there, she might've gone for a walk.

I took a shower—because I needed one, I told myself, not out of any neurotic Freudian motive. Afterward I went outside and sat on the front porch step. Something felt wrong. The sun was too high—it seemed much later than four o'clock. Milking time; Jess would be thinking of me, worrying about me. I wished I could call him, tell him I was all right. But that I'd blown it with Ruth. But that we'd live.

It took a few more seconds before I figured it out, the thing that wasn't quite right. The piece in the landscape that was missing.

My car.

21

Total Bullshit

Raven wasn't home. His mother looked like an old sitcom mom, like Florence Henderson or somebody, and his house was all wrong, too. He should live in, like, the Addams family mansion, not a long rambler with green aluminum siding and white shutters.

"No, I'm sorry, Martin's not here right now," Mrs. Black said, standing in the front door and drying her hands on a paper towel. "He went to Richmond for the weekend. To visit his father," she added, like she thought I looked sick or lost or something and it would help if she gave a longer explanation.

"Oh," I said. Raven's parents were divorced. He lived with his mother, but he saw his dad pretty often. "Okay, well, thanks."

"Can I tell him who came to see him?"

"Oh, Ruth Van Allen. I just was, um, driving around. It's not anything important. I'll see him Monday." I smiled, walked back down the flagstone walk very casually. Got in the car and started it up like nothing was funny, I drove around by myself all the time. In the rearview mirror I saw my gray, pasty face and the sweat on my forehead. I could almost throw up. I kept the window open as I drove, just in case.

Where should I go? Not Jamie's or Caitlin's. Not Becky Driver's. Krystal's was all that was left. I could park the car in the alley where nobody would see—in case somebody came looking for me. It was only four o'clock; the Palace would be open for two more hours, but Krystal would let me lie down upstairs in her apartment. She might even have Midol or something. No, probably not. Well, some more Menstru-Care, then, but so far its unique combination of B-12, black cohosh, and kava-kava wasn't doing squat.

I parked in back of the store, blocking Krystal's garage, but that was okay. Better than trying to parallel park in the alley. Using the key she gave me, I let myself in the back door.

Krystal was up on the ladder, getting a box down from the top shelf in the storeroom. "Ruth!" She almost lost her balance, she was so surprised. "Wow, you startled me. I thought you were home in bed with a heating pad. It's not that busy, you didn't have to come back." Out in the store, the phone rang. "Oh, shit, can you get that?"

I started to go, then stopped. "Um. That might be my mom."

She gave me a funny look. "Okay," she said, coming down the ladder. "So I'll get it. And I should say—?"

"I'm not here. I went home early with cramps, that's all you know."

She raised her eyebrows and pushed her lips out, fishlike: *Interesting*. Then she made a dash for the phone. I'd never asked her to do anything like this before, lie for me or anything, but I wasn't surprised that she was doing it. Krystal was somebody I could trust.

I couldn't hear what she was saying on the phone, and I didn't want to go any farther into the store. After she hung up, she had to wait on a customer, so I sat on a cardboard box and rocked back and forth, hugging my stomach. Having cramps feels like everything is going wrong inside, like a war happening in your guts. I really could throw up. The more I thought of it, the sicker I felt. The bathroom was only about six long steps away, I could make it. But just then Krystal came back, and I got distracted.

"What happened?"

"It was your mom, all right. She asked if you were here and I said no, you went home early because you were sick." She wrinkled her forehead. "The Menstru-Care didn't work?" I shook my head. "Well, so that was about it, she just asked were you here and I said no. What's up?"

"Can I lie down upstairs for a while?"

"Sure. You running away from home?" she said, grinning. The bell over the front door tinkled. "Go on, I'll bring you some cramp bark tea as soon as I get a break. Fix you right up."

"Cramp bark tea?"

"Absolutely. For muscular support during cyclic changes. Go."

Krystal's apartment was awesome, like in a movie from the 1960s only much cooler, not kitschy at all but, like, retro. She had big orange and brown sculptures on the walls that looked like mud pies, and thick tapestries hanging and sort of finger painting artworks, and the rugs that she'd made herself out of yarn and rope. The furniture was really rough and primitive, twig chairs and splintery cabinets with the nails showing and a couch that was just big upholstered pillows piled on top of one another. And everything in earth tones, and for some reason the shades were drawn, plus she had an electric fountain shaped like a grotto and you could hear water dripping. Being in her apartment was like being in a warm, dim, furnished cave.

I had to pee, plus I needed a new tampon. God—what if Krystal didn't use them? What if she used—leaves, or moss, or recycled cloth made out of—hemp or—

Tampax. There it was behind the toilet, the little blue box. Whew. Then I wanted to check out the medicine cabinet, just *see* if she had Bayer aspirin like everybody else, or Listerine, or Crest toothpaste. It felt a little creepy, being a snoop, so I only opened the mirrored door a crack and peeked inside very quickly. Huh. A mixture. She had some Aspergum and a tube of Ben-Gay, but she also had a bottle of Natrol soy isoflavones and some Earth's Bounty Bladderex with the ancient all-herbal Chinese formula. Cool.

The only thing wrong with the pillow-couch was the cat hair all over it. It was hot in the apartment, which must face west because the sun was baking behind the hand-painted shade over the big window. But the heat felt good; I'd been cold and shivery all day. I pulled a knitted throw over my legs and curled up in the fetal position. Rather than think about Mom and Jess in my father's bed, I went to sleep.

Cramp bark tea tasted like dirt. Krystal made me drink a quarter cup every fifteen minutes, and I told her it was working because if it didn't, the next remedy was two eight-ounce glasses of apple-celery-fennel juice. "For the phytoestrogens," she said. "But what you really need is some reflexology."

Reflexology was a pretty good deal. I got to lie back on the sofa and let Krystal rub my feet. The top of my arch controlled the fallopian tube, and behind my inner and outer ankles were the uterus and ovary, respectively. Sure enough, after about ten minutes of stimulating finger massage, my cramps started to get better.

"Hey, this is working," I told Krystal, who was actually drinking a cup of cramp bark tea, too, and there wasn't even anything the matter with her. I gently shifted the white cat, Charmian, a little lower down on my stomach, closer to my pelvis. I liked the warmth, but after a while the pressure didn't feel so great.

"Sure it is," Krystal said. She had her eyes closed; she might be meditating while she did the reflexology. Right now, she was studying healing touch by mail; in two months she'd have her certificate, then she was going to offer it at the store. Forty dollars an hour, which was a lot, but she planned to *guarantee* results. "Nobody leaves unsatisfied" would be the slogan.

I kept waiting for her to ask questions, like what I was doing there and why I couldn't go home. But she didn't, and that was cool, that was the thing I liked best about Krystal, her live-and-let-live attitude. But on the other hand, if you wanted to talk about anything, you had to bring it up yourself. Which was hard.

"So," I said. "Guess what."

"Hmm," she said dreamily. She was doing the finger walk across the top of my left foot, making little snapping sounds with her index finger joint.

"So. So today I go home early, right? Because I'm sick. And nobody's there. But Jess's truck is in front of the Harmons' house, so I figure he's over there talking to Mom, who had to sit for Harry this afternoon."

"Mm hmm."

"So I get a glass of milk and I—"

"Milk? Oh, Ruth." She scrunched up her face. "The worst, the absolute worst. Almond milk, okay, maybe, but *milk*? Oh, baby, no wonder." She shook her head and began to do the finger walk harder.

"Oh. I didn't know. Well, so anyway. So I was feeling really lousy, but I wanted to see Jess, you know, because he's . . . he was like . . ." A friend. "So I was going up to my room first to comb my hair, try to look less sick, you know, put on some blush or whatever. I get to the top of the steps, and what do I hear in my mom's bedroom? Behind the closed door, which she *never* closes?"

"What?"

"Her voice and some guy's." Except it wasn't voices, because they weren't talking. It was sounds.

"Oh—my—God."

"She goes, 'Don't come in, don't open the door!' So I just stand there. Then she opens up, and she's—she's got on her bathrobe. And her hair all messed up and her face red. It was weird—I barely recognized her, it was like she was her own sister or something. And she looked totally in shock, like somebody just shot her."

"So *who was the guy*?"

"It was Jess. My pal Jess."

Krystal stopped rubbing my foot. Her round eyes got big and wide. She whispered, "Oh, no shit."

"Pretty funny, right?" I laughed, and then I almost started to cry, but I kept swallowing until I got over it. No way, they didn't deserve one tear out of me. "Yeah, it turns out they've been carrying on forever, even before my father died."

"Get *out*. Your mother? No way."

"Way. She told me, she admitted it."

"Oh, Ruth. Oh, man, what a bummer. That is really awful. Are you okay? That is so, so heavy. Jeez, how could she do that? So is the guy really hot or what?"

"I don't know. How should I know?" What a dumb question. "I thought he was our friend, I used to go—over to his house—Ugh." I pretended my stomach hurt and stopped talking until my voice got strong again. I wasn't going to be a baby about this, not in front of Krystal.

"Did you talk to him?"

"No, he left. My mother tried to wriggle out of it—"

"What did she say?"

"Just bullshit, about how she's always loved him. *Always*—get that? Oh, but she loved my dad, too."

"Yeah, right."

"Right—I told you it was bullshit. Basically what she told me was to grow up. So I just left, I walked out and stole the car. Screw it."

"Bitch."

I blinked, thinking she meant me. "Oh, yeah," I said when I realized she meant Mom. "What a total bitch." It sounded ugly and mean, and it felt great.

"I mean, really. That's the lowest, to cheat on your husband."

"I know."

"Even if she loves the other guy, it's still cheating."

"I know."

"You must feel awful."

"I keep thinking about my dad. He would never have done that to her, never. He was so good, and he really loved us. He was the best. One time when I was like eight, she had the flu and he did everything—he cleaned the whole house, he did all the cooking, drove me to school, he did everything." Krystal didn't look impressed enough. "I mean, that's just one thing I remember. He never forgot her birthday or Christmas, and he'd always give me money ahead of time so I could get her something. He was *thoughtful.* And I know he never cheated, I *know* it. How could she? How could she hurt him like that when he never did anything to her?"

"You think he knew?"

"No, I'm—" All of a sudden I was freezing again. "What if he did, what if he saw. Oh, my God. And then he died. His heart broke."

"Well, but you said he had coronary disease."

I pulled my feet out of her lap and curled up over my knees. "What if she did it. What if she made him die." I bit one of my knees until it hurt.

"Wow." Krystal kept shaking her head. "That's too much."

"Maybe he didn't know. Maybe it just happened."

"Yeah. Probably. Still. Kind of a coincidence."

My mouth was making too much water, I couldn't swallow fast enough. I stumbled up and ran, willing the nausea back, not letting it escape until the exact second I got the toilet seat up and my head centered over the bowl.

Then—explosion. Garbage and bile and glue, I made myself sick, I nauseated myself. It didn't stop until all I had left was strings of spit.

Krystal stayed in the doorway, but she wouldn't come in. Mom would've come in. She'd've held my arm or touched me on the back while I threw up, and afterward she'd've talked very calmly so I wouldn't be embarrassed or scared or weirded out. Thinking these things gave me a desperate feeling, a mixture of being mad and feeling hurt, some of it was old and childish and some of it was new and grown-up, and I never wanted to feel that combination again.

• • •

Krystal had a date with Kenny, her current boyfriend. She offered to cancel if I was really sick, but of course I said no, go, it's Saturday night, I'm fine. Before she left, I asked if I could park the Chevy overnight in her garage. "Just in case anybody's looking for me." The police, I was thinking, but I didn't want to say that out loud; it might freak Krystal out. She was being so cool about everything, but I worried that if she thought it through very carefully, she might change her mind. She said sure, put the car in the garage right now, so I went down with her and we switched places.

Kenny came at nine, but I didn't see him. Krystal said she'd go downstairs and meet him in the store so I wouldn't be disturbed. I like him, so I was a little disappointed. Kenny's cute, he always talks to me, he tells funny jokes. He's a lineman for the telephone company. Krystal likes him okay, but she's not in love; once she told me her problem with Kenny is that he smokes too much grass.

After they left, I got hungry. Krystal had said I could help myself to anything I wanted, but when I looked in the refrigerator, except for milk, I couldn't recognize anything as food. Even the vegetables were mysteries, not to mention all the stuff in plastic containers. Everything was beige and looked like oatmeal. I found some granola-looking stuff in Baggies in the bread box and put milk on it in a bowl. Yes—cereal. So then I cut up and added a few pieces of a pinkish yellow fruit I'd seen in the grocery store but never tasted before because it wasn't on Mom's boring shopping list. Delicious. But what was it, a persimmon? Pomegranate? Papaya? The fact that I had no idea just went to show, didn't it? I might as well be living my life in prison. Clayborne—what a joke. If you want to know anything or do anything, if you want to *change* anything, you better make it happen yourself, because nobody around here is going to.

I lay back down on the smelly couch and put Charmian on my chest. "I'm blowing this fleabag," I told her. My stomach bumped the cat up and down when I laughed. "You're the fleabag," I said, rubbing her softly between the eyes. The phone rang.

The machine picked up after the fourth ring. After Krystal's message, Mom said, "Hello, it's Carrie Van Allen. I'm just—I wanted to see, make sure—Krystal, if you're there, pick up, will you?"

I sat straight up. The cat made a hissing noise when she hit the floor. I froze—then remembered: Mom couldn't hear anything on this end.

Her voice sounded thin and high, really strung out. "Ruth's not home yet," she said fast, the words falling on top of each other, "and I can't imagine where she is. I can't find her. If she's been there, if you've heard from her, please, please call me. Right away." And she gave the number. Like Krystal didn't already know it. "If you can't reach me, if the line's busy or—I don't know, just—if you can't get me, call my mother." She gave *that* number. "Okay. Thanks. Call if you hear anything. 'Bye."

I lay back slowly, pressing all my fingers against my teeth. Yikes. Yikes. Sweat prickled in my armpits. It felt like all my nerve endings were electrical circuits shooting out sparks. Oh, yikes.

I could get up and go home right now. "Driving around," I could say when Mom asked where I'd been. She'd be mad, but so what? Eventually this would blow over, the fact that I stole the car, and nothing would come of it.

That's what decided me. Fuck it. I wanted consequences, I wanted trouble. The scarier the better—if it wasn't scary as hell, I wouldn't be doing it right.

Krystal got home at 1:37, I saw by the glow-in-the-dark dial of my watch. I wasn't asleep; I'd just turned the TV off, in fact, after watching a million videos on VH-1. I'd turned it off a couple of times before, but each time I got ready to go to sleep, I'd hear my mother's voice, the way it sounded on the machine—it was like it was haunting me or something. Majorly annoying.

I heard the back door slam shut, some bumping around downstairs, Kenny laughing, Krystal going, "*Shh.*" Would she bring him up? I hoped so, even though I was tired. It would be fun to sit around with them and talk about whatever they'd done this evening. Maybe they were drinking. Maybe they'd give me some.

It got quiet, though. Except for the rain on the window, I couldn't hear anything at all.

I got up from the couch and crept over to the door. They'd better not be coming up now, or Kenny would see me in my underpants. I opened the door to the stairs a crack. Nothing. No—a rustling. Krystal's husky voice saying just one word, but I couldn't make out what it was. The stillness got heavier and heavier, fuller and fuller of meaning. *I bet they are. I bet anything.* I wanted to close the door and hear plain, uncomplicated silence again, but I also wanted to stay put until something definite floated up, a sound clue that proved it. Moaning or something. I hung in the doorway until my neck got sore and the wrist I was leaning on started to tingle and my right foot went to sleep. Now my biggest fear was that they'd hear me close the door and tiptoe back to the sofa, and know I'd been eavesdropping, but it was either that or stand there all night, so I shut the door as softly as I could and took slow, huge steps across the carpeted floor to the couch, and when I got to it I coughed really loudly as I sank down on the sighing pillows and pulled the covers over myself. I lay still, feeling stupid and childish.

Everybody's cool about sex but me. Jamie and Caitlin make jokes about it all the time, and underneath the kidding around there's this feeling that they know everything about it and they aren't even that interested in it except as something to snicker about and make fun of. But how can you make fun of something that's a complete mystery? Were they just lying all the time? Was everybody? I myself am afraid to make sex jokes because I might get something wrong, say something that makes no sense and reveal my total and complete ignorance. Not about the act, I get that, but about the . . . the culture of it, the atmosphere. The history and politics, the do's and don't's, the rules. Well, pretty much everything.

Like, why, really, is it all that great? People build their *lives* around it, and not just guys, either. What exactly is the deal? Sometimes I think the only reason I want to do it is because it's not allowed. If I never did it, if I became a nun or something, would I miss it? How many times do you do it if you live to, say, eighty, and you're so-called normal? And how in the world could you get tired of it—that is really a mystery—just because you're married or middle-aged or whatever? It's still sex, and you're still naked, so how could that ever be boring? And how come everybody but me knows the answers to these questions?

Mom having sex with Jess—I don't have to try to not picture it, because I can't picture it. Even if I wanted to. Which I don't. I can't picture Mom with Dad, either, although once I might've heard them—a long time ago, and I didn't know what I was hearing, just funny noises late one night from behind their closed door. But I must've known more than I thought I knew, because instead of going on to the bathroom, I turned around and quietly went back to my room, without peeing.

Mom and Jess. God. Why? They just couldn't stand it? Like in a movie where the two people get so hot they start ripping each other's clothes off? Gross—I almost pictured it, just for a second it flashed in my mind's eye. I set the scene in Jess's barn, the one where they'd made the ark animals, and I imagined naked Mom and naked Jess twisting around in a pile of sawdust.

"Kitty kitty kitty." I hung my arm down and snapped my fingers to call the cat, distract my mind, because I wasn't going there, no way.

Betrayed was how I felt. By my own mother, who turned out to be two-faced and a lying hypocrite. A cheater. Last summer, Mom rented *Hope Floats* and we watched it together, just the two of us because Dad wasn't interested. Poor Sandra Bullock, we said, cheated on by her horrible, wormy husband. How low could you go? Mom sat there and pontificated on fidelity and faithfulness and the seriousness of the marriage vows, blah blah blah, and it was like we were two grown-up women discussing something really worldly, men's wandering ways, and how women were superior because compared to men they hardly ever cheated. (So who are the men cheating with, is what I never get; if men do it all the time and women hardly ever, who are the men's partners? The same handful of women over and over? Boy, what sluts *they* must be.) But—the *hypocrisy* of that conversation, that's what got me. It showed that somebody you trusted could look you in the eye and lie their head off, and you'd never know it. If I thought about Jess teaching me how to fish, talking to me, listening to me talk about my dad . . . if I thought about that I'd explode, I'd hurt myself. It was like I had gas on my hands and Jess was a fire or a hot stove. If I touched it, I'd blow up and burn everybody around me to a crisp.

So I didn't think of it. When all of a sudden the cat jumped out of nowhere onto my stomach, I let it crawl under the covers, and I talked to it and listened to it purr, and told it a story about mice and cheese and a hole in the wall. And I fell asleep before Krystal came up, so I never knew how long she stayed downstairs making love with Kenny.

22

No Sin Goes Unpunished

The police didn't care. Unbelievable—I tried to sound calm, but panic was spreading under my skin like a virus. "Can't you put out an APB or something? She's a missing person. And she's not like this, she's not a runaway, *this is not normal*."

"Yes, ma'am, and you say she's taken your car?" Courteous indifference, that's all I could hear in Officer Springer's voice. It made me clench the phone harder and try not to yell.

"*Yes*. She's gone, it's gone, the keys are gone. It's been more than *five hours*."

"Well, we've got the make and license and we'll be keeping an eye out, but if I were you I wouldn't worry. I know that's—"

"You don't understand, you don't understand, something's happened. Something's wrong."

"But no note, you say, and you and your daughter had a fight?"

"We had—words, yes. She was upset."

"Well, fifteen, they do this, Mrs. Van Allen, they take off."

"Not Ruth. No. She wouldn't."

"First time for everything, you'd be surprised. My guess is she'll turn up any minute, hoping you didn't notice the car was gone. And when she does—"

"Listen to me—are you saying you're not going to do anything?"

"Ma'am, have you got someone you can call?"

"I've been on the phone calling people for five hours. What do you—"

"I meant a family friend, a relative, somebody to sit with you while you wait. I know it's stressful."

"Yes, it's stressful. Anything could've happened. I think she's alone—I've called everybody, no one's seen her—" Officer Springer, who sounded very young, waited through a polite, embarrassed silence while I pulled myself together. "All right," I said when I could. "You're going to call me when you hear anything."

"Yes, ma'am, we certainly will."

"And I'm going to call you. I'll be calling back."

"That's perfectly okay. If it's any help, we get calls like this every day, every single day, and nine times out of ten the kid turns up fine."

"Okay."

"Just remember to give us a call when she comes home, will you?"

"Yes, I will. Thanks."

My left ear ached from pressing the phone to it. I stood in the doorway, listening to the hum of the refrigerator, the tick of the clock over the stove. Ruth wanted a dog clock; every hour a different breed of dog barked. I told her no, it cost money we needed for a hundred other things. Every day, a dozen times, we butted against each other over something that inconsequential. I want this, you can't have it. Yes, no. Inmate, warden. My purpose on earth was to puncture my daughter's dreams. I probably did it out of habit half the time. The parent-child system worked until adolescence, then it broke down. It was fundamentally flawed from the age of thirteen, when it changed from adults guiding children to people bossing around other people. Everyone hated it, both sides, but nobody had a better idea.

I hated the sound of the clock ticking. The smell of fish was vaguely nauseating—Modean had brought over a plate of tuna casserole for my dinner, but I hadn't been able to touch it. Ruth could have it if she came home hungry. No—she could go to bed starving for all I cared. If nothing was wrong, she hadn't been kidnapped or beaten or molested, if she was all right, if she was safe—I'd grab her by her skinny shoulders and shake her till her teeth rattled. Interesting: the only way she was going to get a warm welcome here was if she could produce evidence of abuse.

I could still think like that, dry, sardonic thoughts, because as frightened as I was, I could not make myself believe anything truly horrible had happened. I had to trust that feeling, I had to think of it as higher intuition, not cowardice or denial. My mind swerved between images of catastrophe and images of safety, innocent, prosaic explanations for Ruth absconding with the car. The catastrophe scenarios made my heart race and my skin flush, but deeper down, I knew Officer Springer was right. Any minute she was going to waltz in with a sullen face and a surly explanation, and I was going to kill her.

The phone rang.

"Carrie?"

I sank down on the sofa. "Oh, Jess."

"Bonnie just told me."

"I called her. To see if Ruth was with Becky, but she's not."

"Why didn't you call me? Bonnie said she's been gone since this afternoon."

"I kept thinking she'd come home. I was sure she'd be here by now. I should've called you, I'm sorry, I wish I had."

"It's all right."

"It's dark out now, and she's not used to driving at night."

"Have you called the police?

"Yes, but they're not worried. They just say to wait."

"What happened after I left?"

"I ruined it. I still don't know what I should've said. She was so angry, and I couldn't comfort her, I couldn't do anything but make it worse."

"I'm sure she's okay."

"Why?" I could tell myself that, but I couldn't stand anyone else humoring me. "It's Saturday night, it's almost ten o'clock. She's got the car, she's out, she's gone, she's driving around somewhere—how can you think she's *okay*?"

"Because she's smart, she wouldn't do anything stupid." He didn't sound calm, though. That scared me more than anything—Jess always sounded calm.

"Taking off was stupid," I told him. "Anyway, it's not her stupidity I'm worried about, it's stupid other people. Oh God," I breathed, covering my face with my hand. "No, I know, you're right, she's probably fine, nothing's happened. But she could be with somebody, and I don't know who."

"You've called all her friends?"

"Everyone I can think of. There's a boy—I even made his mother call his father—they're divorced—to make sure he was there and not with Ruth, that he was in Richmond where he's supposed to be, and he is. And all her friends, nobody knows anything—"

"What about Krystal?"

"No, nothing, Ruth left work early because she didn't feel well, and that's all Krystal knows. The police don't care, they say it happens all the time, not to worry—" I laughed, a garbled sound. "I don't think they're doing anything. They say it's nothing, she'll turn up."

"Are you by yourself?"

"Modean was here before."

"Do you want me to come over?"

"No. Yes, but it wouldn't help, there's nothing you can do."

"Why don't I drive around and look for her, look for the car."

"Jess, would you?"

"I'll leave right now. I'll call you in a little while."

"Thanks. Thanks."

"Try not to worry. I know," he said when I tried to laugh. "Just keep thinking about how smart she is."

"I'll *make* her smart when she gets home." Some joke.

I hung up quickly—we'd talked too long, tied up the line, what if Ruth was trying to call? And about thirty seconds later, the phone rang.

"Any word?" my mother's voice boomed in my ear.

"No." I'd called her earlier, on the slim hope that Ruth had gone over to her house.

"Oh, honey."

I told her about the police, that they didn't care.

"I'm coming over."

"No, Mama."

"Your father's home if she calls or comes over here. I'll come and stay with you."

"No, don't, *honestly*, there's nothing for you to do." We argued a little longer, while I tried to figure out what I really wanted. I'd said no to her without thinking, but would it be better to have someone to wait with? Mama would take over everything, no question about it. Would that be bad or good?

"All right, but call me the *minute* you hear anything, you hear?"

"I will, I promise."

"Doesn't matter what time it is, I won't be asleep anyway."

"Well, you might as well go to bed, there's no point in both of us staying up."

That started it all over again. "Then why don't I just come over and we can stay awake together?"

"Because it's too—I'd just rather not, I'd rather—I just want to—"

"All right, never mind," she said stiffly. Wounded.

Shit. "Mama, I'm no good. You don't want to be around me." She clucked her tongue in disgust. "Anyway, she'll probably drag in here any minute. I'm honestly not that worried. Listen, we should get off the phone in case, you know, she's trying to call. Or the police or something."

"All right, Carrie." Still hurt, but bearing up. "You'll call when you hear?"

"I said I would. 'Night, Mama. Thanks. It really—"

But she'd already hung up. *It really helps that you're there*, I'd been going to say. Not to mollify her, either. It was true.

I couldn't sit still. I called Krystal again, got the machine. I hung up after leaving a message, aware of irrational anger. How could she be out when Ruth was missing? Irresponsible airhead. No, that wasn't fair; Ruth was crazy about Krystal, whose only flaw was flakiness. Plenty of worse qualities she could pass on to an impressionable fifteen-year-old. Still, what if Ruth had gone there, gone to the store looking for guidance or help or friendship? And nobody there, just the empty building. I shivered; a hole opened in the pit of my stomach when I pictured her in the car, driving in the dark, hurt and confused, furious over the injustice I'd done to her.

Upstairs in her room, the familiar locker room smell greeted me, and the exasperating rubble and chaos I hated and loved. Although I tried all the time, I couldn't quite remember myself at fifteen, not with any helpful clarity, not to any purpose. Confused and impatient—I remembered being that, but the details were hazy. My strongest memories were of Jess and my mother. What would Ruth's be? Losing Stephen. Finding me with Jess.

Her notebook journal lay halfway under one rumpled pillow. I put my hand on the edge of it and held it there, not thinking about anything. I made my eyes go blind and pulled the notebook out, ran my thumb along the corner, found the last page she'd written on. Saw the date: yesterday. Blinking, blinking, still half blind, I absorbed the last sentence. "So anything above 75 on the final, which I could do with my eyes closed, and I still get a B for the year, not bad for a Francophobe."

I toppled over, resting my head on the pillow. The ripe, sweet smell of Ruth's hair calmed me. Oh, baby, where are you? If she would just come right now. Right now. Every time I heard a car in the street, I froze, listening like an animal. If the front door would just open right now. I started making promises to God. I wanted to read Ruth's diary so badly, I got up and walked across the room. I should've put it back exactly where I'd found it, but I was afraid if I touched it again I'd open it.

I caught sight of my haggard face in the mirror over the bureau, or the small square in the center of the mirror that wasn't covered with stuck-on photographs, ticket stubs, invitations, funny headlines, magazine cutouts. One of the photos was a close-up of Ruth, Jamie, and Caitlin, taken before Christmas by Jamie's amateur photographer brother. Ruth, the tallest, stood in the middle, and they all had their arms draped across one another's shoulders, smiling for the camera. Happy girls, their sweet friendship on display. But Jamie's brother had also caught a look in Ruth's eyes I knew very well, a half-hidden restlessness, a bafflement that didn't match the cocky, wide-mouthed smile. A look that said, *What am I doing here? I think I might rather be* there.

Stephen had had that same thin-veiled impatience with the here and now. It hadn't made him happy. An unfortunate legacy—but Ruth might outgrow it; already she had more resources than Stephen had ever had. Her inner life was quieter. She was sound—I felt that on a bone level, although the details of her inner life these days were beyond mysterious to me. Had we been as close as we were ever going to be? It was one of my terrors—that the paths of our lives had forked for the last time, and now we would begin to grow progressively wider apart, or at best no nearer, until the day I died.

But maybe not. Glimmers of a new kind of closeness with my mother showed through the murk from time to time. Just glimmers, no shining beacon. Our egos kept butting against each other;

too many things couldn't be said, too much was off-limits. Why wasn't love enough? Why wasn't it ever enough?

I wandered back downstairs. Outside, clouds were piling up around a puny moon behind the locust tree. Heat lightning flickered in the west; the air smelled damp and metallic. I left the door open so I could hear the phone, and sat down on the porch steps in the dark. I should've let Jess come over. No lights on at Modean's house, no lights at the Kilkennys' across the street, only one streetlight burning at the corner. Quiet. No dogs, no night birds, not even a cricket. I should've let Jess come. Or even Mama.

This is the pain I should've felt when Stephen died. No sin went unpunished indefinitely, and I had so many sins. Sleeping with Jess wasn't the worst, it was only the one I was focused on tonight. Stephen always said I was too easy with Ruth, and here was the sickening proof that he was right. If I'd been a better mother, she would never have dreamed of running away. Modean had disagreed violently when I'd told her that tonight—in a weak moment. "You're a terrific mother!" she'd insisted, adamant as a cheerleader. "You're not too lax, what are you talking about? *I'm* too lax. This boy's doomed." She put her lips under Harry's chin and blew, making him shriek. "Carrie, you're not too soft on Ruth, I really don't think."

But I did. My excuse was always that I dreaded being like my own mother, so I backed off, time after time, from imposing my will on my daughter—because that would mean imposing my morals, too, my worldview, my principles, my likes, dislikes—everything Mama had smothered *me* with at Ruth's age and ever after, and see what had come of that—resentment, distance, formality. Yearning for closeness and fearing it at the same time, because it came with the risk of being devoured. "For your own good" excused a multitude of little takeovers. It usurped the will of the one you loved, and caused her to make dreadful, long-lasting mistakes.

To save Ruth from that, I'd gone too far the other way and left her rudderless, maybe valueless. No, that wasn't true—but—I was the most wishy-washy of mothers, a dishrag. Except when I caught myself and overcompensated with some unsuitable, out-of-character act of parental tyranny that accomplished nothing except to piss Ruth off.

My own thoughts antagonized me. *All I want is what's best for her, I only want her to be happy, to be what she wants to be, to live a full life*—every word was true, and yet I knew how loaded each one was because my mother had said them all to me, and believed them just as fiercely. It was love's fault again—love simply wasn't enough. How could you find a balance? How could you let a child go and keep her safe? How could you kill your own ego? Unconditional love—was there any such thing except from a dog? I thought of Modean, bouncing Harry on her hip by the hour, laughing with him, listening intently to his gibberish, rocking him to sleep, worrying about him, doting on him—none of that guaranteed anything. He'd grow up and leave her no matter how well she loved him, and unless she was a saint she'd hate it. She'd spend the rest of her life getting over losing him.

I covered my head with my arms, grinding my eye sockets against the bones of my knees. Misery felt like being filled up with black water and drowning. I didn't always believe in God, but I wished he would kill me if that's what it would take, give him my life for Ruth's. Where was she? *Please, God, please, God, please*. For the first time since he died, I missed Stephen, truly missed him. *I've lost our baby*, I confessed, smothering sobs against my thighs. Inside the house, the phone rang.

I ran. I said "Hello!" and Jess said, "Carrie?" in surprise.

"It's me." I didn't sound like myself. My mouth was gluey, the words sticking to each other. "Did you find her?"

"No. I've been all over, everywhere I could think. I'm at a pay phone on Madison. I'll keep trying."

"Okay." I could hear traffic in the background, like whirring static.

"How are you? Are you alone?"

"Jess?"

"Yes?"

"I wish I could do everything over again. I'm so sorry I ruined it for us. If I had a second chance, I'd change everything. I wouldn't let you go."

"Carrie. Let me come there, let me see you."

"No, I'd rather you kept looking for her. Because no one else is doing anything. The police—"

"I'll call them myself. Right now."

"Okay, that's good."

"Call your mother, call a neighbor. You shouldn't be alone."

"I might. Yeah, I might do that. I love you, Jess," I said, and hung up.

A misty rain started to fall. I stood on the porch step with my face tilted up, letting the cold spray prick my skin. A gust of wind pushed me back on my heels. I turned around and leaned against the screen door; the wet mesh smelled like all the warm, rainy days of my childhood. I put out my tongue and tasted the bitter, salty metal, and a memory drifted back, of my mother holding me, both of us staring out through the screen at a greenish storm. I must've been three or four, small enough to pick up but old enough to remember. I could feel Mama's arms tight around my middle, I could see the dogwood tree sway and bend in the front yard of our old house on Pioneer Avenue. I loved storms. Probably from that afternoon, when we'd watched through the screen together, Mama's cheek on my ear.

Ruth loved storms, too. That was a comfort. I let it seep in, a small reassurance that, after all, I hadn't done everything wrong.

Morning.

Two policemen came early, just after eight o'clock. They didn't look smart, they were too young, one had a whitish stain on his lapel, one kept fingering a shaving cut on his jaw. I didn't like them. But I was excessively nice to them, so they would like me and work harder to find Ruth. All night I'd wanted the police to care, to start taking steps, to get worried and take action. Now that they had, I was petrified.

"I've already called all these people," I said when Officer Fitz, the one with the stained lapel, asked for the names and addresses of Ruth's friends. "But no, you talk to them again, that's good," I added in haste, afraid I might have offended him. After they left, I remembered that neither of them had told me not to worry.

I made a fresh pot of coffee, brought the newspaper in. I was tired enough to collapse in a chair at the kitchen table, but too tense to do anything but slurp coffee and stare around at the walls. About three o'clock last night I'd thought a drink might help. I'd poured a glass of white wine, and got down about half of it before tossing it in the sink. It worked too well, made me feel loose and drowsy, and I couldn't have that. I had to stay vigilant. I could direct Ruth's safety with my mind—I almost believed it. If I let down my guard by relaxing or, God forbid, falling asleep, chaos might win. No, the power of worry was my best, really my only weapon.

When the phone rang, I knew it was my mother.

"Hi. No, not yet. I know. Well, they were just here. They . . . yeah. They didn't really say anything, but they're starting to get serious. I know. About time. Well, you can, but—No, it's just that there's nothing for you to—Sure, I want you to. Okay. Okay. No, don't bring anything, just—okay. 'Bye."

"Fun's over," I said to my reflection in the oven window. No more wallowing alone in misery and desolation, no more holding back chaos single-handed. "Mama's coming."

But before she arrived, a carload of Fledergasts pulled up in front of the house. I was sitting at my usual post on the top porch step, alert to the sound of car engines long before they turned in to Leap Street.

Intent on the sound of my own car, I didn't hear Chris's station wagon until it stopped and she got out on the passenger side. I had never seen her in a dress before, a blue and white seersucker shirtwaist, with white high heels that made her look like a giant. She saw me when she was halfway up the walk. Her frowning face cleared; she waved, smiled. She never dropped by like this. What if—

I jumped up.

"Hey. We're on our way—"

I ran down the steps and dodged past her, trying to peer through the streaky car windows. Oz at the wheel, Andy and the little girl, Karen, in the backseat. No Ruth. Disappointment felt like a surprise slap in the face.

"What is it?" Chris said, staring at me. "You okay? You don't look—"

"Ruth's not with you?"

"Ruth?"

I sagged.

"What's wrong? Where's Ruth?"

"She's missing. I just thought maybe she was with you."

"*Missing.*"

"Since yesterday afternoon." Chris gasped. I turned, but she grabbed me back and gave me a hard, long-armed hug. When it began to feel good, I pulled away. "So," I said. "What's up with you? You guys off to church?"

"Have you called the cops?"

"They're looking, they say they'll find her. She's got the car."

"Oh, my God. Well, she's just out joyriding. We used to do that—didn't you do that?"

"All night?"

She made a quick, frightened face. "She'll come home, Carrie. Any minute, I bet."

"Yeah."

"Who's with you? Shall I stay?"

"No, thanks, my mom's on her way over."

"Are you sure? We're on our way to church, yeah, but they can go without me." She gestured at the car. Oz was drumming his fingers on the steering wheel, but stopped and waved when he saw me glance at him.

"No, you go on. Nothing going on here but waiting."

She looked indecisive. "Well, okay, then, but I'll call you later. Oh—the reason I came by. It seems stupid now, but I'll just tell you. I quit."

"You what? You quit?"

"Brian called me at home last night to tell me the news. He sounded so damn *happy*. He just hired your replacement. Guess who it is."

I could hardly remember my job. "Who?"

"Lois Burkhart."

"Lois—from the bank?"

"Lois from the bank! Can you believe it?"

"No. Well—she's an accountant, isn't she?"

"Brian has an accountant, Carrie, that's not why he hired her."

"Why—"

"They're dating!"

"They are? But isn't she married?"

Chris wriggled her eyebrows. "Oz saw them at the Ramada Inn last week, having breakfast."

"Oh."

"So I quit. I don't need that. We talked about it all night. Oz didn't want me to leave, not right away, but I just couldn't keep it up, not with this on top of what he did to you. I've lost all respect for him, Carrie. I called this morning and told him."

"Oh, Chris."

"He didn't even argue. Three years I've worked for that man. We started that school *together*. I'm not saying he couldn't have done it without me. I'm—"

"Well, he couldn't have!"

"No, but I just thought loyalty counted for more than this," she said, blinking moist eyes. "I guess I'm naive. I guess I was stupid."

"It's Brian who's stupid."

She flapped her hand, taking a step back. "I just wanted to tell you. I don't need cheering up, and anyway, you've got enough to worry about. I'll call you later, when we get home from church. I just know Ruth is fine."

"Chris, I'm so sorry."

"It's not your fault."

It felt as if it was, though. "Do you have any plans, any idea what you'll do?"

"No!" She laughed, a little wildly. "Something will turn up, I'm not worried." Obviously not true. "Andy says we should all pray for a miracle, so that's what we're going to do." She combed nervous fingers through her spiky, dirty-blonde hair. "I don't know where he gets that," she leaned closer to say. "We don't even go to church that often. I'm scared to death he's going to be a priest." She moved in for another hug. "Okay, gotta go, but I'll call you. Try not to worry, okay?"

"Okay."

"Andy'll put Ruth on his prayer list."

"Great."

She walked away, stiff-legged in the clacking white heels. She had nice legs. Standing on the curb, she was twice as tall as her car. She bent over, folded herself into the passenger seat clumsily, knees pressed together. The whole family waved to me as they drove away.

"I can't believe she'd go and do this of her own free will." Mama plumped up a sofa cushion by pushing it against her stomach and pounding it with her fist. "She's not like that, she would not deliberately cause this kind of worry. I just *feel* it."

"I think she did, though."

"No, I don't believe it. The police are not approaching this right. That child did not run away. Something happened. I don't know what," she said, steering away from her worst imaginings again, remembering at the last second that she was supposed to be comforting me, not ratcheting my anxieties up higher. "I'm just saying, if they still think she's out joyriding—for nineteen hours!—they're seriously barking up the wrong tree. When did you talk to them last?"

"I told you, they came by this morning. They—"

"That's the last time? Hell, *I'll* call them. This is a runaround, pure and simple."

I thought, *Good, you call,* because even that little bit of responsibility lifted—as futile as I was sure calling the police again would be—felt like a sack of rocks off my shoulders. And deep down, some childlike faith still lay under the irritation and fatigue and hopelessness that, as awful as everything was, Mama could fix it.

But she plopped down on the couch and didn't reach for the phone. She was vain about her appearance, wouldn't dream of leaving the house without lipstick and mascara; even today she'd taken pains to match her eye shadow to her gray blouse. But I'd never seen her look so old. It wasn't lines or wrinkles as much as the color of her skin, yellow from sleeplessness, and the sag of her flesh from worry and fatigue. Drawn by protectiveness, I started to sit beside her.

"I'm telling you, something's *wrong,*" she roused herself to say, for at least the fourth time since she'd gotten here, and I veered away and sat down in a chair. "How would you know if anything's missing from that room? It's World War Three in there. This is what comes of letting a child have dominion over her own space."

"What?" She must've heard that on a talk show. "Mama, what's her room got to do with anything?"

"Someone could've come in here and stolen her things, her valuables, and you wouldn't even know it."

"She doesn't have any valuables."

"She has a stereo, doesn't she?"

"Yes, but—"

"A camera?"

I shrugged.

"A bank? A telephone, a cashmere sweater, leather boots—"

"She doesn't have a cashmere sweater. *I* don't have a cashmere sweater. Anyway, what's that got—"

"Someone could've robbed her. I'm just saying, I can't see Ruth walking out of this house by herself. Something else happened."

"Mama, nothing else happened."

"How do you know?"

"I know."

"You don't know."

"I do."

"You don't."

I squeezed my eyes shut. "Will you stop? She wasn't kidnapped."

"Don't even say that word!"

"Well, isn't that what you keep hinting at?"

"I'm not hinting at anything."

"You *are.*" I stood up, vexed beyond caution. "You're saying somebody came in the house, stole her four-year-old stereo—which is still there, by the way, I saw it—and stole Ruth too while they were at it."

"Carrie, there are weirdos all over the place. I'm not trying to scare you, honey, but that boy she spends too much time with, that vampire person—"

"He's in Richmond with his father, I know that for a fact."

She waved that away. "They're plenty more weirdos where he came from, the high school's crawling with them. They ought to have a dress code, they ought to wear uniforms. But that's not the point—"

"No, it's not."

"The point is, she wouldn't have walked out and stolen the car for no reason. *That's* what the police need to focus on."

"She didn't walk out for nothing. You're right, she didn't."

"There had to be a reason, she wouldn't have just—" She looked at me sharply. "What?"

No going back now. But no going forward, either: when I opened my mouth to finish it, no brilliant explanation came out.

"You had a fight," my mother realized. "Oh, Carrie!" She whacked the flat of her hand against the sofa arm. "For Pete's sake, why didn't you just say so? Lord, Carrie, *damn* it, if you knew what I've been thinking, what I've been through. Well? What happened, what did you fight about?"

Telling her would be as bad as Ruth finding Jess and me in bed. Worse, because she'd zapped me back into my childhood again—as easy as that. I took a deep breath. And jumped when the phone rang.

I hurried around my chair, but Mama was closer and got to it first. "Hello. Yes—no, but this is her mother."

"Mama, give it to me."

"Who?"

"Mama!"

"It's the police," she snapped, shoving the receiver at me.

I turned my back on her. "Hello?"

"Mrs. Van Allen?"

"Yes?"

"It's Officer Springer. Got some news for you this morning."

"You found her." Everything went gray and grainy, little dots of static in front of my eyes. Mama's sharp fingers squeezing the back of my arm kept me upright. "Where is she?"

"Uh, no, ma'am, we haven't exactly found her, but at least we know where she spent the night last night."

"Wait. Mama, *stop*." She was trying to hug me from behind. I twisted away. She saw my face and froze. "Sorry," I said into the phone. "What were you saying?"

"Ma'am, we interviewed your daughter's friends from the list you gave us, and we also talked to Ms. Bukowski there at the, uh, the Mother Earth Palace and Natural Healing Salon, and Ms. Bukowski was suddenly able to recollect that Ruth stayed with her last night."

"Ruth stayed at *Krystal's?*"

"Yes, ma'am, looks like it. Officer Fitz said she was evasive until he reminded her that hiding or harboring a minor's against the law, after which she recalled your daughter sleeping there overnight but leaving the residence early this morning."

"Where did she go?"

"Well, we don't know yet. Officer Fitz said Ms. Bukowski was evasive on that point also."

"*Evasive?*"

"Yes, ma'am. Could be she doesn't know, like she's saying, or could be she's keeping it to herself. Some kind of loyalty."

"Loyalty!" My mother kept dragging at my arm and hissing, "What? What's he saying?" "Can't you make her tell? Can't you *arrest* her?"

"We'll certainly be talking to her again, yes, ma'am. But chances are your daughter will turn up soon, either way. That's how it usually is—they stay out one night just to get your attention, then they go home. You be sure and give us a call when that happens. Some people forget, and that wastes our time because we keep looking."

I said I would, and we hung up.

"Who's evasive?" Mama demanded, finally letting go of me.

"Ruth stayed at Krystal's last night—"

"I got that."

"And she's telling the police she doesn't know where Ruth went, but they think she might be lying."

"Where's the car?"

"I don't know. Not there, I guess, or he'd have said."

"So she took it and she went somewhere. Where?"

"I don't know."

"What's her number?"

"Whose number? Krystal's? I don't know, it's on the—speed dial thing, you press—"

"I know how speed dial works."

She took the phone from me, checked the name printed on the receiver, and dialed. She stood with her feet apart, head up and bust out, the hand not holding the phone clenched in a fist on her hip. Not a trace of fatigue showed on her firm, sturdy body. The Clayborne Women's Club had made a grave error.

"Hello? Krystal Bukowski? This is Dana Danziger, I'm Ruth Van Allen's grandmother. Where is she? What? I think you do. Oh, I doubt that. Listen very carefully, if anything happens to my granddaughter, if she gets a *hangnail* this morning and I find out you know where she is—Pardon? I don't care about that, the police can do whatever they like, I'm telling you what *I'll* do. I'll sue you. No, in *civil* court. For violating my grandchild's civil rights. Yes, I can. Oh, yes, I can. Before I get through with you, you won't have two soybeans to rub together. You think that's funny? I'm perfectly serious—you won't have a vitamin left, you won't have a pinch of wheat germ—"

"Mama—"

"What's that? Call it anything you like, I'm telling you what I am going to do. I'll ask you one more time: *Where did Ruth go*?" Her eyes blazed into mine. Suddenly she grabbed my hand, her knees flexed, and stood up on her toes. Her voice went up an octave. "And you *let her*? You idiot! You silly—fruitcake! Yes, you could've! You could've called her mother, you could've called the police—"

"Where's Ruth? What's she saying?"

"I'm too angry to talk to you, you moronic woman, but this is not the end of it, I promise you. I beg your pardon? What did you say to me?" She took the phone from her ear and stared at it, bug-eyed. Then she slammed it down hard enough to break it.

"What?"

"Do you know what she just said to me?"

"*What?*"

"'Have a nice day.'"

"Mama, where's Ruth?"

"She's gone to Georgetown."

"Georgetown! In Washington? Oh, my God! By herself? Why?"

"So she could get a tattoo." She wilted. She flopped down on the couch, slack jawed, shaking her head from side to side. "A tattoo." She closed her eyes. "My God, how unbelievably tacky."

23

Flash

The hitchhiker looked like Billy Zane. The girl was no fool; she wouldn't have picked him up if it hadn't been pouring rain. And bitter cold. He had a dangerous look, something wild and careless in his steel blue eyes, but his mouth was kind. Rainwater dripped from his slick black hair into the collar of his Tommy Hilfiger shirt. No, his worn, creased, black leather jacket. They rode for a long time without talking, nothing but the slap of the windshield wipers and the hiss of the tires on the wet pavement breaking the sex-charged silence. Finally, outside Tulsa—no—at the beginning of the Badlands, in the middle of nowhere, he turned to her and said in a low, warm, rough voice, "You're going to help me, I know it." Because he was on the run from the law. But he didn't even have to say it—she knew. And they both knew that she knew.

They kept driving. She played Lauryn Hill on the car stereo, and he knew then how cool she was and how perfect they were for each other. They rented two rooms that night in a sleazy motel, the kind Mulder and Scully stay in. He came in her room when she was in her underwear, cream-colored bikini bottoms and a matching tank top, like Nikita in *La Femme Nikita*. He couldn't take his eyes off her. He told her the truth—he worked for Operations and he was on a job *pretending* to be running from the law, and she had to start working for him. She had stick-straight blonde hair and she always wore black. She could do karate. She was beautiful and feminine, but she could throw men around like stuffed animals.

Her name was Jade. Jada. Her name was Kara. Her name was . . . Ally. Never mess with Ally because she will kill you. Ally has long legs and she slouches in chairs, and when she gets up it's like watching a cat stretch after a nap. She wears tight black leather pants. Wherever she goes, people stare at her. Which makes it harder to work undercover, but . . . she's a master of disguise, so . . .

Three guys in a red Pontiac wouldn't pass, they just drove at exactly the same speed I was going (sixty-five exactly) and stayed next to me in the left lane. I didn't look at them after the first time, because they were scruffy and stupid-looking, probably locals, probably farm boys from Fredericksburg or Stafford. I was driving to D.C. on I-95 instead of the back way because I wanted to go fast, and yet everybody but me was going around ninety. I *would've* gone ninety, but I was keeping a low profile. If I got stopped—disaster.

Out of the corner of my left eye, I could see the Pontiac guys waving or something, gesturing. They had to think I was at least sixteen, probably older, they had to. I had on, from yesterday, my new long-sleeved black and white striped pullover, and I'd pushed my hair behind my left ear so my gold hoop earrings and one silver stud were visible. My watch was dumb, I should put it on my right hand for driving, but my extremely cool silver and onyx ring made up for it. What I couldn't make up my mind about was my baseball cap. There were two ways you could look at ball caps: one, that they were totally out and had always, in retrospect, looked lame, especially when worn backward, and two, they were a fashion basic like T-shirts and would never go out, and wearing them backward if you looked cool in every other respect—that was key—made you cute and sassy, like Cameron Diaz, and sort of like you didn't care. Which was, of course, the ultimate.

A huge truck came up behind the Pontiac and flashed its lights. I let my foot off the gas a little. The Pontiac guys did something I didn't look at, either waved or flipped me off, and roared away. Good riddance. Now everything was perfect. I turned the radio up and tried to find a noncountry station. I stuck my elbow out the window. I rested my temple on my fingertips. A woman with interesting, serious thoughts on her mind. After a while, the mist coming down turned into droplets, I had to close the window. Shit, was it going to rain? Mom's umbrella was in the backseat, but it was so incredibly queer, one of those tiny pastel Totes only old ladies or insane people carried.

Maybe I should stop at a gas station and buy cigarettes. Except I didn't have any I.D. Caitlin got cigarettes sometimes, Marlboros, but she didn't really smoke and neither did Jamie, so I didn't either. So far. But if I was ever going to take up smoking, now was the time, today was the day. I couldn't figure out why I wasn't more worried. I should be, like, a nervous wreck. But it was like I had a shield around me. Mom was the one who'd broken the rules, not me. If I got caught—so what? Nobody could touch me. I was immune.

The radio was full of static, but I could hear "Take It Easy," the old Eagles song. "I'm runnin' down the road," I sang along, and slipped into my second favorite daydream. I was driving by myself in a convertible on a long, straight highway in the midwest with Tracer beside me on the front seat. A girl and her dog. Men fell in love with me, but I never stayed anywhere for long, I was always leaving them, it was just me and my dog. Sometimes I'd take odd jobs for the hell of it, but then I was gone, and the people left behind in the small town said, "Who was she, where did she come from? Do you think she'll ever come back?"

Wow, it was really raining. Stupid car, the windshield wipers only had two speeds, regular and maniac. Maniac went so fast you couldn't see anything but the wiper blades, plus the *whack whack whack* made you nuts after about two minutes. This was going to make it harder to see the turnoff. Especially since I wasn't quite sure where the turnoff was. Maybe I should've gone the back way. I *sort* of knew that way—you hit 66, and then somehow you were in

D.C. But there were bound to be signs, right, when I got close, and if I just stayed in the slow lane, nothing could happen. Theoretically. Driving on a superhighway was much easier than driving in town or on windy two-lane roads, because all you had to do was steer.

There was a gas station exit with fast-food signs, Burger King, McDonald's. I'd left Krystal's at eight and hadn't bothered with breakfast. Should I stop? Nah, I'd wait. I was hungry, but it would be more fun to eat in Georgetown.

There was a lot more traffic all of a sudden. Where were all these people going on a Sunday morning? Not church. Now a lot of signs were preparing me to do something. Backlick Road. Franconia or Old Keene Mill Road. I was still in Virginia, I didn't have to do anything yet. But the Beltway was coming up. Gram hated the Beltway, she wouldn't get on it for anything. "Killers, nuts, they'd rather murder you than slow down." Yikes, here it was! Now what? I was on 95, and 95 turned into the Beltway! Ninety-five turned into 495 if you went to Alexandria, and 495 was the Beltway. Did I want Alexandria? Baltimore? No, but I was in the wrong lane, I had to get one lane over to the left.

God. They wouldn't let me! I put on my turn signal, but a million cars roared past, bumper to bumper, not a single one would let me in. I stepped on the gas, but the exit was coming, coming—I slowed and hit the brakes, and the guy behind honked and almost hit me. "Shit, shit, shit," I yelled, and then I did it—jerked the Chevy into the next lane over, *knowing* there wasn't enough room. But it worked and I got in and the Beltway exit flew by and I was safe.

My hands were sweating and my right foot was jerking on the accelerator because my leg was shaking, but I was in the right lane and I was safe and invisible and *this was how everybody drove*. They just went where they wanted to go, never mind if it was safe or they had enough room or the car behind was going a hundred miles an hour. Drive defensively? Yeah, right! "My ass," I yelled, and my heart was still beating like a drum.

Okay. Okay, settle down. Three ninety-five, I was on 395, and here came Pentagon, no, Arlington Cemetery, no, Memorial Bridge, no. Or maybe. I knew that bridge, it went right to the Lincoln Memorial, which was definitely in D.C. But you had to get off 395 if you went that way, and I didn't want to get off anything. No turns. This went to D.C., too, the sign said so.

Rosslyn, no, Airport, no, Crystal City, no. Jeez, another Memorial Bridge exit. No, I wasn't getting off 395—and look, George Mason Bridge, 395 went right over it. Ha! I was crossing the Potomac, there it was, and there was Washington, dead ahead. And the Jefferson Memorial, my second favorite, right there on the left. So cool. I'd be in Georgetown any minute now. I couldn't wait to park this car and get the hell out. Terra firma.

Nothing looked familiar, though. Did I want Fourteenth Street? Too late, wrong lane, I was going under another bridge. Yikes, the Southeast Freeway. Freeway, I didn't want a freeway. Ninth Street? Too late. My hands were, like, frozen on the steering wheel, I could only go straight. Did I want the Capitol? No. Not South Capitol Street, not the Navy Yard. Where the hell was I? This was wrong, this was completely the wrong part of town.

Okay, Eleventh Street Bridge? What the hell, just get out of here. I was shooting over the river again, but that was okay, even though it was the Anacostia and not even the Potomac. South, okay, that was backward, but now I could start over. *Two*-ninety-five, and the sign said I could hit the Beltway going this way. So if I went south, or west, I should hit 95 again. No panic. Everything was just going to take a little longer.

I got a map at the Exxon in Annandale (exit 6), because the guy at the Mobil on Braddock Road (exit 5) was Indian or something and I couldn't understand his directions, but I was afraid to hurt his feelings, so I just nodded a lot and said, "Uh huh, okay," and drove to the next exit. Maps were better anyway, you were more in control. You never saw Nikita asking anybody for directions.

Okay, now I saw my problem. I should've come in on 66, which went right into town, you got on Memorial Bridge and turned left or something and there you were in Georgetown. Or was that the Roosevelt Bridge? What I needed was a D.C. map, but all they had was Virginia. But this was good enough. Sixty-six, that was the ticket. Also, six was my lucky number.

Okay, the Theodore Roosevelt Bridge, not the Memorial. Now—E Street? That didn't sound right. Stay in the right lane, that was always safest. This was a pretty street, but what was it? Constitution Avenue. Shit, this was wrong! There was the Washington Monument, tourists crawling all over. Didn't people have anything to do? At least I had a Virginia license plate. These people came from Minnesota, North Carolina, Oregon. Hah. They had to be even more lost than I was.

A nice-looking lady in the passenger seat of the car next to me was stopped at the same red light. I rolled down my window. "Excuse me!" The lady heard and rolled down her window. "Do you know how to get to Georgetown?"

The light changed. The lady turned to the guy driving, probably her husband. The car behind them and the car behind me both honked. "Turn here!" the lady said, and she and her husband drove away.

Turn here? Twenty-third Street? O-kay.

Shit! Shit! This was the circle around the Lincoln Memorial, and I couldn't get out of the right lane. Should I keep going around? Start over? But what if the guy in the car knew something, maybe this was—

No! Memorial Bridge, and I had to get on it, they wouldn't let me over. I was going over the river again, back to Virginia.

"Shit, crap, fuck, bastard—" Staying in the right lane blew. Now what? Arlington Cemetery, no. Route 50, no. George Washington Memorial Parkway? No, but I was on it anyway. "God!" Balls, crap, piss. I tried to read the map and stay in my lane and not speed and not go too slow so the giant SUV in the rearview mirror wouldn't crawl into my trunk. "I hate tailgaters!" I yelled, beating my fist on the wheel. I could see Georgetown—right there, right *there*, I recognized the red brick buildings of the university. So close. "And yet so far." I laughed, but it sounded hysterical.

Chain Bridge? Too late, I was in the wrong lane. Nobody was going forty-five, the speed limit, but me, so no wonder. Now a long, long, long, long stretch with nowhere to get off. Well, the CIA, but I wasn't going to get off at the CIA, no way. Finally—495, Maryland. Fine, Maryland. Virginia kept screwing me, why not try Maryland. I couldn't tell if it was hunger or nerves that was making my hands shake. Once I got on the Beltway, I'd take the first exit, find a gas station, and buy a candy bar. And look at the goddamn map.

I'd never parked in an underground lot before. I had a heart attack driving under some low pipes, thinking they'd shear off the top of the car, but they didn't even hit the antenna. On purpose I found a place about three miles from the elevator, so nobody was around and I could forward and reverse, forward and reverse, as long as it took to get the Chevy perfectly straight between two gigantic concrete pillars. When I turned the key and the engine hacked and coughed and finally died, it was like washing up on some island after you've been shipwrecked and swimming in the shark-infested ocean for a week.

At least now I knew how to get to Georgetown: you took the Beltway to River Road and then you got on Wisconsin Avenue and just went straight. It was longer, especially if you got in the left lane for Massachusetts Avenue by accident and had to turn around at the Naval Observatory, which was not allowed, but in theory it was a straight shot, and then you just turned right into Georgetown Park's parking lot and there you were. And it was only four o'clock in the afternoon.

I sort of knew where to go now. Back in March with Gram, we'd walked by the cutest tattoo parlor on one of the side streets off M Street, and I was pretty sure I could find it. At least I was on foot. Sunday afternoon. The rain had stopped, and it was like everybody in the whole city was out for a walk on M Street. God, walking around Georgetown by yourself, not with your grandmother, that's like nine and a half on the scale of coolness, maybe even ten. No, ten would be walking around with your boyfriend.

Maybe I should eat something before getting tattooed. There weren't any cheap restaurants, though. That place, the Purple Dog, where Gram and I ate before—it was gone, if I was remembering right; now it was the Black Cloak Inn, and the prices on the menu outside looked outrageous. Eight dollars for a little salad! On Wisconsin, I stopped at an open-air grocery and bought an apple and an orange, and ate both of them on my way to the tattoo place.

Karma Chameleon—thank God *it* was still there. The outside was painted neon green and yellow, and it looked like a happy place, psychedelic instead of biker. I wanted to look at the pictures and read the signs in the window, soak up the atmosphere, get the lay of the land, but a couple coming out of the door saw me and the guy held the door for me, so I had to go in.

Wow, oh wow, this place was awesome. It was like an art gallery. It even had a bunch of couches and easy chairs around a coffee table littered with tattoo magazines and photo albums. Tasteful gray walls, gray carpet on the floor. That was Georgetown for you. The only way you'd know you were in a tattoo parlor was the clerk behind the counter, and behind him the big framed blowups of the most amazing tattoos I had ever seen. A bunch of Georgetown University kids—you could tell by their sweatshirts—

were sitting in the chairs, talking and laughing, looking at picture albums. I wandered over to the side, to a low table covered with big portfolio books chained to the wall, like the yellow pages in a phone booth. I opened one called *Tattootek* and started leafing through it. Whoa. These weren't like any tattoos I'd ever seen before. Rainbow colors, the truest reds and greens, I didn't even know they could *do* that on skin. Every page was like an explosion of colors in your face, and bold, wild shapes, sometimes you couldn't even tell what the picture was, high-tech designs like in an art museum, like that guy Léger. Well, I didn't want that, I was thinking more along the lines of a flower or something, and smaller, I didn't want anything covering my whole back, not that I could afford it even if I did.

The next book was completely skulls and bones, unbelievable, some of them were absolutely beautiful, just exquisite, until it hit you that you were looking at, basically, death. Why would you want death printed on your arm? Or your butt—here was a guy with a little coffin on his ass, and on the other cheek two skeletons with their arms around each other. Weird.

Lots of medieval stuff, the whole dungeons and dragons thing, and devils, demons, vampires, witches, a lot of fiery swords. Two whole books of religious tattoos, including one of Jesus on somebody's arm that looked like a black-and-white photograph, it was so real.

Nature stuff—some of these tattoos I could go for. I especially liked a beautifully drawn blue jay surrounded by pink and green flowers, and a moon-sun design right above somebody's collarbone. Now that was classy. Yikes—this lady had thick black Chinese writing on both breasts, plus her nipples were pierced with spikes. Not little thin rings, *spikes*, maybe a quarter of an inch thick!

"That's gotta hurt," said a woman standing next to me. She smiled on one side of her mouth, the side that wasn't pierced with a little silver paper clip. "I've done my tongue and my belly button, my septum, this one"—pointing to the paper clip—"but I gotta draw the line at nipples. I *mean*."

"Yeah, really," I said.

"But that's just me."

"Me, too."

"I don't care what anybody else does, pierce your brain for all I care."

"I was actually looking more for a tattoo," I said.

"That's all they do here, no piercings. I got this done." The woman had black hair shaved to a stubble, so it was hard to tell how old she was, she could've been twenty or she could've been thirty. She pulled the sleeve of her T-shirt up over her shoulder to reveal an Egyptian woman, like a goddess, in gorgeous pinks and oranges.

"Wow, fabulous. You got that here?"

"Like it? Ask for Stella if this is the kind of work you want. She's a genius. She did this, too." She pulled up her shirt.

"Oh my God!" It was like a pen-and-ink anatomy drawing over her whole front, all the internal organs drawn to scale in the correct places, labeled in old-fashioned script, LIVER, GALL BLADDER, SPLEEN. "That's awesome," I breathed.

"Isn't it great?"

"Was it expensive?"

"Oh, God. Because they charge by the hour and this is complicated. This is no Sailor Jerry flash, know what I mean?"

"Really."

"So now I'm thinking biceps, and I'm thinking either phoenix or Pegasus, the whole myth thing, or else something zodiacal. Just not sure I want a crab on my arm for all eternity, know what I mean?"

"Ha, right."

"So what are you getting?" She rested her hip on the counter and folded her arms. Her head looked bluish under the whiskery stubble, and fragile somehow, you could see the veins over her ears and the bones in her skull. Maybe she'd get her head done someday, little labeled drawings of the cerebral cortex, the medulla. "This your first tattoo?" she asked, eyeing my naked arms.

"Yeah. I haven't quite decided what to get. So—what happens if you get something and then you don't like it?"

"Laser."

"Oh, right."

"But it's expensive, about a thousand bucks even for a small tat, and your insurance won't even look at it."

"Oh."

"So you have to be really sure."

"Yeah."

"You have to pick something that totally expresses your inner self, your personal spirituality. Your body is a temple and you decorate it according to its unique nature."

"Right."

"Tattooing's an artistic way of declaring who you are, you know? What you believe in. So people can see what you are on the inside from the outside."

"Right, sure." I turned back to the book lying open on the counter. My hand fluttered over the picture of two sea horses, another of a howling coyote, an Indian chief, a unicorn, crawling bumblebees. Did any of them express my inner self? "It's kind of like picking out wallpaper." The woman raised her eyebrows and didn't smile, and I added quickly, "The books, I mean, big and heavy, you know, like at the wallpaper store."

"Yeah. So have you got I.D.?"

"Pardon me?"

"They don't do minors here." She gestured over her shoulder.

"Oh." I saw the small sign right behind the computer on the big counter: MUST BE 18—WE I.D. "Oh, yeah." Shit.

"I think sometimes they'll do it if you have a guardian, though, like your mother or something."

I smiled weakly. "That'll happen."

The woman shrugged, sympathetic. "Let's go ask Tony." And she turned and walked over to the counter.

I followed.

"Hey, Tone."

"Fay, what's happening."

"I'm looking at your Celtic custom, you've got some wicked stuff. Listen, this lady—"

"Ruth," I said politely.

"Ruth might have a little problem with her age."

"If she's not eighteen, she's got a problem." Tony's whole face and neck were pierced, silver rings and spikes and clips stuck through his nostrils, eyebrows, cheeks, lips, ears, jaw, forehead, throat. I didn't want to stare, but how could you not? "So how old are you?" he asked me.

"Um, not quite eighteen. Almost."

"You got a driver's license?"

"I left it at home."

Tony and Fay smiled. After a second, I had to smile, too, to show them I knew they knew I was lying. Well, that was the end of that.

Tony had heavy silver rings through the webbing between his thumbs and forefingers. His left arm had twenty or thirty tiny tassels puncturing the skin in a straight line, wrist to elbow, like a fringed leather jacket, except he had a fringed silver arm. "What are you looking for," he asked, "flash or custom?"

"Um . . ."

"How much money have you got?"

"Oh. About a hundred dollars." All my savings that I hadn't banked, plus an advance from Krystal on my next paycheck.

"Flash," said Tony.

"Yeah." Okay, I was looking for flash.

"She could go to Southeast," Fay suggested.

"Yeah. The Navy Yard, you got scratchers around there, they'd probably do you," Tony said.

"Southeast?"

"Or Anacostia."

"Yeah, more scratchers on Good Hope Road, in that area. I mean, if all you want is flash."

"You could try Tex's," Tony said doubtfully. "Really watch the needles, though, don't let him slide any used by you."

I didn't like the sound of Tex's. Plus I'd have to get back on 295, I'd have to go across the river again. "Isn't there anyplace else in D.C.?"

Tony and Fay narrowed their eyes in thought, then shook their heads. "Nah. Pretty much in D.C., you need I.D."

"Okay. Well, thanks. I'll try Southeast, I guess."

"Just be sure to pick an image that mirrors your inner self," Fay reminded me. "You know, something that's the real you."

"Right," I said. "I will."

The real me, I mulled on the sidewalk. Some of the religious tattoos—tats—were really beautiful, but I wasn't that religious. An animal, maybe; I liked wildlife. Or flowers. Flowers might be dippy though. Karen Angleman got a rose on her shoulder blade in ninth grade, and already it was kind of stale. Hm. The true Ruth . . . How about a giant question mark on my forehead?

"'Scuse me. Say, 'scuse me."

I turned around. A man was hurrying after me along the brick sidewalk. His face looked so friendly, I thought I must know him. He stopped in front of me and we said, "Hi," together.

"Hi," he repeated, "how are you doing?"

"Fine, thank you." No, I didn't know him. I was sure.

"So you'd like to get a nice tattoo, huh?"

He must've been in the store—funny I hadn't noticed him. "Yeah." He looked old, forty at least, and he was dressed like a nerd in a yellow short-sleeved dress shirt tucked into too-small green pants, and a black belt pulled very tight around his waist. "I could help you," he said in a soft voice, smiling. "I know a place you could go that's not too far from here. I'm familiar with them, I'm sure they'd do it."

"Um, well, I was going to go to Good Hope Road."

"Oh, Ruth, you don't want to be going there," he said, pursing his lips, trying to look sad, which wasn't easy, because he had one of those faces that always smile, that can't not smile. He started walking while I was talking, so I had to walk along with him. "Good Hope Road's no place for a young girl. A young white girl," he lowered his voice to say. "It's not a good neighborhood, Ruth. Believe me, you don't want to be going there by yourself. There's a place on Georgia Avenue I could take you to. They know me there. I could help you."

"Um . . ." I was trying to think fast. It was a little creepy that he knew my name.

"Georgia Avenue is near here?"

"Pretty near. A car ride, though."

"Oh, I've got a car."

He looked surprised. When he raised his eyebrows, his whole forehead went up an inch. He had curly, wavy hair the color of tobacco. It didn't look quite natural. "My car's right here." He waved his hand toward the street.

"Um . . ."

"To get a tattoo, if you're underage, you have to have a 'guardian.'" He laughed, making little quotation marks in the air with his fingers. "We could tell them I'm your brother."

My father, more like. He kept smiling, smiling. He looked at my face instead of my body—that reassured me. We'd stopped beside a gray car, some nondescript sedan. I looked at him covertly, noticing how his rosy cheeks stood out in his pale, freckled face. I couldn't see any tattoos on his arms. Pudgy arms; he was really bulging out of his clothes.

"Listen," he said, "this isn't a pickup. To tell you the truth, the guys who run this shop I'm talking about are friends of mine. They'd appreciate the business."

"Oh."

"Yeah, it's really just me trying to do them a favor. And you too while I'm at it."

"Oh, I see." I had to smile back, I had to, you couldn't not respond to a smile that insistent. "Well, and Georgia Avenue, um, where on Georgia Avenue is this place?"

"Hm? Oh, up toward Silver Spring, but not that far. Missouri Avenue, in that area."

I'd have to look at my map. "Well . . ."

"It's not that they don't do good work. This one guy's an artist, a genius—but he's just starting out, not many customers yet. I bet he'd cut you a deal."

"Really?"

"Yeah, sure, a discount on some really fine work, probably as big as you wanted. And you should see the colors these guys work with. Incredible stuff. That place—" He jerked his thumb back at the Karma Chameleon and gave his head a quick shake, grinning.

Wow. Way, way cool. If this guy was being straight, wouldn't that be something? A large, beautiful tattoo, something really special, and at a price I could pay.

He dug a key from his pocket and unlocked the passenger door to the gray car. "So what do you think? Want to try it?" He kept his hand on the door handle but didn't open it. "Huh? No harm in trying, you figure, right?"

I folded my arms, pressing my pocketbook to my stomach. I looked over his shoulder, wishing he would stop smiling. "How about if I follow you? I'll come out of the parking lot where I am and pull up right behind you, then you go and I'll follow. That way I'll have my car and you won't have to bring me back here."

He never stopped smiling, but his eyes got darker, it was almost as if they stopped seeing me. He licked his lips. "Sure. Yeah, okay, that'll work. What're you driving?"

"White LeBaron. Convertible, but the top's up."

He nodded, watching me. "Nice car."

"Yeah, my dad gave it to me. Sweet sixteen." I smiled back, lying through my teeth and liking it. A kind of rush went through me—it was the best I'd felt all day. "Okay," I said, "sit tight. I'll swing right around behind you, shouldn't take more than five minutes. I'll give a toot in case you're asleep." I laughed, and the man stared at me hard before giving a quick, uncertain laugh in reply. "Thanks a lot, hey, this is really nice of you." I started backing up.

"No problem."

"Wow, a cheap tattoo—I can hardly wait. Okay, I'll see you!" I waved, pivoted, and strode off down the sidewalk. I didn't turn around, not even at the crosswalk on Wisconsin, because if I turned around he'd know. The powerful feeling was already gone. I felt breathless, panicky, like that time Lisa Cromarty and I, my best friend in Chicago, thought a creepy guy from the bowling alley was following us home. In the dim underground parking lot, I kept walking fast, trying to look innocent and determined and empty-headed, but at the elevator I finally had to turn around to look behind me. No guy.

Unless he was hiding behind a car, looking at me through the dark windshield. A lady rolled a baby carriage around the corner. The elevator came, and I held the door for her. We rode down in silence; the baby was fast asleep with its mouth open, bare legs curled like commas. For a few seconds I felt safe, until the doors opened and the lady rolled her baby in the opposite direction from my car.

There it was, alone in the middle of nothing except dusty concrete. The last thirty yards felt like walking across a minefield, or like waiting for a sniper to shoot you in the back. I got my key out way ahead of time, but my hand was slick and shaky, it took two tries to get it in the lock. The door wouldn't close, I had to slam it three times, and then I banged the lock down with my thumb so hard I tore the nail. Then the car wouldn't start. On the fourth try it growled to life, and I put my forehead on the steering wheel, my heart pounding. Shifting into reverse, I stepped on the gas and crashed into the pillar beside the right rear bumper.

I couldn't even swear. This was beyond any bad words I knew. Tears stung behind my eyes as I inched forward and backed out again, this time not hitting anything. Still no sign of the guy, anyway, and when I paid the lady in the booth five bucks (!) for parking, there was no gray car lurking in wait on either side of this block of Wisconsin. I turned right, toward the river, then right again on K Street, with no idea where I was going. Just away from him.

So far, I wasn't having any fun.

24

When She Was Me

"Ruth was there all along. She was in the store, and that woman, that *bitch*, lied to my face."

I'd never seen Carrie this angry. She was rigid with fury, her teeth clamped, red in the face. She had her hands in fists, elbows out, she was hitting her knuckles together in time to the beat of her outraged voice.

"She was there, and Krystal lied to me, and now she's let her *go*?"

"She's prob—"

"Mama, Ruth's driving the car by herself to Washington."

"But she's a good driver," I said as calmly as I could, "she'll be all right."

"She's not that good. All alone in D.C.? Anything could happen to her. *She's fifteen years old.*"

"Honey—"

"And she's in a mood. I know her, she's feeling reckless, she might do something—Oh, that *woman!*" She pivoted around, looking at the floor, the door, the couch, something to kick. "If she were here now I'd strangle her, I swear to God I would. How could anybody be so *stupid*?"

"Why was Ruth in a mood?" I took her by the arm and tried to make her sit on the sofa, but she spun away and went to stand with her back to the rainy window. The look on her face made me decide to sit down by myself. "Why was Ruth in a mood?" I repeated, though now I wasn't sure I wanted to hear. "What did you two fight about?"

She had on yesterday's clothes, baggy white shorts and an old T-shirt of Ruth's with a Roadrunner cartoon on the front. She must've slept in those clothes. If she'd slept at all. She looked pale and limp, way beyond exhausted. "I'll tell you," she said, folding her arms across her middle. She opened her eyes wide, like she was getting ready to jump off a cliff. "We fought about Jess."

"Jess *Deeping*?"

I jumped when she jerked one arm down and slammed the wall behind her with her palm. "Yes, Mama, Jess *Deeping*. Ruth came home yesterday afternoon and found us. In my room."

I let that hit, let it come right in like a punch to the stomach. It hurt, and it rearranged things inside, but I can't say it was any big surprise. I'd seen it coming. I got too old to fight, and he won.

"Well," I said. "Well. I'll take a wild guess and say you weren't building llamas up there."

"No."

"What did Ruth see?"

"If you mean—us in bed—"

"That's what I mean."

"She didn't *see* anything."

"Thank God for small favors." A sweaty weakness passed through me, as if I needed something to eat. "Well, well, well. Are you proud of yourself? That's a fine example to set for a young girl. I'd say that's probably the end of Ruth's childhood, wouldn't you?" Carrie turned her face away, and I lost interest in going on in that vein. You don't need to punish somebody who's already taken care of it for you.

"All right, then," I said. "What's done is done, no use picking at it, it's over. Come over here and sit. You don't look right."

"It's worse than that."

"How could it be? My God. You haven't married him, have you?"

She looked at me steadily, a long, searching gaze. Once she almost smiled. But mostly she looked bitter. "Mama, do you remember when I flew home from Chicago for the high school reunion? The fifteenth?"

"Just you and Ruth? I remember."

"Jess and I got together that night. I slept with him."

Funny, that didn't come as much of a shock, either. Somewhere in the back of my mind, I think I might've known that all along.

"It was our first time. That probably surprises you. I imagine you thought we were intimate in high school, but we weren't. No, I was a virgin to the end."

She kept wetting her lips. She looked me straight in the eye, but I had a hunch if I yelled *boo* she'd hit the ceiling. She looked like a girl to me, scared but determined, she looked like herself twenty-five years ago. Then I blinked, and the middle-aged woman came back in focus.

"At least when it finally happened we didn't enjoy it," she said with a sour smile. "That ought to make you happy." She looked down. "Sorry. The point is. Ruth . . ."

"Ruth? Ruth what? She was five years old!"

"I told her."

"Dear God. Why?"

"I could've lied. Maybe I should've, but she asked me straight out." She made her hair stick up running her hands through it. "I told you it was worse."

"You're right."

"Do you think I should've lied?"

"How should *I* know? Oh my Lord, my Lord. Oh, what a mess."

Carrie came and sat down at the other end of the sofa. "It's not a mess, Mama. It's not an unfortunate domestic situation. I love Jess. It's real."

"You don't even know him anymore."

"You don't know what I know. Now or then—you have no idea."

"Then?"

"I loved him then, too, but that didn't mean anything to you."

I sat back. "You know, I just had a feeling this was going to turn out to be my fault."

"No *fault*. I'm just trying to make you understand."

"Oh, I understand, I don't think it's that complicated. You're having a fling with your old high school flame, and you want to say it's love so you won't feel guilty. Fine, but don't drag me into it." She just stared at me. She'd figured out about the same time I did that I was trying to make her mad. Why? So she'd drop the subject and we could forget it? Fat chance.

"You know he was more than a crush, Mama. You knew it then, too."

"*Then, then*. I never told you to break up with that boy, you can't pin that on me. I won't say I wasn't tickled pink when you did, but you did that all by your little self."

Unexpectedly, she smiled. "I catch myself trying that on Ruth, too. Pretending something she's done is her idea, when I know it's because of me. My influence."

"I have no *idea* what you're talking about."

"Yes, you do. Mama." She reached across and touched me on the arm with one finger. "You were always so strong. Too strong for me. In a way, you took advantage of me. Not on purpose, but I wanted your approval more than anybody's, and you knew it. I'm too old to blame you because I married the wrong man—"

"But you do blame me," I snapped, stung.

"No, I don't. I honestly don't. Or—if I do, I know I shouldn't. But—you put your fears into me."

"I what, now?"

"You made me feel afraid of Jess. You did. Because he wasn't . . . controllable. It was more than just his background you couldn't stand, it was him. You thought he was wild, you—"

"He *was* wild."

"But he wasn't *bad*. And you knew we loved each other—"

"You were eighteen years old!"

"Old enough."

"Say that to me when it happens to *your* child!"

Carrie unwound her legs and stood up. "I'm sorry. I said I didn't blame you—"

"But you do, that's obvious."

"Mama, I just wish you could've let go of me. And it's *me* I blame, not you, for making it so easy for you to hold on."

"Oh, I see. I didn't love you perfectly. Well, forgive me, I do apologize, I see you're doing a *wonderful* job of letting go of Ruth."

Unfair. Carrie blanched. "It's not the right time," she said thickly, "for us to be having this conversation."

"I couldn't agree more." She looked awful, like everything bad had hit her again all at once. It took a lot of willpower not to go and put my arms around her. "I'll get those dishes in the kitchen," I said, and abandoned her.

I made coffee, slamming things around, making a lot of noise. I'd put my *fears* into her? What crap. I hadn't approved of Jess Deeping, and for damn good reasons, solid, motherly reasons. She ought to be thanking, not blaming, me. If it weren't for me she'd have married that boy, had eight kids, and be living on a dairy farm. Lord help us. Deeping, what kind of a name was that anyway? I'd always hated it, it sounded backwoods and common and sinister. Van Allen, that was a name you could be proud of.

I remembered the time, years ago, when Jess Deeping first came to our house, a winter day with the trees bare and ice coating the branches. I watched him and Carrie through the kitchen window while they prowled around the backyard in their heavy coats, liking it better out there than in the warm house where I could've heard them. Once, by the old sandbox, he put his arms around her chest from behind, plucked her off the ground, and twirled her around and around, as fast as he could. She yelled and shrieked, hanging on to his arms, laughing so hard she lost her breath. I could hardly look at her face, or his. Especially his, excited and satisfied, full of his gleeful power. *You're mine, I can have you anytime I want.* I'd pressed up close to the window, chilled and revolted. Men like that, men with "passion," hah, passions they didn't even know enough to hide, they frightened the life out of me, always had. I wasn't sorry for anything. If I had saved Carrie from the likes of Jess Deeping, I was nothing but glad.

"Coffee's ready," I yelled.

She came in, sat down. Blew into her cup with her elbows on the table, back hunched. She's got my shoulders; O'Hara women have handsome shoulders. But her streaky, honey-colored hair had more silver strands in it than I'd ever noticed before. Everybody's getting old.

"It stopped raining," she said. "Just drizzling now. It's supposed to start again, though. Supposed to rain all day tomorrow."

"Won't your animals get wet?"

"It doesn't matter, everything's waterproof. Well—I'm not sure about the owl." She rubbed her forehead tiredly.

The ark sails tomorrow. I could let go of being against it now, I supposed, since it had already served its purpose. Done its worst. "You still going to the sailing?"

"I can't think about it now."

"No, I guess not."

We drank coffee in silence.

"I don't blame *my* mother for anything," I mentioned. "And I could if I wanted to. Negative influence, that's what she had on me. She influenced me not to be anything like her."

Carrie just nodded wearily.

"All I ever wanted for you was happiness, and that's the God's truth."

"I know, Mama."

"And I don't know what you're talking about—I *did* let you go. Don't you remember, I'm the one who said yes when you wanted to go away to college? It was your father who wanted you to go to Remington."

"I remember."

And afterward, sure enough, she didn't come back. She moved around with Stephen, she'd probably *never* have come home if he hadn't needed a job so badly. That didn't sound like any unhealthy mama's hold to me. That sounded like an independent woman making her own way in the world, far away from her mother, nowhere near her mother.

As far away from her mother as she could get.

Well, there it was. We danced around it, pretended it wasn't there, that nothing had changed since the olden days when we used to like each other. A pure kind of love—we did have that when I was young and Carrie was a girl, I know we did. I know it's not realistic to think you can keep it, but oh, that's what I want back, that pure love, when Carrie was all mine. When she was me.

No, I don't mean that, not the way it sounds. *You were too strong for me, Mama*—but how can you be too strong? That sounded like I wanted to overpower her. Be her.

"Another thing," I said. "Isn't it good to be strong? Doesn't every mother want to pass along strength to her children? And isn't the best way by example? Yes to all that," I answered myself when Carrie wouldn't. "Anyway, I'm not that strong. I'm just loud. A million things scare the hell out of me."

"Name one."

"No."

She finally smiled.

"All I ever tried to do was save you from danger," I said.

"Danger."

"But I never get any credit for that, oh, no, you had to find out on your *own* what scares you, you couldn't take my common sense word for it."

"Well, that makes no sense at all—"

"So what if I was in favor of you marrying Stephen? Why shouldn't I have been? If you two didn't have perfect happiness together, I don't believe that's my fault—and anyway, you got Ruth out of it, so you can't call it a failure."

"No."

"And if Stephen *was* too much like your father, that's not my fault, either. Right?"

"Right."

Oh, she just didn't want to fight anymore. But she thought I'd used my influence—my *strength*, ha-ha—to get her to marry some kind of a duplicate copy of the man I married. For company, I guess, so I could feel vindicated or something. Exonerated.

I shuddered, and spit back the last sip of cold coffee. I couldn't remember ever feeling so old. Too old to change. If I was a bad mother, I'd have to die a bad mother. I ran my hand over the smooth top of the oak table, stripped, sanded, stained, and varnished by Carrie, and thought, *Where'd she get this craftiness?* Not from me, and definitely not from George. Well, that's a blessing. Kids have gifts, flaws, quirks, streaks, whole sides of themselves that have nothing to do with their parents. That's a big relief, isn't it? At least you don't have to take the blame for every damn thing.

When the doorbell rang, Carrie jolted up like she'd been electrocuted. "I'll get it." Barefooted, she raced out of the kitchen.

I heard a man's voice on the front porch. I got up more slowly and went in the living room. Peering around the corner, expecting a policeman, I recognized Jess Deeping just before Carrie raised up her arms and put them around his neck.

I couldn't take my eyes off them. He didn't see me, he had his eyes closed, his face half buried in her hair. It was like a movie, and they were as far from me and just as untouchable as stars up on a screen. I don't know how long they stood that way, neither one talking or moving, just holding on, as if . . . I don't know what. As if they were getting blood transfusions from each other. Then I couldn't look anymore. I walked backward into the kitchen, one quiet step at a time.

I went to the sink and ran water, squeezed Joy on my hands, rinsed. I yanked a paper towel off the holder, and over the sound of swishing paper I could hear Carrie's urgent voice, high and full, direct, not careful, overlapping Jess Deeping's baritone comfort. She didn't talk to me like that, I didn't know that tone. With me she held back. She protected herself.

The screen door slammed, and I hurried back into the living room. Empty. I pressed my face to the screen door. Jess Deeping drove a pickup truck. What else? You weren't allowed to say "white trash" anymore, but you still knew it when you saw it, and that's what that whole Deeping family had been, the cow farmer husband and his nutty wife and their slouching, long-haired boy. I'd detested them, Carrie was right about that. They came too close to the kind of people I'd been trying my whole adult life to get away from. I had, too.

The two of them stood by the curb next to the truck, oblivious to the misting rain. He had her hand, he was looking down at it while he talked, and she had her head up, looking full in his face. She came up to his cheekbone. He wasn't a bad-looking man. He'd filled out since the days when he used to skulk around her like a starving crow, singed-looking somehow, wounded, always scrawny as a pitchfork. And always with that look in his eye like he wanted to snatch her up in his beak, his claws, and fly her off to his hiding place. That boy had never wanted anything but Carrie. I knew he was the enemy the minute I set eyes on him.

He leaned down and put his cheek on hers. They were saying good-bye. It looked like they'd kiss when they straightened up, but they didn't. He started around the back of his truck—and stopped when a little silver Honda pulled up behind it. George's.

I told him to stay home, I said there was nothing for him to do, and here he was anyway. Was he my knight, or Carrie's? It didn't seem fair that she got two and I didn't get any. He got out of the car like an old man, his tweed pants loose and ash strewn, his eyeglasses bumping against his chest on a chain. Carrie went and hugged him, but she didn't get much back—his worried smile and some pats on the back, as if he were burping her. He kept his hand on her shoulder, though, while the three of them had a serious-looking conversation. To my knowledge George hadn't seen Jess Deeping in twenty-five years, but if he thought anything was funny about him being at Carrie's house, he didn't show it.

I got tired of watching from afar. I punched open the screen door and marched out to join the party.

Carrie watched me come like I was Sherman bearing down on Atlanta. I saw her take a deep breath and lift her chin, girding herself. Lord, was I that formidable a character? If she only knew. That what I wouldn't mind right now was somebody, preferably my husband, to fold me up in his arms and hold me tight and tell me everything was going to be just fine.

I stood next to George and interrupted him. "What's going on?" He didn't touch me, but I wasn't surprised; I even saw it from his side for a change. You don't hug a woman who *punches* and *marches* and *interrupts*. You move back, out of the way.

Jess Deeping bowed his head to me. "Mrs. Danziger," he said in his low, sympathetic voice. You'd've sworn, if you were an outsider, that he didn't despise me. He'd always been that way, I remembered, soft-spoken and respectful. He'd treated me, and George, too, with a funny kind of gentleness, in fact. It always put me on my guard.

"Hello," I said, and I softened to him for a second, something about his size, the way he stayed turned toward Carrie a few protective degrees. Then I thought of poor Ruth finding him and Carrie upstairs in her mama's bed, and I froze up on him again. Predator, I thought. Ravenous crow.

"Mama, Jess and Pop are driving up to D.C. to look for Ruth."

"What?"

"Jess was going by himself, but I said I'd go along with him."

"I'll be glad for the company."

"We can take my car. Smaller."

"That'll be fine."

They had it all figured out. I didn't care for the way George said "Jess," like he'd known him for ten years, like they were old fishing buddies. I thought of saying I'd go, too, just to make trouble. Things were moving too fast, all this action, everybody taking steps but me.

"You be careful driving, Pop," Carrie said, walking Jess over to his side of the car. I saw her give him a quick, surreptitious kiss on the lips before he folded himself up and climbed in the passenger seat of the Honda. It made me smile in spite of myself. It made my heart sink.

"Got plenty of money? Got your gas credit card? Buckle up," I told George, holding the door open while he settled himself and rooted his keys out of his pants pocket. "Watch out for the maniacs on that Beltway. They'll kill you as soon as look at you."

"We'll be careful," he said. "And we'll call when we get there."

"*And* if you find her," I said.

"The D.C. cops know the license number," Carrie said, leaning in the other window. "I don't know how hard they're looking, but they've got it. Oh, I'm so glad you're going. Thank you, Pop." She said something to Jess Deeping I couldn't hear.

"Keep calling," I said, backing up, "in case she shows up here. Which I fully expect her to do any minute."

"Right-o." George started up the car, took the brake off, waved, and crept away.

"Drives like a goddamn turtle," I muttered, waving back. I wished I'd kissed him, though. On his whiskery old cheek. It wouldn't have killed me. I wished I had.

Back to the house with the women. I liked the *idea* of the men going off to put things right, the women keeping the home fires burning. If it worked, it'd be a miracle. I couldn't touch another cup of coffee, but Carrie poured one for herself and sat up straight to drink it. "I'm so glad you're here. You and Pop. And Jess," she added on purpose. "I don't know what I'd do without you guys."

"Them, maybe. I haven't done a thing."

"That's not true—we know where Ruth is only because you got it out of Krystal." She grinned. "What a terror you were, Mama. She never had a prayer."

"Well, what a pinhead."

"Oh, I'm still so angry! I'd like to brain her, I'd like to go over there and beat her up."

"I'll hold her arms."

We leaned against each other for a minute. I got a thick feeling in the throat. I said, "I don't want us to start up again."

"I don't either."

"But I have something to say. I'm not taking any of the blame for your life."

"No. No, and I don't—"

"But you were right about one thing. I picked your father out on purpose. He's a fine, fine man, but I married him because he was soft and dull, and that's the truth."

"Oh, Mama."

"It's okay, nothing's going to change, we'll never split up. What's done is done. Anyway, I'm not interested in going out and finding Ricardo Montalban. I got exactly what I thought I wanted, and that's the end of it."

Carrie looked at me with glittery, worried eyes.

"It's *okay*. I'm not hard up. I've got a good husband, a wonderful daughter, and a perfect grandchild. Usually perfect. I made my bed fifty years ago, and I swear to God this is the last time you'll ever hear me complain about it."

She laid the length of her forearm against mine. "What about Jess?"

"What about him? What kind of a name is that, anyway, *Jess*?" Never mind Deeping. "Is it Jesse or isn't it? What the heck is his name?"

"Jesse Holmes Deeping. Holmes was his mother's maiden name."

"Holmes. That's not too bad."

"Oh, Mama, he'll be so pleased."

I ignored that. "If you choose him . . ."

"What?"

"I always thought if you ended up with that boy . . ."

"What, Mama?"

"I thought it would mean I'd chosen wrong, all those years ago. I thought it would mean my whole life, everything I picked . . . Well, anyway. I think that's how my thinking went." Carrie's face got pink. She put her head down, but I saw a teardrop hit her on the arm. I put my hand on her back and rubbed her softly between her shoulders. "What kills me is having to admit that Mr. Jesse Holmes Deeping turned out to be a goddamn pillar of the community. For what that's worth."

"He makes me happy."

"I noticed. I guess that can't be all bad."

Carrie gave a wet laugh.

"So let's finish this up. You're not me and I'm not you, and here you've got a second chance to pick somebody who might be good for you. So do whatever you want, because you're not me."

"I know I'm not you."

"I'm saying that for my benefit."

"Oh." She looked at me like she'd never seen me before.

"Meanwhile, don't think I'm done with George. Not by a long shot. I've got plans for that guy."

"What will you do?"

"Torture him. Make him take dance lessons, that's number one. We've got a vacation coming up—could be a second honeymoon." Carrie smiled, not looking at me—I'd gone too far with that one. "Maybe I'll take him to Krystal's," I said. "She owes us one. I'm thinking a deal on aromatherapy. Or better yet, a high colonic."

Carrie heaved a great sigh. "You love him, though, don't you?"

A picture of the narrow, dwindling future opened for a second in my mind's eye. "Of course I do," I said, and pushed it out of sight. I felt Carrie relax against me. "'Course I do. And vice versa. In his way." We were both quiet, and I imagined she was thinking that last over, sizing it up against appearances. Weighing it against the evidence. It was true as far as it went.

Now that is a stingy, miserly phrase. *True as far as it went.* I lived seventy years like that, in most ways. I kept it small and quiet, as if there was somebody I was afraid of whose attention I didn't want to attract. But I wasn't meant to be that way—I should've been bigger and louder. When it came down to it, I didn't fit my own life.

"Hey," I said after a while. "How're you holding up?"

"I'm better. I don't know why. I guess because they went up there. Jess and Pop."

"Somebody's doing something."

"I don't feel so crazy."

"They might find her," I said.

"They might."

"I just hope it's them and not the cops."

"Me, too."

Carrie leaned over and kissed me on the cheek. "I love you, Mama."

"I love you, too."

She folded her arms on the table and put her head down, closed her eyes. She fell asleep almost instantly, while I sat still as a statue and hardly breathed. I was sorry when she jolted awake after only about five minutes.

Go on upstairs and take a nap, I told her, I'll answer the phone if it rings. No, she wouldn't. So we moved around the house together all day, dragging from room to room for a change of scene. The humidity had to be 100 percent. Nothing to see from the windows but gray and rain. George called in the afternoon to say they were in Georgetown, starting their search. After that the police called twice—nothing to report. About six o'clock, Carrie was standing at the screen door staring out at the rain when the phone rang again. I answered.

"Hello," George's mild, uncertain voice said. "That you, Dana? Carrie there?"

Carrie hurried over, hissed, "*Who is it?*"

"It's your father. George, what's going on?"

"Well, no luck so far, I'm very sorry to report."

Carrie was poised over me like a cat, eyes wide, every muscle tense. I shook my head, and she went limp. She slumped beside me on the sofa, leaning on me, pressing her ear to the phone.

"We've been driving around, walking around," George went on. "I think we've been in every store in Georgetown."

"What about tattoo parlors? That's where she was going—did you go to all the tattoo places?"

"Oh, yes, we did that first thing, and that was somewhat fruitful, actually, although disturbing as well."

"How do you mean?" I said. Carrie had a death grip on my wrist; I was losing circulation in my hand.

"Well, we talked to a fellow in one place, quite a colorful shop, who remembered a girl who did look a bit like Ruth. At least she seemed to when he described her."

"And?"

"He wouldn't give her a tattoo because she was too young. She had no proof of age, so he sent her on her way."

"And? So?"

"Well, the worrisome thing is, this fellow in the store says when the girl left—and of course she might not have been Ruth—when she left, he thinks perhaps one of his male customers may have followed her. Gone out after her, in any case. It's probably nothing—I just didn't like the sound of it. Don't tell Carrie about this, will you? That might be best."

Too late. She was already curled up in a ball on the sofa with her hands over her ears.

25

Payback

I drove by Rude Boy's Industrial Tattoos and Piercings four times, and never saw creepy guy's gray car. It was getting dark, though, so every car was starting to look gray. But I didn't think he was there. He thought I'd bolted on him. If he was looking for me at all, which he probably wasn't, he was looking in Anacostia or Southeast, not the very place on Georgia Avenue he'd suggested we should go to together. No, I'd pulled a double-blind on him or whatever you call it. I foiled him.

No way would I have ever gotten into creepy guy's car. What was I, crazy? I wouldn't have gotten in any strange man's car, but especially that guy's. First of all, there was something icky about his body. I hated his stomach, the way the tight round curve of it poked out at me, and the long line of his fly. He was probably harmless—people don't get kidnapped in the middle of Georgetown on a Sunday afternoon, not that I ever heard of. But still, something about that guy's shape scared me. Something about his stomach.

On the fifth pass, I spotted a parking place two doors down from Rude Boy's, in front of a boarded-up wig shop. Too bad I couldn't parallel park. I almost always ended up like two yards away from the curb and had to start over, which I preferred not to do with cars backed up and people gawking at me. Especially today, when I was trying to keep a low profile.

It was kind of a scary neighborhood. Georgia Avenue started out okay, but it got rougher and rougher the farther up you went, and this was the roughest part, these blocks around Rude Boy's. People who looked like drug dealers were hanging out in doorways and on the corners, and I saw two women who might be prostitutes. One, who was black but had platinum blonde hair, wore clear plastic boots with high heels and a leopard skin skirt and a purple tank top. Then again, she could be an entertainer, a singer or something in one of the rundown clubs around here. Maybe she sang the blues. Maybe she was just starting out, like Diana Ross in that movie. Probably not, though. She really looked like a prostitute.

Behind Georgia Avenue was a bumpy, smelly alley with parking areas in back of all the stores. Faded signs that looked like they'd been shot said CUSTOMER PARKING ONLY, BINGO'S ARMY SURPLUS, and RAY'S LIQUORS ONLY, TOWING ENFORCED. All the spaces behind Ray's Liquors were taken, although it was Sunday. Rude Boy's lot was filled, too. I found a tiny, possibly illegal crevice by the garbage Dumpster behind Gloria's Wigs and Beauty, which apparently didn't exist anymore, if being boarded-up meant anything, and it only took five minutes to wedge the Chevy into it. It took almost that long for the engine to die after I turned the key off. So embarrassing. Nothing like chronic bronchitis to make your car stand out in a crowd.

Okay. Moment of truth. If I got a tattoo, which Mom was against and had semiforbidden until I was eighteen, it would be to pay her back. Might as well be clear about that. When you looked at it like that, it seemed kind of immature.

So? I'd never felt like this before. This was a little taste of what it was going to be like to be a grown-up. Before, I'd been able to imagine myself being, say, twenty-one or twenty-five, but that was about it; after that it got hazy and not interesting. But now, because of Mom and Jess, my imaginable age had been jacked up to, like, thirty. This was a totally adult deal, and it made me sick, it made me want to throw up. There used to be an order to things, but it got broken, my life cracked. This was the adult part—I had a very strong feeling that I'd crossed over a line and entered a new phase of myself. It turned out the older you got, the less things made sense. And this was what we were all in such a hurry to get to, me and Jamie and Raven and Caitlin and everybody in my whole school! What a crock! It was like that movie where the guy in the cult has this horrible, grotesque near-death experience and he comes back to tell his friends in the cult not to do it, don't commit suicide, there's no white light, it's all bullshit—but they don't believe him and they kill themselves and it's this big disgusting bloodbath and that's the end.

I had to get out of the car on the passenger side because the driver's door was mashed up too close to the Dumpster. Rap music thumped from somewhere—a car, because now it was fading. Clayborne was humid, but this was ridiculous; this air felt muggy and smelled dirty, full of exhaust and garbage and sweat and no trees. At least it wasn't raining right now. I only had three blocks to walk around to Rude Boy's, but two different guys spoke to me, "Hey, baby, how you doin'?" said one, and the other made kissing noises. I tried to ignore them without looking mean. It worked, because neither of them followed me.

Rude Boy's was freezing cold. It felt great, I could feel the perspiration on my skin drying. A bell above the door rang when I opened it, but I stood in the middle of the bright, empty front room for a whole minute and nobody came. No WE I.D. signs, I noticed; only ones that said NO CHECKS, NO CREDIT, and TIPPING IS ENCOURAGED. I could smell chemicals, alcohol and something else, like airplane glue. Well, that was good, maybe, it probably meant they kept the place really clean. It gave me a queasy feeling, though, like being at the doctor's. So did a sound coming from the open door in the back, a sound like the drill at the dentist's office. Tattoo gun.

My stomach turned over. I could still leave, nobody had even seen me yet.

Screw that. I walked over to the right-hand wall, which was covered from top to bottom with pictures of tattoos. Most of them you could rule out right away, naked ladies, skeletons, devils, motorcycles on fire, grim reapers, snakes, sharks, scorpions, worms, Confederate flags. I wasn't that wild about the girly stuff either, the dream catchers and butterflies and pretty hearts and rosebuds. There must be something here that expressed my inner self. Also something I could afford—Rude Boy had helpfully put the prices next to the tattoos. Marvin the Martian cost seventy-five dollars and took fifty minutes. Demon Skull was twice as much, but you could see why, all that detail in the creepy hollowed-out eyes and the evil grin. I was down to about eighty bucks since parking in Georgetown and filling the Chevy with gas.

A man came through the door in back. He stopped and looked at me but didn't say anything.

"Hi," I said.

He nodded. I guessed he was black because of his hair, which was in thick charcoal dreadlocks caught up in a huge woolen cap, but he was very light-skinned and his eyes were silvery blue, not brown. He was about my height but very slender, with a long, thin, braided goatee tied at the bottom with beads.

He didn't say anything, so I couldn't be sure he worked here. "Lotta tattoos," I said, waving at the walls.

He said, "Yeah," very softly, with a sleepy smile. Maybe he was high on ganja.

"I have seventy dollars," I lied. "I was looking for some flash."

He nodded.

"So. That would be . . ."

He lifted his right arm and did a slow, dreamy pivot, indicating the artwork all around us.

"Oh. So—any of these?"

"Mmm. You're eighteen?"

"Oh, yes. Just today. It's my birthday." Stop talking. "A present to myself, I was thinking. Happy birthday to me."

He didn't say anything, but he smiled. And I knew I was in.

Okay. Okay! Now, what to pick? It was really hard to concentrate with the guy watching me. "I guess something simple. And cheap," I added with a laugh, but he didn't laugh back and he didn't suggest anything, didn't wave me over to the simple but cheap section. He just stood and looked at me. Weird. It made me nervous.

I spotted some plain black designs, crucifixes, the man symbol, an ankh. An ankh? Raven wore one around his neck. It was the Egyptian emblem of life. It was certainly simple, and the one in this drawing only cost fifty-five dollars. Life—I believed in life. I was *for* life, very much so. It summed up one of my primary inner beliefs, no question. True, it was kind of a basic belief; not too many people were *against* life. Ha-ha. No, but think of all the people who got skull or coffin or corpse tattoos—they were antilife, or pretending to be. If you looked at it like that, the ankh was a strong positive statement. I would be setting myself apart from the morbid antilifers, the posers who thought it was cool to be macabre and grisly and negative. And this was only my first tattoo, I'd probably get more later on, the ankh was like the foundation symbol the rest would build on. First life, then . . . whatever.

"This one," I said, pointing.

The man drifted over. "No. This?" He sounded like he didn't believe me. His eyes were beautiful when he opened them wide. He looked at me with a new kind of interest, as if this was the last tattoo in the world he thought I'd pick. Doubts and second thoughts hit me. Not this one? This was uncool?

"Okay," he said lightly. "I can fill it in with a color for seventy dollars."

"With a color?"

"One color. If you like." He had an accent; I could hear it now that he was speaking more than one word at a time. His voice was very musical.

"Umm . . . red?"

He shrugged.

"I want it to really show up."

"Where do you want it?" he asked after a long pause.

This I'd given a lot of thought to. I wanted it highly visible, I wanted it *in your face*. So not my ankle or my boob or my shoulder blade, none of those coy places, even my arm would be covered up with clothes most of the time. "Here, I want it right here." I held up the top of my right hand and ran my finger along the joint. "Half on my hand and half on my wrist, like overlapping. Right next to the bone. And as big as you can make it."

He thought about that for a while before nodding slowly. "Okay," he said. "Let's go."

My stomach did another flip. I was doing it! I was following him through the door in back and moving down a corridor past rooms hidden by plastic shower curtains, and the voices and rap music and the humming tattoo machines that had been barely audible in the outer room were loud and busy-sounding and thrilling—this place was jumping! Other people were behind the curtains getting tattooed right now, which was a relief, it made me feel great, more excited and not as scared. The man stopped at the last door on the right, before the fire exit door in the very back, and stood aside so I could go in first, holding the tattered blue plastic shower curtain back for me. "Thank you," I said, and went in.

It was just a room. I was kind of disappointed. "Have a seat," he said, and I sat down in one of the two regular chairs, just plain wooden chairs. I didn't know what I'd expected—maybe like a barbershop chair, a dentist's chair, something that reclined. I looked around, but there wasn't much to see, drawings tacked on the walls of pretty gaudy tattoos, apparently this guy's custom creations. Oh—his name was Julian; I knew because he'd signed some of the tattoos.

He had his back to me, he was doing something at a table in the corner. He wore baggy corduroys and a bulky, no-color sweater, through which I could see his shoulder blades and his hips and the bony curve of his butt. He seemed very nice. I imagined him inviting me to go home with him after he did the tattoo. He'd live right over the shop. He would make me spicy food, curried rice or something, and serve it to me on his lumpy couch. Afterward, we'd become lovers, and it would be earthy and real because he was foreign and older. I'd learn a great deal from him. We would live over the store and take care of each other until it was time for me to move on. Which would be very sad and very sweet, but inevitable.

He turned around, holding a bottle of alcohol and some cotton swabs. All of a sudden I was freezing; no wonder he wore a sweater, it was probably fifty degrees in here. He pulled up the other chair close to mine and lifted my right hand out of my lap. He started cleaning it with the alcohol and swabs, and I stared at the crown of his head, how the hair grew in neat lines, thick and woolly, out of his clean scalp. When we lived together I'd braid it for him. I'd stand behind him while he sat in a kitchen chair with a cat in his lap, sipping the herbal tea I'd made him.

After he cleaned my hand once, he cleaned it all over again, really scrubbed it, and then he sprayed it with something from a can, probably an antiseptic. So that was good, this was a clean place. I thought of what the guy at Karma Chameleon had said about needles, but I didn't know exactly what to say to Julian, how to ask. *Oh, by the way, are your needles clean?* How rude. Anyway, I trusted him, I'd already decided.

He went back over to the table. I wished he would talk to me, try to set me at ease, like Dr. Lane did before he filled my teeth. There was the tattoo gun, I could see it, shiny silver and smaller than I'd expected. Julian was doing something with little wells, putting ink in them, red and black. I turned away, I couldn't look.

Oh, *God*. I couldn't even stand getting a shot, and this was going to be like a million shots. What if I fainted? I wasn't that great with pain. *Chill*, I told myself, people do this all the time. It's like sex, you can't believe so many people could have it, but look at the evidence, the world has six billion people or something so somebody must be doing it. Same with tattoos, look at all those basketball players, look at Dennis Rodman, look at Madonna, look at the Red Hot Chili Peppers. They weren't babies and neither was I, I could do it if they could, and anyway Raven said it was more like vibration than a pain, he said it was practically nothing, you got used to it and then it was almost pleasant, it was like a drug high or—

"I'll start." Julian wheeled over a little padded platform and put my forearm on top of it. He looked up when he saw my hand trembling. "Are you afraid?"

I tried to smile, but my lips were too stiff. "No. Not really. Does it hurt?" I gave a high, childish laugh, and blushed. I could have bolted then, jumped up, grabbed my purse, and run. I had a feeling I might throw up. I was so scared, my whole body was shaking with every heartbeat.

Julian said softly, "It won't be bad," and I tried to believe him. "I'm working here, not over bone." He pointed with his index finger at my wrist bone, but didn't touch it. "Bone is the worst. I won't be there."

"Okay." I inhaled and licked my lips. "Okay, then. Let's go. Hit me."

He started the machine. The whine went right into me, into the back of my mouth where my teeth were clenched. Out of the side of my eye I saw him dip needles into ink. "I'm going to start a line now," he said in his lilting voice. I shut my eyes tight.

Yeeeee-ow. It really really *hurt*. It really hurt! *Owww!* I wasn't going to be able to stand it. "Don't forget to breathe," Julian said, but he didn't stop drilling. I showed him my teeth and turned my face away. Breathe. La la la la la, I sang in my head. Okay, it wasn't as bad. But it was still bad. But I could do this. As soon as I knew I could do it, the pain got better. A little. La la la la la.

I wished Julian would talk. I could talk to him, but I didn't want to distract him, make him go outside the line or something. I glanced down at my arm. Oh wow, he'd done the circle part on my hand, which was bleeding a little, not too much. I got a queasy feeling and had to look away.

"Easy," he said, "not so good here," and I could feel him coming closer to the bone for the crosspiece. I wasn't prepared for this deep, biting pain. Tears got deeper and deeper in my eyes. I blinked fast to get rid of them, squeezing and relaxing my left fist for a diversion. I thought of all the movies where the guy gets shot and somebody has to dig the bullet out while he bites down on a piece of wood or something that always breaks, *crack*, right before the fadeout. If I had a stick in my mouth it would break right . . . about . . . *now*.

"Better now," Julian said, and started down my arm.

It was better. This was doable. I decided to talk. "Are you the actual Rude Boy?" No, it was better not to talk. What a jerk I was whenever I opened my mouth. Julian shook his head without looking up.

I crossed my legs. I wasn't cold anymore. Where he was drilling felt warm, and the warmth was seeping all through me, my whole body. "Have you always been a tattooer?" Okay, that was it. He shook his head again, exactly as before, and I closed my mouth. Two people, a man and a woman, started talking in the hall. Their voices trailed away quickly—they must've gone out in the lobby. I wished I could've seen them. The rap coming from somewhere changed to steel drums and horns, sort of third world music. Julian didn't even have a radio in his room. He liked to work in silence.

It got bad again when he started on the other crosspiece, which was close to the other bone in my wrist. I was expecting it this time, though, so it wasn't as shocking.

"Okay. Just filling in now. Bad part's over."

Yes. This was what Raven must've been talking about, not pain so much as an electrical heat, a buzz. Plus it was a really pretty red

Julian was using, it had pink in it, a definite color but also soft. Strong but feminine. I loved it.

By the time he finished I was in love with him, too. I fantasized that he was doing this to me naked. His hands were so clean and slender. I wanted to touch his braided beard, pull on it. Pull his mouth to mine and kiss him. I was feeling a little drunk. High on endorphins.

"Done." He turned off the machine and stood up, went over to his table. "Do you like it?"

My arm floated up, weightless. "It's lovely. Thank you so much." Little pinpricks of blood seeped out of the veins on the surface of my hand. Nothing hurt. It was a beautiful tattoo. "You're a true artist."

He smiled, not with humility or gratitude, but as if that amused him. I felt a little insulted.

"How much do I owe?" I leaned over to get my purse.

"Seventy."

I got out three twenties, a ten, and five ones. Tipping was encouraged. That left me a five-dollar bill and some change to get home on, but that should be plenty. I had a full tank of gas.

Before I could give him the money, he put my arm on the little platform again and started taping a gauze bandage over the tattoo. "Only leave this on for about two hours," he instructed. "Then wash with cool water and soap. Rinse. Dry. For three days, spray very lightly with Neosporin, every five hours."

"Okay."

"No direct sunlight, not for two weeks."

"Really? How come?"

"Because it will fade. In five minutes in sun it will start to fade."

"No kidding."

"It may itch. Don't scratch it, slap it."

"Slap it?"

"If it becomes infected, put Listerine."

"Listerine?"

"Three times a day."

"Okay."

"That's it."

I stood up. I wasn't dizzy or anything, in fact I felt fantastic. "Thanks a lot. I really like it."

"Good." He held the shower curtain for me, and after I passed through, he came out, too. I was surprised when he walked with me out into the bright front room. At the door, he looked down at his filthy, unlaced sneakers and said softly, "I wouldn't ever have guessed that you were gay."

I laughed.

He looked up, smiling. "Usually I know. But with you." He smiled, shrugged. "I wouldn't have guessed. Anyway, doesn't matter. Take care."

He waited for me to leave. I stood still, staring at him with my mouth open. When I didn't move, he stepped back. "Okay," he said, and went back to the hallway. He ducked into one of the other cubicles, not his. A humming tattoo machine stopped; I heard men's low, casual voices. A laugh.

My skin felt prickly hot on the inside and icy cold on the outside. I got the door open. Warm, humid air smacked against me, tugged everything in me down. My systems started working again. The shock wore off.

If only I could die. Right now. God. Oh God, I really wanted to die.

Nobody hassled me in the three blocks to the car. The last place I wanted to go was home. But maybe I'd get lucky and have an accident on the way and be killed. I could drive off a bridge or a cliff, drive into a stone wall. The car would burst into flames and I'd be incinerated, and no one would ever know about my tattoo except Julian.

The car wouldn't start.

Well, now everything was perfect. A perfect day from beginning to end. How could I commit suicide in Washington, D.C.? I could run out into the middle of Georgia Avenue and get hit by a car. But with my luck, I'd only be maimed. I could wait on a corner to get mugged and hope it was fatal, not just a wounding. I didn't want to be raped, though. I'd always hoped if I was going to get raped it would be after I lost my virginity.

I remembered a White Tower two blocks down on the corner. Unbelievable, but I was hungry. I went in and sat at the counter in the only seat left, between a fat man and a thin man, both black. Practically everybody in here was black. I ordered a toasted cheese sandwich and a small Sprite, thinking I was never, in Clayborne, the only white person. They must be scared around us, always being in the minority. I was scared, but I wasn't showing it, because for one thing it would be rude.

I saw myself in the murky mirror behind the counter. My skin was gray, my hair was dirty, I looked awful. I looked like a raccoon, dark hollows under my eyes. My hand hurt—good, maybe it was infected. I didn't look eighteen. No way, I looked about fourteen. I hoped Rude Boy's got busted and Julian went to jail.

I was such a tool. What a stupid idiot moron. *Retarded* people knew the difference between the ankh and the female symbol. But—Julian had rushed me by staring at me and not talking. He'd made me so nervous. "That one," I'd said, and he'd opened his beautiful eyes in surprise. Oh, if only I could die.

The sandwich just made me hungrier. I asked for the check before I had to watch the fat man eat his dessert, a piece of cherry pie with vanilla ice cream. If I left a 15 percent tip, I'd have exactly two dollars and ninety cents left. Which still should be plenty. I put a quarter and a nickel next to my plate, thanked the waitress, and left.

A girl was hanging up the receiver of the beat-up pay phone on the street just as I passed behind her. So it was like a sign.

Between the cars going by and the kids who should've been in bed by now playing jump rope in the middle of the side street, I had to stick my finger in my ear to hear the operator. "I want to make a collect call," I said, and gave her the number. "From Ruth. To whoever answers."

Mom answered.

"Hello?"

"Hi."

"Ru-uth?" Her voice broke in the middle. Something happened to my throat, too; I couldn't talk for a second. Then Mom said, "Where the hell are you!"

"I'm not telling. Anyway, what do you care?"

"Jess is looking for you, Jess and Grampa, they drove up there togeth—"

"Jess and *Grampa*?" Incredible.

"Tell me where you are!"

"Okay. I'm in D.C."

"I know that."

"How do you know?"

"Your friend finally told us."

"Who, Krystal did?"

"Are you anywhere near a police station? I want you to—"

"No, I'm not near a police station. The car's broken, so I'm sleeping on the street tonight. This is a really crummy neighborhood, Mom. Can you hear it? It's raining again, though—maybe I'll go home with somebody instead of sleeping on the sidewalk."

"Ruth—"

"I could go with some derelict, they're all over the place. A pedophile already tried to pick me up. He wanted me to get in his car, and I almost did. He wanted to take care of me."

"Listen, listen to me."

"I figured out afterward I should've gone with him. I could've been his little girl." Mom gave this high wailing sound. "Maybe I'll share a needle with some of the guys on this street. Maybe have sex with one of them and get AIDS and die." I kept talking even though I was crying. "Why not? I mean, it turns out I'm gay anyway."

"Ruth, please, oh honey, for the love of God—"

"What would you care? If I was dead you could have your lover all to yourself, you and Jess could live happily ever after."

"Ruth—!"

I hung up. I was shaking, I felt hollow inside, I felt like a straw, nothing in me but air. I didn't even know I was that angry. I scared myself.

Stiff-legged, I marched back to the car. It almost started, but then I flooded it and it died.

I crawled over the seat and lay down in the back. I put my good arm over my eyes to block out the glare of the streetlight. The smell from the garbage Dumpster was stronger in the dark. I was sweating from the breathless heat, but I was afraid to roll down a window. My hand hurt. It was almost time to take off the bandage, but I didn't want to look at my tattoo. I wanted my arm to get gangrene and fall off in the night.

I listened to music and the hiss of car tires and the shouts of children and the dangerous, interesting sound of men and women laughing. I thought about how many minutes our phone conversation probably took off Mom's life, and if it was more or less than the number I'd put on with good deeds when I was little. I thought about calling her back and telling her I was okay. A little after midnight, I fell asleep.

26

Floating the Ark

The police left the house a little after ten on Monday morning. They were beginning to look embarrassed, I thought as I ran water over their half-finished coffee cups, but still not worried. What did it take to make them worry? Body parts? Hanging over the sink on my elbows, I let my eyes go out of focus. My brain felt like the rings of water swirling above the drain, aimless, driven by nothing but physics. You couldn't live with the worst fear you'd ever imagined, the one you'd been pushing to the back of your mind since the day your child was born—you couldn't live with that hour by hour and stay clear in the head. I could feel my mind blurring, not from fatigue but for protection.

What was I doing? Oh. This was happening more frequently, amnesiac episodes when I couldn't remember what I had just said, or thought, why I was in a certain room, what a two-way conversation was about. Except for a sick, disorienting hour early this morning, I hadn't slept in over two days. What was that, how many hours? I tried to count, but got lost in the numbers. What did it matter anyway.

My mother came up behind me—I jumped when she put her hands on my shoulders. "Hard as rocks," she said, digging in with her thumbs, Mama's idea of a massage. "Listen, now, today's the day. She'll either come home by herself or they'll find her. This is it, I'm positive."

I nodded; it was easier than speaking. Along with everything else, for some reason I was losing my voice.

"And she's fine. All that bull—that was just stupid, snotty talk, she did *not* sleep on any street last night. Her idea of paying you back."

My throat hurt, or I'd have said, "You didn't hear it, the noise in the background, she was *on* the street." Nightmare sounds; they'd kept me in a state of dread all night. *My baby is in hell and I can't find her.*

"She's all right, Carrie. Come on, you can't get like this."

"I'm all right."

"Tsk. Let me do that."

"I'm finished. Is Jess still here?" He and Pop had been sitting beside each other on the sofa in the sunroom for the last hour, talking quietly, passing sections of the newspaper back and forth. I knew he was still here—I just wanted Mama to talk to me about him.

"He's here." She stopped the sharp-fingered massage abruptly. "I told him to go, but he wouldn't."

I turned around in dismay. "You told him to go?" She'd been civil to him last night, and almost nice to him this morning. She'd brought him coffee, called him Jess, asked him a polite, fairly astute question about the city council's position on the school tax hike proposal—I thought she was making a real effort.

"To the *sailing*. I told him to go see the ark float."

"Oh."

"But he won't."

"No."

"Rather be here." She sniffed, either in approval or disapproval, I couldn't tell. "It's a shame you both had to go and miss it. After all that work you did."

A stunning concession. I wasn't sure I'd heard right. "It'll be there awhile," I said. That was a sore point with Mama, the fact that the town was allowing Eldon to keep the ark tied up on the river until the twenty-sixth of June—forty days and forty nights.

"It'll be there awhile," she agreed gloomily. "Still. I know you wanted to be there when they put the animals on. I'm sorry, but your daughter has a lot to answer for."

"I just want her to come home. I don't care what she's done anymore."

"I know." She put her arm around my shoulder. "You never worried me like this. It never occurred to me to say thanks."

Oh, I didn't want to cry again. "You're welcome," I said, and tried to laugh. "It's never too late to take credit for being the perfect child."

"Don't push your luck," she said, and hugged me.

The phone rang. She stepped out of the way—she'd learned not to try to answer it herself.

"Hello, Carrie?"

"Yes? Is that—Landy?"

"It's me, I'm calling here from the Point. Things are starting to break up now."

"Oh—how are you? Did everything go all right? Jess is here—I'm sorry we couldn't go down there. I don't know if you heard about Ruth, but—"

"Yeah, I did, Jess told me last night. So she's not there yet?"

"No."

"Well, I wondered about that. I didn't want to call you for nothing, but then again, I figured if you knew she was back you'd be down here. It went real well, by the way. Daddy couldn't stay long after the boarding, but he was just as pleased as could be with everything."

"Oh—good. But what were you saying about Ruth—"

"Well, I saw her about halfway through it, about the time we were putting on the medium-size animals."

"What? What?"

"I couldn't stop what I was doing, and after that I lost sight of her—there was a crowd, even the TV people were down here, we were real pleased—"

"Ruth was *there*? Landy, are you sure?"

"It was her all right. It was still raining and she didn't have no umbrella, so she was quite a—"

"Is she still there?"

"That I can't say for sure. I haven't seen her since then, and that was maybe an hour ago, but she could still be. I wished I could've got her, talked to her, but I didn't know if she'd already gone home and come back and you knew it, or just what. Sorry if I messed up—"

"You didn't. Thank you—I'm coming right down."

"Ruth's *there*?" Mama followed me out of the kitchen, into the living room, the sunroom, while I called all the way, "She's back! We found her!"

The men jumped up from the couch. "She's down at Point Park, or she was, Landy just saw her."

Jess shook his head in amazement.

"Who's Landy?" Pop said, beaming, patting Mama on the shoulder.

"Landy Pletcher, Eldon's son," Jess said. "What's she doing down at the Point?"

"I have no idea. Pop, can I have your car? He said the launch went perfectly," I told Jess, "he said TV people were there."

My father dug his keys out of his trouser pocket and tossed them over. "Want me to come with you?"

"I'll go, too," Mama said, looking around for her purse.

"No, Mama, no. Pop—thanks. I'm going by myself."

In the hall, I grabbed an umbrella from the coatrack. I was halfway through the door when I remembered. "Oh—Jess, can you take my parents home?" They'd all followed me into the hall.

"Glad to," he said. We exchanged a secret look. We were enjoying the same mental picture, I knew: of Mama bouncing along between Jess and Pop in the pickup.

• • •

The Leap River was a glorified creek that began at Culpeper and flowed south through Greene County. The deepest part was at the Point and east for a few miles, past Leap River Farm, Jess's farm; after that it turned back into a stream and finally trickled away into the Rapidan. Point Park, Clayborne's main civic recreation area, started at the bridge and ran adjacent to the river for almost half a mile. It had hiking trails, picnic shelters, a children's playground—soon to be refurbished with Eldon Pletcher's money—pretty views, a jogging path, a band pavilion, ball fields. The centerpiece was two wide, side-by-side fishing piers made out of river rock and stretching halfway to the other side of the Leap. Jess, Landy, and the Arkists had constructed the ark between the two piers, which were slightly less than thirty feet apart—a perfect distance for a nineteen-foot-wide ark; if they'd built it at a shipyard they couldn't have found a more convenient staging area.

From the parking lot, I couldn't see it clearly; too far away, too many trees in the way. But what I could see made me laugh, a quick, nervous explosion at the sight of an ark, an *ark,* bobbing on the khaki-colored river. They'd painted it a light charcoal gray to resemble weathered wood, with gay white and black for the doors and portholes and trim. It was a handsome ark, most impressive, you'd never have guessed it was hollow inside, a mere floating stage. What startled the laugh out of me was a glimpse of my lovely giraffe, head jutting up over the flat top of the third deck, so raffish and silly—and as I drove past, his mate on the flip side looking coy, batting her long black pipe cleaner eyelashes. Oh, it worked. Glory be, it really worked. It could've been such a disaster.

The skies were clearing, but raindrops still fell heavily from the trees overhanging the paved lane leading from parking area to parking area. I turned on the wipers and huddled over the steering wheel, my face close to the steamy windshield. Cars and people still clogged the drive; if the crowd had "broken up," as Landy said, it must've been enormous an hour ago. Food and balloon vendors were closing down their concessions. I passed a white van with a satellite dish on top—a TV crew? I slowed to let a mother and her little boy cross in front of me. In red letters across the chest, the boy's T-shirt said I SAW NOAH'S ARK, and the date. What entrepreneurial genius was selling those? Not the Arkists, I was sure. Thank God Mama wasn't here.

I turned around at the dead end without seeing the Chevrolet. Could Ruth have gone home? We'd have passed each other, though, and I'd been watching carefully. Maybe she was on the other side of the river.

I steered slowly out of the park, across the bridge, and turned in at the gravel drive above the tow path. More people, more cars.

There, I saw it. No—that Chevy Cavalier had a huge dent in the fender. I stopped next to it, blocking a car behind me, and rolled down my bleary window. Ha! There was Stephen's expired faculty parking sticker under the rearview mirror. Ruth was nowhere in sight.

A crumbling concrete lane led steeply up the hill behind the river to Ridge Road, where there was another, smaller parking area. Jess and I, a million years ago, used to go there and park. I found a place for the Honda near the overlook. Just as I was getting out, a fresh rain shower started. I opened my umbrella and started back down the slippery road toward the water. Watching my feet, I didn't see Ruth until we almost walked into each other.

"Oh," she said involuntarily. Her surprised face shut down and turned stony. My impulse to reach out for her sank just as fast—but the dark thing, the deep dread inside finally slithered away, out of sight. Gone.

She looked half-drowned. "Are you all right?" She gave a nonchalant nod. "Come on," I said, and turned around. I tried to share the umbrella, but she made a point of slouching up the hill beside me in the downpour. *Drown, then,* I thought. Anger was working hard to overwhelm my relief; the urge to slap my daughter's sullen face had never been stronger. But neither had the urge to grab and hold and never let go.

Inside Pop's car, I fumbled in the glove compartment until I found a clean handkerchief. "Here, dry your hair. At least dry your face." She turned around to comply, surliness in every move, every line of her body. For a second I felt drunk on it, the old familiar sneering meanness, the intimacy, the dearness of it filling my throat like honey, like tears. *We will get through this, and it will be awful, but oh I love you, I love you.*

The rain slacked off again, reduced to trickling streams down the windows. Through the murk and the trees, the little bit of river visible from here was only a muddy, moving blur. "Are you cold?"

She shook her head, staring straight ahead. She looked exhausted, red-eyed and disheveled, the wrinkled knit of her shirt sticking to her childish breasts. She wouldn't look at me. I couldn't stop looking at her.

"Why did you come here? Why didn't you go home?"

"I drove by, saw a million cars. Including the cops."

She must've seen Jess's truck, too. "Are you all right?" I asked again.

She shrugged one shoulder and stared out the window.

"Did you get a tattoo?"

Her nostrils flared. "I don't have to tell you anything."

In spite of everything, I wasn't prepared for more hostility. She leaned forward to wipe the condensation off her side of the window, then switched the wipers on for one swipe and turned them off. The message: anything outside this car is more interesting than anything inside.

"I'm sorry for what happened," I said. "Sorry for the way it happened. I know you're hurt. But if you're waiting for me to apologize for being in love with Jess, that's not going to happen."

"Who cares, Mom, I don't give a damn anyway."

I sighed when she folded her arms across her chest; fortifying the stockade. There was nothing to do but start further back. "You know Jess and I went to school together. When we were in high school, we fell in love. Eleventh grade."

"How come you never told me?" She made her voice sarcastic, as if the answer would be obvious to a child. "How come you kept it a secret?"

"I told your father," I evaded. "It wasn't a secret."

"Oh, yeah, what did he say?"

"Nothing. He—didn't think anything of it."

"Poor bastard."

I blanched, not at *bastard* but at the casual cynicism. I'd never wanted her to be this grown-up.

"Ruth. I know how you feel."

"Bullshit, you don't know anything."

"Then tell me."

"No."

I took hold of the wheel and turned it back and forth until the steering lock clicked. "I'll tell you how I feel, then. I'm sorry I hurt you. I'd rather hurt myself. If you wanted to punish me, you couldn't have picked a better way. And I'm angry about that. Ruth, I am so mad at you."

She scowled straight ahead.

"I *do* know how you feel. You think I dishonored your father. You think the two people you trusted most have been false to you, tricked you. You're furious and you're hurt." Her cheeks turned bright red. She looked out the side window to hide her face. "How was I supposed to tell you?" I said thickly. "Do you think I did any of this on purpose? I didn't want to fall in love with Jess again."

She said through a stuffy nose, "Why didn't you just marry him in the first place?"

"I should have."

She turned on me with burning eyes. "Oh, that's great, Mom, then I wouldn't even exist. Then you and Jess could have everything."

"Oh, stop it. I should've married him because he was right for me. I fell in love with Jess when I was seventeen. No—eleven, the first time we met." I couldn't help smiling, but that only made her flounce around in disgust. "The reason I didn't marry him is because I chickened out. He was . . . a wild boy. Your grandmother couldn't stand him," I said with a careful laugh. Ruth wouldn't look at me, but I could tell she was listening closely. "But he wasn't wild, not like that. I doubt if he ever even broke the law—speeding, maybe. He was just different, he unsettled some people."

"Like Gram."

"Yes."

"Maybe she thought . . ." She stopped, remembering she wasn't talking to me. But then she had to finish. "Maybe she thought it was catching. Jess's mom's disease or whatever."

He'd told Ruth about his mother? I hid my surprise. "I think you're right, I think that was part of it. And I think that's why he changed when he got older. Partly. Became more sedate. Cooler."

"All grown-ups do that."

"I suppose." I gave up; I couldn't explain Jess, it was beyond me. Especially to Ruth, especially now. And what a dangerous job, clarifying for my daughter why I loved someone else and not her father. However I phrased it, how could that do anything but wound?

"Mom?" She fiddled with the radio dials, the heater knobs, hunched forward, giving me her closed profile. "When you, um, whatchacallit. Committed adultery, did Dad know? Was it . . . is that why he crashed the car?"

"No."

"How do you know?"

"Because—it was years before—you were a *baby*." She gawked at me, finally more amazed than angry. "But I'm not—this isn't something I want to talk to you about. I told you, one time, and never after. It was a mistake, and I suffered for it."

"Oh yeah, I'll bet."

"Ruth, listen. People can't always choose who they love, sometimes it just happens. Sometimes we—"

"We can choose who we sleep with!"

Ah, the knife in the heart. She wouldn't look at me, so I let my face crumple, breathing through my mouth, hoping I wouldn't cry. "We can," I said, voice fluttery. "You're right."

"And you were wrong." Implacable.

"That's what I've been trying to tell you."

She wiped the windshield with Pop's handkerchief and turned on the wipers again. Needlessly; the sun was breaking out in patches. A billowy wind chopped the surface of the river, dulling the shine. It was clammy in the car; I rolled my window down a few inches. Finally I had no choice but to find a tissue in my pocket and blow my nose. When I did, Ruth glanced at me.

"*Jeez*, Mom."

I couldn't hear any sympathy. I wiped my face, sniffed in the rest of the tears. Amazing, how prodigiously well I was botching this job. "I was wrong, I admit it. But not only for what happened with Jess. I was guilty of a kind of cowardice, too." But was she old enough for that revelation? No, I decided, backing off; let Stephen stay the innocent, injured party a while longer. Forever, maybe. Yes.

"The important thing is that your father never knew about us."

"How do you know?"

"Because I know. I swear—you can let that go."

She stared at me fixedly for a long minute. "Okay," she said, and we both relaxed slightly. A little light slanted through the murk.

"Here's the thing," I said. "Eventually we have to forgive ourselves. I know you think I'm a hypocrite, a liar, a—a jezebel—"

"What's a jezebel?"

"It's kind of a . . ."

"Slut?" But she blushed when she said it, and smirked, trying to make it sound like a joke.

"The things you think I've done wrong—I did them out of love, and so I forgive myself." Her mouth pulled sideways; I could practically hear her thinking, *How convenient.* "That's not an excuse. Or—it's the *only* excuse. Listen to me. If Stephen had lived, I don't believe we'd have stayed together. Not because of Jess—don't think that. And I know you don't want to hear it, but I *can't* explain this to you until you're older."

"Why not?"

"Because it's not fair to your father. But Ruth—Jess is for me, I can't do anything about it. Do you think it takes anything away from how much I love you? It doesn't. It doesn't. You're the best part of my life, you've always been, that can't ever change. Even if you—tattooed your whole body."

She snorted. And colored again, and stared down at her lap. She almost smiled.

"I know I've been too easy with you sometimes. That's been my biggest failing as a mother, but the reason—"

"No, you haven't."

"The reason—and it's hard for me to tell you, but I'm going to—it's because I've always tried so hard not to be like *my* mother. Who, frankly, wanted to run my life for me—and this I'm telling you in confidence, woman to woman. But she did it out of love—again—so I've forgiven her, too." The reality wasn't as neat and tidy as these linked, symmetrical revelations implied, but I wasn't trying to illuminate a moral lesson, I was just trying to tell the truth. Finally. "But that's beside the point, we're not talking about my mother, we're talking about yours. I've tried—" I sighed, suddenly exhausted. I put my head back. "I've tried to be a good mother. And I know, I can *hear* that that doesn't sound like much. And I'm sorry if I've been permissive or loose or if it's felt to you as if I don't care—"

"Mom—"

"—or I'm uninvolved. Because, believe me, I couldn't *be* more—"

"Mom. You're not lax. I don't even know where you get that."

"I'm not?" I got it from Stephen.

"*No. Jeez.* You're a lot of things that aren't so great, but permissive isn't one of them."

"Oh." That stopped my momentum. "I thought I was. As a reaction."

"Well, you're not. *God.*"

"Okay. Well."

Was she trying to make me feel better? Worse? I was thinking of what to say next when Ruth said, "I didn't mean there's a *lot* of things. You know, that aren't so great. Some, a few things. That's all."

My heart swelled at this overture. "Oh," I said, low-keying it. "Well, that's good. Some; that's better than a lot. There are . . . almost no things about you that aren't so great. To me. Well, one thing. That I'm thinking of right now, but that's it."

Suspenseful pause.

"What? The car, right? That was an accident. I was backing up—"

"No, not the car. Last night. The things you said on the phone. And I didn't know where you were, and I couldn't find you, and I didn't know what to do." The deadliest time of my life. Like being buried alive.

"I know." Her pale face flushed. "That was, like, a really bad time for me."

"I know," I said, anxious to forgive.

"Sorry," she mumbled, playing with the door handle. "I thought about calling back. I knew it was rotten, and I just—did it anyway." She shook her head, looking baffled, as if that instance of adult cruelty didn't fit with her idea of herself.

I reached out to stroke a dark, wet strand of hair behind her ear, something I'd been wanting to do for fifteen minutes. "It's all right. It's okay." I'd have worried I was being too lax, but apparently that wasn't one of my failings after all. On the other hand, Ruth's perspective might not be totally objective.

"God, I'm tired. I'll tell you everything that happened, but not right now, okay?" Her face, bland and accepting as she suffered my increasingly affectionate caress, sharpened all at once. "Oh—I forgot."

"What?"

"The car died. I think. I parked it down there—"

"I saw it."

"And now it won't start. I think this time it's really dead."

Were we finished? For the time being? Ruth had a lot of explaining to do; I had a lot of discipline to mete out. Neither of us was in the mood to get on with either of those. "Let's go see if it starts," I said. "If not, we'll come back for it later."

"Okay. Look, the sun's out."

I started the car and drove down the hill. Double-parked, I waited while Ruth got out and tried to start the Chevy. No luck. "Nope," she reported, getting back in. "All it does is make a clicking sound."

"Could be the battery."

"Or maybe the starter."

We drove out to the highway and across the river bridge.

"Mom, I gotta say, it looks really cool." She meant the ark. I glanced over, suspicious. She didn't *look* sarcastic. "Too bad you missed all the action," she continued, with breathtaking casualness. "Stop here for a sec, okay—look how it looks from here."

I pulled up behind a line of cars parked on the verge, just beyond the bridge, and we gazed down at the floating, bobbing ark, tied with taut, multiple lines between the two long piers. "Let's get out," Ruth said, and so we did, and stood on the grass with our backs against the car, looking down at the ark. "So it's hollow inside? Because guys were walking on it when they put the animals in. Isn't it cool that it rained just for the boarding part? Like, symbolic."

"It's got a solid deck, but no hull, nothing underneath," I said. "It's a raft, basically—"

"But I can see it going down, I can see the sides under water."

"I know, but there's nothing behind, it's just painted sheets of plywood, and they only go down about two feet. It's an illusion."

"Cool."

"It's a raft with two hollow boxes on top. You can stand on the main deck, but the other two are fake. You never saw anybody walking on them, I'll bet."

"No, they went inside with the animals, and then put them out through the windows on the two upper stories. I figured there were stairs in there."

"Nope. A ladder."

"Wow. Everybody really liked it."

"Did they?"

"There were a million people at least, I mean, it was like the Fourth of July almost, you should've . . ." She pulled on her hair, a childish habit, and usually an indication of moral uncertainty.

"I got here about nine-thirty or so," she started again, speaking slowly. A news report. "They were just starting to put the animals on. Some TV cameras were here, and people doing radio interviews, I guess—they just had tape recorders and microphones. I saw Landy, he was with about six guys, I guess Arkists, rolling animals up the gangplank or whatever you call it—which is gone now, they took it away when they were done. Everybody thought the animals were great. For a while I was standing near this family, the parents and these two little girls and one boy. They went nuts over the monkeys especially, Mom, but also that flying cat and the elephant. And the owl. Everybody liked the polar bear. I think the big animals were more, like, crowd pleasers, but that's because most people were far back—anybody on either one of the piers could see the little animals perfectly. I like the prairie dog a lot. And the chicken. The mouse—that was cool how you had it going up the chain.

"I heard this guy near me saying how there was only one of everything, how come there weren't two, so I told him about the different sides. He thought that was neat. I didn't tell him I was related to the person who made everything. I was going to, but then, I don't know, I just didn't.

"I saw Mr. Pletcher. And his wife. He had on a black suit and she had on a navy blue suit and a flowered hat. In fact you could tell all the women who were Arkists because they all wore hats. They had cameras on Mr. Pletcher; I think he gave an interview. He looked pretty, you know, blissed out. Maybe he was on drugs. Landy went and stood with him when they were finished with the animals, and then he gave a speech."

"Landy gave a speech?"

"Yeah, and it wasn't bad. But you could tell he was nervous. He stood right down there, right there, on this raised box thing, right by the water. He just said thanks to everybody for coming out, and he named the people who had helped. He named you. And—Jess. And some others. He read the ark story from the Bible. Then he carried the microphone over to his dad, who was behind him. The P.A. system must've been really cheap, at first all you could hear was squeaks and squeals. Landy held the umbrella over the old guy and he said something, but we couldn't hear him. Everybody got really quiet. His voice was so weak, and it took him forever to say what he said. Which wasn't much, but I can't quote it or anything. Just about how the ark doesn't mean God's wrath, it means forgiveness, and like, starting over from scratch.

Purification. And then something about how kind people were to him, all his dear friends and his family. How much love he felt. Their generosity to him. Because they saved him. Then he said good-bye, and—some people cried, which was weird because, before, it had been like a carnival, almost. The Arkists sang one song, a hymn, and it was really . . . how can I say this . . . terrible. So then the ceremony part was over, and people just crowded around the ark as close as they could get and looked at it. Anybody who had a camera took about a million pictures. They really . . . they really liked it." She paused, thinking. "I guess that's about it," she said, and sat back.

I gazed down, easily imagining, thanks to Ruth, a milling crowd under umbrellas around a makeshift platform in the rain. Landy mumbling into a squawky microphone, screwing up his courage to read the story of Noah to hundreds of strangers. And Eldon, struggling to say his piece in the little bit of time left. Giving thanks for a singular act of love, the expression of which was floating on the river in front of him. An ark.

"Hey, Mom. Wanna see my tattoo?"

"Oh." I tried to sound thrilled. "I definitely do. Is it wonderful?"

She laughed.

"I've been thinking maybe I should get one," popped out of my mouth. "Think I'm too old?"

"No *way*. I think you should get one exactly like mine."

"Really?"

"Absolutely. Mother-daughter tattoos."

There was a glint in her eye that tipped me off. Oh Lord, what had she gotten, a swastika? Coiled snakes? I put a light, very tentative hand, just my fingertips, really, on her spine as we turned away from the river. Immediately her arm came up and circled my waist.

"Want to drive?"

She flashed me a look of surprise. "Sure," she mumbled, pleased, coloring. "Thanks." We separated casually.

"We'll come back for the car tomorrow."

"Good deal."

In the car, Ruth showed me her new tattoo. And then we went home.

27

THE LAST STRAW

School's out, finally. For the very last thing in English, Mrs. Fitzgerald told us to make a list in our journals of the two or three major things most on our minds as we say good-bye to sophomore year and look forward to becoming juniors, and then try to develop strategies for dealing with these issues over the summer vacation. Most kids didn't bother because she was never going to check and see if we did it, but I came up with a big list, a huge list. The first item was—

No. 1. *My tattoo.*

This experience continues to suck and be as putrid and humiliating as ever. First I put a bandage over it for school and told people I had a burn. Then I told Jamie the truth after making her swear never to tell a living soul, not even Caitlin. Surprise, surprise—the whole school knew all about it within one day.

Gram hates my tattoo and said she'd pay to have it lasered off, so she and Mom took me to the dermatologist, Dr. Ewing, who said it would be pretty major to remove the whole thing and how about if he just took off the arms and the top of the circle, and after that healed I could go to a reputable tattoo place and have the arms put in lower and the loop more oval, so like a real ankh tattooed over the old one.

Nobody was in favor of this but me. Luckily the money factor kicked in, so that's probably what we're going to do. I'm pretty stoked, but it won't happen until August, and meanwhile I've got this, like, lollipop on my hand. Not to mention a lot of stupid gay jokes to put up with. Some guy at school called it an "all-day sucker." Which, when you think about it, is pretty much what I was.

Meanwhile, I've been thinking. *Why* is the female symbol a lesbian thing? Men wear stupid macho symbols, swords and guns and flaming motorcycles and what-have-you, and nobody says *they're* gay. Just the opposite. I don't know, I'm torn. Sometimes I think screw it, I'm keeping this, it's a sign of my female power. I'm strong in myself, I know who I am, and to hell with what anyone else thinks. Okay, but then I think—but why does it have to be so hard? And do I really want a tattoo I'll always have to be *living down*? And besides, I really *want* an ankh. Because I'm *for* life.

So I don't know. I still have a few more days to decide.

No. 2. *Raven.*

I guess he's not my boyfriend anymore. Not that he ever was, except once for about five minutes. I'd been noticing he wasn't as friendly as before, and I found out why: The Other Woman. "Cindy." She's this total Goth, a sophomore, honest to God she looks like a corpse, they've sent her home twice that I know of for ghoul makeup. I saw her with him in the library two times and once in his car. They're perfect for each other. I don't miss him. In fact it's a relief not to have to hear his atrocity stories anymore.

I can't believe I used to worry about my name, like it wasn't dark enough or something, I should change it to Hecuba—and now this. *Cindy*??

No. 3. *Krystal.*

Mom made me quit working at the Palace. God, she's still so mad. Much madder at Krystal than me, which doesn't make too much sense. "You're not the adult, she is," is all she'll say. I ran into Krystal in the video store one night—luckily Mom wasn't with me. It was weird at first, but after a few minutes of chatting, it was like old times. She broke up with Kenny. Now she's going out with the UPS man—Walt, I've met him plenty of times. "He's a very gentle meat eater," she says. When we finished catching up and all, Krystal said, "You stay in touch now, and don't be a stranger." I said I wouldn't be, and then I thanked her for helping me out, letting me sleep on her couch and everything. She said, "Anytime," and I was about to go on and thank her for the rest, but when I heard in my head how it would come out—"Thank you for lying to my mom and not telling the cops that I took the car and drove by myself illegally to D.C."—I couldn't say it. Like, it almost sounded sarcastic or something.

I'm not saying Mom's right about Krystal—I definitely think her heart was in the right place and she was a true friend when I needed one. Just saying, there are different ways to be a person's friend, and maybe aiding and abetting them no matter what they do is not the best way every single time. That's all.

No. 4. *Punishment.*

I got grounded for three weeks, including all the end-of-school parties I was invited to, and I have to pay for the dent I made in the car out of my allowance. I guess this puts to rest for all time Mom's theory that she's too lax. Ha ha ha ha ha ha ha ha.

The worst was when the cops were going to push back by one year my eligibility to get my driver's license. Which would've been the end, I might as well have committed suicide. But somebody intervened (guess who? Jess, who's like a big effing deal on the city council), so that went away. Thank God.

No. 5. *My new job.*

Grampa hired me to type on disk all the corrections and revisions to the book he and his colleague are writing. So far there aren't very many, so obviously this was a pity hiring. He gives me the minimum wage, same as Krystal, but it's nowhere near as much fun. I have to work in his office at his house for the first few weeks, until I know what I'm doing. It's more or less part-time.

One thing I'm learning, besides more than I ever wanted to about minor English eighteenth-century poetry, is that Grampa isn't as quiet as I've always thought he was. In fact I can't get him to shut up. What does he talk about? The weather a lot; he's got a weather radio, and he likes to watch the weather channel on TV. Yesterday he talked about this incredible deal he got on four radial tires for his Honda. I mean at length. And other stuff, how his lawn is doing, his tomato crop, how lawyers are ruining the country, why the Atlanta Falcons aren't as good as the Carolina something or others. It's boring. But it's sort of nice, too, because it's easy and relaxing, I can listen or not. I can tell he likes me. We're almost getting to be friends. He's nice. I've figured out the reason he doesn't talk to Gram is because she talks all the time. Which is so funny, because she complains to Mom that she can't get a word out of him and she might as well have married a mute. I feel like sending her an anonymous note—"Shut up for a while, why don't you, put a cork in it!" But I bet she wouldn't even see herself. She'd think it was for somebody else.

No. 6. *The Ark.*

Old Mr. Pletcher died. Late in the afternoon on the day of the ark launch, he had to be rushed to the hospital in an ambulance because of his heart. He stayed there for four days, then he said he wanted to go home to die. And that's exactly what he did, two days later. The Clayborne paper did another long story, and more people than you'd think showed up for his funeral, including Mom, and afterward the ark was even more popular. The Richmond paper did this sort of tongue-in-cheek article that made fun of the whole situation, but not in a mean way, and they said the "animal constructions are imaginative and delightful" and "unexpectedly affecting." Mom was dancing on the ceiling. The only bad part was one night when some kids from out of town (the paper said, but since they never caught them how do they *know*?) threw a burning stick from the pier onto the ark and started a fire that did damage to the owl, the pelican, the panther, and the grizzly bear. Well, that stirred people up and ended up causing even more visitors to come and look at it. It was a genuine tourist attraction.

But then the forty days and forty nights were over, and they dismantled it and sold it for scrap lumber, proceeds going to the Arkists. Up until then, nobody had thought about what would happen to the animals. (I thought they'd just throw them away, but that was before I realized how *imaginative and delightful* they were.) Mrs. Pletcher, who is the actual owner of them, called up one night and told Mom a big petting zoo in Pennsylvania, which happens to be called Noah's Ark, had offered to buy the whole menagerie for three thousand dollars, to put in their welcome building. She wanted to know what she should do—sell them to the zoo and give Mom the three thousand minus expenses for materials, which takes it down to about two thousand, or give them to the new Church of the Sons of Noah she's having built out on Route 634 in her husband's memory. We could really use two thousand dollars. But Mom told her the church should have them—especially since the petting zoo could never have used all of them and would've ended up throwing some away. Plus Mom likes the idea of them decorating the aisles in the Church of the Sons of Noah. Sort of like Stations of the Cross, she says.

No. 7. *Mom's Job.*

She doesn't have a real one yet, but everybody is hopeful. Her friend Chris, who is also unemployed, had an idea that Mom could do illustrations for these kids' books Chris wrote. First it was just an experiment, to see if it would work at all, and Mom only did some pen and ink drawings. But they were good and Chris liked them a lot, so next she tried some watercolors. Well, they were a hit, too, so now they've teamed up. Who knows what will happen, but at least for now they're going to see if they can write and illustrate books for children who are between the ages of four and seven. I read the one they finished and it wasn't bad.

So that's one thing. Another is that some professor's wife in Clayborne wants Mom to paint a mural in her dining room of people sitting at a big table and eating. She wants it to take up two whole walls and be sort of old-fashioned and French, like Renoir or Toulouse-Lautrec or somebody, with lots of French bread and wine bottles and candles on the table and the people dressed like the nineteenth century—EXCEPT—she would like four of the diners to look like herself, her husband, and her two kids! Mom thinks it's a riot! She's probably going to do it. The lady will pay big bucks, even more than the petting zoo would have, so she's going to give it a try.

The third thing is—Mr. Wright asked if she'd teach a course in art next semester at the Other School!! No one could believe the balls on this guy. She said no, of course, especially since he was paying squat, but now she's actually rethinking her decision. She could do it for "practice," she says, because maybe Gram's been right all along and what she should really do is go back to school for a teaching degree and then teach art. Jeez. I'm just glad I'll be out of here by then and there's no way she could ever be my teacher. Who knows if this will happen or not. It's sort of a last resort, as I get it, in case the other gigs don't work out. "Something to fall back on," Gram keeps saying. Mom says she doesn't hate the idea as much as she used to. I guess that's something. But me—whatever I end up doing, I know it won't be the thing I hate the least. It'll be the thing I love the most. Whatever that may be. I said that to Mom the other night, as a matter of fact, but she didn't pick up on it or defend herself or anything. She just said, "Good for you," and let it go. So that made me think. Easy for me to say. I don't have a kid to send to college in two years.

No. 8. *Jess.*

I'm grounded, so naturally I'm in my room last night doing E-mail when Mom comes in and sits on the bed. She's got her serious face, so I know we're going to Talk, and I'm even pretty sure what about, but I say nothing, to make it harder for her to start. This doesn't work, because she says right out, "What are you going to do about Jess?"

I'm not really mad anymore, I'm more like, oblivious. Or trying to be. Just trying to live my life without any of that in my face, and until now she's been okay with it. I mean, maybe she sneaks over to his house all the time, maybe they have hot phone sex every night—I don't know and I don't care to know. (I still can't believe he rode up to D.C. with Grampa. I wish I'd been a fly on that windshield!)

So anyway, I try to cut the conversation short by saying I'm not doing anything about Jess, and if she wants to bring him around and be his girlfriend, hey, be my guest, no skin off my nose. I mean it's not like he needs my permission to come a-courtin', right? This doesn't amuse Mom. We go around for a while, and finally she admits that what she really wants me to do is talk to him.

Long story short, Jess calls today and invites me to go for a ride with him and Tracer in his pickup truck, and I get to drive. Yee-ha, big deal. I outgrew that stupid cowgirl fantasy a long time ago. But I don't point that out or act smart, in fact I am incredibly polite. Butter, as they say, won't melt in my mouth. It's much better to peace out in these situations and act like nothing is going on under the surface, no mental alternative dramas. You've got a lot more clout when you chill than when you act sullen or argue or show your hand. This I have learned over the years and at tremendous personal expense.

Jess freaked me, though. We were going south on back roads, down toward Orange, which is a pretty little town, and I was being extra careful not to speed so he couldn't get anything on me. It was hot, but we didn't turn on the AC, the air smelled so good, even the fertilizer smell when we went by the new fields. Cows everywhere—I used to ask him what the different breeds were and he'd tell me, Hereford, Guernsey, Brown Swiss, Jersey, etc., but today I didn't ask because already I could see how easy it would be to slide back into our old friendship as if nothing had happened. I think it's partly the silences, which are weird with other people unless they're like your parents or your best friend, but they're never weird with Jess. Why is that?

So it's a beautiful day and we're driving along, not talking much because I am being cool, when all of a sudden he goes, "I'll get lost if you want me to." I say something brilliant like, "Huh?" and he says, "It's up to you."

I'm thinking, Shit! I didn't know what to say. Finally I told him I didn't think my mom would agree with him, I seriously didn't think she'd say it was up to me. He said she was taking a lot for granted with me, she was making an assumption that eventually I was going to be okay with them being together, but it was because that's what she wanted to happen. But that he could see clearer. He said, "Ruth, I'll do whatever you want."

Oh, great! I go, "Look, it's none of my business what you do, you're two consenting adults." He smiled when I said that, "two consenting adults," and I just kind of, I don't know, I went mooshy inside. I liked him again, the same as before, and it was so totally annoying, like I was a pushover for anybody who thinks I'm funny or lovable or whatever, which I am. A pushover, I mean.

We drove around Orange for a while, but when he said do you want to get something to eat at the café, I said no thanks. Because this was not a social occasion. I turned around and started driving home on Route 15 because it's faster.

He goes, "I've been thinking." Tracer was sprawled across his lap and halfway out the window, tongue out, ears flying. I didn't want to hear what Jess was thinking, and I almost turned on the radio, but that would've been incredibly rude, plus I didn't have the nerve. He said, "I've been wondering how I'd have felt if my father loved someone after my mother died." (Or before, I thought, but I kept my mouth shut.) He said he thought he'd have pretended to be glad for his father, but inside it wouldn't have made any sense to him, because his mother was the center of their lives, she was what made his family work.

So I said it's not the same. I said my father wasn't like that.

I hated admitting that to him. But he was trying to make some kind of a circle, some parallel story about his life, and it didn't work. These days when I try to think about my dad, it's strange, but I can only picture him in his study in the old place in Chicago, doing his work. I can't see him anywhere else in the house, I can't put him in the kitchen or the bathroom or the yard. I just see him sitting at his desk. He's wearing his light green shirt with his tie undone, and he doesn't look up when anybody comes in. He's busy. He puts his left hand on his forehead to shield his eyes, and keeps writing.

I changed the subject, started talking about Mom and Chris's new book, about a little duck named Schwartz who never cleans up his room so he can't find his winning lottery ticket. I wasn't interested in talking to Jess about my father. That's private. All the way home he kept trying to get back to the point—his point—but I wouldn't help him out. I admit I liked seeing him get more and more frustrated. But he didn't press it, he didn't put the screws on or anything.

When we got home, I turned the motor off and just sat there, didn't jump right out and run off. I knew he wasn't finished, and sure enough, he starts saying how those times when we went fishing or just walking around, the times I came over to see him, he really enjoyed himself and he didn't have any, like, motive going on. He said, "I just liked being with you." I'm thinking, now is the time I'm supposed to say, "I liked being with you, too," and us to make up. I *wanted* to say it. But I didn't. I just couldn't. I sat there and played with the steering wheel.

We got out, and I figured he was going to come in the house with me. I even half wanted him to, so this could finally be over. But he didn't, he climbed back in the truck. I mumbled something like, "It doesn't matter to me if you come in or not. I mean, don't stay away on my account, because I just don't give a damn." That was so bad, I couldn't look at him. Why couldn't I be nice? I think it's because it still feels disloyal—like being nice to Jess is cheating on my dad. It's like giving in and being selfish, doing what I want to instead of what I ought to. Jess goes, How about if we take it really slow, and I go, Yeah, that sounds okay. And he says, "I love your mom. I wasn't waiting for her before, because I never thought it would work out. But now I am, and it doesn't matter how long." I don't know what I said. I was embarrassed. I mean, that was so personal.

So then he said, really quietly, "I love you, too." I looked at him. "I do," he said.

Well, I couldn't talk. But it was kind of the last straw. He put his hand on the side of the truck, and that was like a touch on my hand or my arm. Then he started the engine up and drove away.

So who knows what will happen.

Or else it's obvious.

Mom says we have to forgive each other for the things we do out of love. Oh, I guess. She forgave me for telling her I was sleeping on the street with derelicts. Did I do that out of love? I might have, but you have to go pretty far back to see it. And you'd have to really love the person to bother going back that far. Well, I will work on my forgiveness. Jess is cheating somehow, though; he's making it too easy.

So anyway, I guess that's it for items that are on my mind and strategies to deal with them over the summer. It's been a . . . I don't know what. A some kind of a year. It's been the kind of year I'm not going to understand for a few more years. Like the year when I was twelve and I first got my period and we moved from Chicago to here—I can see now how interesting that year was, but at the time it just felt like one stupid thing after another.

This is the year my father died. I turned into a different person. I am forever changed. The problem here is, I didn't know what kind of a person I was before, so how am I supposed to know who I turned into? Time, I guess. "Time will tell" is a true saying. Nevertheless, one of these days I would very much like to understand things about myself *while they're happening*.

I read somewhere that grief is all about the griever, hardly at all about the person you've lost. Thinking over this past year, I can see how true that is.

Okay. Well, that's it.

EXCEPT! No. 9. *There is this guy.* His name is Robbie Warriner, and he's Chris's next-door neighbor and also a year ahead of me at school, a total computer freak, and a major babe. (I think. Becky says no, he's a tool, but she likes Jason Bellinger, so what does she know.) He's so nice, he comes over to Chris's and helps Andy, her kid, with his new computer and teaches him games and stuff. So of course sometimes when I go over there to see Mom, he's there. He's going to study computers and virtual reality in college, he's already decided. I told him I'd like to learn how to do spreadsheets, since I might take statistics next year, and now he's teaching me! He has red hair, but it's dark red, not orange, and he doesn't have freckles. He's taller than me. He has long, graceful fingers and this really intense face, and when he hunches over the keyboard and stares into the monitor at a pie chart it's like watching Van Cliburn or somebody. He chews Dentyne. Sometimes he sits behind me to show me cell formulas or fields or whatever. I smell that peppery-cinnamon smell and forget what I'm doing. According to Chris he's not going out with anybody. I think the guy being a year and a half older than the girl is exactly right. Mom likes him a lot. Not that that matters.

28

Celtic Circle

Ruth said yes.

I couldn't believe how easy it was. I'd phrased my question very casually: "I was thinking I might drive out to Daddy's grave, clean it up, put some fresh flowers. It's such a beautiful day. But you're probably busy, you wouldn't want to come with me. Only for an hour. I just thought since it's so pretty."

"Sure, Mom. I'll drive."

But just as we were leaving, Mama pulled up in her new car, a sporty red compact with a sunroof. "Where're you going?" she yelled out the window, spotting us on the sidewalk. I told her. "Great, I'll go with you. Get in, this car rides like a dream. Ruth honey, you want to drive?"

And that was that. I seethed all the way to Hill Haven. My mother might be bossy, but she wasn't blind, was she? Surely she could see that this particular mother-daughter foray was tricky enough already, fraught with pitfalls, a minefield of possible disasters. Maybe she thought a third party might ease the way, but honestly, couldn't she see that the whole *point* was the intimacy, the privacy—the mother-daughter part?

No. As it turned out, she *was* blind, but I didn't learn why until later. All I knew then was that she was in a rotten mood and she wanted company.

After a week of stifling heat and humidity, it was a mild, gorgeous day, the sky a puffy cloud-filled azure blue that made my chest ache. Ruth said it felt more like Chicago in spring than

Virginia in July. Along with a clutch of zinnias and rudbeckia, the freshest flowers left in my neglected, baking-hot garden, I'd also brought along a blanket and a Thermos of lemonade. I'd had a hopeful but naive vision of Ruth and me sitting hip-to-hip on the blanket, sharing confidences along with the single cup. The fantasy didn't fit three. Neither did the blanket; Mama plopped down on it heavily, tucking her skirt around her calves, perspiring from the short climb from the paved path, while Ruth stood apart and looked off in the distance, hands on her hips, long legs too tan under her black shorts in spite of my incessant sunscreen carping. With a sigh for lost opportunities, I sat down next to my mother.

Presently Ruth dropped to her knees and began to pull back the dry, dead grass from around Stephen's bronze burial plaque. She'd cut her hair for the summer, shorter than mine, a sun-streaked cap of soft, springy curls. I loved it, loved to touch it, even though it made her jerk away and say, "*Mom.*" She'd be sixteen next month. I remembered very well what getting my driver's license had meant to me—freedom, independence, the glorious beginning of my real life. But for a mother it only meant one thing: the beginning of the end.

"Carrie, you look tired." Mama poured half a cup of lemonade from the Thermos and drank it. She sounded peevish. "Ruth honey, doesn't your mother look tired?"

Ruth looked up, narrowed her eyes at me. "No. I think she looks pretty." She shrugged and went back to pulling grass.

"Thanks," I said after a startled second. How long had it been since she'd given me a compliment? Resentments were beginning to crumble, maybe from old age, maybe only to make way for new ones, but I loved our truce and didn't care what motivated it. Ruth liking me, being nice to me again—I hadn't known how much I'd missed that.

"Hey," she said, "look."

"Don't point," Mama said severely. "We see them."

"What?" I exchanged a look with Ruth—*What is with her?*—and glanced over my shoulder. "Oh." A funeral service, above us, forty yards away on top of the hill the cemetery was named for. There weren't many mourners. They stood out in black silhouette against the sky, a very old woman in a long-sleeved dress—she must be stifling—two older men, a young woman, and a boy. A minister was reading from a prayer book, and a word or two drifted down on the shifting breeze, *Almighty Lord . . . beloved . . . we ask . . .*

Ruth put her dirty hands on her thighs and stared. "You never know, do you. It looks like an ordinary funeral, the guy's dead and she's the widow, those are the kids and the grandkids, everybody's sad. But it could be something completely different. It could be anything."

My hand paused on the way to the Thermos. Was that a shot? Ruth's way of implying that my grief at Stephen's funeral had been disingenuous? A lie?

"I mean, the old lady could be the mother instead of the widow, and one of those guys could be the husband of the dead person. Or they could be brothers, the two guys, and they've lost their sister. You know. It could be anything."

"Oh." Relief. "It's true," I said, "we do make assumptions about people based on—"

"Stereotypes," Ruth finished. "Everybody jumps to conclusions about people. It's what causes racism and sexism and religious intolerance. I think it's better to not think *any*thing about people. Just try to keep an open mind at all times."

I nodded thoughtfully. *Native Son*, I recalled, was on her summer reading list. I closed my eyes for a few seconds. I had a sensation of rising, floating, hovering over all the graves in the cemetery, all the graves in the round, blue and green world. Millions and billions of the dead and the living, countless people standing over the stones of their loved ones, praying and wishing, weeping, grieving.

"George lied."

I opened my eyes. "What, Mama?"

"Your father has reneged on his promise." She yanked up a tuft of crabgrass and flung it sideways. "I should've known, I should've seen this coming a mile off."

"What happened?" I looked at Ruth, who kept her head down; she crouched over the plaque, blowing on it, rubbing it with the hem of her T-shirt. *She knows*, I thought. Whatever this is, she already knows about it.

"We're not going on our trip," Mama said flatly.

"Oh, no. Why not? I thought Pop finished his book." He had finished it, Ruth had told me so the night before last. As soon as it was done—the book he'd been collaborating on for the better part of two years—he and Mama were supposed to go away together. Only to the Bahamas, and only for a week, but it would be the first vacation they'd taken together in—fifteen years, she claimed, but that seemed impossible, she had to be exaggerating.

"Oh, he finished it all right. He finished it months ago, if you ask me, and all this so-called *editing* is just dicking around."

Dicking around? Ruth did look up at that, doll-eyed.

"But don't you already have tickets and reservations and everything?" This was bad. I hadn't been paying close attention to the minutiae of my mother's life for the last month or so—too many other things on my mind—but I knew this trip meant more to her than a casual getaway. She'd been seeing it as a transition between past and future, her old and her new life—maybe. The beginning of something different, or at least the possibility of it, between her and Pop. "Oh, Mama, why can't he go?"

"A symposium in Toronto. He gets to read a paper. Very prestigious, he says. They asked him at the last minute," she said with sour triumph. Rolling sideways, she got up using her hands, slapping vigorously at the back of her skirt. "I'm so mad I could spit."

She walked away, keeping her back to us. She was getting old lady feet; one navy blue flat was worn down on the outside, the other on the inside, as if her feet were slowly collapsing on each other. She wore long-sleeved blouses no matter the weather—"My arms are ugly," she claimed, "my elbows look like turkey wattles." I hectored her about taking her calcium, but she was still losing height; after forty-two years, I was finally taller.

Ruth looked up, blank-faced, from the absorbing task of rubbing dirt from her fingernails. These days her loyalties were divided. I loved it when she came home from her sinecure of a summer job and reported snippets of conversations with her grandfather, Grampa said this, Grampa thinks this about that. She was finally getting to know him, even growing close to him, and I envied her for it. But the experience was naturally muddying what had always been clear and uncomplicated, the family line: Gram was fun, lively, and interesting, Grampa was pretty much not there. Grampa was a rumor.

My mother's bowed head worried me. Surely she wasn't crying. I strolled over to where she was running her hands over the pointed stakes of an old iron fence. "Mama?"

"I'm fine."

"I know."

"I'm just mad. I wanted to go. Damn it to hell, I wanted to go on that dumb trip."

"I know you did."

"I feel like going anyway. Not to have fun, just to spite him." She smiled, grim humor returning. "I could ask Calvin Mintz to go with me. Bet he's lonely without Helen to boss around anymore. What a pair we'd make, huh?"

The hard fence spike made a dent in the fleshy pad of the thumb I was pressing into it. For me the summer was passing in a haze, a kind of golden liquid balm, nothing remotely like it had ever happened to me before. I hadn't lost myself in love or lust, I was still me, I could see Jess's flaws—moodiness, self-containment bordering on aloofness—and he could see mine—too numerous to mention. But we fit, we always had, and our time together was filling up places in me that had been empty for so long, years and years. We were still in the chemical dependency stage, addicted to each other. That wouldn't last, but I even looked forward, with curiosity, not dread, to what came next. To leave him now would be like . . . a drought that begins again after one long, healing rain.

"I'll go with you."

"What? Oh, no." Mama laughed self-consciously, dabbing at the perspiration under her nose with the edge of a tissue. In the slant of her downcast eyes, I could see the idea taking root.

"Why not? I haven't been anywhere in ages. Ruth could stay with Pop part of the time, part of the time at Modean's."

"I can stay by myself," Ruth called over. "*Jeez.*"

"You don't need a trip right now," Mama scoffed, striding away a few paces, pivoting, coming back. "You're in the middle of all that business with Chris, you've got"—she flung her hand out—"things going on." Jess, that meant. She'd all but reconciled herself to him. He was like arthritis in a new location, a psoriasis flare-up, one more old age-related affliction she had to accept with grace and dignity.

"Well, nothing's going to collapse in a week. Come on, we'll have fun."

"Oh, shoo." Still playing hard to get. "You don't want to go on a vacation with your old mother."

I did, though. I wanted to give her what she wanted, freely and for nothing. From the heart. For so long Mama had squeezed love out of me like toothpaste from a tube, and see where that had gotten us—at a prickly distance from each other, the hunter and the hunted, her starving, me scared of being eaten. Jess was mixed up in there, too. Loving him, choosing and acknowledging him—that was when I'd finally gotten free, when I was the most bound and committed. Now I could make this not-so-little sacrifice for my mother, give her this gift, for the very reason that she didn't expect it and hadn't asked for it. Hadn't squeezed it out of me.

"I do, Mama. I want to go away for a week in the Bahamas with my old mother. We'll lie on the beach and read all the books we've been saving up."

"Oh . . ."

"We'll eat fish every night, and we'll go shopping, we'll go to the movies, we'll fat-ass. We won't do a damn thing if we don't feel like it. And if we meet two nice-looking guys in the bar, we'll let 'em buy us mai-tais."

She gave a giddy, girlish laugh. "Well, that would serve him right, wouldn't it? Oh, honey." She took my arm and gave it a hard squeeze. "You know what, I'm gonna ask Birdie."

"Birdie? What—to go with you?"

"She needs a trip, she's been down in the dumps."

"*I* need a trip." Now I felt hurt. "You can't ask Birdie, she'll drive you nuts."

"She will, Gram," Ruth agreed, sidling over. "She'll drive you nuts."

"She probably will." She laughed again, a gay sound, and I thought, *I love your face, I love you, Mama.* "I think that's what I'll do, though. Carrie, you are a sweetheart, but you've got enough going on right now. I'll call Bird this afternoon, perk her up. Now, who's doing these flowers? Ruth honey, you know how the little holder in the plaque works? You pull it out of the ground and turn it over and it's a vase. Oh now, aren't those pretty. Carrie, are they from your garden or Modean's?"

So we arranged the flowers on Stephen's grave, and I mused on the interesting fact that my mother could still surprise me, still had tricks up her sleeve. Say what you would, families never got boring. And mothering never got less complicated. All you could do was hope, like a doctor, to do no harm. But it was a futile hope, because harm was inevitable, and then you just hoped someone, someday (Ruth, soon) took into account your good intentions.

My mother shoved up from her knees with a grunt and took a few stiff paces away, pressing both hands to the small of her back, stretching, jutting her chin out. I stayed where I was, barely brushing Ruth's arm with mine. I stroked a finger over the raised letters, STEPHEN EDWARD VAN ALLEN, BELOVED HUSBAND, FATHER, and tried to marshal my thoughts. Now was my chance to say something wise or true or conciliatory about Stephen. Squeezing Ruth's tennis shoe, I said, "Your father—"

"Mom, do you think he can see us? Or hear us? Do you think he's, like, aware of us right now?"

"Hmm. Well, I don't know, but it's possible, it's entirely—"

"Because sometimes I can really feel him near me, but other times . . ." She lowered her voice to a whisper. "I can almost not even remember what he looked like. If I concentrate on that green corduroy shirt, I can still see him." She drew in a deep breath and blew it out. "But for how much longer, you know? What if he becomes invisible?"

"Well, then—"

"Then I guess I'll just carry him around like a feeling. I'll always have that, right, the *sense* of my father."

"You look like him," I said. "Here." I traced my finger along the neat, decisive line of her jaw. "You'll never lose him, because he's in you." She smiled. "That's why I could never not love him. Why I never stopped."

"Yeah, but . . ." A faint pink colored her cheek. Embarrassment? I'd take that over outrage any day. I started to speak, but she said, "Don't talk about that here, Mom, okay? You know." She ran her palm across the brittle grass on top of the grave. "Just in case."

Of course. Just in case. I felt embarrassed by my own indelicacy.

On the hill above us, the service was breaking up. We were ready to go home, but out of respect, we waited for the mourning family to drift down the path to their cars and mill around for a few minutes, getting organized—*you go with him and we'll go with them, see you at the house*—the necessary social business of grief. Then we three strolled down to Mama's car. *We've had our funeral*, I caught myself thinking, *we're safe for a while.* As if loss were apportioned fairly, predictably, at convenient intervals. But hope was a deft deceiver, and I was nothing if not full of hope on this savory, soft, sweet-smelling midsummer day in the Hill Haven Cemetery. The future had vistas, potential, it looked like a pastel sky. The only cloud was that everybody I loved wasn't as full of sappy, sanguine expectation as me. There was something to be said for starting over, for filling your boat with fresh progenitors and sailing off into the downpour. Your new day wouldn't last long, but that was the nature of new days. Grudges resurfaced, bad habits recurred, slights and hurts and meannesses were bound to muddy the floodwaters before they could even start to recede. But then you started over again. As long as you could love and as long as you could forgive, it never had to end. Good thing, because you'd never get it right for long.

"Mama, let me go with you," I said again from the backseat of the car, leaning forward, careful to stay out of Ruth's rearview mirror. "We could have such a good time. Come on. I'd really like to go."

But she wouldn't budge. She was going with Birdie, period, and I wasn't sure why. It wasn't for the pleasure of martyrdom—I knew exactly how that role played out, and today Mama wasn't playing it. Generosity of spirit? A belated demonstration, better late than never, of the art of letting go? I enjoyed not knowing. I liked giving her the benefit of the doubt.

"I've got this great idea," Ruth said, flicking on the turn signal and slowing down smoothly, conscientiously, for the stoplight. She was going to be an excellent driver. Either that or she had her entire family fooled and she was going to be a holy terror. Absently, I reached around for my purse; we were coming into town, and Ruth's great ideas in this vicinity usually had to do with the Dairy Queen or McDonald's. But she said, "Let's *all* get tattoos."

I snorted. Mama rolled her eyes.

"Yeah, no, I mean, wouldn't that be incredible? When I get mine fixed, we could all three get new tattoos. Just a little one for you, Gram, a little bit of flash. It doesn't really hurt, not that much, and if we do it together it would be, like, a distraction. What do you think?" Her eyes danced in the mirror, daring me. "Mom, you could get a sexy one, you could get a butterfly on your ass."

Mama hooted with laughter. "What would I get?" She pushed up her sleeve, holding out her spotty, mottled forearm. "A big bleeding heart with an arrow through it? And underneath, 'George, Forever and Ever.'"

Ruth guffawed, bouncing in her seat. "Cool, or a skull and crossbones, Gram, right on your collarbone or something. Or your boob! Wouldn't that blow them away at the garden club?"

They cackled and snickered, thinking up wilder tattoos and more vulgar places to put them. The idea that my daughter was contemplating, had actually suggested, apparently not in jest, getting group-tattooed with her mother and her grandmother—that hadn't quite sunk in yet. Something to think about later.

Meanwhile, I thought about the tattoo I would get if I ever really did it. Not a butterfly on my ass. What was it called, that symbol of the serpent eating its own tail? It probably signified infinity, endlessness, timelessness. But for me it would mean the effort to love well going on and on, round and round, always imperfect and always forgivable. The best we could ever do for each other.

In the front seat, they'd made decisions. A perfect ankh for Ruth, some kind of flower for Mama—not a rose, though: too common. "Are you in, Mom?" Ruth took her right hand off the steering wheel and lifted it in a fist. Poor hand, still pink and sore from the last laser treatment. Mama clasped it, chuckling. I surrounded it gently with my hand, and the three of us stuck our joined fists through the sunroof and shook them in the air.

I sat back, wistful, feeling a little heavy from all my fond, precarious hopes. Pastel sky or not, the future came too fast sometimes. It flew by in a blur—not unlike the Dairy Queen. But what could you do? Nothing. Hope for the best. Relax, enjoy, and let your daughter, the expert, drive you home.